ALSO BY MARILYN LUDWIG

SEARCHING FOR JULIETTE

HASTE YE BACK

THE SECRET OF KENDALL MOUNTAIN

IT'S PERFECTLY SAFE . . . THE RULISON MATTER

TRUST THE MAGIC

THE GEESE THAT WON THE WAR

THE GHOST OF A TREE REMEMBERED

THE BORROWED DAYS

WAITING GAMES

No Small Parts

A Novel in Three Acts

MARILYN LUDWIG

ISBN: 9780996742283
LCCN: 2020907974

ZAFA PUBLISHING
Downers Grove, Illinois

In Memory of
    Valerie D. Sokol
    Who found the Key to the Curtain
    And kept a mighty clean costume cage.

For hundreds of Highland, Herrick, and North High students
Thank you for years of dramatic moments!

And for Nancy.

ACT ONE – A ROARING MOUSE

Remember: there are no small parts, only small actors.
— Constantin Stanislavski

DREAMILY, KYLIE KENNEDY DOODLED THE theater masks of comedy and tragedy in her science notebook. Which one of you guys will win? she asked herself. Am I going to be happy or sad in less than an hour? She tried to zero back in on the teacher's boring lesson on one-celled organisms. Who cared? The euglena was definitely her candidate for loser of the day. Kylie hadn't written a single note. Instead, the notebook was filled with tentative cast lists, with her as lead, of course, and sketches of the beautiful gowns she might wear. She exchanged glances with long-time neighbor and sometimes-best friend, Rosita Santos, who was twisting a strand of her long black hair around a pencil. Roe's nervous, too, Kylie thought. She wants the part almost as much as I do. She took a deep breath and glared at the classroom clock.

Finally at 2:40, the feared but longed-for announcement came over the intercom. First, a clearing of the throat, and then Vice Principal Willard Hasting's nasal voice whined into every classroom of Castle Bluff Middle School.

"Excuse me, teachers and students, for interrupting your studies for this short announcement." Mr. Tanning, the science teacher, made a face while the class tittered. Mr. Hasting's announcements were never short. "The cast list for CBT's fall production of *The Mouse That Roared* is posted outside the office. You may examine it at the termination of classes today. Please refrain from crowding the hallway. I'll expect you to behave like ladies and gentlemen. Remember, you can't all be winners. Good luck—What? Excuse me a second. Oh, I see. Students, I apologize. I should have said, 'Break a Leg!'"

Mr. Tanning groaned. It was his turn to stare at the clock.

Soon she would know. Kylie felt her stomach flutter. Stage fright, and she wasn't even on stage yet. She had had a large part last year in seventh grade, so maybe Miss Armstrong would decide to give her a small one in *Mouse*. Or maybe no part at all.

While Mr. Hasting went on to give the scores of sporting events, Roe gave herself a firm lecture. *Try to act casual. Don't look as nervous as you feel. See Kylie, though, pretending to act so stressed out. As if she didn't know she was Armstrong's favorite. Being in competition with her closest friend was proving difficult.* Roe sighed. *If only they could both have leads!*

"That is all, students. Again, teachers, please excuse the interruption."

Mr. Tanning, relieved that the short message was finally over, returned to his presentation of the life cycle of the euglena.

Normally, no one worried about talking in Tanning's science class. His fascination with his own words kept him from noticing. Roe decided to take a chance. "Kylie," she whispered, "don't worry. You'll be Glorianna."

"I'm not so sure," Kylie whispered back. "Remember last year how the eighth graders acted when I got a good part? Miss Armstrong might have decided to give it to someone else. I won't mind, really. I guess we should be happy with any part we get."

Roe scowled. "Speak for yourself. That part I had last year was a big nothing. Armstrong owes me."

"I doubt if she sees it that way." Surprisingly, Mr. Tanning had left a world meaningful only to him. All six feet towered over Roe's desk, and using the sarcastic tone he had mastered after too many years of teaching said, "Your career as a thespian will have to wait. Remain behind and write a summary of what we covered today."

Tanning wasn't fair, of course—Kylie had been talking, too. He always picked on kids with ethnic-sounding names, especially Hispanic and Latino ones, but it wouldn't make sense for both of them to stay. Besides, Kylie had promised to meet Beth Walters at her locker, which would be easier without Roe along. Her friendship with Beth was a sore point with Roe, especially now that Beth was in seventh grade. But Kylie had known Beth for a long time, too, and their moms had been friends foreverl. Just because Roe lived next door didn't give her special privileges.

Kylie noticed the crowds of students fighting their way to the office window. She could easily tell who had parts and who didn't. Some of the girls were crying.

"Hey, Kyle!"

"Hey, Beth." Kylie crossed her fingers. She hoped tiny red-haired Beth would get something. Usually seventh graders were lucky to even make X-tras. Unlike me last year, she thought. "Are you ready? Shall we push our way through?"

"I guess. Where's Roe?"

"Had to stay after."

Beth held up a shaking hand. "I am so nervous. Let's wait until the hall clears. Then it won't be so embarrassing when I don't find my name there. My audition was awful."

"So was mine," Kylie said, only to be polite.

"I thought you were terrific. You're certain to get Glorianna."

"Here's hoping." She crossed her fingers.

The single-spaced cast list looked innocent enough, taped on the office window next to notices announcing the new volleyball team, lunchroom menus, and library fines. Kylie urged Beth forward. "Go on. I'm too nervous. Read it, and then tell me—gently."

"Hmmm." Beth scanned the list. "Hey, that cute Kurt Brockway got the lead."

"That's no surprise," Kylie said. "He's super-talented."

"Cute, too."

Kylie giggled. "I'll tell him you said so."

"I wouldn't mind." Then she shrieked. "Kyle, I got a part. I'm Fran! Who's Fran?"

"One of the tourists who wanders into the land of Grand Fenwick. It's not big, but it's fun. Oh, I can't take it anymore. Look ahead. Who is Glorianna?"

"Glorianna is—drumroll, please. Glorianna is—wait for it. Glorianna is Kylie Kennedy!"

"Really? Where?" She pushed Beth aside. "Oh, I can't believe it!"

"We both got in!" Beth screamed and hugged Kylie, who screamed and hugged back.

"We'll have so much fun. Oh, but what about Roe?" Kylie searched until she found it.

Jane . . . . *Rosita Santos.*

"Uh-oh," she said.

"What's the matter? Isn't it a good part?"

Kylie hedged. "Yes and no. It's good if you're in seventh. Jane is also a tourist, but all the others went to seventh graders. Roe is the only one in eighth."

Beth shrugged. "Well, at least she got a part. Most people didn't get anything."

"She's not going to see it that way," Kylie said. "Poor Roe."

It was four when Roe convinced Mr. Tanning that she would pay better attention in class. Of all days to have to stay after school, she thought, making her way down the empty hall. At least she could look at the list alone. "Please let me be Glorianna," she whispered. "I've got to be Glorianna!"

Roe skimmed the list, pausing at the leads. So, that stuck-up Kurt is Tully Bascom. Then she looked for the only part that mattered.

Glorianna . . . . *Kylie Kennedy*

Disappointment and jealousy flooded through her. Kylie—Golden Girl Kylie! And what made things worse, Glorianna was the only decent part for a girl in the whole play. Did she get anything? She looked again.

Jane . . . . *Rosita Santos*

One of the tourists? Oh, great. A bit part with a bunch of seventh-grade babies!

Roe's dark eyes smoldered as she stalked to her locker. "Miss Armstrong has it in for me," she muttered. "Maybe I'll quit."

A locker door slammed near her. It was Marla Gray's. Roe couldn't remember seeing Marla's name on the cast list, although she had auditioned. "Talking to yourself, plain Jane?" Marla sneered. "Going to hang out with seventh graders this year, are we?"

"At least I got a part, unlike some people." Roe slammed her locker, too, ensuring it would be jammed the next day, and walked proudly out of the building.

Once outside, her false pride disappeared. She couldn't face the late activity bus—not with her classmates gossiping about who made the play and who hadn't. She'd walk, clearing her head in the cool fall afternoon.

She'd been counting on Glorianna, not only because she loved the part, but also because playing it would give her a better chance of winning a scholarship to Crofts Performing Arts High School. By the time Roe arrived home, she'd reached a decision. "I'm still mad at Miss Armstrong, but I won't have a chance of getting into Crofts if I quit."

As usual, her mother was lying on the couch staring at the TV. Did she even know what she was watching? Roe tried to tell her about the play but was cut off. "I'm tired. Fix us something to eat. Your father isn't coming home tonight."

"I don't blame him," Roe muttered, as she went into the kitchen to stretch the leftovers one more time. Why couldn't her parents be like Kylie's?

After eating a lonely meal and before turning to her science book, Roe decided to phone next door. She should at least pretend to be happy for Kylie. It wasn't like she had friends to spare. Besides, she didn't want Kylie to dump her for that little ditz, Beth.

"Great news! Congratulations," Roe said, once she heard Kylie's excited voice.

"Thanks, Roe." Did Kylie sound surprised? "Both my cell phone and the landline have been ringing all evening. Everyone's been so kind."

So kind? La-dee-dah! Give me a break. But she said, "I just wanted to say you'll make an awesome Glorianna." Actually, she meant that. Kylie would be perfect.

"Congratulations to you, too, Roe."

"Thanks, but it's not much of a part."

"Now, now," Kylie scolded. "Remember what Miss Armstrong always says, 'There are no small parts—'"

"—'there are only small actors.'" Roe made a gagging noise. But, surprisingly, she felt better. "I gotta study. See you tomorrow, Kylie."

KYLIE OPENED THE AUDITORIUM DOOR for a quick peek at the stage. She could see Miss Armstrong setting the chairs. "Need help?" she called.

Miss Armstrong ran her fingers through her short brown cap of hair and wiped the perspiration from her forehead. "Hi there, Kylie. Shouldn't you be in class?"

"Student Council, but we finished early. I'll give you a hand."

"Fine. A few more chairs, and then I'll treat us to a soda. I wonder why the auditorium is so overheated today."

Kylie admired Miss Armstrong, who'd been hired as Castle Bluff Middle School's director because she had once directed and acted professionally in Chicago. It was strange she'd come to Castle Bluff and had given it all up. Kylie was certain she'd never give up acting—especially not to teach.

"That should do it," Miss Armstrong announced, as Kylie put the last chair in the circle. "Let's go have that soda."

"The janitors should help you set up," Kylie insisted, settling into an overstuffed couch in the Green Room next to the stage. Miss Armstrong purchased the two bottles and joined her.

"I've surrendered that battle. Being a director also means being a part-time custodian. So tell me, Kylie, were your parents pleased by your part in the play?"

"Were they? Dad bought ice cream to celebrate." Kylie didn't tell her that she had overheard Mom bragging on the phone about how her daughter had won "the lead." It was embarrassing but fun. Even Kylie's ten-year-old brother stopped thinking about Batman long enough to be impressed, or at least excited about the ice cream.

But a later phone call Mom made to Grandma bothered her. "I wish she didn't have her heart set on going to Crofts. I don't think we can possibly afford to send her there unless she earns a scholarship." Then she sighed. "Yes, I'll try to be positive. Perhaps Dan will find something soon, but it's been so long . . ."

Kylie, deep in thought remembering, didn't notice Miss Armstrong talking to her. "Earth to Kylie—can you hear me?"

"Oh, sorry, Miss Armstrong."

"Glorianna is a challenging part. You be careful not to let your schoolwork suffer."

"I will. Are the scripts ready?"

"Yes. Each one has the character's name printed on it and a copy of the schedule stapled inside."

Organized as always, Kylie thought. She knew that for the next eight weeks, the land of Grand Fenwick would be Miss Armstrong's real home, and the characters her family.

"I promised to meet Beth and Roe. I'll be right back, Miss Armstrong."

Miss Armstrong frowned. "Is Roe all right? Concerning her part, I mean."

"I guess so," Kylie said, even though it wasn't true.

"Roe worries me," Miss Armstrong pursued. "Sometimes I wonder— are there problems at home? Is there anything you can tell me?"

"Uh—I don't think so. I've got to go. I'm late."

Kylie hurried down the hall. Roe would never forgive her if she said, "Roe's mom spends the whole day staring into space, and her father is never home."

Poor Roe. No wonder she was so grouchy lately. But she was talented. Why hadn't she received a larger part? Well, Miss Armstrong was the director and knew best.

Kylie smiled as she remembered her conversation with Mom and Dad. "Don't worry about winning scholarships. You keep on being the best person you can be. That's what's important," Mom said.

"We'll find a way to send you to Crofts, if that's what you want," Dad had added.

Dad always tried to make her feel better, but Kylie wished he would just level with her. If going depended on a scholarship, she needed to know.

Beth and Roe were waiting beside her locker, acting as if they were strangers waiting for a bus in a dangerous neighborhood. Honestly, she thought, *if those two don't start getting along, I might dump both of them and find myself some new friends.*

"Hi, guys," she greeted. "All set for read-through?"

The stage was crowded when Roe, Kylie, and Beth arrived. Miss Armstrong required everyone, even crew, to attend read-through. Jaimie Jelinek, Miss Armstrong's student director and stage manager, passed out the scripts, and Roe searched for her part. Kylie began highlighting her lines. *What a showoff,* Roe thought.

Miss Armstrong gave the traditional welcoming speech. "I could have cast this play a dozen ways. If you're disappointed, remember, there are no small parts, there are only small actors." Roe kept her eyes down but was certain Miss Armstrong was looking straight at her.

There were a few audible groans, but Miss Armstrong chuckled. "I realize it sounds corny, but it's true. You'll find out."

Roe already knew the basic plot of the play—how a tiny backward European nation, Grand Fenwick, dares to declare war on the United States because it would certainly lose and then receive financial aid. Then, because of a comedy of errors, it wins! How will Grand Fenwick ever manage to rehabilitate the USA?

For the next two hours, the newly formed cast dragged themselves through the first reading of *The Mouse That Roared.* Some of the actors sounded as if they had never read aloud in their whole lives.

"This is awful," Roe heard Beth whisper.

"Don't worry," she assured the younger girl, "this is the way read-through always is." Beth looked startled. *Probably surprised I was decent to her,* Roe thought, feeling a little guilty.

Roe had to admit Kylie made a perfect Glorianna. She wondered if the play had been chosen with her friend in mind. In a way, she was in awe of Kylie's ability, but mainly she was jealous. At first, Roe put little energy into the part of Jane. Then it occurred to her she should prove to Miss Armstrong that she had made a colossal mistake in not giving her something larger. She began to read her part in a clear, confident voice and was rewarded by several admiring glances, including Beth's. *Maybe I can teach these seventh graders something,* she thought.

"So, what do you think?" Miss Armstrong asked, after the character, Chet Beston, gave the final line of the show.

The cast applauded.

"It's great!"

"It's awfully long. Are you sure we can do it?"

"I've got some props we can use."

"I've got the perfect dress for Glorianna."

"I'm glad you're pleased. We have lots of work ahead of us. Be sure to follow your schedule. We'll block the first scene tomorrow. You're dismissed, but I would like to see Roe for a few minutes."

Maybe she's changed her mind, Roe thought. *Maybe she will give me a better part.* "Wait for me in the hall," she told Kylie.

Miss Armstrong smiled uncertainly. "Roe, I'm afraid you're disappointed by the size of your role. I'm sure you'll find, though, that it will give you an excellent opportunity to improve your projection and timing."

Roe forced herself to remain calm. She made her face a blank and said nothing.

Miss Armstrong tried again. "Trust me, Roe," she said softly.

Roe refused to make eye contact. "It's not a problem, Miss Armstrong." She walked away.

"What did she want?" Kylie asked.

"Nothing important," Roe said.

"You want to go get a Coke to celebrate? I'll treat."

Celebrate what, Kylie? You? But Roe forced herself to smile. "Thanks. I've got enough money, but I've got some stuff to do in the library." She didn't want to do homework, but she wanted to go home even less."

"You're probably smart," Kylie admitted, "but I want to have some fun. How about it, Beth?"

"You're on!"

Roe watched them turn the hall corner before making her way, head down, to the library.

SCENE 3—BLOCKING, BOOKS, AND BOYS

GOOD THING ENGLISH IS JUST a movie, Kylie thought, as she sat back and relaxed in the darkened auditorium where her class was meeting. If we were watching the old *The Mouse That Roared* movie, I could concentrate, but as it is, a nap would be nice.

"Kylie, wake up," a voice whispered. Then a hand bearing a multi-folded note appeared on Kylie's right shoulder.

"Thanks," Kylie whispered back.

The note's wrinkled condition and many folds indicated that other eyes had read it before it reached its destination. Kylie unfolded it eagerly. Fortunately, there was enough light to read.

> *Hi Glorianna!*
> *Want to go to Smithy's after school? We could get a snack and work on our lines.*
> *Your uncle,*
> *Count Mountjoy.*

Brad Michaels, the tallest, best-looking boy in the whole eighth grade was asking her out! Kylie managed not to shriek. While chewing the eraser off her pencil, she decided on the perfect reply.

> *Dear Uncle Mountjoy,*
> *Yes, a strategy meeting at Smithy's to plan Grand Fenwick's next move. Do you think Smithy's serves*

pomegranates? They are my favorite food. Where shall we meet?

Your niece, Glorianna

Kylie folded the note again before sending it on its way. Pity they didn't have each other's cell phone numbers so they could text, but no, this was better. The teachers were down on texting during class and were even taking away kids' phones. Wait until she told Roe and Beth! She had been sorry her first blocking rehearsal wasn't until tomorrow, but now she had something to look forward to. "Yes," she breathed, waking the boy seated next to her.

The film ended, and the houselights put an end to the students' mail service. "Class, your assignment tonight is to write a one-page summary of the film you just saw. Due at the beginning of class tomorrow."

Uh-oh! Kylie had no idea what they had been watching. I'll ask Brad, she decided. She followed the restless surge into the hall. Brad pushed his way through to whisper in her ear, "I'll meet you at your locker after eighth period."

He knows where my locker is! Hugging her books, Kylie continued down the hall to science.

Roe placed her books on the top shelf of her locker. Don't slam the door, she reminded herself. The custodian had told her she would be in big trouble if he had to pry it open again. She wouldn't close it all the way, she decided, grabbing her script.

"Hey, Roe." Beth joined her. Both were scheduled for the first blocking rehearsal. "Did you hear that Brad asked Kylie out?"

"Everyone's heard," Roe snapped. I'd better make some new friends, even if they are seventh graders, she decided. Otherwise I'll be stuck with this baby.

As Roe and Beth entered the auditorium, they saw Kurt Brockway running around the stage dragging an object on a string. Jaimie Jelinek, the student director, was laughing at his antics, almost to the point of tears.

"What's going on?" Beth asked.

Kurt growled at them. "It's the rat that roared!" As a joke, Kurt had brought a large rubber rat to rehearsal.

Honestly, Roe thought, Kurt always has to be the center of attention.

"Actually, I think we'll use it," Miss Armstrong said. "The play begins with the sound of a roar, and then Tully enters and talks to an invisible mouse. It might be fun if the audience sees a mouse dashing across the stage."

"It's a rat." Kurt sounded annoyed that his joke was being treated seriously.

"From a distance, it will look like a mouse," Jaimie said. "Great idea, Miss Armstrong."

Soon all who appeared in the first scene of the play had arrived. "Even those who were in Castle Bluff Theater last year," Miss Armstrong looked straight at Roe, "could use a blocking review. Don't worry, newcomers, stage geography is simple if you know the difference between up and down and right and left."

Roe knew it wasn't that simple, and even directors can become confused. Miss Armstrong explained that the stage was divided into invisible sections. Upstage was the term for away from the audience, while Downstage meant towards it. Back in the old days, stages were built on a slope, and sometimes the scenery and furniture had to be nailed down. Today, stages are level and the audience raked. But the terms "Up" and "Down" remain.

Miss Armstrong asked Kurt to demonstrate walking Upstage and Downstage. Kurt, always the clown, walked like a chicken, causing the cast to laugh again—especially Beth.

Uh-oh, Roe thought. Beth doesn't realize Kurt likes to have lots of girlfriends. Poor kid. Maybe she should be warned. Nah, let her find out for herself. It wasn't Roe's job to advise seventh graders.

Next, they practiced walking Right and Left. On the stage, right always meant the actor's right and left, the actor's left. "It's only confusing when you're in the audience," Miss Armstrong explained.

The seventh graders practiced walking Upstage Right, Downstage Right, and Downstage Center. As Miss Armstrong gave directions, the cast rushed to respond. Roe couldn't imagine anything more silly or boring.

"We'll learn new stage terminology at each rehearsal," Miss Armstrong said, "but we'd better start blocking so we can stay on schedule. Let's start with Tully. The rest of you may take a break."

Roe, Beth, and the two other tourists, Priyanka and Imani, stood in line for sodas at the machine in the Green Room. Roe knew Priyanka slightly but had never met Imani. Roe loved the name and learned it meant Faith in Swahili. It was cool that each tourist had a different skin color, ranging from pale-white Beth to dark-chocolate Imani. Grudgingly, Roe admitted it was clever casting.

"I think we're lucky to be tourists," Priyanka said. "We don't have many lines, so we'll still have time for other things."

Beth nodded. "And the parts are cute. If we do a good job, no one will notice they're small."

Imani agreed. "We have a great family room, if you guys want to come over and practice sometime."

"Would you ask Kurt?" Beth asked, blushing slightly.

Imani laughed. "Definitely."

"Then let's make it definite," Priyanka said. "Otherwise, we'll never get around to it."

"Friday night at seven? I'll check with my mom, but I'm sure it's okay. I'll let you know tomorrow."

Roe forgot her aversion to seventh graders. Imani was nice. Maybe she would be able to go Friday night. Before returning to the stage, the girls wrote each other's phone numbers on their script covers and pooled their extra money for sodas for Kurt, Jaimie, and Miss Armstrong.

"An oasis in the desert," Kurt declared, when Beth handed him his drink. He pretended to kiss her hand while she laughed in obvious delight.

"Take it from the top," Miss Armstrong instructed, and Kurt opened the play. He entered Stage Left, crossed to Stage Right, and began scolding the invisible mouse.

Roe remembered from last year that blocking meant planning all large stage movements. The director would place the actors where they belonged and show them how to move around. Each moment on stage had to look like a picture.

"Tourists enter Stage Left."

Roe carefully wrote "n'tr S.L." in her script.

"Cross to Tully in this order: Mary, Jane, Fran, and Pam."

Roe wrote, "X to T after M." She showed her script to the seventh graders, so they could mark their own copies.

After the four tourists were on stage, Miss Armstrong arranged them into a pleasing stage picture. Roe drew a little sketch of what they looked like. "Don't stand in a straight line unless I tell you to," Miss Armstrong said. "Straight lines are for cancan dancers."

To Roe's disgust, Kurt quickly organized the seventh graders into an impromptu cancan dance.

Miss Armstrong laughed. "Save it for the variety show."

They practiced the tourists' entrance over and over again. The girls made fun of the tiny country of Grand Fenwick that was only five miles long by three miles wide.

No wonder you're left alone, Roe, in her role of Jane, told an insulted Tully Bascom.

"Excellent first rehearsal," the director said. "Next time we do this scene, be Off Book."

"What does that mean?" Imani whispered.

"Lines memorized," Roe whispered back. "We'll work on it Friday night." She crossed her fingers.

Smithy's, the hangout for the theater crowd of both Castle Bluff's middle and high schools, as well as Crofts Performing Arts, was crowded by the time Kylie and Brad arrived. There were shouts of "Hi" and "Congratulations" for both Glorianna and Count Mountjoy. Kylie noticed some of Crofts' students looking at them with interest.

They both ordered chocolate milkshakes.

"My treat," Brad insisted.

"Okay, thanks. But I'll treat next time." She'd save her money rather than frittering it away as usual.

"Next time," Brad agreed.

Glorianna and the Count tried to settle the affairs of their tiny country but soon gave it up for the laughter and fun of Smithy's. Kylie finally felt a part of this crowd—accepted, popular.

"We should find a more private place to practice," Brad said, "but we'll be okay at tomorrow's rehearsal."

A private place? That sounded fine to Kylie.

Five o'clock came too soon. "We'd better hurry if we're going to catch the late activity bus."

"Darn," Kylie said. "I don't have time to go back to my locker. I left my books there, and I have a huge science test tomorrow."

"Can't help. I don't have Tanning or any science homework tonight."

Kylie shrugged. "Oh, well. Roe lives next door to me. I can always borrow her book."

Roe said goodbye to her cast mates and headed for the school library. She spread her books out on an empty library table and reached for her least favorite subject, math. Other students were also taking advantage of Castle Bluff's new policy of keeping the library open in the evening. Roe wrinkled her forehead and concentrated on an especially difficult algebra problem.

Science next. A major test on one-celled animals; Mr. Tanning had promised it would be a killer. Roe reviewed her notes, and then opened her book to the end of the chapter. After quizzing herself on the vocabulary, she made sure she could answer the questions without peeking back.

"I should be all right," she whispered.

"Hey, Roe." It was Eric Stein, who had received the role of Page. Another small part, Roe thought.

"Oh, hi."

"Ready for the test?"

"I think so."

"Would you quiz me?" Eric sat next to her. "I never can tell what I've learned until someone asks me."

"All right. It might help me, too."

They took turns. "What's the name of the one-celled animal that changes form?"

"Amoeba."

"What's the name of the one-celled animal that looks like it has a tail?"

"Euglena, of course. Tanning's favorite."

They continued like this for another half hour until Eric glanced at his watch. "Are you going home now? We could walk together."

"I've still got English. I'll take the last bus."

"Maybe some other time, See ya."

Should she change her mind? Eric was really nice. No, she couldn't count on being able to finish her homework at home. If she didn't do laundry, there wouldn't be anything clean to wear tomorrow. She sighed. "I wonder if Mom has eaten anything today."

Roe had saved her favorite subject for last. Eagerly she opened *The Diary of Anne Frank* and left the world of Castle Bluff Middle School far behind.

"Roe, the library is about to close. Didn't you want to take the bus?"

"Oh, thank you, Mrs. Erickson. I totally lost track of time."

"With that book, I can see why," the librarian said. "Did you know it's also an award-winning play and that Crofts will perform it this winter?"

Roe sighed. "Oh, I wish they were doing it next year and I could be in it." If she went to Crofts, that is.

"Would you like a copy of the script? I'll check it out for you while you gather your things."

"That would be great, Mrs. Erickson."

Then Roe had a wonderful idea. For her class project, she could compare the diary with the script—show how the book had been adapted into a play. Maybe she could learn about the actors who had first created the roles.

Before leaving the building, Roe stopped at her locker. Marla was at her locker, too. Strange, Marla hadn't been in the library. "What are you doing here so late?" she asked, although she couldn't stand the girl.

"None of your business, plain Jane," Marla snarled and walked away.

Roe checked over her books. I'll take the diary and script home, she decided, but I won't need math or science. She put the texts into her locker and closed the door.

SCENE 4—A TROUBLESOME DAY

KYLIE SLIPPED INTO HER SEAT as the final bell rang. That was cutting it close, she thought. It would be awful if a detention kept her from attending rehearsal. Worriedly, she watched the pile of homework papers make its way to the front of the room—the first time she'd ever failed to turn in an assignment. If only she had remembered to ask Brad to explain the movie. She looked over at him. Brad shrugged, indicating that he too, hadn't done his homework.

Kylie tried to console herself. The general opinion was that Mrs. Simmons didn't grade half the papers she collected. Maybe she wouldn't notice. Instead of listening to the class discussion of *The Diary of Anne Frank*, Kylie turned to the science notes carefully concealed in her English notebook.

I'll study for the test, she decided. Was it my fault an assembly wiped out my only study hall? Oh, gosh, I'm doomed. I wouldn't recognize a paramecium if it bit me on the nose. This is Roe's fault. Why didn't she take her book home last night?

"Psst, Kylie. Beth asked me to give this to you."

"Thanks." Kylie took the note. Beth and the boy had lockers next to each other. She must have given it to him there. She opened it eagerly, not hearing Mrs. Simmons giving directions for a pop quiz.

> *Kylie, don't tell anyone! Music room trashed last night. Hasting thinks someone in cast did it! Call tonight! Destroy note! Beth*

Kylie shrugged. Probably a simple explanation. Beth always over-reacted. Better study. She looked down at her desk and found another paper.

While she had been reading, a quiz had been placed on her desk. Was she going to fail two tests in one day? This couldn't be happening!

Today I'm almost glad I'm me, Roe thought, as she walked into the gym. Her math teacher had commented on her improvement, and she knew she would do well on the science test later. In English, Mrs. Simmons had approved and seemed excited about her idea for the Anne Frank project.

That was weird, she thought, remembering her conversation with Mrs. Simmons right after class. Miss Armstrong was there, asking for Mrs. Simmons' help with costumes, and overheard Roe discussing her plan to compare the diary with the script. "What a coincidence," Miss Armstrong said. Then, a note was delivered to her, and she turned pale and left the room.

"What did Miss Armstrong mean by a coincidence?" Roe asked.

"Oh, probably because Crofts is doing the play this winter," Mrs. Simmons responded vaguely.

Maybe, Roe thought, but it was still weird.

Roe's PE class had begun its first lap around the indoor track when the loud speaker took charge.

"Excuse me, teachers and students, for interrupting your studies." Roe made a face. Hasting needed a new opening line. "Please send the following students to the office immediately." A few of the students exchanged worried glances. *Immediately* meant trouble.

Mr. Hasting read off a list of names: Kurt Brockway, Rosita Santos, Elizabeth Walters, Imani Jones, Priyanka Patel, Jaimie Jelinek. Roe flushed as all eyes turned on her. "These students are to report to the office immediately. Again, teachers, please excuse the interruption."

"It must be connected with the play," Roe told the teacher, who looked as if it were a plot to get out of running. PE teachers are paranoid, Roe thought, as she walked down the hall.

"Roe, wait up!" Beth, more freckle-faced than usual, seemed totally distraught. "I've never been called to the office before. My parents will kill me."

Roe scowled. "Chill, Beth. It's not like we've done anything wrong."

All of Act 1 Scene 1, plus the student director, Jaimie, arrived at approximately the same time. Miss Armstrong seemed tense as she stood waiting silently with a livid Mr. Hasting.

"Don't try to pretend you don't know why you're here," Mr. Hasting bellowed, as they took seats in his office.

The actors shook their heads. Kurt became spokesperson. "Honest, Mr. Hasting, we don't know. Does it have anything to do with the play?"

Mr. Hasting cleared his throat. "Yesterday afternoon, between the end of the school day and six p.m., the music room adjacent to the Green Room was—" Mr. Hasting paused for effect—"vandalized."

"Vandalized?" Jaimie asked. "How?"

"The choir's music was strewn all over the floor," Miss Armstrong explained.

Mr. Hasting threw the director a look that clearly said, "Keep quiet." His eyes blazed, and his nose turned red. "Someone ripped up, and then poured soft drinks over valuable sheet music."

"You don't think we did it?" Roe protested.

"You had the use of the stage and Green Room yesterday afternoon. I don't need to remind you the soft drink machine is in the Green Room. The night custodian discovered the violation when he began cleaning at seven."

"We left the building together at five," Miss Armstrong said. "I'm certain my students aren't responsible."

Roe flinched. She'd been in the library until six-thirty. Should she say so? No, better wait.

"There will be a full investigation, and the perpetrators shall be suspended." The principal checked his watch and then waved them out of the room.

Miss Armstrong had a request. "May I talk with my students before they return to their classes?"

"Very well, Miss Armstrong. See if you can get to the bottom of this outrage. Sabotage has no place at Castle Bluff Middle School!"

They walked silently to the Green Room. Priyanka and Beth sniffled, on the verge of tears. There, they all talked at once.

Miss Armstrong demanded silence. "You must keep this quiet," she cautioned. "Don't gossip, even to other cast members, and keep your eyes and ears open."

"I'll bet it was revenge," Kurt said. "Someone who didn't get a part wanted to frame CBT."

"I thought of that," Miss Armstrong said. "Or perhaps someone who isn't happy with their part."

Does she mean me? Roe wondered. "Couldn't someone in the chorus have done it?"

"It's possible, although there was no choir rehearsal yesterday. As I said, keep your eyes and ears open. We must try to clear CBT."

"So, what do we say when people ask why we were called to the office?" Priyanka asked, as they left the Green Room and were beyond the director's hearing.

Jaimie had an answer. "Say we got into trouble because we left chairs on the stage after rehearsal."

Beth brushed back tears. "What if they don't believe us?"

Kurt growled. "That's their problem!"

SCENE 5—TGIF

"TGIF!" DANNY KENNEDY ANNOUNCED THE next morning. He looked at his sister in a superior ten-year-old way. "Bet you don't know what that means, Kylie."

"It means, Thank God It's Friday." Kylie sighed as she sliced bananas onto her cornflakes and drowned both in two-percent milk. She gazed at the flames coming from the electric log in the stone fireplace in the Kennedy's country kitchen. If only she could wrap herself in Grandma's quilt and bask in its comfort all day. She watched the rainbow prisms on the carpet, cast by the firelight shining through her mother's colored glass collection on the kitchen counter. Sometimes home was the best place to be, she thought, remembering her stress-filled yesterday.

"We say, Thank *Goodness* it's Friday," Danny explained. "Sister gets mad if we say God, unless it's in a prayerful way, of course."

Kylie almost longed for the simplicity of Sister Mary Margaret's fifth grade.

"For heaven's sake, stop chattering and finish your breakfast." Mrs. Kennedy, frazzled as she always seemed to be lately, surveyed the hard surfaces in the kitchen in such a way Kylie knew she had misplaced her keys again. "Danny, you'll miss your bus, and Kylie, you've had a late start every morning this week."

"That's because it's so cold. I can't remember September ever being like this. I want to snuggle in my blanket and go back to sleep."

Mom was not in a sympathetic mood. "Set your alarm for a half hour earlier. Then you'll have more wake-up time."

"See ya." Danny gulped down the rest of his orange juice, gave his mother a quick peck, and bolted.

"You come straight home from school today!" But Danny was beyond hearing range. "Oh, darn!" Mom noticed the forgotten math book on the floor next to the table. "I'll have to stop off at St. Joseph's before going to work."

"Bad idea, Mom. He'll never learn if you keep doing everything for him."

Mrs. Kennedy shook her head. "Well, I'm not sure. Getting started in real estate has been more difficult than I expected. I can't seem to get organized."

"Tell me about it. Eighth grade is much harder than seventh. Mom, I know we're supposed to go see Aunt Gerry's photos of her Ireland trip tonight, but I'd like to stay home and study."

"On a Friday night? Really, Kylie, you've always managed beautifully. If I had a penny for every time you swore you were going to fail right before you ended up with an A plus, I could go to Ireland, too."

Kylie tried again. Why couldn't her mother understand without having everything spelled out? "Please let me stay home. Between assemblies and Student Council meetings, I hardly had any study periods this week. Sometimes I wish I'd never run for secretary." And in the evenings, she admitted to herself, she'd been so swept away by the glory of the lead and being Brad's new girlfriend, she hadn't given schoolwork a thought.

"I'm sure you'll do a wonderful job with whatever you do. As for staying home tonight, your father would never approve of your being here alone. But if you invite someone over, I guess it will be all right—this time."

"Thanks, Mom. I'll ask Beth." Kylie gave her mother a hug before making a quick escape.

She ran next door and rang the Santos's doorbell. No answer. Kylie peeked in the window and saw Roe's mother sitting on the couch, staring at the television. Kylie could hear the program's familiar theme song. Kylie shook her head, worried. Mrs. Santos was getting weirder and weirder. In a way Kylie was relieved that Roe hadn't waited for her. How could she have pretended not to notice Mrs. Santos was totally immersed in Sesame Street?

In the next block, she spotted Beth far ahead. By jogging, she managed to catch up. "Hey, Beth. Why didn't you come to rehearsal yesterday?"

"Orthodontist," Beth explained. "Miss Armstrong was cool with it. How was rehearsal? Did Miss Armstrong mention the music room?"

"Main topic of conversation."

"That's strange. She told *us* not to talk about it."

Kylie made a face. "Too late. It's all over school. Mr. Hasting wants the teachers to talk with their homerooms—about the *Dreadful Prankster*."

Beth giggled. "Sounds like a character in a Batman movie."

"Yeah, but I have a feeling it's not going to be funny."

"Did Miss Armstrong say she suspected Roe?"

Kylie shook her head. "Hardly. But she ignored her the whole rehearsal, and Roe could tell. It was too bad because she was trying really hard. She was hysterical during the part when the tourists try to speak French. If Miss Armstrong had only complimented her, I'll bet Roe would have been okay with her small part."

"Miss Armstrong thinks Roe did it," Beth said.

"I'm afraid you're right."

As they approached the school, Kylie remembered to invite Beth over for the night.

"Sorry, Kyle. Imani has invited the tourists over for a line rehearsal, but I'm sure she wouldn't mind if you came, too."

"No, that's all right. I should stay home and study. As usual, Mom has over-booked us for the entire weekend. I'm not allowed to stay alone tonight, but I'll ask Roe—if she's not going to Imani's, too."

Kylie was starting to feel left out. What had happened to the week that had begun so happily?

Roe had left for school early in order to avoid Kylie. Yesterday at rehearsal, it had taken her awhile to notice that people were treating her strangely. They were either too nice, like Kylie and Eric, or they ignored her, like Miss Armstrong. At first Miss Armstrong's behavior hadn't bothered her. After all, Roe hadn't been very pleasant, either. But she had tried to make amends by working hard on her part, small as it was, and had been certain Miss Armstrong would notice. Suddenly she knew. Miss Armstrong suspected her of vandalizing the music room! The rest of the rehearsal passed in a confusing blur.

Well, I didn't do it, and I can prove it, Roe thought. Plenty of people saw me in the library, including Mrs. Erickson. She'll vouch for me.

Roe walked alone for two blocks before she heard footsteps behind her. She turned and saw a girl she recognized, Cress Morgan, a junior at Crofts. Nice enough, but she always acted like she knew everything. Roe almost crossed to the other side of the street. Don't be silly, she scolded herself, slowing her pace to allow Cress to join her.

"Hi there," Cress said. "You're in CBT at the middle school, aren't you? I never forget a face."

"I know who you are," Roe said shyly. "I've seen you in lots of plays at Crofts."

"Now I remember!" Cress sounded triumphant. "You were in Armstrong's fall play last year."

"I'm Roe Santos."

"See? I never forget. You're a good actress, Roe."

"Thanks, but Miss Armstrong doesn't seem to think so. This year, I'm Jane, one of the tourists—a bit part. Miss Armstrong thinks—" Roe cleared her throat—"the part will give me an excellent opportunity to work on my projection."

Cress laughed. "You sound just like her. She could be right, though. You have a lot of natural ability. Your stage movement and expressions are excellent, but your voice is too soft—doesn't carry. A part that will force you to project and work on comic timing could be your ticket into Crofts."

Roe stared at the opinionated girl. "But I need a lead—a part that will show Crofts what I can do."

Cress looked disgusted. "You CBT kids don't get it. Crofts isn't looking for prima donnas. We need people with all-around theatrical ability. No small parts in theater, girl. Actually, you probably have a better chance at a scholarship than your golden-haired friend. What's her name? You know, the one who always plays the same kind of part but never improves. We call actors like that one-trick ponies."

"You mean Kylie Kennedy? She's playing Glorianna. She's the best actor we've got!"

"Ya think? I'll bet if you close your eyes when she says her lines, without paying attention to meaning, you'll think you're hearing her in last year's play."

Roe thought it over. Cress might have a point.

Cress continued to lecture. Roe thought she made some good points, although the way she did it was awfully irritating. "What crew are you on, Roe?"

"I'm not on any crew. I've got a part."

"Big mistake. Crofts is interested in the technical side of theater, too. Get yourself on a crew and start your project."

"I guess I could sign up for props, but what project?"

Cress patted the thick folder she was carrying. "These are the scholarship applications for Camp Shimmer Lake. I'm on my way to give them to Miss Armstrong. One of the requirements is a project to improve theater in your school."

"Camp? I don't know."

"Oh, Roe, it's not just any camp! It's my favorite place in the world!" For a minute, Cress's eyes glowed with pleasure and longing, and she became an ordinary teen, not a pretentious authority figure. "This will be my last summer there, unless I can get a staff job the following summer. Mrs. Crofts-Baker runs it. It's in Michigan, right along the dunes. We do three shows in three weeks and learn so much! You've just got to go!"

"Sounds great," Roe said, "but I may not be able to. I'll need a scholarship to go to Crofts next year. I don't think my parents would be willing to spend the money when I could go to the regular high school for nothing. It's not the money, exactly. They're just not big on theater."

"Then you want a Shimmer Lake scholarship. Practically everyone who gets one is offered another one to Crofts. You almost have to bomb out not to."

"There is a props meeting after school today," Roe said slowly. "They're looking for more volunteers."

"There you go." Cress summarized. "Work on props, part, and project, and you'll land at Crofts next September."

The three Ps, Roe thought, as they entered the building. Filled with her own importance, Cress bustled off to the Green Room.

Roe found Kylie waiting at her locker after school. "I went to your house this morning, but you'd already left," Kylie said.

"I had stuff to do."

"I rang the doorbell, but your mom didn't answer. I could see her through the window watching TV."

Roe nodded. "And that's where she'll be when I get home." *If only Dad comes back tonight,* she thought. *He's got to listen to me. It can't go on this way.*

Kylie looked flustered. "Uh, I was going to ask you to stay over at my house tonight—if you aren't going to Imani's."

Roe's eyes filled, and she turned away, embarrassed. "No, I wanted to, but my father is supposed to come home. Maybe I could go to your house later—like eight or nine."

"That would work," Kylie said. "We haven't had a sleepover in ages. Not since our birthdays."

Roe still couldn't look at Kylie. "Okay. I'm going to the props meeting, but I'll let you know when I know."

"We might see each other on the bus. I'm meeting Brad at Smithy's. But tonight, Roe, I should do some homework. I haven't had much time this week. If you come, do you think you could explain that diary thing we're reading for English? I haven't even started it."

Roe's tears disappeared. "That diary thing? Do you mean *The Diary of Anne Frank*? Don't you know what it's about?"

Kylie shook her head.

"Oh, Kylie. Time to wake up!"

Kylie and Brad rushed over to Smithy's. Hoping not to be discovered by the Friday afternoon crowd, they sank into the most private booth they could find. The date had been made in English class, and Kylie had counted the minutes until the 3:15 bell. *Thank goodness it's Friday,* she thought, remembering Danny's proclamation that morning.

"I'll buy the milkshakes today," Kylie promised, grateful she would receive her allowance the next day. Mom had hinted, though, that Kylie should start using it for essentials. *This is essential,* she decided.

Brad nodded. "Chocolate with extra whipped cream."

Fortunately, Miss Armstrong never scheduled Friday afternoon rehearsals but reserved that time for crew meetings. Kylie and Brad opened their scripts. They were required to be Off Book Scene Two by Monday.

"Someone should prompt us," Brad said. "I can't tell if I've learned my lines or not."

Kylie nodded. "That's okay. I know mine, even though I bombed on everything else this week. I'll read my part and prompt you."

"Ryan should be here," Brad complained. "How can we practice this scene without the prime minister?"

So far, Ryan Cotner had been a disappointment. He didn't seem interested in giving any extra time to his challenging role.

"He's on the tennis team, too," Brad continued. "He's a good actor, but I think Armstrong might have made a mistake in casting him."

Kylie noticed Eric Stein sitting alone at the counter and beckoned him over. Eric seemed pleased to be asked to read Ryan's part.

"You're Roe Santos's friend, aren't you?" Eric asked Kylie.

She grinned. "Best friend—most of the time."

"Is she coming?"

"No, she went to a props meeting in the Green Room, but I'll tell her you were asking." Kylie made her voice sound suggestive.

But Eric shook his head worriedly.

"Something wrong?" Brad asked.

"I'm not sure. I don't know Roe very well, but she helped me study for the science test. I just don't think she should be staying after school so much."

"Why not?" Kylie asked. "She likes to do her homework in the library."

Eric tried to explain. "I was in the office after school, and I overheard the new head custodian talking with Hasting. Man, was he hot! Seems most of the custodians' food was stolen from their refrigerator last night. Well, their room is right next to the Green Room."

Brad groaned. "Oh, no, not more trouble?"

"Yup. Hasting's Dreadful Prankster has struck again."

"But how does that have anything to do with Roe?" Kylie wondered. "There were tons of people at rehearsal yesterday. I was there myself."

"Beats me, but you saw how Armstrong treated Roe, and I heard Hasting mention her name. I don't know why they suspect her, but they do."

After ordering soda and fries, Eric held Brad's script and read the part of David Benter while Glorianna and Count Mountjoy practiced their lines. Kylie didn't do well, though. Her heart wasn't in it. She couldn't stop thinking about Roe.

"Hurry, Roe. You'll miss the activity bus," Samantha Bates, the props committee chair, urged. "Remember, it's the only one running on Fridays."

Roe dumped the entire contents of her locker onto the hall floor and frantically searched through the debris.

"I'll have to catch up. Go ahead without me, Sam. I've lost something important."

At a nearby locker, Jaimie Jelinek gathered music for her voice lesson. "What did you lose, Roe?"

"My silver bracelet." Roe continued to search. "I left it in my locker yesterday before PE, but I don't remember putting it back on again."

"You mean your ID bracelet? The one with the rose engraved next to your initials?"

Roe nodded. The bracelet had been from her father—the only present she could remember that was just from him.

"Too bad," Jaimie said. "Do you think it was stolen? You hardly ever close your locker all the way."

"It jams if I do, but I doubt anyone took it. I probably did wear it home and forgot taking it off." She returned the contents to the locker and set the combination lock to the last number. "Honestly, this locker is nothing but trouble. It either jams or doesn't lock."

"You've missed the bus. My voice lesson lasts until five. If you want to hang around, my mom could give you a ride home."

"Thanks. That sounds great."

"The library is closed on Fridays. Where will you wait?"

"I'll crash in the Green Room. Could you get me there, in case I fall asleep?"

"Sure thing. See you in an hour."

The Green Room was empty. Roe treated herself to a soda, then crashed on an overstuffed chair and closed her eyes. She was more worried about her bracelet than she cared to admit, and she dreaded the conversation she must have with her father—if he came home.

But I've got to do it. I can't take care of Mother by myself.

In this quiet, dim place, she allowed herself to remember the accident that had destroyed her family, although remembering usually confused her more than it helped.

Almost two years had passed since the dreary December night her brother Mateo and two of his friends had plunged to their deaths off the old Markey Bridge. Seventeen-year-old Mateo had had the use of the family car that night, with the understanding he was to first drive Roe home from her sixth grade play rehearsal. Then he could go off with his friends. The dress rehearsal for a play, in which she played the lead, ended at seven-thirty after a pizza party. What a wonderful time it had been!

Roe's friends, especially Kylie, had looked on with envy when handsome Mateo and his friends had walked into the auditorium to meet her. Roe had noticed the expression on Kylie's face and almost offered her a ride. Her stubborn, selfish act probably saved Kylie's life.

The boys had been laughing and cracking jokes as they crossed Markey Bridge. Then it was sort of a blur. When Roe awoke, she found herself in a bed at St. Anthony's Hospital, alone, her head pounding and her arm in a cast.

According to the police, the car had skidded on the icy bridge and crashed through the railing. They found Roe unconscious on the bridge next to the break-through. It took hours to retrieve the bodies of two of the boys, but Mateo's was never recovered. How Roe had escaped from the car remained a mystery to others. Roe knew, but she would never tell. It would only make things worse.

Roe's whole world had changed by the time she came home from the hospital—no Mateo, and a mother and father numb with shock and grief. Mrs. Santos hardly noticed she had a daughter. Roe wondered if her mother blamed her for Mateo's death—or maybe she wished Roe had died instead.

Mrs. Santos locked Mateo's room and allowed no one but herself to enter. Then she quit her job and stayed home. On the few occasions she did speak to Roe, it was to issue brief orders. Mr. Santos, always somewhat distant, became more so, and his business trips became more and more frequent. Sometimes he mentioned returning to Mexico, a place where Roe had never been. Did he want to return alone? Roe didn't know.

Other families cope with tragedies. Why can't mine? she often asked herself.

She missed being in the play, of course. Kylie took on Roe's lead role and was noticed by Miss Armstrong, who came to see the performance.

"Everything changed," Roe whispered, before drifting off into a troubled sleep.

At four, Eric said goodbye and rushed to catch the activity bus. In spite of the distance, Brad walked Kylie home. "Would you like to come over to my house tonight? We could work on lines and watch a show."

"Your house?" How she wished she hadn't invited Roe, but maybe she could change the invitation to another night. "I'm not sure. My parents won't be home, but they might say I can. They could pick me up on their way back. I'll text you later after I find out."

After Brad left, Kylie thought of Roe. She had noticed the tears. The invitation had been important to her, and now Kylie was planning to dump her.

"A fine friend I am!" Kylie flung her jacket onto a living room chair, although she knew she'd hear words on the subject later. The closet is too far away, she thought. She was considering taking a quick nap on the couch when the study door opened.

"Oh, hi, Dad. You're home early." Then she gulped. The expression on her father's face meant something was wrong.

"Kylie, please come here a minute. I want to speak with you."

Roe woke with a start and looked around in a daze. What was that? Had she dreamed the odd shuffling noise? She noticed the clock. Almost six? Jaimie must have forgotten her. She'd have to walk home, and it would be dark by the time she arrived. If only she got there before Dad grew frustrated with Mother and left again.

"What are you doing here?"

She jumped. "Oh, sorry, Mr. Jacobs, I fell asleep. My friend was supposed to meet me. She must have forgotten."

"Get along with you," said the night custodian. "I got work to do."

All the lights were on at home. That never happened. In the living room, Roe found her father seated at his desk, bent over, his head resting on his hands. Her mother was no longer on the couch. "Where is she?" Roe demanded.

"Sit down, Rosita."

"Where's mother?" she repeated, not obeying.

"That's what I'm about to tell you. I came home early, around noon, and found her lying on the couch staring at the TV."

How dare he? "That's not news. It's where she is most of the time." If you were at home more, you might have noticed. But she didn't say that, of course.

"Rosita, she didn't respond. I don't think she knew I was there. I called 911, and an ambulance took her to the hospital."

"Hospital?" Roe began to shake.

"I don't understand the technical terms," her father continued. "Dr. Rao says she's terribly depressed, possibly suicidal."

"Suicide? Mother?" An odd numbness crept over her.

"She never came to terms with Mateo's death. I'm afraid I haven't either," he added quietly. "Dr. Rao recommended a hospital in Michigan, and we took her there this afternoon. She'll get the best possible care," he said robotically, sounding as if he were quoting a brochure.

Softly, Roe began to cry. "Everything keeps getting worse—not better. How long will she be there?"

"I don't know, honey." Mr. Santos stood and held out his arms. But Roe didn't respond. Her father had become a stranger. He lowered them again. "I'm going to rent an apartment near the hospital so I can be near her. So much of this is my fault."

Roe wiped away the tears with the back of her hand. "What about me? I can't go to Michigan."

"Of course you can't. I've made arrangements for you to stay with the Kennedys."

"I'm going to live with Kylie?"

"I've given Dan and Jane money for your care. You may come back here whenever you like, but you'll have your meals and sleep next door." A pained look crossed Mr. Santos's face. "You'll receive better care there than you have here for the past two years."

Kylie greeted Roe at the front door. "Dad told me what happened after I got home. I'm sorry about your mom, Roe, but I'm glad you're coming here to live. We'll be sisters as well as friends."

Roe burst into tears, but they were mainly tears of relief. At last her mother would receive help. She was no longer Roe's responsibility.

Scene 7—Green Room Woes

Kylie stretched lazily, resetting her alarm, pulling the pink and white comforter to her eyebrows. Fifteen more minutes, she promised herself. Through the wall, she could hear Roe in the guest room. Maybe it was good she had her own room. Kylie had wanted Roe in the twin bed next to her own, but Mrs. Kennedy was adamant. "This is more than a sleepover. Roe could be here for some time. You girls need your own space." Mom was right, Kylie decided, hearing drawers being opened and shut. Roe was one of those crazy morning people.

She grabbed her alarm again. An extra ten minutes wouldn't hurt, although going to school today might not be so bad. She was prepared—for a change. She'd even caught up with her schoolwork—thanks to Roe. What a weekend! They must have talked all night on Friday. They were best friends again, maybe for the first time since Mateo's accident.

Saturday had been a typical Kennedy chore-and-everything-else day. After shopping and cleaning and helping Roe move in, the whole family was exhausted. "I'm taking this hard-working crew out for dinner and a movie," Mr. Kennedy announced. "You deserve it."

"Are you sure?" Kylie's mom seemed worried.

"Yes," her husband said firmly.

They went to a new restaurant in town, specializing in spaghetti and chicken, served family style. Kylie was pleased to see Roe finally relax, joking with Dad and Danny. The film they chose starred one of their favorite comedians, and they laughed so hard at his antics they could hardly hear the movie.

Sunday also would have been typically Kennedy—church in the morning, dinner at one, joined by Grandma and Grandpa, followed by a discussion of afternoon and evening plans—if Roe hadn't said, "Please excuse me, but once dinner is over, I've got tons of homework. Our English project is due in a week."

Kylie seized the chance and asked to be excused, too. Her mother had looked at her amazed. "You don't have homework, do you, dear?"

This was her opportunity to be honest. "I haven't even started reading *The Diary of Anne Frank* yet, and I have no ideas for a project. I've got to work, too. With Roe."

Both girls went next door to study. Roe's house was sad and eerie but, unlike Kylie's, quiet. Roe sat at the dining room table and dug into math. At first, Kylie tried to talk but seeing Roe's determined expression, finally opened the book. Hours passed as she read from cover to cover. It was almost suppertime when she finished, tears streaming down her face.

"That was the saddest, most wonderful thing I ever read," she said. "Everyone should read this book."

Roe put down her pencil. She had finished the rough draft for her project. "I wish Crofts would wait until next year to put on the play," she sighed. "Not that I'll be there, of course."

"Probably neither of us will." Kylie shook her head. "Your idea of comparing the diary and the script is super. I wish I knew what to do."

"Some of the boys are working together on a model of the Secret Annex where Anne and her family lived." Roe had looked thoughtful. "You're a fast reader, Kylie. It took me much longer to read the diary." She paused, still thinking. "I know, maybe you could get Miep Gies's book, *Anne Frank Remembered,* from the library. It's about how Miep helped the Franks and other families. She was extremely brave and nearly got caught lots of times. You could read it, and then write about what was going on outside the Secret Annex— what people went through to help Anne's family and other Jews."

It was a wonderful idea; she liked it even better than Roe's project. Kylie determined to go to the library first thing to check out the book. The alarm rang again. As she reached over to continue her game with the clock, there was a loud rap on the door.

"Kylie, if you don't hurry, I'm leaving without you!"

Roe said goodbye to Kylie at the library door before going alone to the office. In spite of the confusion over the weekend, she had remembered to search for her bracelet but didn't find it. Maybe someone had turned it in to Lost and Found.

Mrs. Schultz, the secretary, looked from her desk and smiled, but the smile faded when she saw Roe. "What is it, Rosita?"

Roe was startled by the secretary's cold manner. Mrs. Schultz had always been sweet to her. "I've lost my bracelet," she explained. "It's silver and has a rose and my initials on it. I was wondering if it had been turned in."

"One minute." Mrs. Schultz left her desk and went into Mr. Hasting's office. She returned quickly. "Mr. Hasting will see you," she said, without looking at Roe.

Puzzled, Roe walked into the principal's office. A stern Mr. Hasting sat at his desk, dangling a silver object. "What do you have to say regarding this?" he demanded.

Roe sighed in relief. "My bracelet! Thank you, Mr. Hasting. I've looked everywhere for it."

"And where do you think it was found?"

Roe shook her head.

"The night custodian discovered your bracelet in the custodian's room Thursday night, right after he noticed food had been stolen. What do you have to say for yourself?" Mr. Hasting practically shrieked.

"I didn't do it!" Roe raised her voice, but it was no match for Mr. Hasting's. "I've never been in the custodian's room. I put my bracelet in my locker before going to PE on Thursday. That was the last time I saw it."

"Mr. Jacobs also saw you, all alone, in the Green Room on Friday evening," Mr. Hasting persisted. "He said you were acting strange."

Roe gasped. "I was acting sleepy. I missed the bus and was waiting for a ride from Jaimie Jelinek, but she forgot about me, and I fell asleep. When I woke up it was dark, and I had to walk home. Jaimie will tell you, Mr. Hasting. I didn't do anything wrong."

"The Green Room was found vandalized this morning," Mr. Hasting bellowed, "and you, young lady, are our prime suspect." He shoved the phone toward Roe, who had begun to cry. "Call your parents at once. This is ample grounds for suspension."

Roe sobbed. "I can't call my parents. My mother is sick, and my father took her to a hospital in Michigan."

"Leaving you here alone?"

"I'm staying with the Kennedys. Honest, Mr. Hasting, I didn't do it."

"Then phone the Kennedys."

"They're not home."

Mr. Hasting sneered. "I see you have an answer for everything. Go on to class, but make sure they contact me first thing tomorrow. You may have your bracelet back, but I'll hold you responsible for returning the Green Room to proper order. Today's rehearsal is cancelled."

Trembling, Roe asked Mrs. Schultz for a late pass to her first period class. On the way, she stopped off at the girls' room to wash her tear-stained face. Jaimie was standing at the mirror brushing her hair.

Roe swallowed hard before speaking. "I'm rounding up some kids to help clean the Green Room after school today. Will you come, Jaimie?"

Jaimie crammed the brush back into her purse. "You've got to be kidding. Clean it yourself!" She marched out.

Morning classes passed in a blur of hostile faces, accusing glances, and whispers that stopped when she drew near. They knew! Who had Mr. Hasting told? Or was someone else spreading the rumors? But eventually lunchtime came. Roe felt better when she saw the anger on Kylie's face.

"How dare he accuse you? My dad will be furious."

"Hasting thinks my bracelet is proof. He says I have to clean the Green Room. I've asked some people to help, but no one will talk to me."

"Don't worry, Roe. I'll take charge of finding a cleanup committee. You concentrate on getting through the day."

Before going to her first afternoon class, Roe stopped off at her locker. Marla Gray was nearby closing hers. Roe almost didn't say anything, but she knew how it felt to be ignored. "Hi, Marla," she said.

Marla turned and smiled—an evil smile—and the dark eyes above it were full of malice. It was obvious Marla was responsible for the trouble. She had stolen the bracelet. Marla, who hadn't been cast in the play—who hadn't even received a small part. Roe had no proof, of course. She just knew.

Kylie was first to arrive in the Green Room. What a time she'd had organizing a cleanup crew. She shuddered, remembering. Thank goodness she had been the one to ask. How could they have turned against Roe so quickly? She wondered if they would have done the same thing to her. Well, the thing to do was make it like a party. They must show Roe their support and cheer her up.

Soon the only other recruits, Beth, Brad, Kurt, and Eric arrived. Roe came last. It was obvious she had been crying. The usually calm Eric was white with fury. He does like Roe, Kylie thought.

Beth dropped fifty cents into the soda machine and handed Roe a Coke. "I know you didn't do it, Roe," she said. "I'm with you all the way."

Kurt chuckled. "She sure is and can prove it. Beth has detention for decking Jaimie Jelinek."

"He exaggerates," Beth said. "I merely shoved her."

Kylie couldn't help feeling satisfied when she saw the embarrassed look on Roe's face. Roe had been nasty to the younger girl.

"Beth, I don't want you to get into trouble because of me!" Roe started to cry again.

"Hey, that's what friends are for." Eric's words were light, and Kylie and the rest took the hint. Time to put a lid on emotions.

Brad organized them, and the Green Room soon was back to normal. (Fortunately, the custodians had taken care of the clogged toilet.) Then they purchased a round of sodas, another one for Roe, and began to plan.

"Do you have any idea who did this?" Eric asked.

"Maybe, but I don't have proof," Roe said softly, "so I won't say anything." She wasn't going to be like the people who were accusing her.

"We've go to find out for sure," Kylie insisted, "not only for Roe's sake, but for all of us. This is wrecking CBT's reputation, and it's hard on the play. We needed that rehearsal Hasting cancelled."

"So, any suggestions?" Beth asked.

They thought.

"I've got it," Eric said. "Those of us who have rehearsal tomorrow can stay behind afterwards and hide in the Green Room. Maybe we'll get lucky and catch someone in the act."

"That might work," Kylie said. "Who has rehearsal besides Brad and me?"

"The tourists don't," Beth said. "That lets me out, and Roe, too. Besides, I've got that detention."

"I've got rehearsal," Kurt said, "but I've got to go home afterwards and study for a math test. Parents' orders. My grades are slipping because of the play, and Dad said I'll have to quit if I don't turn things around fast."

"I don't have a rehearsal, but I'm staying anyway." The expression on Eric's face dared anyone to disagree.

"What about me?" Roe wondered.

"You've got to stay in the building," Kurt said. "Otherwise nothing will happen. You're the one being framed."

Kylie shook her head. "I don't think she should be in the Green Room, though. If anything goes wrong, we don't want her blamed again."

"She can work in the library," Brad said.

They all nodded—including Roe.

Planning together made everything different. Kylie couldn't wait for the next day. The situation was serious, but it was awfully exciting, too.

SCENE 8—CAUGHT!

Kylie tried to ignore the persistent itch on her lower back, but the more she ignored it, the worse it became. "Sorry, guys, but I've got to scratch," she said.

"Are you nuts?" Eric stage-whispered. "Get down!"

"Phew!" Kylie breathed, tackling the tickle before resuming her tight position.

She glanced at the Green Room clock, its hands still visible in the dark room. Only fifteen minutes since she, Brad, and Eric had taken their places behind the shabby couch and overstuffed chairs. What had begun as an exciting adventure had become an uncomfortable, silent bore.

A rustle broke the silence. "What was that?" Eric whispered.

"It was the cat," Brad answered, in a spooky, hissing voice.

Kylie couldn't help giggling.

Eric growled. "You're going to blow the whole thing."

"Sor-ry, but I happen to be getting a cramp in my foot."

"At least you've got some feeling. My whole leg has gone to sleep."

"Shhh!" Eric warned. "This could be our last chance to clear Roe."

With that, they crouched down again. Things were officially serious, Kylie reflected. Not only was Roe in trouble, but today's rehearsal was terrible. The dirty tricks were on their minds and morale was low. *We've got to solve this mystery before the play is ruined.* Her parents were being great, though. Last night after the dishes were loaded and Danny was distracted by the TV, Kylie and Roe confided in Mom and Dad, telling them everything—except for the plan to catch the guilty person, of course.

"I'll do more than phone," Dad had promised. "I'll pay Mr. Hasting a visit first thing tomorrow morning." Kylie nearly laughed out loud as she remembered seeing her father storm into the vice principal's office that morning. She wished she could have seen Dad giving it to that awful bully.

After school, Roe had watched the rehearsal from the back of the auditorium. Totally depressing. No one remembered lines or blocking or anything. The play's going to be a disaster, she predicted. Then on the way down the hall to the library, she passed Mr. Hasting. He glared at her without speaking. She wondered what Mr. Kennedy had said to him. It felt good to have a father on her side—even a borrowed father.

The Kennedys had talked Roe into revealing her suspicions. "We understand you don't want to accuse anyone unjustly," Mrs. Kennedy said, "but we should know what you're thinking. The conversation needn't leave this room."

So Roe told them about the late afternoons she had bumped into Marla at their hall lockers. "I don't know why she was even in the building. I don't think she joined anything but Drama Club." Roe mentioned Marla's taunts and evil expressions. "Of course, that's not proof of anything."

Mr. Kennedy gave a long, low whistle before speaking. "Marla Gray. Wouldn't that be a fine kettle of fish with her father the treasurer of the school board?" He hesitated. "Now this *really* can't leave the room. If it weren't for Charles Gray, I don't think Willard Hasting could keep his job. There have been many complaints regarding his strong-arm tactics. His treatment of you, Roe, and other minorities, seems typical. But for some reason, Charles Gray is Mr. Hasting's staunchest supporter."

Roe sighed, wondering what was happening in the Green Room. She spread her books and papers on the library table. Concentrating wouldn't be easy, but it sure would be nice not to have any homework tonight. She'd start with science.

Behind the couch, Kylie shifted to make herself more comfortable. Darn, I'm getting a cramp, too, she thought. She had her own theories about the identity of the culprit. It could have been Marla. She was pissed off enough about not making the play, but Jaimie's behavior was strange, too. Jaimie had "forgotten" to awaken Roe and had become surprisingly hostile toward her former friend. Kylie shuddered, remembering her effort to recruit Jaimie in the clean-up. Why had she turned against Roe?

She'd decided to give up when the Green Room door opened. Kylie held her breath. She could hear someone whisper—"Shh."

Kylie was all set to jump when—"Relax, guys. It's only me."

"Beth, what are you doing here?"

"I'm not the prankster, if that's what you think. Detention is over, and I knew I would go crazy waiting at home, so I came here."

"Well, hurry and get down," Eric growled. "Let's hope you didn't wreck the whole thing."

Roe closed her science book and opened algebra. She groaned. The problems were tricky. Too hard to concentrate. Instead, she'd proofread her Anne Frank project again. She felt herself identifying more and more with the young war victim. Anne had problems with her mother, too, and she was being punished for something that wasn't her fault. Anne was Jewish; Roe was half Latina. Could Uncle Dan—he'd asked her to call him that—be right? Surely Mr. Hasting didn't have a problem with where her father had come from. Roe wished she could talk to Anne about many things. And if she heard about Roe's mom, maybe she'd appreciate her own more. At least Mrs. Frank cared about her daughters.

Roe's father had phoned last night but didn't give her a chance to discuss her own troubles, even if she would. "Rosita, I'd like you to clear Mateo's room. Your mother won't be home anytime soon, but I want there to be no reminders when that time comes."

Roe had gasped. "What do you want me to do with everything?"

"Box up whatever you think meaningful and store it in the attic. Give the rest to charity. Use your own discretion. That room must stop being a shrine."

Roe agreed but dreaded the task. Didn't she have enough to handle? She could ask Kylie to help but was afraid of what the forbidden room might reveal.

She returned to her project. At least Anne had a terrific father.

Kylie was ready to give up when it happened. The door opened, slowly and quietly. Then one small lamp came on. She longed to end the suspense but forced herself to stay in the cramped position. They must catch the person actually doing something.

She heard an odd striking noise, smelled burning, and then heard Brad shout, "That's enough, Marla. Put it out!"

Leaving her hiding place, Kylie saw Marla Gray preparing to set off a smoke bomb. Eric grabbed it, stepped on the wick, and then took matches away from the startled girl.

"So it was you," Kylie said. "Just because you didn't get a part, you tried to wreck the play and Roe's reputation."

"And almost succeeded," Eric said.

"Someone should get Roe and Mr. Hasting," Brad said.

"I'll get Roe," Beth offered.

"And I'll get Hasting," Kylie said.

Marla glared scornfully at her captors. "I don't have to stay here." She headed for the door.

Brad and Eric each grabbed one of Marla's arms. "Oh yes you do," Eric said.

"Don't you know who my father is?"

Brad held on tighter. "We don't care who your father is. You're not going anywhere!"

Kylie found Mr. Hasting working late in his office. "So, you've caught the perpetrator. Good work. Rosita Santos, I suppose."

She saw the anger fade from the vice principal's face when she told him Marla Gray was setting off a smoke bomb. Oddly, he seemed frightened.

Then Mr. Hasting began to chuckle. "I guess it's one of those adolescent things. Why, when I was a boy . . ." he began confidentially.

Kylie stared at him. Was he going to let Marla get away with it?

"They're in the Green Room," she said, interrupting Mr. Hasting's story about what he and his friends had done with firecrackers when he was *just a lad.* "I've got to go, Mr. Hasting. I'll see you there."

In the hall, Kylie grabbed her cell phone. Roe needs her own father, she thought, but mine will have to do. She punched in the numbers. "Please pick up, Dad," she whispered. "No voice mail, please!"

Fortunately, Mr. Kennedy answered the phone and promised to drive to the school immediately. Then, impulsively, she called Miss Armstrong. Their director should be a part of this, Kylie decided.

Roe was on problem twelve when she heard Beth's voice behind her. "It worked, Roe. We caught her."

Roe closed the book. "Marla?" she whispered.

"She was trying to set off a smoke bomb." Quickly, Beth filled Roe in, and they hurried back.

But if they expected to find a defeated Marla and an apologetic Mr. Hasting, they were disappointed. Instead, they saw Brad squirming in discomfort, Eric looking as if he were on the verge of a stroke, and Marla sitting quietly on the couch with a superior smirk on her sour face.

Roe gasped. Was Mr. Hasting defending Marla?

"I'm sure you can understand how disappointed Marla must have been not to have received any part in the play," he said.

Marla nodded her head in agreement before switching to a mournful expression.

"Only because she wrote on her audition form she wouldn't accept anything but Glorianna," Eric said. "Jaimie told me."

Noiselessly, Roe began to cry. She scarcely noticed that Beth, who'd put an arm around her, was crying, too.

"I'm sure we can put this behind us," Mr. Hasting purred. "So much fuss over practical jokes."

"Jokes? Roe would have been suspended, if not worse," Eric roared. Roe hardly recognized him.

"A smoke bomb would have affected the whole school," Brad said quietly. "This isn't a joke, Mr. Hasting."

The vice principal shrugged impatiently. "Well, it didn't happen, did it?"

Eric was not going to stop. "Isn't Roe's father important enough for you?"

The students gasped at Eric's nerve.

"I will not allow you to say such things to me!" Mr. Hasting bellowed.

"Time that somebody did, Willard,' said a voice at the Green Room door. Mr. Kennedy had heard the whole conversation. Standing with him was Kylie and next to her, Miss Armstrong, mouth open in disbelief.

Roe let out a sigh of relief that, mixed with her sobs, soon turned into hiccups.

"There was no need for you to come," Mr. Hasting said. "This is a simple matter I will handle."

"Yes, you will—in your office with me watching," Mr. Kennedy said. "Either you call Marla's parents and follow the school district's disciplinary procedure, or I will contact the police."

Mr. Hasting began to sputter, but Kylie's father held firm. "Marla, you come with Mr. Hasting and me," he said to the girl who looked uncertain for the first time. "Anna," Mr. Kennedy addressed Miss Armstrong, "Will you see that these young people get home?"

"I certainly will," she said.

In a shaky voice, Roe spoke. "Wait a minute, please. I want to know. Marla, I can understand why you were upset about not getting Glorianna, but you didn't want my part. Why did you try to make me look guilty? I've never done anything to you."

Marla sneered, then laughed. "Actually, I wanted people to suspect Kylie because I should be Glorianna. I'm a much better actor. But you were too easy to resist. Everyone knew you were mad at Miss Armstrong, and you were always staying late to study. Your habit of not closing your locker made it simple for me to take your bracelet. And you framed yourself when you fell asleep in here."

Even Mr. Hasting looked stunned by the cold cruelty of Marla's words as he, Mr. Kennedy, and Marla left the Green Room.

Miss Armstrong grabbed Roe into a hug. "Roe, I am so sorry I ever believed it was you."

Roe returned the embrace. "I don't blame you," she said. "I'm sorry I was a poor sport. I'm starting to see what you mean about small parts. All of our small parts were important tonight. And Beth, I'll never forget how you stuck up for me, even though I've been mean to you."

"Let's be friends," Beth said, with a teary smile and a hug.

Then it was Kylie's turn. "Oh, Roe, I'm so happy for you."

"I'm feeling left out. Group hug," Brad said, and he and Eric joined in.

Miss Armstrong laughed. "Now I suggest we put this behind us. We've got a show to do!"

SCENE 9—REHEARSE! REHEARSE! REHEARSE!

THE FOLLOWING WEEKS FLEW BY. Soon tech rehearsal was only days away. "It's always like this," Miss Armstrong explained to her nervous actors. "You think you have all the time in the world, and then—well, you don't. No matter what, I always think I need two more weeks."

The stage no longer seemed foreign. The actors were as comfortable moving around on it as they were in their own homes. The scenery crew, led by a tech theater class from the local high school, was constructing the complex set that had to move quickly between the castle in Grand Fenwick, a science lab in New York City, and the White House in Washington DC—with the curtain closing only between acts. As Miss Armstrong said, "Pacing is essential, both for actors and crew."

Kylie had learned her lines, but not everyone else had managed. Brad made so many mistakes in his role of Count Mountjoy that she had a difficult time playing opposite him. For a while, this put a strain on their friendship.

Miss Armstrong took her aside one day. "Don't be so hard on Brad," she cautioned. "He'll have his lines memorized in time. People learn them in different ways and at different rates."

After this conversation, Kylie backed off. She didn't want to lose her first boyfriend over a play. On stage, Count Mountjoy was prompted through his scenes with Glorianna. During their Friday night rehearsals at cast members' homes, she let someone else drill Brad on his part.

Beth was becoming disillusioned. "This isn't fun anymore—no one is getting along. I don't think the show is going to be any good."

Kylie tried to lift her spirits. "This is normal. Just wait. The excitement will come back during dress rehearsals."

Beth wasn't convinced. "Maybe, but hanging around for only a couple of scenes is boring. I'll be glad when the play is over."

Not long after Marla was caught in the Green Room, Ryan Cotner, who played the role of Prime Minister David Benter, quit. He was in danger of being dropped from the tennis team because of low grades. His parents hired a tutor and gave him a choice—tennis or the play? Tennis won.

Miss Armstrong fumed. "He made the play first, and the play should come first."

Eric Stein saved the day. By helping Kylie and Brad, he almost knew the lines by heart. And because of watching so many rehearsals, he also knew the blocking. Miss Armstrong gave Eric a quick audition, and he became the new David Benter.

"But the Page?" Miss Armstrong moaned. "It's not a big part, but it's important. Eric was perfect."

Kylie had been thinking. "How about Roe? Jane and the Page are never on stage at the same time. It would be possible for her to play both parts—with a quick costume change, of course."

"I wanted the Page to be a boy," Miss Armstrong complained, but she really had no choice, and Roe was more than capable of handling the double role.

Ryan wasn't the only one affected by looming report card time. One Friday afternoon, Kylie walked home alone, leaving Roe behind to attend an emergency props meeting. She walked slowly, without her usual confidence. Many students had received their report cards in the mail the day before, and hers was bound to be waiting for her. While her work had improved since Roe had come to live with them, Kylie was not optimistic.

Sure enough. No sooner had she taken off her jacket than her mother called her into the kitchen and presented her with an ominous piece of paper. Kylie studied it. Not even one A. B in English, D in science, C- in math, and the rest were Cs.

"What do you have to say?" her mother demanded.

"Actually, it's better than I expected." Kylie tried to ignore her mother's shocked expression. "I totally messed up this quarter, Mom. A lot of it was my fault, but each time I tried to study, it was impossible—Student Council meetings, special assemblies, things like that. I hardly ever have a study hall anymore."

Kylie also admitted to having been more interested in her social life than in paying attention in class. While she took the blame for her poor report card, she pointed out the number of times she had asked her mother to be excused from family activities in order to study but hadn't been allowed to.

"You've always managed before."

"Before is over. My grades are better, now that I'm studying with Roe. I got an A on my Anne Frank project, thanks to Roe giving me the idea. But if I don't make more time for homework, I won't get into Crofts even if they like my acting."

By putting their heads together and finally listening to each other, Kylie and her mother worked out a plan. Kylie would request a substitute whenever Student Council meetings took place during her study hall rather than after school, and Mrs. Kennedy would check with her daughter before committing her to weekend activities.

"If I study on school nights and on Sunday afternoons, I'm sure I'll pull up my grades by the end of the semester." It had been a difficult conversation, but Kylie thought she was back on track.

If it wasn't for the constant dark cloud of her family's problems, Roe thought she would be perfectly happy. Sometimes she wished she could stay at Kylie's forever. The Kennedy's home was light and clean—filled with the smells of delicious food and sparkling with laughter and love. Most important was Kylie, who had become as close as a sister. When their homework was done each night, she, Kylie, and Mrs. Kennedy, whom she now called Aunt Jane, worked on their costumes.

Roe felt a twinge of jealousy return when she first saw Kylie's gowns. They were beautiful! One of peach organdy edged with cream lace made Kylie's complexion and golden hair even more striking. The other gown was a blue and white floral with a high, stiff, taffeta neck. Roe felt better when Kylie informed her the neck itched unbearably.

"If I breathe, it will be over," Kylie said, as she was zipped into the floral gown. "I'd better lose a few pounds."

"You'll do no such thing," her mother said. "I'll see if I can take it out a bit."

Roe had almost finished hemming her Page outfit, a mustard-colored velvet tunic with a white ruffle down the front, to be worn over a black turtleneck. Black tights and a black cap with a long white feather completed the costume.

Kylie sighed. "I never could wear that. I wish I were as slim as you."

Roe grinned. "I wouldn't mind switching places." Her costume change was simple. All that was needed to turn the Page into the outlandish tourist, Jane, was to take off the tunic and cap and add an orange vinyl mini-skirt and owl-like sunglasses. Her prop was a pair of binoculars.

Costumes, Roe thought, as she made her way to the Green Room for the props meeting, were almost done, but props were another matter. She had turned in the two assigned to her, but no one else had. Samantha Bates, the props chair, wasn't much of a leader, but maybe things would go better today. At least she would be meeting Eric at Smithy's after the meeting—the first time it was officially *a date*. She smiled.

Other than her family, the only other big problem Roe had was Jaimie Jelinek. Marla had been sent away to a private school, and most people knew Roe was innocent. Even Mr. Hasting was attempting to be civil, and his "short" announcements weren't as long anymore. But Jaimie still treated her as if she had a rare disease. Whenever Roe confronted her, Jaimie would say, "I don't know what you're talking about," and walk away. Finally, Roe gave up, but Jaimie's behavior hurt.

Miss Armstrong and most of the members of the props committee were seated and silent when Roe arrived. Strange that Miss Armstrong had joined them. "What's wrong? Where's Sam?" she asked, looking around the Green Room.

"You've put your finger on it," Priyanka, another tourist, said.

Miss Armstrong broke the news. "Samantha has resigned as chair of the props committee."

"Oh, no," Roe moaned. "Hardly anything has been done. I think my two props are the only ones we have."

"By now, the actors should be rehearsing with them," Miss Armstrong scolded, "and since it appears, Roe, that you are the only one who has done anything, suppose you take over as chair?"

Roe hesitated. It would mean a lot of work, but she had yet to decide on a project for the camp scholarship. Maybe it could deal with props. "All right," she said.

The committee cheered.

"Wait a minute," Roe cautioned. "I'm going to need your help. This isn't all Sam's fault, you know."

"Scavenge around and get those props as soon as possible." Miss Armstrong gave Roe a smile before rushing off to another committee meeting.

Roe stared after the busy director. "That's it!" And then she laughed at the startled faces. "I've got the best idea. We can get the props and have fun at the same time." *And do my project,* she thought. But that would be her secret. "Now, where's the list?"

Someone thrust the props list into her face. "Heather," Roe ordered, "go to the LRC and run off twenty copies. That's a lot, but let's be on the safe side." Quickly, she told the excited girls her plan. "Let's talk more in private tonight. The line rehearsal is at my house. Please try to come, whether or not you're in the cast." Roe wasn't aware she'd claimed the Kennedy's home as her own.

Kylie, urged by Beth and Roe, had agreed that organizing Friday Night Line Parties would be her special project for the Crofts' camp scholarship. She gave her long curly hair one more brushing and admired her tan *Mouse* sweatshirt. The front, picturing a large mouse, advertised in brown letters, "*The Mouse That Roared* Castle Bluff Theater" and the names of everyone connected with the production were printed on the back.

Downstairs in the family room, all was ready. Her guests would find chilled sodas in coolers and large bowls of chips on the table. Mom had taken Danny and a few of his friends to a movie while Dad stayed home to chaperone.

Kylie should have been happy but wasn't. It was her turn to be jealous. She had accepted the responsibility for her poor report card and was doing better, but Roe's joy at receiving all A's had been a little hard to take. Kylie could still hear her shriek of delight. She even got a comment from her counselor. "This would have been a remarkable achievement even without the difficulties you have faced this term. You are to be commended." And now Roe was bubbling over about her secret project idea.

It was as if their positions had been reversed, Kylie thought. They should call Roe the golden girl, in spite of her dark hair. Then she remembered Roe's mother and was ashamed of herself. And when she thought of her own mother and how disappointed she'd been, Kylie sat on her bed and began to cry.

A knock interrupted the tears. The door opened. "What's this? Crying? Still over a report card?"

Kylie wiped away the tears. "It's not only that, Dad. I deserved those low grades. I didn't try. Now that I'm working again, my grades are better. I know I can do it."

Her father sat next to her. "I know you can, too. So what's the trouble?"

Kylie sighed. "It's hard to explain."

"Maybe I can help. It seems to me you got used to everything going your way—of always being Number One."

"That's part of it. Mainly, I don't feel creative anymore."

"You? That's surprising. Why not?"

"My scholarship project for one thing—the line rehearsal nights. That was Imani's idea. She turned it over to me because I didn't know what to do, and seventh graders won't do projects until next year. Roe gave me the idea for the Anne Frank report. I got an A on it, too."

"Good girl!"

"But I would have failed if it hadn't been for Roe. And she found out we needed to be on a crew to be eligible for a camp scholarship, so I volunteered for publicity. I can't remember when I had an idea all my own. I feel like I'm cheating." Kylie choked up again.

Dad put his arm around her. "First thing, stop knocking down my girl. You've managed to learn a valuable lesson many talented people don't discover until they're much older. As you take part in more activities, you're bound to meet people more talented and creative than you. I've certainly learned that the hard way. But I don't think that's what's happening. You've been too busy to be creative. When was the last time you had a quiet time to yourself?"

Kylie nodded. "I used to get the best ideas right before falling asleep. Now I'm out cold the minute my head touches the pillow."

"I thought so. Keep in mind something else," her father continued. "Remember the things you have done this year. There are many ways to be creative, you know. Who stood by Roe when almost everyone else turned against her? Who suspected Mr. Hasting might cover up for Marla and phoned me? Who won the lead in the play, never missed a rehearsal, and was the first to have her lines memorized?"

The sound of the doorbell put an end to Mr. Kennedy's list. "And who," he concluded, "is going downstairs to host the most successful line rehearsal party ever?"

Giggling, Kylie gave him a hug. "You are the best daddy in the world," she said.

SCENE 10—BRAINSTORMS AND PROJECTS

ROE SHIVERED BOTH FROM DELIGHT and the falling temperatures as she and other members of the cast and crew gathered on the front steps of Castle Bluff Middle School the following Friday morning. All held invitations. Many were asking questions. This had better be good was the general feeling. No school because of a teacher's institute. If it weren't for Roe, they would still be in bed this cold, cold morning.

Roe pulled her new CBT sweatshirt down over her hips, cleared her throat, and concentrated on projection as she explained her project. "Without knowing it, Miss Armstrong gave me the idea. As you probably know, I'm the new props chair. We hardly have any props, and our all-day tech rehearsal is tomorrow."

A few people groaned. Roe's project sounded like work.

Roe grinned. "Just wait," she promised. "Miss Armstrong told us we should scavenge around and find props. And that is what we're going to do." She formed a megaphone with her hands. "Ladeez and Gentlemen," she announced, "welcome to Castle Bluff Theater's first scavenger hunt!"

All cheered while Kylie gave her a thumbs-up. Roe hadn't even told Kylie but had gone around with such a Cheshire Cat expression, Kylie had threatened to smack her. Like the others, Kylie had received an envelope covered with red and blue question marks and yellow smiley faces.

Inside was the invitation, which included Roe's cell phone number.

CELEBRATE TEACHERS' INSTITUTE WITH A DAY OF FUN!
AND HELP *MOUSE!*
MEET ROE SANTOS ON THE CBMS STEPS,
9:00 AM FRIDAY RSVP.
BRING YOUR INVITATION WITH YOU!

"If you look at your invitation carefully," Roe continued, once the noise died down, "you'll find a letter printed on the lower right-hand corner. That's your group letter. What we're going to do is divide into four groups of six, three boys and three girls, except for one that will be all girls since more girls responded." There was some grumbling at this.

"Hey, are we too late?" Jaimie Jelinek and a girl Roe didn't recognize came up the walk and joined them. "This is my friend, Barb. She's not in CBT but wants to help."

"B-but you never responded." Had Jaimie done this on purpose?

"Oh, I guess I forgot," Jaimie said in a smug voice, almost daring Roe to exclude her. "But of course, the stage manager should participate, if it's about the play."

"Give me a second." Roe tried to study her list again, but she was too flustered to concentrate. What did Jaimie have against her, anyway?

Like a guard, Eric stood next to her. "Let me see if I can help," he said, taking the list from her.

Coming to the rescue again, Roe thought. "Thanks," she whispered. "We've got to figure it out fast."

"Piece of cake," Eric whispered back. "Okay," he said, addressing the crowd. "Here's the new plan. Jaimie and Barb will take Roe and my place in the B group. We'll stay behind to take care of things here."

A sensible solution, Roe thought, although she was sorry not to be a part of the hunt. There were many things to do at the meeting place, though, and it would be nice to spend time with Eric. Another pleasant thing was seeing Jaimie looking so annoyed. She was watching Eric in a strange way. Not angrily, exactly, but—I've got it! Jaimie likes Eric! Well, we'll see about that! She threw Jaimie a victorious smile.

"The A group will stand here," Roe commanded, back in charge. Soon the four groups were separated, eagerly awaiting further instructions. "I will distribute a different list of props to each group. Your goal is to find every item on it and report back to Smithy's. Smithy is letting us use one of his banquet rooms, so be sure to thank him."

"Three cheers for Smithy," Kurt yelled.

"Shhh," Beth ordered. "This is Roe's show."

Roe smiled at Beth and resumed her instructions. "If any props are too large for you to carry back, write down their locations. Mr. Kennedy has offered to go back with his truck. The first group to arrive at Smithy's with all their props will be treated to ice cream sundaes provided by the CBT budget." She held up her hands to stop the applause. "Hey, you're going to need all the time you've got. If you haven't found your props by three, go to Smithy's anyway. We'll put our heads together and figure out how to find the rest."

"You're awesome, Roe," Kylie whispered, as Roe handed her a list. Roe gave her a quick hug of thanks.

Kylie was pleased to be in Group C with Brad, Beth, and Kurt, as well as Don Barber and Jennifer Yu, whom she didn't know well. She grabbed Beth's arm and whispered, "I guess Eric showed her."

"Unbelievable," Beth said. "Jaimie's acting like a jerk because a boy she likes, likes someone else. Did you see her face when Eric said he'd stay with Roe? Serves her right for being so nasty."

"We're wasting time," Don complained, leading them off the school steps. "Gossip later."

"Read the list out loud, Kylie," Brad suggested.

"Okay. 1. *A basket of artificial flowers.* For Mrs. Tully to carry. My mom has plenty of fake flowers. 2. *A shaving kit.* Chet Beston uses one in the third scene. If they're all this simple, we'll be done before lunch."

"Don't comment, Kylie, just read."

Kylie frowned. "Well, sor-ry. 3. *A red telephone.* 4. *A hat with an arrow sticking through it.* For General Snippet, of course. That's you, Don. 5. *Five crossbows with arrows.*"

Brad shook his head. "Do they still seem so simple?"

"I can get the basket and flowers," Kylie said, "No problem there. But the shaving kit?"

"I've got one," Kurt said.

"You?" They all laughed.

Kurt grinned. "You should see my beard when I forget. No, it's an old one of my dad's. I put toothpaste and stuff in it when I go places."

Kylie checked off the flower basket and the shaving kit. "We'll get those two items on our way back to Smithy's."

"Here, let me read the rest of the list," Kurt said. "Kylie will take all day. 6. *Four cameras with cases.* 7. *A bowl of fruit, including a pomegranate.* 8. *A scroll for the page.* 9. *The Q-bomb.* 10. *A shortwave radio.*"

"Wow!" Jen said. "This is going to be tough."

"Each group must have been assigned ten props," Don said. "Miss Armstrong warned us this was a props-heavy show."

Kylie shook her head. "Looks like we've got to make some of the things ourselves. Any ideas for the hat with the arrow?"

"We've got boxes of Halloween junk in our attic," Don said. "I'm almost certain we have one of those curved arrows you wear over your head, so it looks like the arrow is piercing right through your skull."

"Perfect," Brad said. "What about the hat?"

Quiet Jen spoke. "There are plenty of military hats in the CBT costume cage. Wait for me. I'll go get one."

Kylie stopped her. "Wait, Jen. We need a plan. I'll go with you, but there's no sense in the rest of you waiting."

"I'll find the arrow," Don said.

"I'll go with you," Brad said.

"My mom's got fake fruit," Beth said, "but I don't think we'll find a fake pomegranate."

"They're in season, though," Kurt said. "I'll go with you. Let's go to your house for the fake fruit, and then to a market to buy a pomegranate."

"And we'll meet where?" Brad wondered.

"Don's house," Kurt said. "You can look for other stuff in your attic. Besides, Don lives right near my grandmother. She never throws anything away."

"We'd better hurry," Kylie said. "We're the only group still here."

They made sure of Don's address before departing.

"Thanks for coming with me, Kylie. I don't have a boyfriend like you and Beth do."

"Really, Jen? Do you think Kurt is Beth's boyfriend? I hadn't noticed."

Jen laughed. "Then you're blind."

It took awhile before they found a hat matching the one General Snippet would wear as part of his costume. Kylie hoped they wouldn't have to destroy the hat when they added the arrow. She also grabbed a remnant of material.

"It's practically the same color as the hat. We'll camouflage it so the audience won't see the bent wire."

"If the boys find the arrow," Jen cautioned.

"They have to. It's almost ten already."

After the C group finally left the school steps, Roe turned to Eric. "Smithy's won't open until 11:30. What should we do first?"

"The cafeteria is open. Why don't we have hot chocolate and donuts while making plans?"

"Good idea. It's been hours since I had breakfast. I could use a second one."

"Hey, Roe," Eric asked, as soon as they were seated in the empty cafeteria. "What would you have done if Jaimie had come without Barb? Let her take your place and be with me?"

"I guess so. I wouldn't have had much choice. I had to keep the numbers even for the competition to be fair." Roe hesitated before going on. "I never noticed before that Jaimie likes you."

"Did you see the expression on her face when we pulled the big switch?" He laughed but then grew serious. "We played together when we were little, and our parents are good friends. But I never thought of her as a girlfriend."

"Well, I wish Jaimie wouldn't take it out on me. We used to get along fine."

"Don't worry about it," was Eric's unhelpful advice. "Let's plan."

"We'll make a list," Roe said. "I've got crepe paper streamers and balloons. We'll make Smithy's look gorgeous."

"We'll need a long table for the props, but how are we going to get them to school after the party?"

Roe explained that Mr. Kennedy would come to Smithy's at five to pick things up. "He's been great. All the Kennedys have."

"How much longer are you going to live there? Isn't your mom better yet?"

"No, and it could take a long time. It might never happen. Sometimes I wish I could stay with the Kennedys forever, but then I feel guilty because it sounds like I don't love my parents. I do, but our lives changed after my brother died."

"Kylie filled me in some. It must have been awful."

"It was," Roe admitted. "That reminds me. Dad wants me to pack the stuff in Mateo's room. I haven't had the nerve to go in there, much less to start."

"I could help if you want," Eric offered. "We'd have time after we decorate, if you don't think it's too private."

Roe shrugged. "I don't know if it's private. I haven't been in Mateo's room for over two years. Dad told me where the key is. I didn't want to ask Kylie because she knew Mateo. You never met him, so it feels different."

The whole gang was waiting for them at Don's house. "Where's the arrow?" Kylie asked.

Don opened an oversized laundry bag, and they saw the arrow, fake fruit, and a real pomegranate.

"Perfect." Kylie added the hat and material.

"Now let's go to my Grandma's," Kurt said.

"As long as we ring doorbells on the way," Kylie said. "That's what you're supposed to do on a scavenger hunt."

No one responded at the first two houses. At the third, a woman, her hair in curlers, peeked from the living room drapes and yelled, "No solicitors!" She pointed to a sign on the door before closing the blinds.

"But madam, this is a marvelous vacuum cleaner," Kurt joked.

"And for only $50,000 more, we'll throw in a used car," Brad added.

Kylie giggled. "Let's try the next house. Our luck is bound to change." However, a small child slammed the door in their faces before they could say a word.

"Let's ring doorbells," Don mimicked. "That's what you're supposed to do on scavenger hunts."

"If you want to lose, that is. Let's go to my grandmother's. I'll bet she has everything we're missing."

For some reason, Kylie had expected Kurt's grandma to be a little old lady with puffy blue-gray hair. She was surprised when an attractive woman, maybe in her sixties, wearing blue jeans and a plaid shirt, opened the door. Kurt made introductions. "And this is Gee," he said. "Call her that. Everyone does."

"After Gee greeted them, she turned to Beth. "So this is Beth. I've heard about you."

"You have?" Beth asked, clearly puzzled.

All of them looked at Kurt and laughed, but he'd turned his back. All they could see was the tip of his left ear, which had turned bright pink. I guess Jen was right, Kylie thought.

Kurt changed the subject by showing Gee their props list. "Oh my, this does look complicated."

Kylie gasped when she saw Gee's living room. Every inch of space, not devoted to sitting or walking, was filled with Gee's collections—porcelain figurines, old children's books, kewpie dolls, teddy bears, photographs in silver frames, German beer steins. Amazingly, everything was clean and in order. Gee's house could be an antique store, if the items were for sale. Kylie wished she had time to browse.

"First things first. You must be hungry. I'll fix some hot chocolate and a platter of cookies."

The boys and girls protested, but Gee waved them off. "You must keep up your strength. Kurt, you take everyone down to the basement and look around."

"My grandma," Kurt said proudly as they walked down the steep stairs.

"Why do you call her Gee?" Beth asked.

"'Cause her last name is Grainger, and my other grandma's name is Brockway, like mine. When my sister and I were little, we called them by the letters of their last names—G and B—Grandma G and Grandma B. Now, it's just G-e-e and B-e-e. Gee and Bee."

"Cute," Jen said.

The basement was not like any Kylie had ever seen. Gee's collections were boxed, labeled, and stored alphabetically on shelves.

"Cool," Don said.

"Gee likes to change her displays. She cleans everything and brings it down here. Then she takes new stuff upstairs and cleans it again."

"She'd make a great props chair," Beth said.

It was the box labeled "Cigar Boxes and Cases" that gave them the idea for the Q-bomb. "Yes!" Kurt eagerly opened the box. Inside were bomb-shaped aluminum tubes that had been used to hold cigars.

"Absolutely perfect," Kylie breathed. "The bomb has to be small enough to fit into the scientist's pocket."

"Don't forget a plank," Jen reminded them.

"A lightweight board would work,' Brad said. "We've got plenty of lumber in my basement. The soldiers can tape the bomb to the plank when they march back into Grand Fenwick."

"Anyone in the audience who recognizes that the bomb is a cigar case will have a laugh," Kurt said. He took one labeled White Owl.

Beth noticed a crate labeled "Cameras" and selected four. "We'll ask Gee if we can borrow these."

"Here's a scroll that would work," Brad said, "and a basket and some flowers, so we won't have to go to Kylie's house."

"But no red telephone, crossbows, or shortwave radio."

"Let's go upstairs and ask Gee," Kurt suggested.

Hot chocolate and cookies awaited them. "Yummy," Beth said.

"I hope you come again, dear."

Gee approved of their findings but was unable to help with the missing items. "Why don't you start ringing doorbells? That's what you're supposed to do on scavenger hunts."

While they laughed, Kylie explained their streak of bad luck. "Maybe we will try again," she said.

SCENE 11—A DIFFERENT KIND OF WINNING

ERIC HELPED THE ICE CREAM PARLOR owner carry in a long, heavy table and set it against one wall. "Thanks, Smithy, this table is fine."

Smithy was panting. "How many props do you expect?"

"Lots," Roe said. "There are over forty in the show. The hardest part will be keeping track of them, making sure they're in repair, and that no one forgets when they're supposed to be on stage. Most important, we must be sure to return them to their owners once the play is over."

"You children are certainly gluttons for punishment."

Roe and Eric grinned. They didn't mind Smithy calling them children, as long as no one else did. They assured him they could do the rest of the decorating on their own and thanked him once again.

"Always glad to be useful." Smithy returned to his lunchtime customers.

Then they hung blue and white streamers, Castle Bluff Middle School's colors, and used a helium tank to blow up blue and white balloons until Roe announced the room looked perfect.

"Let's grab a sandwich before we tackle your brother's room," Eric said.

"Now what?" Kylie asked, after they left Gee's house. "How are we going to get the crossbows and arrows?"

Brad shook his head. "I saw some toy bows and arrows in Don's attic, but they'd look lame in the play."

"I have an idea." Startled, they looked at Jen, who was usually so quiet they forgot she was around. She came to life on stage, though, in her role as the nervous secretary, Miss Wilkins. "My dad is a PE teacher at Community," Jen explained, referring to Castle Bluff's junior college. "They teach archery, but the classes won't start until spring."

"Community isn't far," Kurt said, "but do you think your dad will have time to see us?"

Jen shrugged. "Worth a try."

Fortunately, Mr. Yu had a free period and was busy at his desk grading papers. He smiled at his daughter and her friends. "Playing hooky again?" He winked at Kylie.

"Teacher's Institute, Dad." Jen explained the scavenger hunt project and the need for crossbows and arrows.

"Well, we won't use them until spring. They aren't toys, though. Anyone who fools around with them could get hurt. Are you sure you need the arrows?"

"Just once," Brad explained. "But we don't have to pull back on the strings."

"I'm not sure—"

"I have an idea." They looked at Kylie hopefully. "We have locked cabinets on both sides of the stage. The soldiers only use the arrows once. They come in from Stage Right, have a short scene holding the bows with the arrows in position, and then exit Stage Left. We could keep the arrows locked in the Off Right cabinet until their entrance. Then we could unlock it, hand the soldiers the arrows, and then lock them up again in the Off Left cabinet when the soldiers exit. Props crew could handle it."

Jen's dad nodded, and they sighed in relief. "I could lend you some quivers, too. If you attach feathers to the tops of dowel rods and carry them in the quivers, they'll look like arrows from the audience."

It was a great idea. Mr. Yu said he had late afternoon classes but would help Mr. Kennedy load his truck when he finished teaching. The boys and girls thanked him and were on their way once more.

The campus, with its old-fashioned ivy-covered buildings, looked like a scene from a movie. I wouldn't mind going here someday if they have a decent theater department, Kylie thought, vowing to find out. She had time. College was a long way away. "What's left?" she asked.

Brad reported on their progress. "We still need a shortwave radio and a red telephone. Then we have to get the shaving kit at Kurt's house. My dad's a Cub Scout leader. He's sure to have dowel rods and feathers in the basement."

"And the plank for the Q-bomb," Don reminded him.

Beth wailed. "But how are we going to find a red telephone?"

No one had any suggestions.

On their way back toward town, they stopped to admire Castle Bluff's most famous landmark. "Doesn't Markey Castle look beautiful today?" Kylie asked. "Out of place, of course, but beautiful."

They all knew the story of how Mr. Markey's great great grandfather had built the small castle on the bluff to remind him of the ones he'd known as a boy in the "old country." It was from the castle that the town was named. Kylie didn't think it really looked like a castle, unless it was a gingerbread one you might make from a kit at Christmas time. Markey Castle was a rambling, four-story brownstone mansion with latticework and turrets. It was rumored that the entire top floor was a ballroom, complete with crystal chandeliers and a grand piano. You would think the entire cast of Grimm's Fairy Tales lived there, or maybe just the witch in Hansel and Gretel—certainly not a shy, frail man in his nineties.

Kylie's eyes twinkled. "Do you suppose Mr. Markey has a red telephone?"

Jen gasped. "You're kidding?"

"Why not? After all, you're supposed to ring doorbells on scavenger hunts."

Everyone groaned.

Roe stacked a dusty set of science encyclopedias—the kind people used to buy at the supermarket for $2.99 per volume after a $10.00 purchase—in one box, and then reached for a similar set on car maintenance. Then she began to sneeze, and Eric, as if to be companionable, sneezed, too. The sad room was dusty.

She sat at Mateo's desk and waited for the sneezing fit to end. Then, without thinking, she opened one of the photo albums her brother had always kept on the shelf above his desk. There he stood, holding the fish he'd caught during an early camping trip with Dad. Another was his basketball team. One of the last ones showed Mateo holding his driver's license. He looked innocent and happy—before he turned into a stranger. Most of the photos were of Mateo and his friends, but there were a few of the family. One of Roe's mother standing next to Mateo at his eighth-grade graduation made her gasp. Roe couldn't remember Mother ever looking so lovely. She closed the album and bowed her head.

Eric touched her shoulder. "Roe, it's none of my business, and I wouldn't blame you for getting mad at me for interfering, but I don't think this is fair. Your father isn't being fair to you."

"Fair?" Roe repeated. The word seemed odd applied to her. "What do you mean?"

"He had no right to ask you to do this. Your mother couldn't do it, and your father won't. It's too painful for him, so he asked you. He's the grown-up. It's his job."

Roe stared at him. Could Eric be right? "But what can I do? Dad wants Mateo's things gone before mother comes home."

"Which you said might not be for a long time. Why don't you ask Mr. and Mrs. Kennedy? Maybe they could pack things up and store them in the attic. Then your father can go through everything himself sometime."

Roe sighed. "I guess you're right. I didn't know it would be this hard." She grabbed another photo album and a notebook she found in the top drawer. "I'll take these with me," she said, shoving them into her backpack.

Firmly, Eric led her from the haunted bedroom. "Let's go back to Smithy's," he said.

The scavengers made their way to the front door of the mansion and soon stood on the enormous wrap-around porch. Kylie looked for the doorbell, but where the bell should have been, there was nothing but a grotesque sculpture.

"It's a troll," Brad said. "I've seen pictures of them."

Kurt lifted the troll's nose. "It's also a doorknocker. You do the honors, Kylie. This is your idea."

"Gross," but Kylie gingerly grabbed the troll's nose and rapped softly.

No sounds from inside. She tried again—louder this time.

"Forget it, Kylie," Beth said. "Let's get out of here."

But the door opened. A man who looked like Jeeves, a butler on a British TV show Kylie's parents watched, stood waiting expectantly. She didn't think butlers existed in America.

"How may I help you?" he asked.

He wasn't British, Kylie decided, just formal. She explained they were theater students from the middle school and were looking for props for a play. "We wondered if you might have anything we could borrow . . ." Her voice faltered. Maybe this wasn't such a good idea.

"Who is it, Leland? Do we have company?"

"It's a crowd of young people, sir. They're looking for property items for their theater production."

"A play? How splendid," said a voice Kylie assumed was Mr. Markey. "Do show them in."

Leland stepped aside, allowing Group C into the gingerbread castle.

Kylie couldn't help staring at Mr. Markey. He was the oldest person she had ever seen, with flyaway wispy white hair, not much taller than tiny Jen. Covering his pale blue eyes were thick round glasses that kept slipping down to the bottom of his sharp nose. His lips were thin but when they turned up into a delighted smile, he glowed, causing him to look years younger—and fun!

"It's a fine thing to have visitors, " he said. "Leland and I don't have them often. Wouldn't lunch be nice?"

They nodded but stared daggers at Kylie. They couldn't disappoint the old man, but Kylie's mischievous suggestion was going to cost them valuable time.

Mr. Markey took the unwilling but curious students farther inside. "Come into the parlor. Leland will make sandwiches and lemonade." Again, he smiled happily at them.

Come into my parlor said the spider to the fly, Kylie thought, remembering an old nursery rhyme. Not that Mr. Markey was a spider; he was a dear. But he was going to make them lose the scavenger hunt, and it was her fault.

"What do you need for your play?" he asked, as soon as they were uncomfortably seated on antique chairs.

"A shortwave radio and a red telephone," Kylie said.

"Must the radio work?"

"No, sir," Brad said. "It's a prop. The sound crew will take care of the noise."

"I have an old one you may have. My nephew used it fifty years ago. Leland will fetch it from the study when he's finished preparing your sandwiches."

"And the telephone?" Beth asked.

Mr. Markey chuckled. "Leland and I don't have much use for telephones, but you might check the storage room. I'm sure I put one in there some years ago. It's yours if you can find it. It's tan, I believe."

"We need a red one," Don reminded him gently.

"Couldn't you paint it?"

"What?" they shrieked.

"Paint it," Mr. Markey repeated. "If it wouldn't be too much trouble, of course."

Brad slapped his head. "Boy, are we dumb! Of course we can paint it. There's a can of red spray paint in our garage."

"That's a wonderful idea, Mr. Markey," Kylie said. "Thank you. You've saved the day!"

Their new friend beamed his pleasure.

"We won't have time to paint it before the scavenger hunt ends," Jen said. "But if we have the phone and the can of paint and say we'll do the work ourselves, I'm sure it will count."

Mr. Markey gave directions to the storage room on the third floor. "I rarely go upstairs nowadays," he said. "Be sure to bring down anything you can use."

Kylie gathered her courage. "Mr. Markey, I've always wondered about your fourth floor. Is it true it's a ballroom?"

Mr. Markey laughed. "Indeed, yes. Oh, the parties we had when I was young. Why don't you take a peek inside? There's a small stage."

"Imagine having a stage in your own home," Kylie said.

"We'll be careful," Brad promised.

The old man gestured toward the stairs. "Take your time. When you come down, your luncheon will be ready. I haven't had this much fun in years."

"I don't know if we should slug you or hug you, Kylie," Kurt said, as they climbed the staircase to the third floor.

"Well, I don't care if we do lose," Beth said. "Mr. Markey is lonely, and I wouldn't have missed this for anything."

Kylie agreed. "He's a sweetheart. Maybe we can help him in some way. He may not have anyone but Leland." Kylie didn't know why exactly, but she had a negative feeling about the butler, or whatever his role was.

The ballroom was grander than they had imagined, although the stage was not much more than a platform. Amazingly, the room was clean, and the hardwood floor looked freshly polished. Leland was either a good worker or Mr. Markey had other help. The storage room was overwhelming, but they did manage to locate the tan telephone.

"Look at this armor," Kurt cried, pointing to medieval shields, helmets, and swords. "Wouldn't this be fantastic on the set?"

Don shook his head. "Too heavy. The stage crew has to change the scenery quickly and quietly."

Jen sighed. "Wouldn't the armor be a great decoration for a cast party?"

Not having cast parties had always been a sore point for CBT members. The cafeteria and gym were reserved for other functions, and parents weren't willing to entertain such a crowd in their homes.

That's it! Kylie thought, as an amazing idea came to her. Come to think of it, she had been having super thoughts all day. "Listen, everybody. Thanks to Jen, I've got an idea." She ignored Brad's groan. "It's going to make us lose the scavenger hunt, but we might win something more important than ice cream. I'm going to ask Mr. Markey if we can have our cast party in his ballroom."

"No way!" Brad exclaimed.

"You're crazy," Kurt added.

Beth shook her head. "He'll never give permission."

"I think he will. Mr. Markey likes us, and he's lonely. I think we're exactly what he needs!"

"You're the best props chair I've ever had!" Miss Armstrong told Roe. "Are you certain we've got everything?"

"We will if Group C comes through. They're the only ones not back, but it's only three o'clock now."

"Here they come," Miss Armstrong said. "Just in time."

Group C forged its way through streamers and balloons to the crowded props table, so Roe could check off their findings.

"That's it," she announced. "As soon as Mr. Kennedy delivers the items too large to carry, we'll have all the props for *The Mouse That Roared*. The scavenger hunt is a success!"

"Hooray for Roe!" someone shouted. Then everyone echoed, "Hooray for Roe!"

"Who won?" Kylie screamed over the racket.

"We did!" came a cry from the corner. Jaimie's group displayed their ice cream spoons as proof. Roe thought she looked pleasant, for a change.

"You only think you won," Brad said. "Wait until you hear Kylie's news."

He helped her onto an empty chair. "Quiet, please," she said, and then waited until all eyes were on her. "What would make our performance absolutely perfect?"

"Certain people remembering their lines," Miss Armstrong suggested.

"The scenery not falling over," Jaimie said.

"A cast party!" Eric yelled.

"Eric's got it," Kylie said. "As you know we can't use the school, and none of our parents want to entertain such a rowdy bunch. Well, when we were looking for props, we met someone who will let us use his place for a party."

"Who? Where?"

"Get ready! Drumroll, please!" Kylie waited for the noise to subside before continuing. "The *Who* is Mr. Markey. And the *Where* is—the ballroom in Markey Castle!"

After that, there was too much excitement for Kylie to explain further. Then Roe jumped up on another chair and led the cheer. "Hooray for Kylie!"

SCENE 12—TECHNICALLY, A DISASTER

THAT NOISE AGAIN! WHAT WAS it? Oh, right. Kylie reached over to play her usual morning game with the alarm clock. Wait, it's Saturday. Why had she set the alarm? She turned over and was almost asleep when she remembered. Oh, rats! The tech rehearsal! Kylie reset the alarm when she was stopped by—total silence. How odd. Roe was always up first. Why weren't the drawers slamming? Reluctantly, Kylie stretched her legs toward the floor. I'll have to check, she thought, grabbing her always-comforting robe.

All was dark and still, and the lump under the quilt made it clear Roe was still asleep. Kylie shook her. "Roe, we've got to get ready for tech. Come on!"

Roe barely opened her eyes. She spoke so softly Kylie could barely hear. "I feel awful. I don't—oh no," she croaked, "I've lost my voice." Tears of frustration and disappointment rolled down her cheeks.

"I'll get Mom," although Kylie doubted even her mother could solve this problem.

Mrs. Kennedy took Roe's temperature, shook her head, and made the pronouncement. "You're not going anywhere this weekend."

Kylie patted Roe's shoulder. "I'll tell Miss Armstrong. Don't worry about anything. Just get better."

While grabbing a quick breakfast, Kylie expressed her concern. "She's got to be well by dress rehearsal."

Mrs. Kennedy promised to contact Roe's doctor, and Kylie hurried off to school alone.

The lights crew was on the job when she arrived. Some of the eighth-grade members were teaching seventh graders the light board while others were on tall ladders changing the focus of the lights so all acting areas would be lit without casting shadows.

Rob Gardiner, the lights chair, asked Kylie to walk around the stage while making adjustments. She admired the completed set as she examined the interior of a medieval castle. Outstanding, she thought. She felt the lush red velvet cushion on her gold spray-painted throne and almost felt a stirring of patriotism at the sight of the flags of Grand Fenwick hanging from the light poles overhead. Other scenes, those in New York and Washington D.C., would be played Down Right and Left on the apron of the stage.

"Thanks, Kylie, that should do it," Rob yelled down from his high ladder. Kylie waved to him and resumed her search for Miss Armstrong.

She found the busy director backstage opening the props cabinet. "Poor Roe," Miss Armstrong said, once she heard the news. "So much has happened to her this year. I'm glad to say that things are going to get better. I can't say anything more, but soon something wonderful is going to happen."

Roe must have won a camp scholarship, Kylie thought. "I hope she gets better for the play."

"Dress rehearsal isn't until Tuesday," Miss Armstrong said. "I'm sure she'll be fine by then. But in the meantime, I'm missing a props chair. Could you set them, Kylie?"

"I guess so."

Miss Armstrong gave her a list. "Put each prop on the Stage Left or Stage Right tables. Let me know immediately if anything is missing." Miss Armstrong handed her a key. "After checking, make sure the cabinets with arrows are locked again."

Kylie promised to do her best, and Miss Armstrong rushed off to check the sound cues. She was always amazed by how much work went into putting on a play. The audience has no idea what's going on backstage, she reflected.

At eleven, the light and sound crews completed their work, and the technical run-through, often referred to as a Q-2-Q, was ready to begin.

Although the rehearsal was mainly about making sure the crews were solid on their cues, Kylie felt her first pangs of stage fright.

The sounds of a deep roar, followed by the trilling of birds, filled the dark theater. Backstage, Kylie watched Kurt waiting for his entrance cue, a spotlight on the front curtain. The birds stopped singing and a bugle prematurely announced the wrong scene, but the stage remained dark. The protests began. "Hey, lights!" someone yelled to the light booth.

"We'll have to take that again," Jaimie blared from the house. "Bring up the lights as soon as you hear the bird sounds."

Out went the work and houselights, followed by deafening sounds of jet planes. Cast and crew groaned. "Cue back to the beginning, sound crew," Miss Armstrong ordered.

"This is not a good sign," Kurt whispered.

Eventually, Kylie's first scenes began and were going smoothly until Brad threw her an exit cue line far too early. Kylie responded by sweeping regally off the stage, leaving a few bewildered actors behind.

"What are you doing here?" Sharon, the curtain puller, asked.

When Kylie realized what had happened, she whispered, "Oh, gosh, what if I did that during a performance? The audience wouldn't even understand why Grand Fenwick decided to declare war."

"It wasn't your fault," Sharon consoled. "Brad gave the wrong line."

Kylie shook her head. "It *was* my fault. I took the cue. I should have known it was wrong and covered for him."

"Good girl," said a superior voice. "You're growing up." She didn't say the word, "finally," but it was implied.

Cress Morgan, that uppity junior from Crofts. What was she doing backstage? "Hi, Cress," Kylie whispered. "Why are you here?"

"Writing an article for Crofts Chronicle. Should make interesting reading."

Swell, Kylie thought. At least she wouldn't be on stage again for a while. She'd grab a couple of sodas and join Beth in the audience.

"Thanks," Beth said, accepting the offered root beer.

Kylie sat next to her, just as lights missed their cue again and plunged the stage into darkness. "What a mess!" she said.

"I wish my family wasn't coming opening night. We've worked so hard, and everyone was doing fine. What happened?" Beth and her fellow tourists were only in a few scenes, so they had plenty of time to observe from the audience. "At first the mistakes were funny," she said, "but they aren't anymore."

"Cheer up. It's only the end of the world," Kurt said, plopping himself next to her.

"Are you sure you have time?" Beth wondered. "We're just doing cue to cue, not whole scenes."

"Plenty of time. I wanted to tell you both that Gee is coming opening night, and she's going to help at the cast party."

"Great!" Kylie said. "She'll be a big help at the castle."

"I like your grandmother," Beth said.

"Everyone does. She likes you, too."

"Tully Bascom—late entrance!" Jaimie screamed.

"Uh-oh! See you later." Kurt further disgraced himself by jumping onto the stage from the audience and going right into his lines.

Beth shook her head. "Jaimie is definitely losing it."

"Can't say I blame her," Kylie said, as the phone kept ringing even after it had been answered. When the Fifth Soldier tripped and dropped the Q-Bomb, powerful enough to destroy the world, they covered their eyes and groaned.

"I'm on next," Kylie said. "Wish me luck!"

By the time the curtain closed, too slowly, on the land of Grand Fenwick, everyone was either overcome with mirth or had dissolved in tears.

Miss Armstrong summoned the entire cast and crew out front. "Not bad," she said smiling.

"What?" they cried. Jaimie was the loudest.

"Trust me. I've seen a lot worse. What will help is a half-hour lunch break. Then we'll run another Q-2-Q. You'll see a big improvement."

Kylie and the others exchanged glances. Again? They were hoping to go home.

"Two more things," Miss Armstrong continued. "Don't worry about the mistakes you made this morning. You won't make them again." She grinned at her exhausted cast. "You'll make different ones next time."

Everyone either laughed or groaned, depending on their mood.

"And the second thing," Miss Armstrong concluded. "I've ordered pizza and sodas. They're waiting for you in the cafeteria. So enjoy, and be back ready to go in a half hour."

This time, there were cheers all around.

All morning Roe tossed and turned. Her head ached—her whole body was sore. Sometimes she slept, sometimes she half-slept. Delightful memories of yesterday traveled through her head. The best was Miss Armstrong's excitement when she realized the scavenger hunt was successful. "You're the best props chair I've ever had!" As promised, Mr. Kennedy had driven his truck to Smithy's, and later Roe and Kylie had joined him for the trip to Community to pick up the bows and arrows for the tech rehearsal—which Roe was missing right now. Who would make sure the props were in place? That was her job.

Like everyone else, Roe was excited about the cast party and proud of Kylie for having the courage to ask Mr. Markey. "I've got to get well," she said in a hoarse whisper.

Aunt Jane came into the room with a cup of apple cinnamon tea. "Not much change," she said, feeling Roe's forehead. "I can't give you more Tylenol for a while, though."

"Did you reach Dr. Rao?" Roe croaked.

"I couldn't get an appointment until four. Try to rest. I'll wake you in plenty of time."

"Thanks," Roe whispered.

She drifted back to sleep, and the nightmares about Mateo began. First, he pointed to various objects in his room. *Don't you dare touch my stuff! You have no right to be in my room. It's private. Get out!* She tried to ignore him, not wanting to tell him he was dead. She grabbed a sweater and threw it into a box marked "Charity." *Hey, that's my favorite!* Mateo's dark eyes glared. Throughout the dream, she heard a voice saying over and over, *It's not fair—it's not fair!*

Roe woke with a start. She hadn't dreamed of Mateo in a long time. The voice, of course, was Eric's. "Fair." Ever since he'd said that word, it had been stuck in her head. Nothing about the situation was fair. What Mateo had done wasn't fair. Her father walking away from the family wasn't fair. Mother having a breakdown wasn't fair. Most of all, it wasn't fair she was the only one who knew what had happened—who carried the burden of that awful night, alone.

She was awake now. Maybe she felt a little better, at least physically. She turned on the bedside lamp and reached for Mateo's notebook—her first opportunity to look through it. It was a journal of sorts, started several years before the accident. The earlier pages gave glimpses of the Mateo she knew. When the two of them got along, before he turned mean. Most were brief accounts of Mateo's day. *Asked Sue to homecoming. She said YES! An A on my science project!*

Then Matteo got his driver's license and changed. *I ditched them last night. Who needs them? Bunch of losers. I need my own wheels, but no, the parents can't understand because they didn't have a car when they were my age. Do they think I'm anything like them? No, Mother and Father, I do not want to take my brainy sister anywhere! Not that anyone would ever think she is my sister. What a pain in the ass she is!*

Roe's eyes filled, not that she was surprised by his words. She blew her nose. Crying would only make her feel worse.

And then, finally, on the last page there it was. *Got a dependable supplier now. Some excellent shit coming our way. Greg will ditch school this afternoon to get it, and then party!!! We've talked Angel into trying it. He's bringing the booze. Only problem is I've got to take Senorita Rosita home from her rehearsal. Then we'll dump the little bitch fast.*

There was a little more, but then the journal came to an end—the end of Mateo, Greg, and Angel, too. And almost Roe, the only one who knew what had happened. Or was she?

"Oh, no!" she whispered. Was she really the only one who knew? Mother had locked the room and wouldn't allow anyone inside. What if she had discovered the notebook? What if that's why she got sick?

All at once, Roe was certain. Her mother had read the horrifying words before locking two doors—the one to Mateo's bedroom, and the other a secret one within herself. Trembling, Roe turned off the light and buried herself under the covers.

"I've got to tell someone," she whispered.

After rehearsal, Kylie and a few others stayed behind to help Miss Armstrong. The auditorium and Green Room must be spotless before the director could leave, so they surveyed the area once more for soda cans and candy wrappers. There had been enough hostility already between the custodians and CBT.

"Miss Armstrong, do you think we'll pull it off? *Mouse*, I mean."

     MARILYN LUDWIG

The director smiled. "I think it's going to be wonderful, Kylie, as long as we have at least one strong dress rehearsal. You've heard the superstition that a bad dress rehearsal means a good performance—don't believe it!"

Miss Armstrong continued sweeping, and Kylie crushed a few more cans. "A bunch of us are going to the castle Sunday afternoon to decorate for the party," Kylie said. "I'm going, if I get my homework done in time, but I wish Roe could come, too."

"Yes, it is too bad about Roe. I'll be there. I'm looking forward to seeing this famous castle." Miss Armstrong sighed. "Soon it will be over. It's going to seem strange going home from school at a regular time. We'll still have Drama Club, of course, but there's always such a letdown when a show ends."

Kylie nodded. "I wish we could do a winter play. I'll help with the spring musical, but I'm not much of a singer."

"I feel the same about another play," Miss Armstrong said. "There's a short one I'd like to do—an audience participation play of Cinderella. But we won't have the space. It will be the band and orchestra's turn to use the stage for their holiday concerts."

"Would you direct again if we had a place to rehearse and perform?"

Miss Armstrong nodded. "I certainly would."

It was almost six when Kylie arrived home. But was this her house? What had happened to the sounds of the blaring TV programs Danny always watched at this time? Kylie checked in the kitchen, where she found her mother preparing dinner. At least that was normal.

"How's Roe?" She sampled a homemade biscuit and gave the chicken soup an appreciative sniff.

"Probably sleeping again. Dr. Rao says she has a mild case of bronchitis but is overtired and suffering from too much stress. No wonder, poor kid."

"Will she be okay?"

"She's on antibiotics. I sent your brother over to Grandma's for the night."

"No wonder it's so quiet. But the play?"

"Her voice should return in time. She'll stay in bed all day tomorrow and will remain home from school on Monday and Tuesday. I'll clear it with the school. I'm sure she'll be allowed to attend dress rehearsal on Tuesday afternoon if she's well enough."

Kylie gave Mom a hug. "It must have been hard for you to take off work today. You and Dad are wonderful, and I'll bet your chicken soup will do Roe more good than any medicine."

"Always nice to be appreciated. Why don't you go upstairs and check on her. I'll bet she'd like an update on the tech rehearsal."

Kylie found Roe sitting on her bed, holding a notebook, and staring straight ahead. She looked scared, Kylie thought. "Roe?"

Roe gave a deep sigh. "Kylie, I'm glad you're home. I need to talk to you!"

SCENE 13—EVERYTHING GOOD IS HAPPENING

"IT WAS RAINING," ROE REMINDED Kylie. "Mateo, Doug, and Angel were in a great mood. At first, I felt important being with them, and also a little guilty for not offering you a ride home from rehearsal."

"I was mad at you," Kylie admitted. "Not later, after the accident, of course. But I don't understand, Roe. Why are you going through this again? And why now?"

"Because of this." Roe showed her the notebook. "It's a journal I found in Mateo's room. I kind of knew most of what was in it, but I didn't know it existed—that Mateo had put down so much in writing."

"I don't understand."

"Drugs, Kylie. Fentanyl—although I didn't know what kind until I read it—it's even worse than heroin. That's what caused the accident. The weather might have been a factor, but the accident really happened because Mateo and his friends were high. He wrote about it in the journal. He also said horrible things about our parents and me. He basically said he didn't want me to be his sister." Roe was through with tears. She told her story in a cold, matter-of-fact tone.

"You knew?"

"Shortly after I got into the car, Mateo started bragging. He and Doug were totally wild and out of control."

"Who was driving?"

"Mateo. Doug was in front with him, and I was in the backseat with Angel." Angel had tried to convince Mateo to let him drive. *Come on, man.*

I've got my license, and I'm in better shape than you. But Mateo had refused. *Oh, no. My so-called daddy wouldn't like it. I must protect his precious little girl.* But Roe was not ready to tell Kylie that part.

"We were getting close to Markey Bridge when things got weird. Mateo's mood changed. He turned mean after Angel wanted to drive, but then he went crazy. He had this high-pitched voice. 'I'll bet I can make this baby fly,' he said. 'I'll bet we can soar right off this bridge.' Then he put his foot down hard on the accelerator, and Doug giggled. The road was icy, of course."

"Then how did Mateo push you out of the car? That's what I've always heard happened. That he had saved your life."

Roe didn't answer. "What I'm wondering now is about Mother. I kept quiet about most of what happened because I thought it would make things worse for my parents. The autopsy results showed drugs in Doug, of course, but Mateo's body was never recovered, so we pretended Mateo was clean. Angel had some alcohol in him. But this notebook—" Roe coughed. She'd been talking too much.

Kylie poured her some water. "The notebook, Roe?"

"Mother. Mother locked Mateo's bedroom door and wouldn't let anyone go inside. Now I'm wondering . . ."

Kylie gasped. "Roe, do you think that's why your mother had a breakdown? Because she read the awful things Mateo wrote about your family and the drugs?"

Roe nodded. Her throat hurt too much to talk.

"Roe, this is important. As soon as my dad gets home, you've got to tell my parents. Okay?"

Roe nodded again. She would rest, and then she'd tell the Kennedys most of it. She couldn't handle this alone anymore.

When Sunday afternoon arrived, Kylie was reluctant to leave Roe while she was off to have fun at the castle. It didn't seem fair. Roe had talked with Mom and Dad, who insisted Roe's father be contacted immediately.

"Carlos must come here," Dad had said. "Roe is too ill for me to take her there." Mr. Santos was driving down from Michigan, but they were not certain when he would arrive.

"Are you sure you'll be okay?" Kylie asked.

Roe, who had wrapped herself in a soft quilt on the couch in the family room, smiled at Kylie. "I'll be fine. I don't need a babysitter. It's a relief to be downstairs. I'll watch some of the DVDs your mom got from the library. Besides, I wouldn't go if I could. I must be here when my father comes."

Kylie examined the DVDs. One was *The Diary of Anne Frank*. How thoughtful of her mother.

"It's the original black and white version," Roe said. "I've heard it's the best. Your mother told me there was a nation-wide contest for the girl who played Anne. A teenage model named Millie Perkins won the part."

"Cress Morgan told me Crofts auditions have started."

Roe sighed. "I wish they'd wait until next year." She turned on the movie, and Kylie watched with her until Brad's mother arrived to drive her to the castle.

"See you later," she said, grabbing her jacket. No response. Roe was too engrossed in the film to notice her departure.

"Rosita?" The film had ended. As hard as Anne's world was, it almost seemed preferable to her own.

"Dad, you're back."

"Yes, I've been driving since early this morning. I'm afraid I must return right after we talk, though. How are you feeling?"

"Maybe a little better. I should be able to make dress rehearsal and the performances. You won't be able to come, will you." Roe didn't bother to make it a question. She already knew the answer.

Mr. Santos shook his head. "I'm sorry. Let's hope I'll attend your next play. May I see the notebook, please?"

Roe handed it to him and both were silent for a long time. The pain on his face was too much to bear, and she looked away.

Finally, he closed it. "I knew he had changed and that I didn't like what he was becoming. Of course I never dreamed the situation was that bad. You knew?"

"Yes. Once we were in the car I could tell they were in bad shape. It only got worse."

"Why didn't you tell us?"

"I didn't think it would help. I thought it would be better if you and Mother didn't know. Then I found the notebook, and I was afraid—"

"—that she already knew?"

Roe nodded. "And it could be the reason she locked the door. Maybe it caused her breakdown."

"I will take this notebook to her psychiatrist and counselors, although I think there may be more going on with her. But Roe, I promise things will be better. It's not going to be easy, but at least you and I will be a family again."

Just the two of them? "How is Mother?"

"Still unresponsive. Perhaps in time this will help. She must face and deal with the truth—about everything. I imagine all of us are going to need some guidance. For the present, you concentrate on getting well and having a wonderful year with the Kennedys. It's a long drive. I should be on my way."

Roe almost let him go, but there was one more thing she hadn't told anyone. "Dad, before you go, there's more. This is hard."

"Take your time," he said.

She paused for a long moment. "You and Mother think Mateo pushed me out of the car to safety. He didn't. He was driving; I was in the back seat. Mateo didn't care about me. I'm not sure he ever did. It was Angel, Dad. He was drunk, but he wasn't on drugs."

They came to Markey Bridge. "I'm going to make this baby fly."

"Hey, cut it out, man," Angel said. "The roads are icy." Mateo applied his foot again, and the car spun wildly. Angel slid closer to Roe and whispered. "They're both crazy. We've got to get out of here. When I open the door, jump. He was barely loud enough for her to hear. "I'll be right behind you."

"I can't," she said, terrified.

Angel reached over and cracked open the door. The wind caught it and blew it open to the hinges. "Jump, or I'll push."

Roe jumped. The sound of the car hitting the water was the last thing she heard before losing consciousness.

"It was Angel, Dad. He saved my life, but he couldn't save himself. Will you tell Mother?"

Dad? She had never seen him cry before, and she turned her head quickly. It took him awhile to respond.

"I don't know. Her doctors must decide whether or not it would be too much for her. You're strong, Rosita. I'm not sure how you handled it. I couldn't have at your age." He gave her a long, silent hug, and then he was gone.

Roe's throat hurt. She was glad she didn't have to talk anymore. She was glad it was no longer just her problem. She started the DVD again. She didn't want to think about herself. Better to think about Anne Frank.

Kylie and Brad were not the first to arrive at Markey Castle. Leland opened the front door, pointed upstairs, and sighed. What had happened to the polite butler?

On their way, they met Kurt and Eric, dragging a heavy piece of medieval armor from the storage room. "Hey, you two," Kurt greeted. "Grab a sword or two. We need all the workers we can get."

"How's Roe?" Eric asked.

"Still sick but a little better." Kylie wished she could tell Eric what was going on, but that would be up to Roe. She wondered what was happening back at the house. Had Roe's father arrived yet?

"I sure hope she'll be okay for the play," Eric said.

"We think she will." Kylie crossed her fingers.

She stopped off at the storage room for a shield before climbing the rest of the way. Already, the ballroom had been transformed. Two knights, in full armor, were standing guard on both sides of the platform stage.

"Hi, Kylie," Beth greeted her. She was talking with Kurt's Grandma Gee. "We thought we'd hang our Grand Fenwick flag over the stage as soon as the play is over. What do you think?"

"You'll need an awfully tall ladder," Kylie said.

"I'll bet we can borrow one from Community," Gee said, pulling out her cell phone. "I'll take care of it."

"Oh, there's Miss Armstrong," Kylie said. "See you later."

The director was pacing back and forth on the platform stage, not nervously, more like she was marking the space. "This place is great, Kylie," she said. "Look, the kitchen in back extends the full length of the stage and could be used for dressing rooms and a backstage area. The doors at both sides of the kitchen would work for entrances and exits. And the steps from the house to the stage are wide enough to be safe for youngsters."

"There's no curtain," Kylie objected.

"You don't need a curtain for most children's plays."

Miss Armstrong's intentions were becoming clear. Kylie gasped. "Are you thinking what I think you're thinking?"

Miss Armstrong grinned. "We'd need chairs for the audience, of course, but I think we could borrow or rent them from the college."

"You're thinking of doing *Cinderella* here? Have you asked Mr. Markey?" A party was different from a play involving weeks of rehearsal.

"Not exactly," Miss Armstrong admitted. "I only met him a few minutes ago." She gestured toward two people. "Do you think it would be too much for him?"

With Leland's help, Mr. Markey had climbed the stairs and was having an animated discussion with Brad. They seemed to be arguing about where to hang a set of banners. Evidently Mr. Markey won because he burst into a triumphant laugh. Kylie remembered the first time she had seen him—a shy little man peeking at them from behind a door. We *are* good for him, she decided, without answering Miss Armstrong's question.

Soon the ballroom looked even grander than the stage set at school. Kylie finally found time to talk with Mr. Markey.

"A play here? On this stage?" The old man shook his head, although his eyes sparkled. "Oh, dear. I don't know, I'm sure. I'll discuss it with Leland." Kylie crossed her fingers.

"Whatever you decide is fine, Mr. Markey. We're your friends, no matter what you decide."

At nine, Miss Armstrong gathered the cast. "Ask your parents if we can borrow card tables and folding chairs. Be sure to notify Leland before bringing them here." She smiled at the unhappy man, who bowed in an attempt to maintain his dignity.

In addition to Kurt and Beth, Gee offered to drive Kylie and Brad home, saving Brad's mother the trip. "I'll come back during the week and help," Gee promised. "Don't worry about your party."

"You're terrific," Beth said.

"You read and hear about this all the time," Uncle Dan said. Both he and Kylie's mother were in the family room trying to comfort Roe. "Sometimes people have to accept that a person they loved did something terrible. The grieving may never completely end, but they have to get over their anger and guilt. It's easier when that person is still alive, of course, and could possibly change for the better."

Aunt Jane put her arm around her. "In time, Roe, it will hurt less, and you will be able to focus on your positive memories of Mateo. Remember, drug abuse is a disease. It was the drug, not Mateo, doing the harmful things."

Roe wasn't certain she agreed but nodded anyway.

"And just think," Aunt Jane continued, "thanks to you, your mother may be able to come to terms and eventually accept what happened. She may return, finally in good health."

Roe smiled. "Yes, that would be wonderful."

"And the party is going to be wonderful!" Kylie, who must have heard Roe's last word, burst in on the scene, stopping at seeing the serious faces. "Oh, I'm sorry. Is everything okay?"

"Much better," Roe said. "My dad thinks facing the truth will help Mother."

"Oh, I do hope so. Roe, I've got so much to tell you. Everything good is happening. And the play is only four days away!"

SCENE 14—BREAK A LEG!

"STOP!" KYLIE GRABBED BETH'S ARM and pulled her away from the curtain. "Don't you know it's bad luck to peek at the audience before a performance?"

"Why?" Beth joined Kylie at the Stage Left props table.

"I don't know why, but it is. Come on, we're supposed to meet in the Green Room as soon as we're in costume."

"What else is bad luck?" Beth asked, as they made their way to the girls' changing room.

"Oh, there are lots of superstitions in the theater. For instance, a good dress rehearsal means a bad performance, only Miss Armstrong says she doesn't believe in that one."

"Good thing," Beth said. "Our final dress rehearsal was great, but the first was awful."

Kylie smiled, remembering last night. No one, not even Brad, had missed a line. Even lights and sound were practically perfect. Miss Armstrong had been pleased, too, although she didn't think it was as wonderful as they did.

"There's still room to grow. Too often, actors reach their peak before the first performance. Now it's time for the audience to bring our play to life."

Maybe that's what the superstition means, Kylie thought. If you put all of your energy into a perfect dress rehearsal, you might not have enough left for opening night.

Surprisingly, the changing room wasn't crowded. "Most of the girls must be in costume already," Kylie said, removing her jeans and T-shirt, before drowning herself in the peach organdy gown. Beth helped with the tricky back zipper and placed the crown on Kylie's head.

"Know any other superstitions?"

"Well, it's supposed to be bad luck to whistle in the dressing rooms."

"How about the Green Room? Is it bad luck to whistle there?"

Kylie laughed. "It certainly is at this school. If anyone whistles in our Green Room, it can be heard on stage."

"Why is it called the Green Room? It isn't green. It's sort of a sick-looking yellow."

"I read somewhere that long ago at the Drury Lane Theatre in London, the room where actors met was painted green. Now it's sort of a tradition, even though it doesn't make sense."

"Speaking of green, I'd better hustle." Beth changed into her tourist costume, a mint-green mini dress. The style had enjoyed a brief popularity in the sixties, the time period in which Miss Armstrong had chosen to set their production, and was not much more comfortable than Kylie's outfit. "Are there any good luck superstitions?" Beth asked.

"It used to be good luck to use a rabbit's foot to apply your powder," Kylie said.

Beth grimaced. "I say it's bad luck for the rabbit."

"Spoken like a true vegetarian." Both girls giggled.

"Hey guys, let's go. Armstrong's waiting." Roe, wearing her cute tourist outfit, stage-whispered into the locker room. Kylie was pleased to see that Roe's stage makeup camouflaged the dark circles under her eyes, signs of her recent illness and worry.

"I checked the Stage Left props against the list," Kylie told Roe. "We're all set."

"Thanks. Stage Right props are ready to go, too. The auditorium is filling fast. We're going to have a full house."

"Don't peek," Beth warned. "It's bad luck."

Most of the cast had assembled when Kylie, Beth, and Roe squeezed into the tiny Green Room.

Imani greeted them. "I am so nervous, I'm going to be sick. How can you stay so calm, Kylie?"

"I haven't had time to think about it. I'll be plenty scared soon. But try not to worry. Usually, once you've said your first line, you stop being nervous and just relax and have fun. At least, that's the way it is for me."

Miss Armstrong asked the cast to form a circle. Kylie stood between Roe and Beth, rather than next to Brad. On this special occasion, it seemed right to be with her two best friends.

Miss Armstrong told the cast how much she had enjoyed working with them. "You are the most talented cast I've ever directed," she said. There were a few snickers at that. Miss Armstrong had said the same thing last year. Then she asked an odd question. "Who is the star of this play?"

"It's Kylie—that is, Glorianna," Imani said.

"Wrong," Miss Armstrong said.

"Then it must be Kurt, as Tully Bascom," Kylie said.

"Wrong again."

"Is it Count Mountjoy or David Benter?" Roe suggested, although that didn't seem likely.

Miss Armstrong shook her head.

The cast looked at each other, puzzled. There were no other possibilities. A lot of the other parts were good, but they weren't leads.

Miss Armstrong chuckled before explaining. "The star of this play and every play is the audience. Without the audience, there is no show. Put them first, and your play will be a success. Make sure your audience can see and hear you. Allow them to laugh by not continuing to speak while they're laughing."

"Hold for laughs," Kurt said, looking dashing in his Swiss hiker's costume.

"That's right," Miss Armstrong said. "Now, let's hold hands, close our eyes, and pass around a special squeeze for the success of *The Mouse That Roared.*"

For almost a whole minute, there was complete silence in the Green Room. Kylie winced at the strength of Roe's squeeze.

"Places!" Miss Armstrong cried. Everyone dropped hands. "Now, go break a leg!"

"Break a leg?" Beth asked.

Kylie explained "It's bad luck to say good luck, so we say 'break a leg!'" Kylie knew the expression probably started long ago when performers were paid only if they made it onto the stage. They hid behind the side curtains called legs. Then they would have to cross, or break, the leg line, until the audience could see them. If they could break a leg, they were successful. She'd explain later.

"Places" meant that cast members should go to the backstage area closest to their first entrance. For Beth and Roe, this meant backstage Left. Kylie's place was on the stage itself, behind the closed curtain. Cast members who didn't appear until later scenes remained in the Green Room, listening to the play over the intercom.

Soon the school orchestra completed a medley of peace songs from the sixties. The audience applauded, and then received a warning bell before the lights went out. The mighty roar of Grand Fenwick's mythical mouse resounded through the darkness, and Kurt took his place on the apron of the stage. The lights came up again, and the play began.

Kylie felt the blood drain from her face and her stomach churn. Soon it would be her turn. She could hear the audience chuckle at the tourists' insults. They were beginning to warm up and enjoy the play. Time to get into character. Kylie remembered Miss Armstrong's advice. *Start thinking like the person you're playing even before you appear. Give your character thought lines as well as spoken ones.*

Whatever shall we do about our economy? Kylie began to pace slightly. If the vineyards in California steal our ideas, Grand Fenwick will be ruined, and then how will I afford pomegranates?

Roe appeared in her Page costume and the curtain opened. She had successfully managed the hardest costume change in the show. *The Duchess Glorianna the Second!* she announced, and Glorianna swept grandly to her throne.

Pray be seated, she ordered Count Mountjoy and Prime Minister David Benter. *The meeting of the privy council will now begin.*

Roe returned to the Green Room to wait for her next scene, still as the Page. She was pleased to find Beth and a few others there, too. No, she shook her head at the offer of a soda. "Not a good idea." Burping, hiccups—any kind of indigestion—was a risk she was unwilling to take. She welcomed this break, though. After giving the Page's announcements and proclamations, her throat hurt. She knew she hadn't recovered entirely, but, as Miss Armstrong said, the show must go on.

"It's going well, don't you think?" Beth asked. "Kylie did a great job of covering when Brad blew that important line."

"Yes," Roe said, "but Brad didn't break character or let it throw him. Sometimes that's harder than covering."

They grinned at each other when the audience roared approval at the antics of Grand Fenwick's five soldiers. Dressed in medieval attire, they were hysterical as they prepared to attack New York City with bows and arrows.

"It's so much fun," Beth said, "but I think I'll be tired of it after three performances. I don't see how real actors can keep on doing it, show after show after show."

"I can. I wish I could keep on doing this for a whole year. Each time, I'd have to keep up the energy and make my parts interesting."

Beth sighed. "I don't think I care enough to ever want to do this professionally. There's a rumor going around that CBT might be able to do a show called *Cinderella, Cinderella* this winter. It would be fun to tackle something new."

Roe smiled but wasn't sure she agreed, not that she begrudged Kylie, her dearest friend, who would no doubt be cast as Cinderella. Roe wasn't the right type—not a Disney Princess. Who could she be? A wicked stepsister? That didn't appeal to her. Maybe if they were able to do the show, she'd volunteer to be props chair or work on the set. Creating a pumpkin carriage would be challenging.

"Hi!" Kylie, too, had a break. She carried a huge arrangement of red roses.

"Flowers already?" Roe asked. "It's bad luck to get flowers before the show is over. Who sent them to you?"

"Not for me, silly. They're for you. Roses for Rosita. And I think you'll decide they mean good luck for you." Kylie handed her the fragrant bouquet. "A messenger brought them. Read the card."

Roe's heart sank. "They must be from my father." Although Dad told her he couldn't come, she'd still hoped. No one was in the audience just for her. But at least he remembered.

"Just read it," Kylie insisted

Roe read the message aloud.

> *Dear Rosita,*
>
> *We wish we could be with you tonight. We'll be sure to attend your next play. Break a leg!*
> *Love, Dad and Mother*

Roe stared at the signatures. "Kylie," she cried. "Look at this! My mother signed it. Dad wrote the rest, but she signed it, too!"

Mother was written in a different handwriting from the rest of the note. "That's what I thought," Kylie said. "She must be getting better, Roe. This is such good news! It's even better than your dad being in the audience!"

Roe and Kylie hugged each other and danced around the room, although a few of the roses received a beating.

"Are you guys nuts?" Beth asked, although she was smiling. "Have you forgotten there's a play out there?"

"Roe," Jaimie hissed from the doorway, "you're on in four lines."

"Yikes!" Roe flung the roses at Kylie and dashed for the stage.

From her throne Center Stage, Kylie observed the play's closing scene. In her role as Glorianna, she acknowledged the efforts of her loyal subjects in bringing peace and stability to Grand Fenwick and announced her engagement to Tully Bascom. In her real-life role as Kylie, she couldn't wait for curtain call when she would be the last person on stage to bow to the audience. Then she would signal the cast to join her for one more bow.

Finally, Secretary of State Chet Beston gave the closing line of the play.

> *And able to tell the rest of the world—No war!*
> *This microscopic little mouse of a country!*

The curtain closed slowly, and the audience cheered.

We did it, Kylie thought. We really did it!

SCENE 15—WON'T IT BE WONDERFUL?

"A RE YOU SURE YOU WANT to walk?" Brad asked. "My dad offered to drive us."

The final performance was over, a Sunday matinee. The set had been struck, and Kylie and Brad were on their way to the cast party. Because of no school the next day, the parents had approved the Sunday night event. Kylie wouldn't consider a ride. "No thanks. The fresh air feels wonderful after being cooped up in a hot theater for how long?"

"It seemed endless," Brad admitted. "But wasn't it great?"

"The best play ever. But, as Miss Armstrong said, it's time to put the show to bed and look ahead. The party is a perfect way to begin."

The first frost of the season had made the ground firm and easy to walk on this late November afternoon. The sky was overcast and still. Last leaves had drifted to the ground, and the odor of illicit bonfires filled the air. Kylie felt like she and Brad were in a special world of their own.

"We'll have snow soon," Brad predicted.

"Cinderella in a castle in the snow," Kylie breathed. "Wouldn't it be wonderful? Do you think Mr. Markey will let us use his stage?"

"Not if Leland has a say."

Kylie and Brad continued to walk in silence, each involved in private thoughts. She knew Brad hoped for a theater camp scholarship even more than she did. With so many brothers and sisters, she doubted his parents could afford Crofts' high tuition. Of course if Dad didn't find work soon, her parents probably couldn't either. While a theater camp scholarship was no guarantee for another one to the high school, those who received them seemed to have a better chance.

"Do you think scholarships will be awarded tonight?" she asked.

"Yup." That was all Brad said, but he took her hand and gave it a squeeze.

Brad was an ideal boyfriend, Kylie thought. They liked the same things and knew when it was time to talk and when it was time to be still. She never had to worry if Brad really liked her, as Beth did with Kurt. Nor did she have the bother of a jealous ex-girlfriend as Roe had with Eric. Eric insisted that Jaimie had never been his girlfriend, but try telling that to Jaimie. Kylie smiled at Brad. He was just perfect. Brad smiled back and kept her hand in his the rest of the way. She wished they could keep on walking forever until—

"It looks like a fairytale!" Kylie dropped Brad's hand and gasped at her first glimpse of the castle.

A team of dads had strung white lights on the drainpipes and window frames. The lights outlined the castle in the autumn twilight. Extended across the front lawn, a red and golden banner read, WELCOME MOUSE CAST AND CREW!

Brad took Kylie's hand again, and they rushed up the castle steps.

"Look Roe, the programs are ready." Jen Yu handed Roe a cream-colored piece of card stock covered with exquisite calligraphy.

GOODBYE MOUSE!

Castle Bluff Theater Cast Party

Dinner—Roast Chicken or Spinach Lasagna, Caesar Salad, Rolls, Sundaes

Awards—Dr. Hazel Harper

Presentations—Miss Anna Armstrong, Mr. Harold MacLean Markey

Entertainment—Dancing

Music provided by
Castle Bluff Middle School's Rock & Jazz Band

"You do beautiful work, Jen."

Jen's dark eyes sparkled. Roe marveled at the change in her. Jen had been a different person since the scavenger hunt. She had put her shyness aside and had become a valuable member of the theater.

"Everything looks gorgeous," Jen said.

Roe agreed. The ballroom resembled a medieval Grand Hall, decorated with the brightly colored banners, swords, and other props from Mr. Markey's storage room. The area in front of the stage remained clear for dancing while card tables and chairs formed a semi-circle around the dance area. Each table, covered with a soft yellow tablecloth, boasted an arrangement of candles and fall-colored mums. On stage, chairs and a podium with a microphone had been prepared for honored guests.

Beth, carrying her dress in a garment bag, joined them. "This is going to be the coolest party ever," she said. She looked at how Roe and Jen were dressed. "Did you bring your dresses, too?"

"We did," Roe said. "So did Kylie. She's in the bathroom changing."

"Let's join her," Beth said. "The party will start soon."

Roe hummed along with the band. They were doing a great job. No wonder they received awards as the best middle school band in the state. She glanced away from Eric to watch Kylie dancing with Brad. She looked beautiful, of course, in her new deep blue strapless, the first one she'd ever worn. The dress was gorgeous but couldn't compare to Roe's more modest red satin and black lace. What a surprise it had been when the large check and note arrived from her father, instructing both girls to find the most fabulous dresses in the world to wear to the cast party. Roe's only accessory was her gold bracelet, specially engraved just for her. The dress makes two things Dad has given me, she thought. Three, counting the rose bouquet.

"You look like the gypsy we studied in music class," Eric observed.

Roe laughed. "Carmen? Maybe that is who I am tonight."

The dance ended, and she and Eric applauded the band's fine efforts.

"You seem awfully calm," Eric said. "Aren't you nervous about the scholarship announcement? I am."

"Not really," Roe said. "I did the best I could with my small parts—"

"No small parts—you were great," Eric interrupted.

Roe smiled. "Thanks. My project and grades are good. It's out of my hands. No sense in being nervous."

She meant that. Living with Kylie's family had made her less driven to make changes in her life. Her mother was where she might get better, her father loved her after all, and she had true friends. I'll be okay, she thought, whether I go to Crofts or not.

"Let's just have a good time tonight," she said.

"Please take your seats again for dessert and some special announcements."

Kylie and Brad rushed to the table they were sharing with Roe and Eric. "This is it," Kylie said.

As soon as the guests settled down, Miss Armstrong resumed. "First, I would like to welcome you to the best cast party Castle Bluff Theater has ever had."

"I think it's the only one," Brad whispered.

"And I would like to thank the people responsible." They all cheered as Mr. Markey, Gee, the band director Mr. Nance, and even Leland, stood after their names were called. Kylie almost shivered at the sight of Leland's expression. She had always thought he was too serious. Now, he looked almost miserable, as if he were seeing the end of his life as he knew it. Probably that's exactly what's happening, Kylie thought, vowing that Mr. Markey would never be lonely again.

Those at Kylie's table had chosen hot fudge sundaes. She and Roe exchanged warning glances, reminding each other not to drip chocolate onto their new dresses.

Miss Armstrong commanded their attention again. "I would like to introduce a special guest whose face will become a familiar one to some of you. A big hand, please, for Dr. Hazel Harper, the head of the theater department at Crofts Performing Arts High School."

Kylie clapped enthusiastically. In spite of her nervousness, she couldn't help being amused by Miss Armstrong's formality. Perhaps the atmosphere of the elegant ballroom was responsible, or maybe she was in awe of Dr. Harper. Kylie had heard somewhere that Miss Armstrong had wanted to be hired by Crofts and had settled for Castle Bluff Middle School. Thank heavens she had!

Dr. Harper was a tiny grim-faced woman with steel-gray hair. She had a voice larger than expected, waving Miss Armstrong away when the microphone was offered to her. "Never use the things," she said.

Roe giggled. "Talk about projection."

"It's my great pleasure," Dr. Harper boomed forth, "to award the Crofts' scholarships to the 61st session of our theater camp, located on beautiful Shimmer Lake in Michigan."

"Isn't that near where your mother is?" Kylie whispered. Roe nodded but held a finger to her lips.

While the audience held its collective breath, Dr. Harper explained that students who had shown exceptional ability would spend the last three weeks of June taking master classes in acting and other areas of theater, while preparing a polished final production. Directors and teachers were Crofts' distinguished alumni, who had found success in the theater world. Outstanding eighth grade students throughout the Midwest were eligible for full, partial, or partial-with-conditions scholarships.

"Conditions?" Kylie asked quietly.

As if she'd heard Kylie, Dr. Harper responded. "A conditional scholarship means we expect the student's academic grades to improve before eighth grade graduation. Those students will be monitored closely. A partial scholarship means Crofts will pay half of the tuition. This year, it is my great pleasure to award five scholarships. That is a great number for any one school, and you should be proud. The winners of the partial scholarships are—Brad Michaels, Eric Stein, and Kylie Kennedy."

Kylie gasped as the crowd applauded. She made it! A partial might be okay with her parents, even if Dad didn't find a job. She hoped it would be all right with Brad's, too. He looked worried. But what about Roe? She glanced over at her friend, but Roe's head was bowed.

"And the recipients of full scholarships are Kurt Brockway and Rosita Santos."

At that, everyone cheered. Kurt was extremely popular and, thanks to the successful scavenger hunt, so was Roe. Kylie gave her a hug as the scholarship winners made their way to the stage to receive their certificates and scholarship information. She shook Dr. Harper's hand as she was given the precious envelope.

As soon as Kylie returned to her seat, she took a quick peek. She was afraid of that. Stamped on the scholarship letter was the word "Conditional." Well, she would do it. Her grades had improved. They'd be perfect by May, or she'd die trying. Brad didn't look happy, and Kylie wondered if he also had received a conditional. She sighed. Too many milkshakes at Smithy's!

Gazing at Roe's shining face and tear-filled eyes, Kylie stopped thinking of herself. No one deserved this more than she. "Oh, Roe," she whispered, "won't it be wonderful?"

Miss Armstrong resumed her position on the podium and waited for the applause to stop. "Congratulations. I hope you five come back in the fall and share your experiences with next year's CBT members. Perhaps we'll have even more students trying for scholarships. Next I have an announcement that will come as a complete surprise."

Kylie shook her head. Putting on *Cinderella, Cinderella* wouldn't be a complete surprise. Lots of kids knew it was a possibility.

"Last August," Miss Armstrong continued, "a friend of mine, who is also a director at Crofts, approached me with an unusual request. He asked me to search for a particular type of actor from the eighth grade class. This student was not to be given a large part in CBT this year. My friend wanted an unfamiliar face, partly because of the history of the show he planned to direct, and also because he did not want the actor closely associated with any other specific role. Instead, the person I chose would play a small part and concentrate on specified weaknesses. I agreed and decided not tell anyone what I was doing." She sighed. "Keeping the secret turned out to be difficult at times."

What was she talking about? Miss Armstrong smiled at the puzzled faces. "I don't mean to sound mysterious. I'm happy to finally make it clear. Crofts has completed casting for *The Diary of Anne Frank*, with the exception of one important role. The part of Anne Frank will be played by our own Roe Santos—that is, if she's willing."

"Willing?" Kylie blurted. "It's her dream come true!"

At that, they burst into laughter and applause, and Roe, who still hadn't recovered from the scholarship announcement, blushed and nodded furiously.

"Roe and I will work out the details later," Miss Armstrong said smiling. "Our last announcement of the evening will be given by our host, Mr. Harold MacLean Markey."

Leland helped the old gentleman to the stage and adjusted the microphone. "Can you hear me?" Mr. Markey's thin voice filled the room.

"Yes," they shouted good-naturedly. Mr. Markey had become popular with everyone.

"I just want to say," Mr. Markey continued, "I am happy to announce that CBT's next play, *Cinderella, Cinderella*, will be presented right here on this stage!"

A loud "Whoop" came from several tables, including Kylie's.

Mr. Markey then held up a large old-fashioned key before handing it to Miss Armstrong. "This is to the back door to the stairs leading to the kitchen behind the stage. You'll be able to come anytime you like without having to ring the front door."

Kylie couldn't believe the trust Mr. Markey was giving them and could tell by her stunned and proud look, Miss Armstrong felt the same way.

"Now, carry on with your party," Mr. Markey concluded. "You deserve it!"

Most people returned to the dance floor, but Kylie asked Brad to wait. "I've got to talk to Roe first."

Roe still seemed stunned. Kylie put an arm around her. "Are you okay?"

"You mean, after being handed the moon? Okay isn't the word." Roe's voice trembled. "I can't believe it. Winning a scholarship and the part of Anne—in one evening? No wonder Miss Armstrong asked me to trust her. But I'm embarrassed to say that for the longest time, I didn't."

"Miss Armstrong understood," Kylie said. "And while you're rehearsing at Crofts, the rest of us will be in this fairytale castle. Won't it be wonderful?"

Just then Eric claimed Roe for his dancing partner, and Kylie felt a tap on her shoulder. She expected Brad, but it was Mr. Markey.

"May I have this dance?" he asked shyly.

Kylie smiled. "I'd love to. Thank you for asking. Thank you for everything, Mr. Markey."

"My pleasure, Miss Kennedy. "Congratulations on your scholarship."

"It's only conditional," Kylie confessed.

"So what in life isn't?" The old man laughed and led her onto the floor. "Now suppose we concentrate on that dance—on the condition, of course, that you promise to hold me up."

ACT TWO – Cinderella in the Castle

Act Well Your Part. There all the honor lies.
—Motto of the International Thespian Society

Scene 1 — Too Many Changes

R OE SANTOS SHIVERED. SHE AND Kylie Kennedy had been caught in a freezing rain that was turning quickly to snow. They were using the back entrance—called the mudroom for good reason—to keep from dripping water onto Mrs. Kennedy's hardwood floors. "I can't believe only two weeks ago we were cleaning up after the cast party."

Kylie agreed. "It feels like a month at least, or maybe even a brand-new year. Everything seems different now. You're rehearsing at Crofts, and soon we'll have auditions for Cinderella in the castle. And then Winter Break. Can't wait!"

Well, she couldn't wait either, Roe thought, although for a different reason. At some point, she would confide in Kylie that rehearsals for *The Diary of Anne Frank* were not living up to expectations. Oh, she still loved the play and the part—that wasn't the problem—but she was beginning to wonder if the rest of the cast would ever accept her, never mind like her. Roe shrugged. At least the weekend had officially started. No rehearsal today.

She and Kylie removed their wet clothes and were about to enter the kitchen when they heard voices. Aunt Jane and Uncle Dan, as Roe now called Kylie's parents, were arguing.

"Shhh!" Kylie cautioned. Miserably, they stood and waited, not sure what to do next.

"I'm doing the best I can," Kylie's normally calm father whined. "Do you think I like going out every single day, coming back with nothing?"

"But you've had so many interviews. I don't understand why no one is interested."

"I guess I'm not good enough."

"Of course you are, Dan. I wasn't suggesting . . . But I am worried about the kids, with Kylie's camp scholarship being only a partial and Danny wanting to stay at his school and have hockey lessons."

"Those things are the least of our problems, Jane. We're living way beyond our means. We don't need a truck, a van, and a station wagon. You'll keep the wagon, but I'm going to turn in the others for something smaller that's not a gas-guzzler."

"Well, I don't know—"

"Well, I do. I'll keep on trying, but even with your working again, if something doesn't break soon, we could lose the house. And your nagging sure doesn't help!"

Roe and Kylie heard the kitchen door slam, followed by tears from Kylie's mom. Soon, another door slammed, and the kitchen was empty.

Embarrassed, Roe and Kylie hardly looked at each other. "Let's sneak upstairs and change," Kylie whispered.

That was the best they could do for now, Roe thought. It wasn't as if this were the first time they'd overheard problems discussed. Mortgages, taxes, and school tuition were becoming standard topics. She felt guilty, stuck in the middle of this big mess. Here she was, basically living off the Kennedys, while her father, a CEO for a pharmaceutical company, was living in Michigan, so he could be near his wife, presently housed in an insane asylum. Roe didn't belong with them, but she didn't belong here either—or at Crofts—or maybe not anywhere. She knew Dad sent Uncle Dan money, but how much and how often? Surely it wasn't enough. Lose their house, when there was a perfectly good one with no mortgage, empty, right next door?

Buzzing with excitement, Beth set down her heavy bag of beauty equipment before ringing the Kennedy's doorbell. She would be the bearer of the latest gossip, for a change, instead of the last one to know anything juicy. Since becoming a seventh grader, she was practically invisible, although it helped somewhat that Kylie and Kurt, two popular eighth graders, were her friends. Wait until they heard the news!

So cold! She rubbed her arms and stomped her feet. Kylie knew she was coming to dye her hair. How much longer must she wait? She leaned on the bell until finally Mrs. Kennedy, bundled up ready to leave, answered the door. Odd, Kylie's mother looked as if she'd been crying. Maybe she'd been slicing onions. That's what always happened to Beth's mom.

"Hello, Beth. The girls are expecting you." Mrs. Kennedy continued down the porch stairs without explanation.

Beth dashed upstairs, where she heard voices coming from Kylie's closed door. She flung it open. "She's back!" Beth announced grandly.

"Obviously," Kylie said. "It's about time."

There was a strange tension in the room. Something was off. Both girls seemed relieved to see her, and Beth didn't think it was about dying hair. Her announcement didn't seem as momentous as it had been before. "Hey, not me," she said. "Of course I'm back, or at least I'm here. Someone else is officially back, and you're not going to be happy about it. Entering Stage Left and crossing Center is—ta da!—Roe's worst enemy, Marla Gray!"

"What?"

"Well, I haven't seen her yet, but my little sister Kelly is a friend of Marla's sister. Believe me, Marta isn't thrilled. Marla and Marta! What were her parents thinking?"

Kylie shrugged. "Probably thought it was cute. I'll bet Marla got kicked out of boarding school." She put an arm around Roe. "Well, we won't let her bother us, right? We'll ignore her."

Roe nodded soberly before changing the subject. "I guess if you're going to destroy Goldilocks's golden locks, you'd better get busy. Personally, I plan to stay out of it. I'll be far away when Aunt Jane and Uncle Dan explode."

"But aren't you going to help?" Beth asked.

"Unh-uh. Doing homework, and I'm going to try to phone my dad. See you later."

Kylie looked worriedly at the closed door. She and Roe hadn't discussed what they'd overheard in the kitchen. Too embarrassing, and what could they say? She shivered, even though her room was warm. Everything was changing. Some of those changes she knew; others she sensed were coming—unknown and somehow scary.

"Are you sure you want to go through with this, Kylie? Do you really want me to dye your hair?"

"Oh, sorry, Beth. You're sure it will wash out if I don't like it or Mom and Dad go ballistic?"

"Well, that's what the package says. I can't understand why you want to. Your hair is so pretty."

"Monday's auditions. I don't want Miss Armstrong to cast me as Cinderella. She probably won't, but I can't take a chance. I've got to get a part—just not that one. Maybe I could be the wicked stepmother."

"The fairy godmother is great, too, but why not Cinderella?"

"I've been type-cast. Roe told me Crofts calls actors like me one-trick ponies, like I can do only one kind of part. Well, I think I could do lots if given the chance."

"Call yourself a pony or just plain lucky." Beth shook her head. "Look at me. The only part I have a chance at might be a stepsister, and even that's not likely. But Mr. Carroll doesn't think I should try out at all. He thinks I should concentrate on my writing." She heaved a great sigh.

Kylie looked at her warily. Beth's crush on the new social studies teacher was becoming really annoying. "Time for my hair," she said.

A half hour later, with Kylie's head sopping wet, black dye dripping down her face, the doorbell rang. Kylie shrugged. Roe would get it.

But soon Roe related the bad news. "Kylie, Brad is here. He says he's got something important to tell you."

"Brad? I can't see him like this! See what he wants. Please?"

"Okay, I'll try."

"I haven't seen him forever. I hope he doesn't want to break up."

"Unlikely," Beth said, "and he'd hardly tell Roe."

"Roe, wait. Beth, hand me a towel." Quickly, Kylie fashioned a turban. "I'll hide behind the door and listen."

Beth nodded. "We'll finish the job when you come back."

Kylie was already regretting the hair fiasco. Her parents would not approve, and she'd miss her chance to see Brad. Carefully, she hid behind the front door.

"Brad," Roe said, "I was wrong. She isn't home."

Brad stood there, uncomfortable, probably because of Roe's lack of hospitality as well as the frigid weather. Normally, she would have asked him in.

"Well, tell her Marla Gray is back."

"Yes, we heard," Roe said, starting to close the door.

"That's not all. Her father skipped town and the cops are looking for him, and Mr. Hasting was fired. Both were indicted. Looks like they helped themselves to money belonging to the school district. I guess that's why Hasting defended Marla. He wanted Mr. Gray to keep on being treasurer."

"Gosh! I'll tell Kylie. Thanks for letting me know, Brad."

"Yeah, well, it's freezing out here. Gotta go. See ya." The door finally closed.

Kylie stepped from behind the door. "Thanks, Roe."

"Not sure I did you any favors. Brad kept staring at the door. I think he sensed you were there." Roe sniffed. "Or maybe he smelled you."

"Terrific. Well, I guess I'll ask Beth to wash this stuff out of my hair. It wasn't such a good idea after all." Too many changes, Kylie thought again.

KYLIE PULLED HER BLUE WOOLEN cap over her ears and took matching mittens from her jacket pocket. "It's only snowing a little. I don't see why Mom said I couldn't walk." Kylie had been grumpy all day, and a walk to the castle might have lifted her spirits. So what if the weather report that morning had been grim? It wasn't like the weatherman was always right—or even most of the time.

Waiting alone on the front steps, she felt on display—part of an exhibit of the definitely unpopular. It was Brad's fault she was so down. Not even one note in English class. "I guess he doesn't like me anymore."

All in all, it had been an unsettling day, ending with an announcement from the new acting vice principal, Mrs. Warde. "Will the following students report to the office?" Just an impersonal voice reading a list of names. No long apologies about disrupting the class, no sports scores, not even a reminder of the CBT auditions at the castle.

Did she miss Mr. Hasting? No, but as mean and unfair as he was, Kylie was accustomed to him. As Dad said—"You might be better off with the devil you know." She shivered. Something was going to happen. She could feel it. She could also feel a tap on her shoulder.

"Hey, Kylie, do you have room in your car?"

"Brad," she said coolly. "Are you sure you want to go with me?"

"Oh, come on, Kyle. You know I can't afford to fool around in class anymore. Plus, I've got to get a job. My parents can't pay the half tuition to camp. I need to raise a thousand bucks."

"That much?" Kylie had never been able to save more than twenty dollars without blowing it. Would she be in the same situation? If Dad didn't find a job soon, could her parents afford to send her? She needed to grow up—starting now.

"Sorry, Brad. I guess I haven't been thinking clearly. It's just that everything is different. I miss passing notes. I might even miss old Hasting."

Brad grinned. "I agree about the notes anyway. But think of the fun we'll have at camp together."

"If you get the money." And me, too, Kylie added silently. "What are you going to do?"

"Not sure yet. I'm not old enough for a real job, but I've got some snow shoveling lined up for early mornings and weekends."

"Sounds exhausting. Anything else?"

"I might ask Mr. Markey if he could use me at the castle for a few hours after rehearsals. Custodian-type stuff. My dad is willing to come get me when the weather is bad."

"Will you have time to be in the play?"

"If I want to be accepted at Crofts, I'll make time."

"You will," Kylie said. "And so will I." Perhaps she could earn money babysitting. But that much?

Then Roe and her boyfriend Eric Stein joined them.

"Room for more in your car?" Eric asked.

Kylie laughed, suddenly forgiving her mother. "Room for six more. Mom is bringing the van." She wondered how much longer they'd have the van, if Dad made good on his threat.

By the time Mrs. Kennedy arrived, a vanload of hopeful actors awaited her. The weather forecast had proved accurate after all. Temperatures were dropping rapidly, and the snow was no longer the light fall Kylie had dismissed.

Kylie couldn't help feeling proud. Much of what was happening was her doing. Back during the scavenger hunt, she had insisted that her group ask for props at the castle Kylie had marched up the imposing front steps and pounded the troll-shaped doorknocker. Not only had they succeeded, they'd made friends with the reclusive Mr. Markey. Later, he allowed them to use his beautiful ballroom for their cast party and gave them permission to use the small stage for their next production. Miss Armstrong, their director, now had a key to a private entrance, so Leland, the stuffy man who cared for Mr. Markey, wouldn't be disturbed by groups of students traipsing over his entryway.

"Looks like a gingerbread fairyland, doesn't it?" Brad said as they arrived. "Like home for a cookie witch."

Kylie gazed at the castle standing alone on the bluff. Someone, Leland perhaps, had turned on the lights left from the cast party. The whole castle, even the turrets and cupolas, twinkled in the snow. Kylie shivered again— this time in delight.

Kylie waved goodbye to her mother and Roe before entering the castle. I'll bet Roe wishes she could do both plays, she thought.

Roe's thoughts were similar but not quite what Kylie had imagined. She gave a great sigh.

Mrs. Kennedy chuckled. "That doesn't sound like someone getting ready to rehearse her favorite role. Do you regret not being in *Cinderella, Cinderella?*"

How much should she say? "That's not it exactly, Aunt Jane. There aren't any parts right for me, and I do love playing Anne Frank. It's just—"

"Your friends are all excited about performing in the castle, and a part of you wants to be with them?"

Roe nodded. "Yes." And that was the truth, only not the whole truth. She hadn't heard from her father all weekend. He hadn't called, and her efforts had been unsuccessful. How long had it been since they'd talked? Not since right after *Mouse* ended, she figured, and even then only briefly. She must talk to him about doing more to help the Kennedys.

"How are the Anne rehearsals going, Roe? Are you enjoying yourself?" Aunt Jane gave Roe a sharp look. "You don't seem very happy."

"Rehearsals are okay, and the director, Mr. Warner, is nice."

"But?"

"Well, it's like the other kids in the cast resent me. They don't think I should be there."

Aunt Jane nodded. "I was afraid of something like that. You received a great honor, but I can understand how Crofts' students might see it differently."

"I'll be okay, Aunt Jane. Don't worry."

The weather had become severe. Traffic and road conditions became Mrs. Kennedy's only concern.

The stone stairs leading up to the kitchen and ballroom were narrow and winding, and the air, chilly and damp. "Feels like a dungeon," Beth's boyfriend Kurt said.

Beth agreed. "It's creepy. I'm glad I'm not alone." If it weren't for Kurt she would have preferred not coming. What was the point? She wasn't going to be cast.

At least the atmosphere changed the instant they entered the large upstairs kitchen. A group of students, including Kylie, Brad, and Eric, had already arrived and had discovered homemade donuts and hot chocolate waiting for them.

Miss Armstrong greeted them. "Welcome. Look what Gee has done."

"I decided to put this old stove to work," Kurt's grandma said, offering a fresh platter of cinnamon-covered donut holes to the newcomers. The aroma almost made Beth swoon.

"We thought it would be warmer and friendlier if we held auditions here," Miss Armstrong explained.

Beth noticed that chairs had been set up in the circle Miss Armstrong seemed to favor for auditions. She counted quickly. Only fifteen students had come. Maybe she had a chance after all. Mr. Carroll wouldn't be pleased with her, but she'd try to explain that her friends were important, too. He had seemed angry she'd decided to audition. Surely she was mistaken. Why should he care? "Where is everybody?" she asked.

Miss Armstrong laughed. "I think this is it. Having rehearsals so far from school and during vacation time made many people reconsider. Actually, I'm pleased. I think we can find spots in the cast or crew for everyone here today."

Crew? That wouldn't take so much time. Maybe it would work out after all. She could please her friends and Mr. Carroll. And you, Beth? What do you want? She ignored that inner intrusive voice.

"As you know," Miss Armstrong began, "this version of Cinderella is an audience participation play."

She stopped at the sound of steps on the stairs. When the door opened, there stood Marla Gray, covered with snow, looking frozen and miserable. "I'm sorry I'm late," she said. "I had to walk; I didn't have a ride."

"She's b-a-a-ck," Beth stage-whispered to Kylie.

Kylie looked down—her face hot. She hadn't seen Marla since that awful night she'd almost set fire to the Green Room, intending to let Roe take the blame.

"Come in, Marla," Miss Armstrong said with forced friendliness. Gee helped Marla out of her wet coat, and then poured her some hot chocolate.

In spite of herself, Kylie admired Marla. It took courage to come here, especially alone. But how could anyone forgive her for what she'd done?

"Let me continue," Miss Armstrong said. "A participation play is a challenging experience, even scary at times."

"Scary?" The students looked bewildered.

"During the performance, the audience is invited to take part, and since they don't have lines, anything can happen. For instance, children will come up on stage and help Cinderella clean the room. Later, they'll help her get ready for the ball. One child will brush her hair while another helps her put on the glass slippers. What the children say and do makes each performance entirely new and unpredictable."

"Cool," someone said. Kylie agreed. It sounded hard, but fun.

"One of the characters will even be chosen from the audience," Miss Armstrong said. "The actor playing the king chooses his own queen and seats her next to him onstage. Audience participation means the actors must be so solid with their lines and know the play so well, they can be flexible and keep the play moving no matter what happens. They have to enjoy the audience and help them have a good time."

For the first time, the play meant more to Kylie than a ticket to Crofts. It sounded awesome! She had to make it—but what if she didn't?

"Now for the characters. There's Cinderella, of course, and her wicked stepmother and two stepsisters. There's also a king, the prince, and a comical duke who goes through all kinds of antics to force the glass slippers onto the stepsisters' feet."

Everyone looked at Kurt, who grinned and crossed his fingers in the air.

"Finally, there's the fairy godmother. She's an important character because she does most of the talking with the audience and even encourages them to dance at the ball."

Kylie brightened. The fairy godmother part sounded interesting. Good thing she decided against black hair. Hers could easily be powdered gray, if that was the look Miss Armstrong wanted. Miss Armstrong was too smart to choose her for Cinderella. The director must know Kylie's chances for Crofts could be hurt if she played a role similar to Gloriana.

"Decide what part you'd like to try for," Miss Armstrong said, "and don't worry. If you make a mistake choosing, I'll ask you to read something different. Also, if I haven't worked with you before, I might ask you to move a little or perhaps do an improv."

Kylie wasn't worried. She hated improv, but Miss Armstrong knew her. She wouldn't be asked.

"Improvisation can show me your ability to concentrate and use your imagination. Kylie, suppose you demonstrate in order to help the group relax."

Except for me. I won't relax. Goodbye fairy godmother, Kylie thought. All of her friends, knowing how she felt, looked sympathetic.

Definitely sensing her thoughts, Kurt bounced to her side. "Let me do one with Kylie," he insisted. "It's more fun that way." Miss Armstrong nodded.

They put their heads together for a quick whispered conference. At Kurt's suggestion, Kylie pretended to be a teacher questioning a student as to why he had failed to turn in his homework. Kurt mimed being a dog eating the assignment, a small child flushing it down the toilet, and finally, a monster ripping it up. Kylie showed shocked disbelief at each excuse, and then grabbed Kurt by the ear and threw him out of her classroom.

The whole group laughed and cheered.

"I guess you've relaxed us." Miss Armstrong said.

As they returned to their seats, Kylie whispered, "Thanks, I owe you."

Kurt grinned. "No problem."

Gee passed out the audition sides. "So raise your hands if you want to be Cinderella?" Gee sounded like a barker at the circus. She continued in this fashion until everyone had a part to read.

Kylie noticed with relief that Marla had chosen to read the part of the wicked stepmother. Type casting? Well, at least they wouldn't be competing. They began with Cinderella. Four girls wished to try. Kylie decided to pretend she was the director. Who would she pick if she were Miss Armstrong?

Oh, no, Kylie groaned inwardly as Beth joined the group. In addition to her appearance—bright red hair, pale face and freckles—Beth's high-pitched voice was completely wrong for Cinderella. She might make a funny stepsister, though. Maybe Miss Armstrong would ask her to read again.

Petite Jen Yu, whose father had supplied bows and arrows for the last play, read next. She did a worse job than Beth, but Miss Armstrong asked her to read later for a stepsister. What about Beth?

The students watching started to squirm. Only two Cinderellas to go. Maybe it was a problem more people weren't auditioning.

Priyanka Patel tried next. She read well, but her short, dark, straight hair didn't fit Kylie's vision of Cinderella. And she was almost as tall as Brad!

Jaimie Jelinek read last, and Kylie nodded. Jaimie's sweet pure voice and fragile face framed by pale white-blonde hair gave an instant picture of Cinderella. Kylie mentally cast her in the part. She wished she liked Jaimie better. Recently, Jaimie had received a surprise letter, stating that a mistake had been made and that she had received a full scholarship to Crofts' Camp Shimmer Lake. "Boy, did they ever apologize," Jaimie said. Most people were happy for Jaimie but had grown tired of hearing her brag about it.

"King!" Gee announced loudly, forcing Kylie back to the present. Again, there was no contest. Two boys tried out—a tiny seventh grader and Brad, the tallest boy in the eighth grade. Brad read the part as if the crown were already on his head.

Three boys tried for the duke. While they were all good, Kylie thought that Kurt, the funniest and probably the most popular boy in the whole school, would get it.

All four who tried out for the prince were outstanding, but Kylie cast her mental vote for dark, slim, serious Eric Stein. Wouldn't it be something if Roe's boyfriend played opposite Jaimie? From the smug expression on Jaimie's face, Kylie thought she was thinking the same thing.

Miss Armstrong asked Jen Yu to reread, this time for one of the stepsisters. Shy Jen came to life in the comic role. A new girl named Gabrielle Soleigh also gave a terrific reading. Beth was not called again.

Kylie hated to admit that Marla gave the best audition for the wicked stepmother. Her natural haughty manner brought elegance to the role. Unless Miss Armstrong decided to hold the past against her, Marla would be cast.

Finally came Kylie's turn. Reaching out to the audience, she made her fairy godmother warm and witty. Kylie crossed her fingers. She had auditioned well, but one more person still needed to read.

Imani Jones also wanted that part. She turned her godmother into an old-fashioned mammy from the Deep South, right out of *Gone with the Wind.* Everyone seemed stunned and a little uncomfortable that Imani drew attention to her race. However, Imani was so funny and convincing that soon they began to laugh and applaud. Miss Armstrong frowned, but how could she not like the audition? Imani was so good!

Kylie's heart dropped. She knew who she would pick if she were director. Imani's interpretation would give the play a whole new look. The audience would love it. Oh, well, she thought. *I can always do props or costumes. I hope the people who gave me a conditional scholarship don't change their minds when they find out I didn't make the play.*

Miss Armstrong stood and applauded the group. "This is for all of you. You've done splendidly, and I wish you could all have parts. I'll post the cast list some time tomorrow, and read-through will take place here Wednesday after school. Those of you not cast, please let me know what crews might interest you."

Kylie, Beth, and Kurt began to help Gee clean up. Brad whispered to Kylie that he was going to ask Mr. Markey for a job in the castle. "My dad will pick me up. I'll call you later."

Soon the kitchen was back in shape. As they prepared to leave, Miss Armstrong asked Imani to remain. *Probably wants to give her the part right now,* Kylie thought. Then Kylie saw Marla struggling into her still-wet coat and swallowed hard before speaking.

"Marla, we're going right by your house, if you'd like a ride."

Marla stared at Kylie. "Are you sure?"

"It's only a ride. The weather's too miserable for anyone to walk."

"Thanks," Marla murmured, following Kylie to the Kennedy's van.

SCENE 3—SOMETIMES IT'S LIKE THAT

K YLIE STARED AT HER NAME in disbelief. It's not fair, she thought. It's just not fair! Embarrassed, she turned away from the excited group of students examining the cast list. "Thank you," she said automatically to her friends' shouts of congratulations and tried to ignore others' puzzled looks.

She pushed opened the school's heavy front door at the same moment Miss Armstrong rushed out of the office. The two nearly collided. "Oops," the director said, before continuing out of the building. She's certainly in a hurry, Kylie thought.

Abandoned and lonely, Kylie stood shivering, trying to make a decision. Should she take the bus? Roe and Beth were busy, and Brad had headed straight for the castle to begin his new job as Mr. Markey's handyman. Kylie wasn't sure he'd even seen his name next to "King." No, she couldn't face any more fake congratulations. She'd walk home—by herself.

But before she took the decisive step, the front door opened abruptly. "Did you see the girl who just left?" It was Mr. Carroll, the new social studies teacher, who now sponsored the school newspaper and had convinced Beth she was heading for the New York Times. "Who was she?" he demanded impatiently.

"You mean Miss Armstrong?"

"Oh, I thought—" Mr. Carroll looked closely at Kylie. "And who are you?"

Kylie blushed. She did not like the way he was looking at her. "I'm Kylie Kennedy."

"Oh, so you're Beth Walters' so-called friend."

She attempted a laugh. "Hardly so-called. Beth is one of my best friends. Well, see you, Mr. Carroll. I'm late." She hurried off.

Creepy, she thought. Why does Beth like him?

Kylie had reached the end of the circle drive when a voice called out. "Kylie, wait up!" Breathlessly, Imani Jones rushed to join her.

"I didn't think you'd ever want to speak to me again."

"We've got to talk," Imani insisted, "but it's too cold out here. Can you come to my house?"

"Let's just go to Smithy's. I'm starving."

Smithy's Grill and Ice Cream Parlor was the special hang-out for theater students. Kylie and Imani were greeted immediately by friends and acquaintances.

"Great news, Kylie. Congratulations!"

"Too bad, Imani. I heard your audition was awesome. Next time!"

The two girls pushed through the crowd to an empty booth. Imani had ordered a hamburger, fries, and a chocolate milkshake while Kylie settled for fries and a Coke. Mom had made it clear she would no longer advance Kylie's allowance. She would have to make ten dollars a week do. She sighed. That should be enough money, but somehow it never was. It seemed strange to be here without Brad.

"Imani," she began, at the same time Imani said, "Kylie." Both girls giggled. "Let me start," Imani insisted.

Imani explained that Miss Armstrong had told her right after auditions that Kylie would receive the part. "She was complementary but thought people would be offended by the way I played the fairy godmother. Maybe she was afraid people would think she was racist. She definitely thought the administration would."

"I disagree," Kylie said. "You could have toned it down. The audience would have loved you."

Imani smiled. "Thanks. Mrs. Armstrong didn't think so, but I'll bet that wasn't Miss Armstrong's only reason. Could you keep your camp scholarship if you didn't get a part?"

Kylie shook her head. "Probably not. Now I really feel bad. Imani, you know you were better."

"No, I wasn't, silly. I was just different. You were everyone's idea of a fairy godmother. No one was surprised you got it. Besides, Beth and I are going to co-chair the props committee. Maybe we'll have another scavenger hunt—if she can forget about . . ." Her voice drifted off.

Kylie nodded, smiling. Maybe it was going to be okay. After all, Miss Armstrong knew best; she was the director. All the people Kylie had predicted, except for Imani, were in the cast. Jaimie would be Cinderella and Eric the prince. Wait until Roe found out! Kurt would make a terrific duke, and Marla an especially wicked stepmother—if she didn't continue the part offstage. Best of all, Kylie would be rehearsing with Brad practically everyday.

Evidently Imani had been deep in her own thoughts, for she chuckled. "Miss Armstrong didn't mention it, of course, but I think I know what she was thinking. I won't have any trouble getting into Crofts if that's what I decide to do. My parents work there, and my sister is one of their best dancers. Crofts is like that. A lot depends on family connections."

Kylie gasped. "That's awful."

"Maybe," Imani admitted, "but if you make it and your brother wants to go someday, he'll have an easier time getting in. And being a boy doesn't hurt."

Kylie grinned. "Danny at Crofts. Hard to imagine. But you said if you decide to go. If?"

Imani shrugged. "There are things about it I don't like. A lot of cliques—and total snobs. Aniya, my sister, says some students have been knocking Roe down, saying nasty things because she got Anne."

"Roe hasn't said anything." Not that they'd had time lately to talk much.

Imani noisily polished off her shake while surveying the crowd entering Smithy's. "Kylie, isn't that Brad?"

"He went to the castle after school." But she turned to look. No mistake. Coming from the counter, carrying two chocolate shakes and wearing a huge smile, was Brad. Mr. Markey must not have needed him, so he'd tracked her down. Oh, my, could she handle a shake on top of Coke and fries?

But instead of joining her, he sat at another table—next to a girl! Kylie had never seen her before but had to admit the only word for her was *Gorgeous!* She looked like someone Kylie had met before, but who? Long wavy chestnut hair and the creamiest complexion ever. Probably a great figure, too. The pleased expression on Brad's face said clearly he had also noticed and, worse, shared her opinion.

Dizzily, Kylie stood. "I've got to go. Mom will wonder where I am."

Imani protested, but Kylie cut her off. "I can't stay. Thanks for explaining. See you tomorrow."

Kylie pushed her way through the crowd to the exit. She could hear Brad's voice yelling behind her. "Kylie, stop! You don't understand!"

I understand perfectly, Kylie thought, rushing out into the cold December air.

Close to tears, Beth left the newspaper workroom. Normally, Mr. Carroll was nice, always making her feel good about herself when no one else thought she was special at anything. Today, all he did was scowl after she explained she had to go to the read-through at the Castle.

"But you didn't make the cast," he objected. "No, I shall expect you here promptly tomorrow after school."

"But I can't let my friends down, and Imani and I are props chairs," she said. "I promised her I'd come."

"Imani," he said. "That's the girl who won't join the newspaper staff. Just as well, perhaps."

That didn't make sense. Imani received good grades in his class. "I'll come next time," she said.

"Maybe," he said. "Maybe not. It could be I'll find someone else instead. And what's so wonderful about this Miss Armstrong? She didn't even cast you. How long has she been teaching here?"

"Uh, four years, I think."

Then he kept quizzing her, asking where Miss Armstrong had come from, what were her qualifications, things Beth couldn't possibly know. She was close to saying she'd stay when Kurt peeked into the room.

"Beth? Oh, sorry for interrupting. I thought if your meeting is over, I'd walk you home."

Mr. Carroll waved her out of the room, saying nothing.

"I don't like that guy," Kurt said, as they left the building.

"He's all right. I think he's annoyed because I can't attend a newspaper meeting tomorrow. He's planning on taking photos."

"Tomorrow? We have read-through," Kurt said.

"Yes, I'll be there."

"You okay not getting a part?"

"I am, Kurt. Really."

Beth had done what Mom always advised. She asked Miss Armstrong how she might improve, and the director had been kind but honest. "You did fine, Beth. This wasn't the right play for you. Sometimes it's like that." Exactly what Beth had figured. Sometimes it was like that.

After a quiet, tense supper, Roe retreated to her room. The whole family had been gloomy. Another *You're-Over-Qualified* day for Uncle Dan, and Aunt Jane seemed just plain weary. Danny was angry because his parents told him they couldn't afford to have him play hockey, and Kylie was bummed over something.

And once again, Roe was having no luck reaching her father. She'd left a message on his cell saying it was urgent. Could he be ignoring her? If so, why? Sighing, she turned to her algebra. A test tomorrow—to make her miserable life complete.

A knock on the door. "Come in," Roe barked.

Kylie entered uncertainly. "Sorry to bother you."

"No, that's okay. I'm sorry I'm grumpy. Got a wicked math test tomorrow. Congrats on the part."

"Thanks. Imani was better, but she's being awfully nice about it. We went to Smithy's after school. That's why I want to talk. She said something about you."

"Me? I haven't seen her in ages."

"No, but Imani's older sister goes to Crofts. Well, Aniya said she'd overheard some mean things about you."

Roe nodded. "They don't want me there." A long pause. She didn't want to talk about it, but Kylie was waiting. "Let's talk another time, Kylie. I've really got to study."

"Well, okay. But whenever you're ready, you know where I live."

Roe gave her a brief smile and watched Kylie leave the room. Then she put her head down on her desk and cried silently.

SCENE 4—WHERE IS MISS ARMSTRONG?

KYLIE RAPPED ON THE CASTLE door and waited for Leland to answer. Where was Miss Armstrong? Shivering, impatient, the entire cast of eight plus a small crew had waited outside the locked backdoor for at least twenty minutes before unanimously electing Kylie to seek help from Mr. Markey. Actually, Kylie didn't mind. She needed a break from pretending Brad was invisible.

She knocked again, just as Leland opened the door. "What might I do for you?" he asked coldly.

"Who is it?" asked a pleased voice. "Do we have company?"

Kylie remembered the first time she had met Mr. Markey. He'd said almost the same words then.

"It's only me, Mr. Markey. Kylie Kennedy. We're here for rehearsal, but Miss Armstrong hasn't shown up with the key. Could I go upstairs and let the cast in?"

"Of course. Do come in." Mr. Markey appeared, happy to see her. "Miss Armstrong must have been detained. Would you like a cup of tea?"

"I'd love one," Kylie assured him, "but could it be later? They're freezing waiting."

Mr. Markey chuckled. "Don't let me keep you. Leave a note for Miss Armstrong and invite everyone down. Leland and I will be delighted to have you join us."

Leland scowled. Did he ever look delighted? "Thanks, Mr. Markey." Kylie rushed up the wide staircase to the fourth floor ballroom.

No Miss Armstrong yet. After turning on the lights, Kylie went through the kitchen and down the steep back stairs.

The cast cheered when she opened the door. "Finally," Marla cried, pushing Kylie aside.

"Any sign of her?" Kurt asked, as the rest followed Marla up the dreary passage.

Kylie shook her head. "None. All the lights were off, and Mr. Markey doesn't know anything."

The cast explored the stage, noticing that Miss Armstrong had prepared for the rehearsal. All their scripts were numbered and stacked on a table. "She must be running late," Kylie said, echoing Mr. Markey. Then she remembered. "Mr. Markey invited us for tea while we wait. Do you want to go?"

"Do we ever." Kurt rubbed his stomach. "He's sure to have more than tea. Lead us to it!"

"I'll leave a note for Miss Armstrong," Brad said, the first words Kylie had heard from him since they'd arrived. She looked at him, but he turned away. Well, fine. Who cared anyway?

Reluctantly, Beth followed the group downstairs. She should have stayed for the newspaper meeting after all. Mr. Carroll had ignored her completely in class, even though she raised her hand to answer lots of times. And he made it a point to talk to another group of girls after class. She was being punished. Maybe she should resign as props co-chair, she thought, although she didn't want to let Imani and the cast down. *Or maybe you should quit the newspaper,* that annoying inner voice suggested. Oh, really? Then what kind of grades will I get? *Do you think Mr. Carroll would try to get even with you? A teacher?* Be quiet, she scolded the voice.

Usually, Beth and her conscience were in agreement. But she had never cared for a teacher like this before; actually, no teacher had ever paid much attention to her. She was cute little Beth, an adequate student, nothing special—until recently. She hoped Miss Armstrong would come soon or that Mr. Markey's treats would cheer her up.

"Welcome," Mr. Markey greeted them. "Welcome all." In anticipation of their visit, he had attempted to brush down his wispy white hair and had changed into a pale green sweater, rather than his old brown standby. His blue eyes twinkled and his face beamed in pleasure. "Sit down and make yourselves comfortable," he said. "Leland will be along soon with refreshments."

Representing the group, Brad thanked Mr. Markey and apologized for the inconvenience.

"No trouble at all. Just because you have your own entryway doesn't mean you're not free to come down and visit any time you like. Leland and I have missed you."

On cue, Leland entered, pushing a serving tray. He attempted to smile, but Beth thought he succeeded only in looking as if he had a toothache.

Mr. Markey invited the cast to sit on the fragile antique chairs in one of the castle's many parlors. Soon they were juggling cups of sweet tea and delicious, dainty cookies. The girls ate with small bites until they noticed the boys consuming far more than their share. Protesting, the girls ate faster.

"Let the cookie race begin!" Kurt declared. Beth frowned, afraid Mr. Markey would be offended. But he tittered with glee. Leland, however, left the room.

On her way to Crofts' vending machines, Roe stopped when she heard raucous laughter and words clearly not meant for her ears. "Laugh all you want, but I am not going to kiss a dirty Mexican." It was Devin, the boy who played Peter, Anne's boyfriend.

"You can't avoid it," said Laura Lee, who played Margot, Anne's sister. "Now if I were playing Anne as I should be—"

"This whole contest idea is ridiculous," a girl interrupted, but Roe hurried back to the rehearsal room, the longed-for soda forgotten.

Robotically, she wrote her blocking into the script, just going through the motions until rehearsal was over and she could dash outside to where Aunt Jane would be waiting. Tonight she would call Dad again and insist he come down to see her, or better still, let her go there, maybe this weekend— if she reached him. And she would talk with Kylie, who already knew something was wrong. I should be with the others at the castle. I don't fit in here, and I never will. Sometimes she thought she didn't belong anywhere.

"Let's go home," Jen Yu said, looking at her watch. A full hour had passed since their arrival at the castle. "I don't think Miss Armstrong is coming."

Gabrielle Soleigh objected. "We've got over an hour of rehearsal left. My mom is coming for me, and there's no one home I can call." Most members of the cast and crew were in the same boat.

Kylie had a suggestion. "Miss Armstrong left our scripts. Why don't we go back up and have our own read-through?"

Eric agreed. "It's something to do. Miss Armstrong can start blocking tomorrow."

All heads nodded slowly. It wouldn't be as much fun without their director, but it beat hanging around waiting for their rides.

Mr. Markey had an idea, too. "Leland will contact Mrs. Grainger to come and be with you. I'm sure you don't think you need a chaperone, but it would make me feel better." Actually, everyone looked relieved at the thought of Gee, Kurt's grandmother, joining them.

To their amazement, Leland pulled a cell phone from his pocket. "I think they should have a phone upstairs. Do you want me to arrange it?"

Mr. Markey agreed immediately. Although several of the students had cell phones, a landline made sense.

On their way out of the parlor, Kylie overheard Brad talking to Leland. "Do you need me again today?"

"No, thank you," Leland said, "but would you come tomorrow?"

"Sure thing."

"She had a wonderful time. Thank you, Brad."

Who had a wonderful time? For the first time since leaving Smithy's, Kylie had doubts.

Back in the ballroom, Kylie asked the cast to sit in a circle of chairs, and then began to pass out scripts. "Well, look who made herself director," said Marla.

"Fine," Kylie said, handing the scripts to her.

Wordlessly, Marla handed them back and sat down.

At first, the readings were lackluster, bad even for a read-through. They missed the director.

"Come on," Kylie pleaded. "What would Miss Armstrong say? She'd be disappointed in us."

Surprisingly, Brad backed her. "Kylie's right. Put some energy into this. Some of us can't afford to waste an entire afternoon."

After that, read-through went amazingly well, especially as soon as the cast realized how terrific the script and all the parts were.

Kylie loved the fairy godmother but kept remembering Imani's interpretation. Imani should have this part, she thought again, before tackling a long monologue.

"Greetings!" Gee had arrived. "Still no director?" She frowned, looking around. "Well, carry on."

The cast finished reading just as cars were heard at the back of the castle.

"Mr. Markey gave me an extra key," Gee told them. "I'll come early tomorrow, just in case." Then she cautioned. "If I were you, I wouldn't mention to anyone that Miss Armstrong wasn't here. First, let's find out what happened. We don't want to cause Miss Armstrong any embarrassment."

Kylie noticed Marla brightening at this. Gee noticed, too. "That could mean no Cinderella in the castle and no stepmother part, Marla," Gee whispered. Marla finally nodded.

It wasn't like Gee to over-react, Kylie thought, as she put on her winter coat. Where was Miss Armstrong?

" **A** ND THAT'S WHAT'S GOING ON," Roe said.

Kylie gasped. "He called you a—"

"Dirty Mexican. Yeah, the guy who is playing a Jew during the Holocaust is a bigot. Nice, huh? Any ideas besides quitting the play? A definite possibility."

"Could you talk to the director?"

"Maybe, but it might make things worse. If Mr. Warner scolded the whole cast, they'd blame me."

Kylie nodded. Yes, that probably would happen. "You've got to talk to Mom and Dad."

She was right, of course, and Roe knew it. But Aunt Jane and Uncle Dan had their own problems. "I'll wait a few more days," she said. "I'd tell my dad what's going on, if he'd only answer or return my calls. Well, enough about me. How did read-through go?"

Quickly, Kylie brought her up to date. "So we have no idea why Miss Armstrong didn't show. I sure hope she's back in school tomorrow."

Then they both confessed to having a ton of homework, so Kylie returned to her room.

The phone rang as Kylie completed French. Could be Brad—to apologize maybe? She waited for someone downstairs to answer and then strained to hear the sound of her name. She shrugged. Must be for someone else. Brad would have called her cell, anyway. She double-checked her homework to make sure the French accent marks were going in the right directions. Her grades were much better now. She finished loading her backpack for the next day when her mother entered.

"That was Mrs. Grainger on the phone, Kylie." Mom sounded puzzled. "She seemed excited about some costumes she found in the attic and wants you and the rest of the cast to go to her house to look at them and to join her for dessert. Roe is invited, too. You'd think the costumes could wait. Perhaps she's lonely."

Kylie suppressed a grin. The word, "lonely," hardly fit Gee. Besides, Gee didn't keep costumes in her attic. She did have a small sewing room, but all of her collections, which didn't include costumes, were stored in the basement, boxed and labeled carefully. Obviously, Gee was up to something.

"I don't want Gee to be lonely, and I'm all done with my homework. May I go? I won't unless Roe can come, too."

Roe's reaction to the invitation was to stuff her books into her bag. "I may regret this tomorrow, but I'm definitely going. I haven't seen Gee since the cast party, and I could use some fun for a change."

As Mrs. Kennedy parked in front of Gee's neat bungalow, Kylie and Roe saw Beth, Kurt, and Eric heading up the walk. Kylie's mother laughed. "Looks like a cast reunion. Text me when you're ready to come home. Not too late," she warned, as Roe left the car first to join Eric.

Mom held out her hand to stop her daughter. "Kylie—" she hesitated, seemingly searching for the right words—"Kylie, Mrs. Grainger is a dear old lady, but she does tend to make up life as she goes along. She follows her own set of rules. I want you to remember that. Do you understand?"

Kylie nodded yes, so Mom would leave. Actually, she didn't have a clue what her mother meant. She caught up with Roe, happily talking with Eric on the front steps. Roe didn't seem bothered by her boyfriend playing opposite Jaimie. She's not the jealous goof I am, Kylie thought miserably.

Soon Gee's tiny kitchen was full. The boys and girls exchanged puzzled glances as they watched Gee pouring Cokes and emptying bags of chips into bowls. Dessert?

Gee laughed at their bewildered faces, then confessed. "You're here under false pretenses," she admitted. "No dessert and no costumes, either."

Gee had invited the whole cast of eight, but Kurt, Eric, and Kylie were the only ones able to come. "I asked Roe because I've missed her."

Roe nodded. "Me, too."

"And me?" Beth asked. "I'm not in the cast."

"Well, Kurt insisted."

"Okay, Grandmother," Kurt ordered, trying to ignore the laughter. "Why have we been summoned here in this sneaky fashion?"

"It's about Miss Armstrong, isn't it?" Roe guessed.

Gee nodded. "Leland called to tell me they received a special delivery package from her early this evening. I drove over to the castle to get it before contacting you."

Kylie gasped. "Is she all right?"

Gee frowned. "That's a hard question to answer. Frankly, I'm worried. Here, read for yourself."

Gee handed her a letter and a binder, which turned out to be Miss Armstrong's promptbook for *Cinderella, Cinderella,* complete with all the blocking and notes for the production. Had Miss Armstrong quit?

Fearfully, Kylie read Miss Armstrong's message aloud.

> *Dear Cast,*
>
> *I'm sure you remember that in theater Break a Leg means good luck. Well, this time, it's not good luck for us. After I left school today, I tripped and broke mine. It's somewhat severe, and I must rest. Also, my aunt has not been well and needs my company. While recovering, I will stay with her. I have contacted the school, and a substitute will be assigned to my English classes. I didn't mention the play. Perhaps a new director can be found. You'll find all my notes in this script. I'll try to return soon.*
>
> *Love and Best Wishes,*
> *Anna Armstrong*

The group was silent for a full minute. Then Eric spoke quietly. "This is terrible."

"What are we going to do?" Kylie cried. "We can't put on a play without a director!"

"And the vice principal is brand new. She won't be able to find someone else," Beth added.

Roe nodded. "I doubt if she'd even try, and the principal is always at meetings and doesn't care about theater, anyway."

"Especially with most of the rehearsals taking place over vacation and not at school," Kurt agreed. "They'll cancel the show. It's over, folks."

Roe shook her head. "Something's wrong. This doesn't sound like Miss Armstrong at all."

"The last time I saw her," Kylie recalled, "she was rushing out of school and in such a hurry she bumped into me. She must have broken her leg right afterward."

"But where is this mysterious aunt?" Beth wondered. "And why should a broken leg stop everything? A broken leg isn't that serious."

"Sure it is, especially if you have to climb lots of steep stairs." Kylie opened the script and examined Miss Armstrong's notes. The director was almost daring them to continue without her. The blocking diagrams were clear, and she followed Miss Armstrong's ideas easily.

"We'll have to go to the office tomorrow," Eric said. "The play will be canceled, but we'd better make it official."

"Unless . . ." Kylie continued studying the script. Kurt and Eric peeked over her shoulders.

"Looks like Greek to me," Kurt said.

"I don't see how you can tell anything," Eric agreed.

"Well I can," Kylie said. "It's like Miss Armstrong taught us to mark our own scripts, not that most people paid attention. I've prompted lots of times when I wasn't in a scene being rehearsed. I know how Miss Armstrong does things. At least I used to," she finished ruefully.

Roe looked thoughtful. "You could direct this play, Kylie."

"That's what I've been thinking," Gee said.

The rest of the group nodded. "We can't cancel," Kurt said. "It's not just about us. Think how disappointed Mr. Markey will be."

"And Leland." Eric grinned.

"I'll help, Kylie," Beth offered.

The rest of them nodded. They would all help.

Kylie felt flattered but also scared. "I . . . I guess I could. I'd really need the cast's cooperation, though. Everyone's help—not only yours. They'd have to agree to follow my directions."

"I'll knock their heads together if they don't," Kurt said.

Eric flattened their enthusiasm. 'It won't work. Not that I don't think Kylie is capable. She'd be great. But we can't keep what we're doing a secret from the school, and none of our parents would be willing to have us rehearse at the castle without adult supervision. Think it through. Would you want to keep this from your parents?"

They all retreated into silence and gloom. "The play will be canceled," Kylie stated flatly.

"Unless—" Gee piped up.

"Unless?" they prompted.

"Unless I go to school tomorrow and offer myself as a director. I used to teach. It won't matter that the subject was home economics. My teaching certificate is up to date—that's all Mrs. Warde will care about. And who knows? Miss Armstrong might return soon."

"You direct, Grandma dear?"

"Of course not. I'll be the designated adult. Kylie will be the director, but only the cast will know. What do you think?"

They nodded slowly. Gee had a way with her, and the vice-principal would agree. Mrs. Warde would not want phone calls from unhappy parents, upset that the play had been canceled.

"Kylie?" Eric asked.

"All right," she said. "Let's not tell the rest of the cast until tomorrow's rehearsal. Then we'll know for sure if Mrs. Warde will accept Gee as our leader. If she says yes, we'll have a serious talk about cooperation."

"It's late," Roe said. "We'd better call for our rides."

Back home, Uncle Dan handed Roe an envelope. "You missed your father's call, Roe. You'll be pleased, though. He Fedexed your plane tickets. You'll see your parents again this weekend." Roe didn't burst out crying exactly, but she looked weepy enough for Uncle Dan to take her into his arms.

Before falling asleep, she could hear Kylie in the next room making a phone call. "Imani? This is Kylie. How would you like a part in a play?"

Roe smiled. She thought that might happen.

SCENE 6—KYLIE TAKES CHARGE

"AND THAT'S IT," GEE SUMMED up for the solemn faces staring at her. "Officially, I will be the director; unofficially, Kylie—until Miss Armstrong returns. Isn't that right, Kylie?"

Kylie flushed. This was so embarrassing. "Well, I guess I could, if that's okay with all of you, and if Imani is willing to take over my part."

"Maybe." Imani had joined the cast members at the castle. "But when Miss Armstrong comes back—"

"If she comes back," Gabrielle inserted.

Kylie handed Imani the fairy godmother's script. "The part is yours," she said firmly. "I won't take it back, no matter what happens."

"And I'll be here to make sure y'all mind Kylie and behave yourselves." Gee grinned with anticipation.

Those who didn't know Gee looked doubtful. How much fun would they have with someone's grandmother in charge? They talked among themselves.

"What about your scholarship?" Brad asked softly.

For an instant, Kylie's blue eyes met his concerned gray ones. Maybe he still likes me, she thought. "Not important," she whispered back. "Neither of us will go to camp unless we do this play."

With great enthusiasm, Gee addressed the group. "So, cast? What do you think? About Kylie and me?"

Slowly, they nodded. What choice did they have?

"Remember," Gee cautioned. "Keep this quiet. Not your parents, teachers, or even your friends can know that Kylie is the actual director. We'll keep it from the crew as long as possible."

The cast looked startled. They were not used to having an adult tell them to keep a secret from their parents.

Gee tried to reassure them. "Mr. Markey and Leland approve, and if Miss Armstrong comes back soon, all this fuss will be for nothing. Okay, Kylie, you're in charge, starting now."

How to begin? Kylie examined the uncertain faces of people she considered her friends. What would their relationship be like now? "Let's take a ten-minute break before blocking scene one," she said, trying to imitate Miss Armstrong. "Those of you not in the scene can leave if you want, but be sure to check over the schedule Miss Armstrong gave you."

Most of the cast headed for the fridge in the kitchen. Kylie noticed Gee beckoning to Marla. She could count on Gee to make Marla understand that if she sabotaged the play, she would be harming herself as much as anyone. Marla still had a chance to go to Crofts next year, if she could impress the right people with her acting ability.

Kylie decided to get a glass of water but stopped when she heard her name. "I like Kylie," Jen Yu said, "but we need a real director."

"I agree," Gabrielle said. "This is my first play, and I don't want anyone to screw it up."

"You two are the ones who are going to screw it up," Brad said. "Miss Armstrong taught Kylie practically everything she knows. She understands the prompt book, do you?" He paused, waiting. "Besides, Kylie might be giving up her camp scholarship to do this for us."

"I don't understand," Jen said.

"Don't you remember? Like me, she received a partial with conditions. And she is supposed to act, not direct. Kylie gave Imani her part because she knew it would be too hard to act and direct at the same time. Crofts won't even know Kylie directed. It's a big secret. Her name won't even be in the program. Everyone will think she quit."

"Gosh, I'm sorry," breathed Gabrielle.

"Me, too," Jen echoed.

Brad defending her? As soon as rehearsal is over, I'll talk to him, Kylie decided.

She poked her head into the kitchen, but Brad turned his away. "Places on stage," she announced.

"Quite an adventure for you, flying alone," Uncle Dan observed as he drove Roe to her Crofts rehearsal.

"Yes, although I'm a little nervous. I'm glad you'll be able to take me to the airport."

"Wish I could go inside and wait with you there, but I've got another pesky interview."

"I'll ask people if I get confused," Roe said. "Your interview is more important."

Uncle Dan sighed before retreating into silence. A friendly silence, though, and Roe rather welcomed it. Something was going to happen soon, she thought. Perhaps to her or the Kennedys or maybe even her father and mother. She couldn't tell yet from which direction change was coming, but it was overdue.

The car pulled up in front of the school. "Well, here we are. You have a way to get home?"

"Aunt Jane said I should text." Roe waved as she left the car.

She'd much rather be at the castle helping Kylie than here. Anne rehearsals had become almost a torture. It was like the cast couldn't stand her. Deep in thought, she bumped into Devin, the boy who played Peter.

"Yuck! Watch where you're going, you— "

"Come on, Devin, let's get to rehearsal." Norma Kaplan, who played Miep, stopped him.

Mr. Warner gathered his cast around a long table. Instead of a regular rehearsal, they would do table work. "I'd like to hear how you're relating to your character. What you have learned from your part—through your research as well as rehearsing."

Three of the actors discussed their characters, although Roe didn't think they shared anything insightful. Then the director called on her. She liked Mr. Warner and smiled. But then she saw Devin making a face and nudging the boy who played Anne's father. No more! She'd had enough! Roe didn't care what happened next.

"Sometimes I feel like Anne is me," she began, "or that I'm Anne." A few of the cast members snickered.

Mr. Warner frowned at them. "Interesting," he said. "Go on, please."

"Anne was the victim of prejudice. She even died because of it. Here at Crofts, I think I know how she felt." The cast squirmed.

"Are you comparing Anne's Judaism with—"

"With being half Mexican? With being Latina? Yes, Mr. Warner, I am."

No one in the cast looked at her. They examined their shoes or thumbed through their scripts. But Roe could tell they were listening. She had to continue.

"A few of you are trying to make me feel like I'm not okay—like I should be ashamed my father was born in Mexico. At first, I thought you didn't want me here because I'm still in middle school. That's part of it, I guess, but not all. Maybe Miss Armstrong choosing me wasn't such a good idea, Mr. Warner." She paused, but no one else spoke.

"I'm going away tomorrow and won't be at rehearsal Monday or Tuesday. I'm not scheduled anyway. That should give you time to decide if you want me to be your Anne. I can't stay where I'm ignored or nasty things are said about me. And I can't be in a play where the boy who is supposed to kiss me won't because he says I'm a dirty Mexican." Finished, she rose from the table and left the room.

"I never said—" she heard.

"Oh, yes you did, Devin," Norma said. "I heard you."

Roe didn't turn back. Grabbing her coat, not even putting in on until she left the building, she tapped out a message. "Aunt Jane, please come get me." She hoped the wait wouldn't be too long and that she wouldn't start crying in this icy cold weather.

Beth's afternoon hadn't been much better. After receiving a C- on a social studies assignment, a grade she didn't deserve, she gathered her courage and went to see Mr. Carroll after school. "Sloppy work," he said, dismissing her. "You need to do better."

"Shall I stay and work on the paper?" she asked.

He shook his head. "No, we've got it covered."

Then Beth noticed the four other girls in the room. They had never worked on the newspaper before. Three were seventh graders, one in eighth. She knew them only by reputation—losers, misfits, girls without friends. But Mr. Carroll was beaming at them as if they were the newest stars in his galaxy, looking at them the way he used to look at her.

"I'll go then," she said quietly. Something was wrong. Something she didn't like or understand. I need to talk to someone, she thought. But who?

"This will be a rocking chair." Kylie gestured to a chair Down Right. "There will be a fireplace Up Center. This table and chairs Center Left will do for now, but we'll need a round table for the performance." She noticed Jaimie and Marla exchanging glances and stared at them pointedly. "A round table is in Miss Armstrong's prompt book. I'm just following what I'm reading. Now, Jaimie, please sit in the rocking chair. As the lights begin to come up, Cinderella is rocking. Wait for them to come up all the way, pause, and then look out at the audience. Cross downstage and talk to them."

Jaimie sat in the chair, and Kylie turned to those in the audience who had remained behind to watch. Brad was not among them.

"You can be the children in the audience, okay?"

"Yes, Kylie," the cast chanted back as if they were in first grade.

"Fine. Just do as Jaimie asks. I can't block you because I won't be able to block the real audience. But please try not to be too goofy."

"Who, us?" Kurt grinned.

Kylie grinned back. Kurt had become a good friend and would help keep things fun. "Oh, almost forgot," she said. "Jen and Gabrielle, please wait for your cue Off Right."

"Where's that?" Gabrielle whispered.

"Backstage on the actor's right," Jen said. "Come on, I'll explain everything."

Oh, dear, maybe I should have reviewed stage terms, Kylie thought. Gabrielle probably doesn't even know what blocking means. But the rest do and might think I'm showing off if I explain. Jen can take care of Gabrielle.

"Curtain," Kylie called out, although there was none. "Lights."

Jaimie looked up as if she had been napping and suddenly noticed the audience. She smiled shyly before cautiously crossing downstage and speaking. *Hello. Who are you? You remind me of the friends I used to have before my stepmother drove them all away.*

Kylie smiled. Jaimie was a perfect Cinderella. Too bad she was such a pill in real life.

Soon, Cinderella had the pretend children scrubbing the floor, sweeping out the fireplace, and dusting the furniture.

"Is this clean enough, Cinderella?" Kurt asked.

"You're doing fine, children," Cinderella adlibbed before returning to the script. *But be sure to go back to your seats if you hear my stepsisters coming.*

"That's your cue, Jen," Kylie shouted. Jen raised her voice backstage, and the *children* scurried back to their seats.

Jen and Gabrielle were nasty enough, bossing Cinderella, finding fault with her work. However, they didn't move well on stage. I'll have to give them a private rehearsal sometime soon, Kylie decided. It would be better not to embarrass them in front of everyone, especially since they didn't think she should be directing.

Marla, the wicked Stepmother, swept on stage and took control. Those playing the audience gasped. Marla was easily the most talented person in the cast. Without Cinderella noticing, she threw cherry pits into the fireplace. *You forgot to clean the fireplace, Cinderella. What a shame! Now you won't be able to go to the ball!* Marla rushed the stepsisters Off Left, scolding them as they exited.

Grudgingly, Kylie admitted that she could see why Marla had been so upset not making the last play. She was terrific, even though that didn't excuse what she'd done to Roe. Then Kylie had an idea. "That was great, Marla," she called. "While I'm working with Imani, would you help Jen and Gabrielle with stage movement?"

Marla's normally sour expression was replaced with a pleased smile. She nodded. Three birds with one cherry pit, Kylie thought.

Cinderella returned sadly to her rocking chair. The next person on stage would be the Fairy Godmother. Kylie asked Imani to take her place upstage center. The Fairy Godmother would enter and exit through the fireplace, once it was built. Kylie sighed. It wasn't going to be easy watching someone do her part.

Directing was far more difficult than she had expected. She wasn't used to concentrating so hard. Suppressing a yawn, settling for a stretch, Kylie took a deep breath and walked over to the window while Imani made her way to the stage. Rehearsal would end soon. It was getting dark outside—but not too dark to see two figures walking away from the castle. Brad with the girl from Smithy's—the gorgeous one with the long reddish-brown hair, who reminded Kylie of someone. Brad had even taken her arm. Kylie swallowed hard to hold back tears before returning to the Fairy Godmother.

RARELY HAD FRIDAY AFTERNOON BEEN as welcome. Kylie wanted to go straight home and collapse. Or eat chocolate and watch YouTube. Or do anything but think about plays. But no! Stupidly, she'd left the promptbook at the castle. Now she had to go back and get it. For some reason, Miss Armstrong hadn't blocked the scene scheduled for Monday's rehearsal—the one at the ball, the hardest scene of all. It would take hours to figure it out.

At lunchtime, Kylie called Gee to explain the dilemma. "Mom's working late, and Dad has a job interview. It's too cold out to walk." Not telling her parents what was going on was proving difficult.

Gee promised to meet her at 4:30. "I have an errand to run first, so why don't you gather a crew together and pick out costumes? We can drop them off at the castle when you get your script. Then I'll drive all of you home."

It was a great idea. Kylie was getting used to Gee's rescues. Since no one was at home, no one would expect her. Even Danny was staying with a friend all weekend. She thrust her homework into her backpack and looked for helpers. "Hey, Eric," she called out, and explained her mission.

"I'm sorry, Kylie, but I'm meeting Jamie at Smithy's."

"Jaimie? You're meeting Jaimie? What's going on, Eric?"

Friendly Eric turned cold. "You'll have to ask Roe." He started to walk away, but then turned back. "Not your fault. See you later, Kylie. I'll help next time."

More trouble, Kylie predicted, wondering if Roe knew. She had thought those two were solid. Breaking up with Eric was all Roe needed, but it was up to them to figure it out—if they wanted to. Everything keeps on changing, she thought again. Well, maybe Beth is still in school.

Yes, she was gathering papers at her locker. "Beth, could you stay awhile and help with costumes?"

Beth seemed distracted. "Not today, Kylie. I need to ask for help with one of my essays."

"But it's Friday," Kylie objected. Normally, the teachers practically raced the students out of the building on Friday afternoons. "Can't it wait until Monday?"

"The assignment is important, Kylie, and some of the teachers stay late to help . . ." Beth's voice faltered.

Beth's crush on Mr. Carroll was a darned nuisance. "Beth, you promised to help!"

"And I will, Kylie, really. As soon as vacation starts, I'll help every day." Beth gave a half smile and dashed off.

Odd, Kylie thought. The social studies teacher's classroom was in the opposite direction. The hall was deserted now, except for Marla Gray, who was closing her locker. "Going home?" Marla called out, seeming friendly for a change.

Kylie approached slowly. "I'm going to the costume room if I can get anyone to go with me. Everyone seems to think tech will take care of itself. We've got to get the costumes and props over to the castle before school lets out for vacation."

"I'll help," Marla offered, and then added, "I don't have anything better to do."

"You?"

"Home isn't exactly the most joyous place to be these days."

"Oh?"

"My mother has filed for divorce, and all she and my sister do is cry—when they're not yelling at me."

Kylie wasn't sure what to say. "Sounds awful."

Marla grimaced. "I'll survive. So what do you say? Want some help from your favorite enemy?"

Help from Marla? "Uh, sure, thanks. Let's check out the costume cages. Eight costumes shouldn't be too bad."

"Nine," Marla corrected. "You forgot Cinderella's ball gown."

"And the wedding dress, and bathrobes for you and the stepsisters to wear over your gowns." Kylie groaned. Costumes no longer seemed simple.

"You should have asked for help earlier, Kylie. Announced a Friday crew meeting over the intercom, the way Miss Armstrong always does."

"You're right, of course," Kylie admitted. "But we don't have a tech crew. Miss Armstrong left before she assigned one. Beth said she'd help, and Imani was going to before she joined the cast. I'm not sure what to do. Should we let more people in on the secret?"

Marla whistled. "It's a mess, all right. Looks like the cast will have to double as the crew. Better tell them on Monday, Kylie, and work out a schedule."

"Good idea. Thanks."

They walked companionably to CBT's costume cages. More than once Kylie glanced at Marla. This was the first normal conversation they'd ever had. Could Marla be changing because of her family's troubles? At that moment, Kylie felt almost ready to forgive.

Before encountering Kylie, Beth had already seen Mr. Carroll. She had been polite, asking how she might improve her grade. Again, he waved her away. "Learn to write better, but don't expect me to be your English teacher." This from the man who had said she was so talented she should major in journalism someday. On the basis of what? A couple of measly articles covering sports events and one play review? It didn't make sense.

Beth carried a folder of essays she'd written for his class, as well as the current effort. Mr. Carroll had given her high grades and glowing praise on all the others. There were no comments on the C- paper, and she couldn't see any difference in quality between it and the ones marked A. Would all her papers have low grades now that he'd decided he didn't like her? Mrs. Hunt, her English teacher, was impersonal but always kind and thorough. This wouldn't be easy, but she would ask her for advice—if she, too, hadn't left for the weekend.

Mrs. Hunt was at her desk, looking through the end of a stack of papers. "Beth, how may I help you?" She must have noticed Beth's uncertainty, for she gestured to a chair next to the desk. "Sit down, dear."

"I was wondering if you would look at something," Beth began. "It's an essay I wrote for social studies. Usually, I get good grades, but this one got a C-, and I don't understand why."

"Did you talk with your teacher? That would be the appropriate first step."

"Yes, I asked him how I might improve, but he said he wasn't an English teacher, so I thought I'd come to you."

Mrs. Hunt nodded. "And he is . . ."

"Mr. Carroll."

"Ah, yes, the new teacher." Beth thought she sounded wary. "Very well, I'll look it over. May I take it home with me? I must leave soon."

"Thank you." Beth handed her the folder. "I included other things I'd done well on. I can't see much difference."

Mrs. Hunt smiled. "Well, you have a good weekend, Beth, and try not to worry. I'm pleased you care enough to want to improve."

And that was that, Beth thought. She would try to follow Mrs. Hunt's advice. She considered seeing if Kylie was still there, but she needed to go home and forget about school. At least, try to forget.

Costume cages were located along the hallway behind the stage. They actually were cages—a series of locked wire ones reaching from floor to ceiling. All of CBT's costumes and some small props either hung on hangers in garment bags or were in labeled trunks and boxes. Many of the items had been donated through the years—some purchased, others handmade. Miss Armstrong prided herself on neat, clean costumes and props, and heaven help anyone who messed them up. Kylie took the key from her backpack and opened one of the cages.

"I appreciate the help, Marla," she repeated.

"No problem," Marla said, still gracious. "I'll bet Jen and Gabrielle would have helped, too."

"Their stage movement has improved already, thanks to you," Kylie said.

Marla shrugged. "Let's get to work, Kylie."

The two girls unzipped bags and searched through boxes, stacking possibilities onto a hall table. A purple velvet robe and jeweled gold crown for Brad looked fine. Pants and shoes were a problem. She'd have to talk to him. Dreaming up things to discuss with Brad had become her newest pastime.

"This is for me!" Triumphantly, Marla held up a flowing black-sequined gown with a bodice covered with black feathers. A feather headpiece completed the outfit.

"Looks big, though." Marla was as slim as Roe.

"Gee might alter it. It's perfect!" Marla added the black gown to the stack of costumes.

Kylie found an ivory satin and lace formal for Cinderella. The dress could also serve as a wedding gown. "Someone can make a veil." Costume changes for Jaimie were almost impossible, but the gown was large enough to fit a ragged dress underneath.

"Glass slippers?"

Kylie's happy smile vanished. "I have no idea." Suddenly it was too much. She was expected to direct and to provide costumes, props, and scenery. And lights and sound and tickets and chairs for the audience and all the stuff she hadn't considered yet. "We'll definitely have a tech meeting Monday. I can't do this alone. Beth promised to help, but she hasn't done a thing."

Marla searched frantically through her bag. "Don't tell me I'm out. No, here they are!" She seemed to be talking to herself, but then she looked at Kylie. "I wouldn't count on Beth, if I were you. She's one of Carroll's disciples, if you know what I mean. Man, I could tell you things!"

"What do you mean—" Then, to Kylie's horror, Marla took a cigarette from her bag, lit it, and took a deep drag—in the costume cage—in school!

"What are you doing?" Kylie stage-whispered, glancing both ways down the hall to make sure no one was in sight. "Marla, are you crazy? Put that out!"

Marla laughed. "What's your problem? No one can see me."

"Put it out, Marla, or I'll tell. Even if you don't start a fire, you'll get the costumes smelly. Besides, it's against school rules."

A sneer Kylie hadn't seen for a while reappeared. "You'd never tell. You have too much to lose." Marla blew smoke right into Kylie's face.

"Just try me. Haven't you been in enough trouble for one year? Put it out, Marla."

"Oh, all right." She dropped the cigarette to the floor and snubbed it out with her heel. "I thought you'd changed."

"I thought *you'd* changed, but I see I was wrong."

Without another word, Marla picked up the black sequined outfit and marched down the hall, leaving Kylie alone with a stack of costumes, a messed-up costume cage, and a cigarette butt.

Kylie was close to tears as she wrapped the smelly thing in paper and thrust the wad into her school bag, vowing to find a safe place to dispose of it. Not home or school. Oh, Marla, you are so messed up, she thought. You'd better not smoke in the castle. Something else to worry about!

Now what? Kylie checked her watch. She'd better hustle if she was going to have the costume cage put to rights before Gee came. Darned old Marla, she thought, rehanging a red dress they'd decided was wrong for Imani. If she was going to pull a stunt like that, couldn't she have waited until the work here was finished?

Gee arrived just as Kylie locked the cage. After admiring the costume selections, she changed plans. "Let's take the costumes to my house. That's where I'll make alterations anyway."

"Good idea." Kylie climbed wearily into Gee's car. "Now I have to think about props and lights and sound and—"

Gee's chuckle interrupted the list. 'Hold on," she said. "It's Friday. You've done enough thinking for one week. You're the director, not the producer. We'll sit everyone down on Monday and make some sense of this."

All the lights were on at home. Strange, Kylie thought, waving to Gee. She opened the door to the happiest smiles she'd seen in months.

"Dad? Mom?"

They turned to her. "Your father was offered a job, Kylie!"

"Dad, that's wonderful!" She gave him an enormous hug.

That night in bed, she reviewed her day. Gee was right. I need a break, and this family needs to celebrate. I won't think about the play until Sunday. I'll work on the blocking, and—Oh, no! The prompt book! Mom and Dad were going to Grandma's during the day, and then they'd made plans for Sunday, including reservations for a celebration dinner. I can't ask Gee for another favor, and it's too cold to walk so far. She'd have to face the cast on Monday, unprepared to block the most difficult scene in the play.

"Help!" she cried before turning out the lights.

On the plane, thankfully away from it all, Roe reflected on what had happened at rehearsal and her conversation with Aunt Jane. Kylie's mother was, of course, horrified. "I had no idea this was going on! I knew you were troubled, but this is unbelievable. Why didn't you tell me?"

"It's hard to explain. I kept hoping it would get better." And I knew you were going through your own stuff, Roe added silently. "But today, I just couldn't take it anymore."

"I guess you couldn't. I'll call Crofts first thing on Monday. I wish we could contact Miss Armstrong. Perhaps I should call your vice principal."

"No, she's too new. Please don't do anything yet. Let's see what Mr. Warner does. I sort of left it up to him."

Aunt Jane agreed—for the present. "You certainly gave them an ultimatum. But Roe, no more secrets. This is too serious for you to handle alone. And you must know your Uncle Dan and I think of you as another daughter. We've come to love you."

At that, Roe teared up. "I love you, too, Aunt Jane," she murmured.

Uncle Dan, too, had been supportive on their ride to the airport. "Your father has filled me in on what's going on with your family. You have a home with us for as long as you need one."

Tears again. She and her father must have a long talk. As wonderful as Uncle Dan and Aunt Jane had been, they couldn't afford to keep her. The Kennedys needed help, and so did she.

BETH STARED AT HER CELL phone. I should call Kylie, she thought. She wished she could go over there, but she had to watch her younger brother and baby sister while her parents and sister were out visiting. Yesterday, it had dawned on her how cut off she had become from her friends—thanks to Mr. Carroll. And my stupidity, she added, to be fair.

Finally, she turned to her contacts and punched Kylie's number.

"Hi, Beth." Kylie didn't sound especially friendly.

"Hi. Just wanted to apologize for not helping yesterday."

"Oh, that's okay. Marla helped some, and then Gee and I took a bunch of stuff over to her house. We need lots of help with props, though. You want to come over? But I guess you're too busy with your writing." Yes, Kylie was being sarcastic.

Beth explained why she couldn't, but that wasn't enough. "Kylie, I was so stupid," she confessed. Sparing no details, she told Kylie what had occurred with Mr. Carroll. "I am such a jerk!"

"Oh, wow! Beth, that's awful! But I guess you haven't been the only one taken in by him. Personally, I think he's a creep."

Beth nodded, even though she couldn't be seen. "I'm beginning to also. I don't know why he turned against me."

Baby Zoe cried in the next room. "I've got to go, Kylie."

"I can hear. I'm glad you told me, Beth. Maybe you can come over tomorrow afternoon?"

"I'd like that. Thanks, Kylie."

It was too bad Mom wasn't home. She needed advice. This thing with Mr. Carroll—well, it could be serious. It was good Beth had reached out to her English teacher, but she needed to confide in her parents, too. Suddenly, Kylie remembered two things: Miss Armstrong dashing out of the building, and Mr. Carroll demanding to be told her identity. And Mr. Carroll called Kylie "Beth's so-called friend." That was so weird!

There was nothing more Kylie could do. Turning on the computer, she stared at the cast list. At least she had that at home. Who else might help with the play? No one had done anything so far except—Marla. Then Kylie remembered something else. Before Marla lit the cigarette, she mentioned Mr. Carroll—how she could tell things about him. "I need to know," she whispered, scrolling to where she'd typed the cast's phone numbers.

"Marla! Phone!" a young voice screeched. Right. Marla didn't have a cell. Or if she once had, she no longer did.

"Hello?" asked a bored voice.

"Marla? It's Kylie. Look, I'm sorry I over-reacted yesterday. You know—"

Marla laughed. "You sure got upset. Well, I'm sorry, too. I guess I was trying to push your buttons. Actually, I don't smoke much anymore. And I'm sorry I didn't stick around and help you clean up."

"That's okay. I was wondering if you could come over. We could work on props, and, well, I wanted to ask you about something you started to say yesterday."

"About Beth?"

"Yes."

"I'll be right there."

Don't bring cigarettes, Kylie almost said. What was she thinking—having someone like Marla over when Mom and Dad weren't home? But if she wanted answers . . .

After the joyous announcement, Dad had made the new situation clear. "It's historical research at the University of Wisconsin in Milwaukee," Dad explained. "A heck of a commute but a job I'll enjoy doing. But you need to realize that I won't be making the salary I had before. Also, there's not much room for advancement, so I'll keep my eye out for another position. But—"

"At least more money will be coming in," Mom said, "and we'll be able to pay off our debts and Danny's tuition. We'll still need to be cautious, but we're going to be okay."

"Maybe playing hockey can be Danny's birthday present," Dad had said hopefully, but Mom shook her head in warning.

Kylie understood. Her parents didn't want to show favoritism. "My allowance is fine," she said, "and don't worry about Crofts. CBHS is a good school, too."

Kylie was certain to lose the camp scholarship, and it was wrong not to tell Mom and Dad what was going on. Too complicated to go into it then, but maybe sometime soon. She sighed. Marla coming over and Beth's problems were almost a welcome distraction.

"Mother?" No answer to Roe's knock, but the nurse, nodding encouragement, opened it.

"Go on, dearie. Only a half hour, though. She tires easily."

Her mother was sitting in a chair holding a book. She kept turning pages without seeming to take in words. She looks nice, Roe thought. Clean, a simple dress, a neat hairdo.

Roe put her hand on her mother's arm. "It's me, Mother. Roe. Rosita, your daughter?" Why did she feel an introduction was necessary? Something about her mother seemed vague—as if she weren't really there.

Mother gave a start, and then smiled a strange smile. "Hello. How kind of you to come for a visit. Will you be here long?"

"Only a half hour. The nurse says you get tired."

"Oh? I guess I do. It will be time for a nap soon."

"I'm staying with Dad in his apartment until Tuesday night."

"That's nice. Who did you say you were again?"

Roe's eyes filled. This was awful—a half hour was too long. "I'm Rosita, Mother. Your daughter."

The woman, who had become a stranger, put down the book. Her eyes turned dark and angry. "I don't have a daughter. I had a son once. I think I did. I can't remember his name."

"Mateo."

"Mateo. Yes. I want him. Go get him now!"

"I can't, Mother."

"Oh. Well, maybe later. I want to sleep. I'll do that once I'm finished reading a few more chapters."

Out of Chaos. A fitting title, even though it was obvious her mother hadn't been reading a word.

"You go now. I'm very busy." Holding the book upside down, she began turning the pages again.

Roe stood. "Goodbye," she practically whispered.

Without looking up, her mother muttered, "Have a nice day. Thank you for coming."

Roe rushed into the room where her father was waiting. "Why?" she demanded. "Why didn't you tell me?"

Armed with root beer and popcorn, Kylie and Marla sat at the kitchen table. "I don't know anything definite," Marla admitted. "Just stuff I overheard at the boarding school. And I wasn't there long before I got yanked out again."

"Did you like it?"

"Not really. I don't like it anywhere—except maybe on stage, thanks to you." She gave Kylie an uncertain smile.

Kylie looked down. She and Marla weren't used to being polite to each other. "So about Mr. Carroll."

"Well, he's only been here a couple months, right?"

Kylie nodded. "He came when Mrs. Hill left to have her baby."

"Well, I heard he used to teach at the public school in the same town as my private one, but he left under 'suspicious circumstances.' I'm quoting, of course. That's what some girls told me, and they're so dramatic they could be students at Crofts. I believed them, though. They said Creepy Carroll had a reputation for, shall we say, encouraging girls who weren't pretty or didn't have friends. The rumors were that he took advantage of them."

Kylie gasped. "You mean—" She couldn't quite say what she was thinking. "But he's awfully old, isn't he?"

"Yeah, probably at least forty but still good looking in a teacher kind of way. I don't think age has much to do with it. As far as what you're thinking—rape—I couldn't say. No one ever told me exactly what happened, and I wasn't there long enough to find out. But the girls who are his current groupies sort of fit the pattern. Losers. Except for Beth. She doesn't belong with them."

Not certain she was being wise, Kylie related everything Beth had told her. "I think she's turning off on him, though."

"Hope so. He's scary."

"I agree. But why do you think he dumped Beth?"

"Maybe finding out you are her best friend and Kurt is her boyfriend. Like you two are the most popular kids in school. Creepy Carroll discovered that Beth wasn't a loner after all. As far as his intentions go, I don't think they're good."

Kylie came to a decision. "Marla, would you go to Beth's house with me? She has to watch her siblings."

"All right, but she won't want me there."

"Doesn't matter." She reached for her cell phone. "Beth? Marla and I are coming over. We need to talk."

Scene 9—Too Many Problems

WHO WOULD HAVE THOUGHT MARLA Gray would be the one to make her feel good again? Beth still didn't trust Marla—didn't even like her—but Marla had no reason to lie. She had told Beth exactly what she'd heard about Mr. Carroll, and it all kind of fit in with what Beth had figured out. "Creepy Carroll," Marla called him. Beth determined to say that, over and over, until the hurt went away—or was less painful. "Creepy Carroll, Creepy Carroll, Creepy Carroll."

But that was not the only way Marla had helped. When she and Kylie arrived, Beth and her little brother Porter had been playing a board game that she had invented. It was called Castle Bluff, a rip-off on Monopoly. Beth had hand-drawn all of the squares with scenes from their town, both present day and from history. It had taken ages because she had made two boards: one for her family and one to give Danny Kennedy for his eleventh birthday.

"Hooray! I own Markey Castle!" screamed Porter, as Beth landed on the square.

"Oh, great," Beth moaned, examining her dwindling pile of green construction paper money. "You'll probably charge me a million dollars rent."

Porter grinned. "Not quite. Only three hundred, but you still have to repair Markey Bridge. Why don't you say I won, and then you can go have your private talk?"

Beth gave him an impulsive hug. Occasionally, but only occasionally, Porter showed some small signs of maturing.

In Beth's room, Marla exclaimed over the paintings and sketches on the wall. "These pictures, the Castle Bluff game—why aren't you in Art Club instead of Creepy Carroll's newspaper?"

Beth grinned. "What about CBT?"

"Oh, that's all right. Your friends are in it. But you should be painting sets and making posters. You're talented!"

It was something to think about, Beth decided. For sure, it was time to head in a different direction.

Dad ordered pizza. He and Roe needed to talk privately—not in a restaurant. The small kitchen in his apartment would do. "Why didn't you tell me?" Roe repeated.

"I didn't know how," he admitted. "There's so much to tell, I hardly know where to start."

"Mother didn't act depressed. She talked like she had Alzheimer's or something."

Dad nodded. "Some kind of dementia. The doctors haven't put a label on it yet."

"But isn't she too young?" How old was Mother? Mid-forties, maybe? She'd never told Roe.

"She's young, but it happens. The doctors told me stress can hasten it, and she's certainly experienced plenty."

"Will I get it, too?" Roe's voice shook. "It can be inherited, right?"

Dad shook his head but didn't reply. Instead, he headed to the fridge for another beer. He sat once again but said nothing.

Suddenly she knew. Maybe she had always known. Mother's love had always gone exclusively to Mateo—never to her. *I don't have a daughter,* Mother had said. It all made sense now, but Roe had many questions. But first—"I'm not her daughter, am I?"

Wearily, Dad looked down, resting his chin on his hands. When he raised it again, Roe saw tears. "No," he said, "and Mateo wasn't your brother." Then he told her the story.

"Your real mother died giving birth to you. I met Charlotte a year later. She and her son Mateo had been abandoned by Mateo's father—a man Charlotte never married. They had been, essentially, stranded in Mexico. I fell in love with both of them. You needed a mother, and Mateo needed a father. But not in Mexico. Charlotte insisted we return to her country, to her family."

"But I don't have grandparents or aunts or uncles or anyone."

Dad nodded. "Her family wouldn't accept me or you or even their own grandson. In time, I became an American citizen. Then I watched as Charlotte became more and more bitter and troubled. I knew she had mental problems and that I probably shouldn't have married her. But I did, so here we are."

Here they were indeed. "Tell me about my real mother," Roe said.

"Her name was Sofia and she came to Mexico from Spain. "We'd been married only a year when you were born."

"So I'm not half Latina?"

"Well, yes you are—on my side at least. You're also half Hispanic, if anyone wants to know. How does that make you feel?"

Roe wasn't sure. Her defense against the prejudice was that she was only half Latina, that her mother was white. Was she prejudiced against herself? How crazy was that? It was going to take some getting used to. The problems at Crofts had become distant and unimportant. She had planned to talk it over with Dad, but for now it didn't matter.

"How do you feel?" Dad asked again.

"Homesick." That wasn't the right word, of course. The feeling wasn't homesickness—more like not belonging anywhere, longing for something that didn't exist.

Dad gathered her into his arms. "I know what you mean," he said.

Roe wasn't ready to talk about Crofts, but she did tell him about the Kennedys. "They say I can stay with them for as long as I need to, but Dad, they can't mean that. They can't afford to have me, especially with Uncle Dan not working. Do you still send them money?"

Dad was appalled. "Not often and not enough. I haven't been thinking clearly. Well, we'll correct that."

His first decision was to cancel Roe's return flight. "I'll drive you back," he said. "Then we'll decide with the Kennedys what to do next."

That was fine with Roe. She didn't want to stay one more minute.

Kylie was so bored she gave Danny a splendid welcome when he returned, causing him to become wary. "What's going on? You're happy to see me."

"Well, you've always been my favorite brother."

"I'm your only brother. Okay, what's wrong?"

"I'm lonely. Mom and Dad are still at Grandma's and Roe isn't back. I'm sick of my own company and glad to have anyone's—even yours."

Danny grinned. "All right then. How shall we celebrate this weird occasion?"

He was growing up, Kylie thought, not certain this was a good thing. "Board games, making cookies, whatever," she suggested.

"Let's skip the whatever and eat cookies and watch TV," he said.

Then her cell phone jingled. "It's Roe."

"From Michigan? Cool." Danny waited impatiently until Kylie ended the call. "Well?"

"She didn't say much. Only that her father is driving her back here. She's not flying."

"How's her mom?"

"She said it's complicated."

Danny snorted. "Complicated. That's what people always say when they don't want to talk about it."

Kylie smiled. "You could be right. Oh, I forgot to tell Roe that Dad found a job."

"What? What? Dad got a job?"

Of course he wouldn't know. "Yes, in research—in Milwaukee."

"Yes!" Danny screamed. "Everything is going to be okay now!"

Kylie tried to caution him. "Things will be better," she said, "but we still have to be careful with money." She doubted he heard her, though. She hadn't realized Danny had been worried, too. It was time to stop thinking of him as a little kid. He'd be eleven next weekend, and she hadn't even decided on a present for him. Maybe Roe and I can figure out something together, she thought.

"I'll get the cookies. You pick out what show we should watch," she said. It wouldn't matter what he selected. She wouldn't be able to concentrate. Even though she knew better, she couldn't help sharing Danny's feelings. Everything was going to be okay.

SCENE 10—A REAL FAIRY GODMOTHER

IMPOSSIBLE! KYLIE STARED AT THE promptbook, right where she had left it in the castle. Like magic, the ball scene was covered with blocking diagrams and notes. "It was blank before,' she whispered. "I'm positive." She looked around the room for answers.

Eric arrived. "What's wrong, Kylie? You look like you'd seen a ghost."

"Maybe I did," Kylie said softly.

"Hey, Kylie! Wow! This is something!" It was Kurt calling from the stage. "You must have worked all weekend on this. Who helped you?"

Bewildered, Kylie rushed out of the kitchen, followed by Eric. There, right where it belonged Up Center, was a bigger-than-life fireplace, made of strong cardboard, supported on a wooden frame. The fireplace had been expertly painted to look like stones—black, white, and gray. Imani would have no trouble hiding behind it, and there were even little cubbyholes to store her props. It was perfect!

Kylie shook her head. "Not me. I'm as surprised as you are."

As well as the fireplace, a makeshift but workable dark blue curtain was strung across the stage. Kylie hadn't planned on using any curtain.

"I must have a real fairy godmother," she cried.

"Or a fairy godfather." Jen giggled. "Do you suppose it was Mr. Markey?"

Kurt pushed Gee forward. "You are the one with the key, so you must know something," he said. "Speak!"

"Mr. Markey said he rented a curtain from a theatrical supplier. There's your answer." Gee grinned. "And Leland and Roberta must be especially artistic."

"Leland?" Kurt shouted. "No way!"

"Actually, he's pretty nice," Brad said. Then he looked carefully at the skillfully constructed fireplace. "But not this nice, and Roberta wouldn't be able to, of course."

They continued discussing Leland and the props and scenery until Kylie wanted to scream. Finally, she did scream. "Who's Roberta?"

Everyone stopped and stared at her.

"I'll get her," Brad said quietly before leaving the room.

"You haven't met Robbie?" Gabrielle asked in amazement.

"Figures," Marla muttered. She left the stage and went to the kitchen for a Coke. Or a smoke? Kylie wondered. Honestly, Marla ran hot and cold. Every time she thought they might be friends, Marla returned to type. "Who's Roberta?" she asked again.

Eric explained. "She's Brad's job and Leland's niece. She's visiting here from California. Mr. Markey hired Brad to help her out—until the dog arrived."

"She's sweet but a little shy," Jen said. "No wonder, of course."

Marla stood in the doorway, drinking soda, looking amused. "I'm surprised Brad didn't introduce you."

Kylie turned red. He had tried, she admitted to herself, but she never gave him a chance. Things were starting to make sense. After school that day, Brad had rushed out to the castle to see Mr. Markey, only to appear shortly afterwards at Smithy's with the new girl. I'm an absolute idiot, she thought. That didn't explain, though, why Brad was holding her arm and seemed to be all over her. Kylie would wait and see.

"We've both been busy," she said. "I can't wait to meet her."

"Well, here's your chance." Brad appeared at the door with the lovely girl Kylie had already seen twice. Again, she was caught by the girl's resemblance to someone, but Kylie couldn't quite grasp who. Certainly not Leland. This time, the girl—Roberta—seemed to be escorted by a handsome golden retriever. The dog Eric had mentioned. "This is Roberta. Robbie, this is Kylie Kennedy."

Robbie took a step forward, not really looking at Kylie. "I'm happy to meet you," she said shyly.

Oh my gosh, she's blind! That's a trained seeing-eye dog. No wonder Brad had held her arm. And of course he was kind to her. She's pretty and probably nice, too. But that didn't mean—Kylie took Robbie's hand. "I'm glad to meet you, too," she said.

Brad escorted Robbie to a chair. "Maybe you'd like to attend a rehearsal."

"I would, thanks. I almost feel like I'm part of the play after hearing Brad talk about it and helping with the fireplace."

How was that possible? "Well, thanks for your help," Kylie said.

"She made it easy," Robbie said. "I'm starting to do things I never dreamed I could do again."

She? Kylie wondered. And doing what things? Diagramming blocking in a promptbook you can't see? I don't think so. And the new blocking was in Miss Armstrong's handwriting, and nothing had been there last Thursday.

It was time to rehearse, but Kylie needed a chance to go over the blocking notes first. Unexpectedly, Marla came to the rescue. "We need a tech meeting as much as a rehearsal. Kylie and I were stuck working on costumes alone Friday," she said importantly. "Besides, Imani isn't here yet."

They looked around. It was true. No Imani. "It isn't like her to be late," Gee said.

"I'll call her," Kylie said. "And I need to check over the promptbook one more time. Brad, would you and Marla lead a crew meeting? Over the weekend, she and I began a list of props. Marla and Gee can tell you what costumes we've collected."

Kylie fled for the kitchen, her thoughts too jumbled to think coherently. Calm down, she scolded herself. She'd sort out the mess about Brad and the unlikely set construction crew of Leland and Roberta later. Well, maybe Leland could have built it, but the stonework looked painted by an experienced scene painter. For the present, though, she had to concentrate on the ball. As soon as she had studied the script enough so she wouldn't embarrass herself in front of the cast, she called Imani.

"What's wrong?" Kylie asked, as soon as Imani stopped crying.

"Oh, Kylie, I can't be the fairy godmother!"

"What?"

"My dad overheard me rehearsing and flipped. He says Gee has no right to let me play the part in such a racist way. Mom agrees. They both want to meet with her."

"Oh, no!"

Imani burst out crying again. "Kylie, I'm so sorry. What are you going to do?"

"Try not to worry. I'll talk to Gee, and we'll get back to you after rehearsal. Your parents aren't coming here, are they?"

"No, they said they'd call Gee at home tonight, but if they can't reach her, they'll call school tomorrow."

"Okay. Try to stay calm."

Kylie made another call. This time to her mother to say she'd get a ride home from Gee. She hoped that was true.

The rest of rehearsal passed in a blur. The cast looked at her, puzzled. Kylie was usually much better prepared to direct a scene. However, the cast knew it was a difficult one, especially without Imani, even though Gee had a fine time understudying the fairy godmother role. Kylie told them that Imani wasn't feeling well. That was true, Kylie thought. Imani felt rotten.

Finally, rehearsal ended. The cast hurried out—Jen helped Robbie downstairs, but Brad stood waiting. "There's a problem," Kylie told him. "I'll try to call you later." Kylie gave Brad what she hoped was a meaningful look. He nodded before going downstairs with the others.

Quickly, Kylie filled Gee in on Imani. "I'll meet you at your car, Gee. I want to check the kitchen one more time to make sure we haven't left anything."

Kylie knew she hadn't, but she was planning to intentionally leave something behind—a note for Miss Armstrong. As illogical as it seemed, Miss Armstrong must have been in the castle.

Once Kylie was in the car, Gee told her she wasn't driving her home. Not yet, anyway. They were going to the Joneses—"for damage control," Gee insisted.

On the ride back from Michigan, Roe told her father what had happened at Crofts. After a long silence, Dad said, "I'm proud of you."

That was not the reaction Roe expected—concern, maybe anger, but not pride. "Proud?"

"You stood up for yourself. You expressed your feelings calmly, and then left. Not many people your age or even older could have done that."

Dad was proud of her. Roe found herself feeling more positive than she had in a long time. "But what should I do next?"

Again, Dad surprised her. She thought he'd respond the way the Kennedys had—say they'd call the school and complain. Instead, Dad said, "I don't think you can do anything but wait—as difficult as that might be— wait to hear from the director. You put the ball firmly into his court, which is exactly where it needs to be. Here's a question for you. What would you like to happen?"

Roe hadn't even considered that, but Dad didn't mind silence. She took the time to think. "I would like to play the part," she said finally. "I love it, and I've worked hard. But I can't continue the way things are. Something would need to change a lot. And if I quit, I don't think I should go to camp, even though the scholarship didn't have anything to do with my playing Anne. Too many of the same mean kids would be there."

Dad nodded. "So we wait. I trust you to do what's right for you."

For the first time, Roe saw her father as a real person—not just one of her many problems. He was stranded in a small apartment in order to be close to a wife who often didn't know him. "What's right for you, Dad? What would you like to happen?"

"I don't know anymore. I wish it would all just go away."

That's what Roe wished. Only a few more days before winter break began, she thought. At least that was something to look forward to.

They remained silent for many miles.

Right before social studies, Beth had been called to the office. Why, she couldn't imagine, but she didn't especially care. Anything that would keep her out of Creepy Carroll's classroom was fine. (She had practiced all weekend calling him that.) She hoped that whatever was wrong would take the whole period.

Surprisingly, her English teacher Mrs. Hunt was there, as well as Vice Principal Mrs. Warde. On Mrs. Warde's desk was Beth's folder.

"There you are, Beth." Mrs. Hunt smiled. "I must hurry to my next class, but before I do I wanted to assure you that you're not in trouble. I realize it can be startling to be called to the office."

Beth nodded. Of course she couldn't tell Mrs. Hunt that she was glad to be there. She remembered the only other time she had been summoned. That was when Mr. Hasting thought that CBT had vandalized the sheet music. That was scary; this wasn't. Going to Mr. Carroll's class would be scary.

"Sit down, Beth," Mrs. Warde said. She looked nervous, too, Beth thought. "I've read all of these essays, and I understand why you were troubled. Mrs. Hunt said you asked Mr. Carroll to explain. Please tell me exactly what he said, at least as much as you remember."

Beth hesitated. It was hard to talk about. "Well, I was surprised because I've always had A's from him, so I looked through the paper but there weren't any comments—just the grade. I tried to ask him about it the next day, but he said he was busy and waved me away. That night, I read over my other stuff and honestly thought the latest one was the best yet. So I tried to talk with him again. I asked him how I might improve. He just said that I needed to learn to write but that he wasn't an English teacher. Then he told me I wasn't needed on the newspaper any longer. There were four new girls there I hadn't seen before. I was confused, so that's why I took the papers to Mrs. Hunt."

"I see." Mrs. Warde opened her computer and seemed to be looking at a schedule. "Well, Beth, how do you feel about going back to your regular class?"

Beth squirmed and felt herself growing hot. "I . . . I don't really want to."

Mrs. Warde nodded. "Beth, there seems to be more going on here than your difficulty, and I need to get to the bottom of it. If you haven't already, I think you should talk with your parents. They may call me if they have any questions. In time, I may call them. I would prefer that you not mention this to anyone else. Have you already?"

"Two friends." Well, at least one was a friend. She hadn't decided about Marla.

Mrs. Warde shrugged. "Perhaps they'll be discreet. What did they have to say? No," she said, reading Beth's expression correctly, "It's not necessary for you to tell me their names."

"They don't like Mr. Carroll," Beth admitted. "They say he only pays attention to girls without friends—loners. They think the reason he dumped me was because he found out that I do have friends. Good ones."

A look came over the vice principal's face Beth couldn't interpret. She didn't respond at first. Instead, she wrote out a pass and a short note. "All right, Beth. Concerning your immediate problem—social studies class—it seems you may be lucky. Mrs. Hunt teaches it as well as English, and it's meeting at this hour. Suppose you join her class?"

Beth let out an audible sigh of relief. "Oh, thank you." Then she thought it over. "Do you mean just for today?"

Mrs. Warde smiled, handing Beth the pass and note. "No, I mean for the rest of the year. Go on now, and try not to worry too much." She called Beth back. "Oh, wait a minute. Please, if you know them, give me the names of the other girls you saw with Mr. Carroll."

Mrs. Jones answered the door. "Yes?"

Kylie felt like a solicitor—or like she was selling Girl Scout cookies. She had no idea what to say. Rising to the occasion, Gee took over.

Mrs. Jones managed a polite smile. "Come in," she said. "Imani has told me about you." She escorted them into the living room where Mr. Jones, who looked even less friendly, was seated behind the evening paper. After introductions, he returned to his paper. I guess he wants his wife to handle this, Kylie thought. What a mess! And what would they do if Imani dropped out? Could Kylie both act and direct?

"I'll call Imani," Mrs. Jones said, going to the staircase.

A teary-eyed Imani soon appeared. She brightened, though, at the sight of Kylie and Gee.

"Please sit down," Mrs. Jones said. "Imani has filled us in on all that is going on. We understand that you, Mrs. Grainger, are supervising the students and that Kylie is the actual director until Miss Armstrong returns. It's all most peculiar, but I suppose it's also commendable of you. However . . ."

Kylie wished she were there for a different reason and that she had time to gawk at the beautiful paintings hanging on the walls. She remembered that Mr. Jones was an art teacher at Crofts and wondered if he were the artist. A magnificent grand piano stood in the far corner of the spacious room. Who played it? But someone needed to say something.

Gee began. "I must take responsibility for this misunderstanding," she said. "I just learned from Kylie that Miss Armstrong felt that people might find the way Imani was playing the role offensive."

Uh-oh, Kylie thought, watching Mr. Jones peek over his paper, giving them a stern look. Gee is going to blow the whole thing.

"That is one of the reasons she wasn't cast originally," Kylie said. "But what happened later was my fault. I love the way Imani does the part. Miss Armstrong did cast me as the fairy godmother, not Imani, but then I had to direct, so I talked Imani into playing it. I thought it would be too hard to both act and direct. Also, most of the kids wanted Imani for the part in the first place," she finished lamely.

Mr. Jones put down his paper and opened his mouth, about to speak.

Kylie tried again. "We didn't know anyone would be offended. She was so funny and so different from the usual Imani."

Mrs. Jones gave her husband a look and held out her hand to him as a signal to keep quiet. "I can see you meant no harm," she said kindly. "But what do you propose to do about it?"

Kylie had thought about that in the car. It was time to really direct, not just to follow someone else's blocking. "It's a large important part," she said, "and it's too late to find someone else. We'd have to cancel the show. That wouldn't be fair to the cast or Imani. She has put in a lot of time into it."

"That's true," Gee said.

Kylie turned to Imani. "So what if you played the part differently? It would be hard, but you could do it."

"Different?" Imani asked. "How?"

"Well, you could do it the way I did at auditions—elegant and kind. Or you could play her like an old lady. Kind of a Disney version."

"That might be fun," Imani said.

"Let's try one of your lines," Kylie suggested. She began to recite the one she'd used for audition. She raised an imaginary wand.

Oh, no! This is terrible. I forgot to tell Cinderella what happens at midnight. Her dress will turn into rags, and a clock will sound twelve times like this—Dong-Dong. When I give you the signal, you must go Dong-Dong twelve times.

Mrs. Jones applauded.

"Now you try." Kylie said. Imani tried the same line and the same approach. Oh, no, Kylie groaned inwardly. She's boring.

"Try playing her old," Kylie suggested. "Slow down your speech, stoop your shoulders, and age your voice a bit by lowering it. Don't be insulting, or we'll have old people mad at us, too."

At that, Mr. Jones burst out laughing. Good, thought Kylie. He's beginning to see we're not so awful. She sensed that obtaining Mr. Jones's approval would be their biggest hurdle.

Imani tried again, using a different line. She seemed to age before their eyes, appearing frail and tiny. Her voice was a little shaky but still full of spirit.

I think introductions are in order. I'm Cinderella's fairy godmother. Did you see the nasty trick that stepmother played on my little girl? Just when you all cleaned up so beautifully, too.

Kylie and Gee exchanged grins as Imani continued the long monologue. Kylie wondered if Imani knew she was imitating Mr. Markey. She was more talented than any of them had realized.

Imani's eyes gleamed as she finished. "Oh, I like playing her that way even better. Please, Dad?"

The Joneses looked at each other, then nodded slowly. "Very well," Mrs. Jones said. "As long as you keep your fairy godmother out of the cotton fields. We can see that your cast needs you."

"The day may come when we can all laugh at stereotypes," Mr. Jones said, "although I don't think I'll be alive to see it. There are still too many people, even here in Castle Bluff, who would find Imani's portrayal accurate. At some point I'd like to see Miss Armstrong, though. Something doesn't seem quite—"

"Imani is going to be terrific," Gee interrupted. "You have a talented daughter."

Mrs. Jones smiled. "We certainly do. And now that that's settled, would you like to have supper with us? Simple tonight—just hamburgers."

Kylie's stomach rumbled. Lunch was hours ago.

"Love to," Gee said.

Kylie nodded. "I'll have to call, but I think it will be okay."

"Ask if you can stay awhile afterwards and do your homework with me," Imani pleaded. "Dad could take you home if Gee can't stay. Right, Dad?"

Mr. Jones gave a thumbs-up sign, as Aniya, the older daughter, a ballet student at Crofts, announced that supper was ready.

Later in Imani's bedroom, Imani flopped on her bed while Kylie sat on a pretty blue and white cushioned chair. Imani sighed loudly. "You guys were incredible. Dad was all set to go see the principal."

"The principal?" At CBMS, few people saw the principal. Kylie wasn't sure he existed. The vice principal was the person in charge of problems.

"I was so scared, Kylie."

"Me, too. It was a close one, all right. Look, I need to talk with someone. Do you have much homework?"

Imani shook her head. "I'll be okay. I've got a study hall tomorrow morning."

It would mean a late night for Kylie, but her grades were good, and this was more important. She spilled out practically everything she'd bottled up inside: Brad and Roberta, Beth and Mr. Carroll, Marla . . . "What will I do if she starts smoking in the castle?"

"I don't think she will, Kylie. I'm getting to know Marla. She's not as bad as she wants us to believe. She gets scared every time she sees people starting to like her, and then she gets mean again. It's weird."

Kylie smiled. Talking with Imani was helping. "I can see why Beth likes coming here."

"I hardly see Beth anymore. I thought she would be my best friend, but she hasn't said anything about problems with Mr. Carroll. It hurts that her crush on a teacher is more important being friends with me, but—"

"She's going to need her friends more than ever," Kylie predicted. "It was only by chance that she told me. You're in Carroll's class. What do you think of him?"

"He's a teacher. I do okay in there, but he doesn't pay much attention to me."

"You're probably lucky."

Finally, Kylie told Imani about the sudden appearance of the blocking notes in the promptbook and the fireplace.

"Sounds like you have a real fairy godmother."

"I need one." But was the fairy godmother named Anna Armstrong? If so, how was that possible?

SCENE 11—ADULT INTERFERENCE

LATER THAT NIGHT WHEN KYLIE'S brain was deep into her algebra, she remembered Brad. She had promised to call him. Was it too late? She'd try texting instead. *Sorry. Was at Imani's 2 fix problem. Pls call if not 2 late.*

The text was delivered, and she must wait. She tried to return to math but kept staring at her phone. "Please ring," she whispered. "Please, please, please." As if hearing her, it gave its rollicking little jingle.

"Brad, I'm sorry."

"So am I," he said instantly. "It's my fault, too. I should have found a way to tell you about Robbie."

"And I should have trusted you." Kylie wanted to make excuses, to say how she had been feeling down on herself back then because of Imani's audition, but excuses seemed a bad idea. Sorry was enough.

"Well, I'm sure glad that's settled. Robbie is a nice girl and all, and I'm glad I have the job, but Kylie, she's not my girlfriend. Yeah, she's pretty, but she's too old for one thing. Also, she's so shy she hardly says a word."

"It's okay, Brad. Let me tell you about Imani. Quickly, Kylie caught him up."

"That's a relief," he said. "We can't lose an actor. I sort of see her parents' point of view."

"I do, too," Kylie said. "Now, anyway."

Then, because it was Brad and she needed to talk, Kylie told him about the promptbook, and how the blocking magically appeared. "It was Miss

Armstrong's handwriting," she said, "and I'm positive the scene was blank when I left rehearsal."

"Something funny is going on," Brad said. "Obviously, Miss Armstrong can't climb those stairs with a broken leg. But someone else is living in the castle—someone other than Mr. Markey, Leland, and Robbie. I hear voices sometimes. Voices that aren't theirs."

"Robbie said *she* had helped her. She? I thought that was strange."

"The mysteries keep piling up," Brad said. "There's also the matter of Roe and Eric, and why she never answered Eric's notes."

"What notes? Eric dumped Roe for Jaimie. Roe's feelings are hurt, but she's had so many hurts lately, she doesn't have time to concentrate on any one thing."

"Phew! That's not what I heard. Eric said that he's given Gabrielle a bunch of notes to give Roe, but she's ignored them."

"Gabrielle. You mean, Jaimie's new best friend? Why didn't Eric just call or text?"

"Broke his phone again, and his parents refuse to buy a new one."

"But Eric is acting like he likes Jaimie," Kylie insisted.

"Well, at first he was trying to make Roe jealous because she didn't respond to his notes, but now he can't get Jaimie to leave him alone."

Kylie couldn't help feeling sorry for Jaimie. She didn't like her much, but she hadn't been treated fairly. "And we thought we had problems last fall. Let me tell you about Beth. It's serious, but I'm sure you won't tell anyone."

After hearing what Kylie knew, Brad added what he'd heard. "Kurt says he can't stand Carroll. Says he's a terrible influence on Beth."

"Well, he's not any longer. So, we're caught up on problems. What do you think we should do?"

"Hmmm . . . Well, school lets out on Thursday. Could you have the gang over Friday night?"

"Probably, but who do you mean by the gang?"

Brad thought. "Well, not everyone. Maybe just our best friends: you, me, Roe, Eric, Beth, and Kurt. It would be like a party but also a meeting. Maybe, together, we can figure out what's going on."

She wasn't alone anymore, Kylie thought, after hanging up. Now, as much as she'd like to go to sleep, she would finish her homework.

Sometime in the middle of the night, she was aware of a light next door. Yes, it was coming from the Santos's house. And then she heard a door close much nearer—right on the other side of her bedroom wall. She gave a sigh of relief and turned over. Roe was home from Michigan.

"There you are," Aunt Jane said, as Roe made her way into the kitchen. "Did you have a good sleep?"

Roe gave Kylie's mother a hug. "I'm still half asleep. What time is it?"

"Almost eleven. Sit down, and I'll fix brunch for both of us."

Yawning, Roe followed directions. "Aren't you going to work today?"

Aunt Jane shook her head. "No. Well, actually, yes—in a way. I had a meeting early this morning, but the rest I can handle here. Real Estate is slow. I'm ending up with a lot of 'work from home' days. I thought you and I needed to talk."

Roe nodded, even though she felt all talked out. "Where's Dad?"

"Next door with Dan. They're making some decisions."

Well, that was good. "About money?"

Aunt Jane smiled. "I imagine, yes—possibly other things as well. We do have some good news. Dan found a job."

"That's wonderful!" Roe was thrilled for the Kennedys. It was also a relief for the subject not to be one of her problems. It was only a matter of time before Aunt Jane got to them, of course.

"Roe, we need to talk about Crofts."

"I'm not sure what to say."

Aunt Jane took the dishes to the sink and poured herself another cup of coffee. "I told you I wouldn't interfere, and I haven't. But I think the director or someone from Crofts should have called here by now."

"I told them I'd be gone until Wednesday."

"It doesn't matter. Someone should have been in touch with the adults responsible for you, or at least called your school. We can't let this continue. If you don't hear from Mr. Warner today, your father and I will pay a visit to Crofts tomorrow morning."

"Okay," Roe said softly. She couldn't handle this alone, and she needed an answer. Was she in the play or not? And did she even care? After hearing that she would see her father later, she returned to her room. She'd try to concentrate on schoolwork until Kylie came home.

Beth, too, was having a talk. She had awakened with both a headache and a stomachache, but she didn't think she was sick—at least not that kind of sick. But she couldn't go to school. She just couldn't. Without getting dressed, she went down to the kitchen. "Mom," she said. "I need to tell you something."

No after school rehearsal today. Kylie decided she was pleased after all, in spite of their needing one. The kids had too many conflicts to make rehearsing worthwhile. It wasn't only Christmas activities facing them, but the last-minute teacher assignments before the school doors finally closed at the end of the week.

But such a wild, incredible day! She needed to share everything with Beth and Roe, beginning with Beth. Kylie double-checked that she had all she needed to do her homework and raced to Beth's house.

"Beth," Kylie blurted, pushing her way in out of the cold as soon as the door opened. "Beth, why weren't you in school? Oh, never mind. You'll never guess what happened."

Beth rushed her inside and up the stairs to her room. "What, Kylie? You're about to burst."

Out of breath, Kylie sat on the bed. "This afternoon, seventh period, you might say we were on lockdown."

"What? Someone had a gun?"

"I don't think so. Mr. Stratton, believe it or not, got on the intercom and told the teachers not to let us go to our eighth period classes or to give out passes for any reason. I guess we do have a principal. I don't remember ever hearing his voice before."

"Come on, Kylie! What happened?"

"Well, then we looked out the window and saw cops coming in. That's all I knew until after school."

"Then—"

"Then Priyanka said she had been helping in the office during her study hall and heard commotion coming from Mr. Stratton's office. Then she heard something about an anonymous phone call, and then someone said to call the police. That's all she heard because the secretary gave her a pass and told her to go back to study hall immediately. She said she'd help you with props, by the way."

"That's good, but go on. Did she find out anything else?"

"No, but Eric said his whole class rushed to the window after someone said they saw cops. The teacher couldn't stop them. Well, Eric saw someone in handcuffs taken out of the building and put into a police car. He thinks it was Mr. Carroll. Shortly after that, we were allowed to go to our eighth period."

"I see," Beth said.

"What? You don't sound surprised."

"I guess I'm not, in a way," Beth admitted, "although I didn't think anything like that would happen. I told my parents about Mr. Carroll turning on me, and they went over to school. I don't know how that turned out. I didn't want them to get involved, but maybe it was a good thing they did."

That evening, Roe's father took them out to dinner. Roe had spent the afternoon with him and knew some of his plans. There had been no word from Crofts, so Uncle Dan had called the school, and both he and Dad made an appointment to see the director the next morning. Whatever came next would be resolved soon. Tomorrow was the last day of school before Crofts' winter break. Even if she were to keep the role, she would not rehearse again until after vacation.

Dad planned to return to Michigan after the meeting but would spend Christmas with the Kennedys, promising to visit more often. Roe was welcome to go to Michigan but doubted she would. "If Mother asks for me, I'll see her," she said.

"So here is the plan," Dad said, once they were supplied with burgers, fries, and Cokes. "Jane will be in charge of selling our house and will receive the commission. The proceeds of the sale, though, will go into a special fund for Roe that Jane and Dan can access whenever necessary. Meantime, I have left enough for Roe's care at least through the summer, and then we'll see what's next."

Aunt Jane and Uncle Dan smiled. Roe was certain they wanted her with them, but that they were also relieved.

"And Danny, Roe's and my birthday present to you will be the hockey lessons you've wanted. How does that sound?"

"Oh, boy! Thank you!" And in spite of Danny's age, Mr. Santos received a hug.

Roe and Kylie smiled at each other. They had plans for something else, but it would be their secret. It was all right that the adults had taken over the day, but they wanted to return to their own world as soon as possible.

SCENE 12—THE GANG, BACK IN CHARGE!

"CASTLE BLUFF MIDDLE SCHOOL, HOTBED of crime, passion, and perfidy," Kurt proclaimed.

Kylie giggled. "Perfidy? What's that?"

"I read it somewhere," Kurt answered airily, "but you've got to admit, our school is a pretty dangerous place these days."

"It's not really funny," Brad said, "but you're right. Both Mr. Hasting and Marla Gray's father indicted and Mr. Carroll taken off in handcuffs. Gotta wonder what's next."

Winter break, finally! All had gathered at Kylie's for the party and planning meeting. An uncomfortable gathering, Kylie thought, looking at Brad, Kurt, Eric, Beth, and Roe. She hadn't had an easy time getting Eric to agree to come. He and Roe still weren't speaking. Kylie sighed. Maybe that was the first order of business. She cleared her throat—the hostess and one in charge. "Before we start figuring out what's going on at the castle, we'll have some eats," she said.

"Yippee!" Kurt cried.

"Wait a second," Kylie continued. "While we're doing that, two of you should have it out. Roe, you need to know that Eric gave Gabrielle gobs of notes to give to you. Eric, you need to know that Roe never got any of them."

"What?" both shouted.

Kylie nodded. "Go talk while the rest of us stuff our faces."

"You never got the notes?" Eric asked, although it was obvious what had happened.

"No, I thought you decided you wanted Jaimie to be your girlfriend. I'm sorry, Eric."

"I'm the one who's sorry. I should have my head examined. I wonder if Gabrielle told Jaimie about them?" Eric shook his head. "I hung out with Jamie because at least someone liked me. I should have figured out a way to talk with you."

"Like call?"

"Cell phone broken, and my parents won't get me another one until graduation. Not much privacy at home, and I hardly ever see you at school. I thought you were all involved at Crofts and had made new friends."

Roe snorted. "New friends! Let me tell you what's been going on with me, Eric." And Roe filled him in on everything—Crofts, Devin, and her parents. "It's been awful, and I haven't felt good about myself. I should have tried to tell you."

"Roe, I am so sorry! Especially about your mother. But what about Crofts? Are you going to stay in the show?"

Roe nodded. "Dad and Uncle Dan had a meeting there Wednesday morning, and I saw Mr. Warner later after school. Big apologies and stuff like that. I'll keep the part, and they're getting someone else to play Peter. Devin was dropped from the show. Won't that be pleasant for me? Still, I'm going to do it anyway. I'll go back after break, and there might be a rehearsal at someone's house after Christmas."

"Not like it was, though," Eric said. "The excitement is gone."

Eric was right, of course. It no longer seemed special—an honor. "At least we're friends again," Roe said, "and I can help out with *Cinderella* over vacation."

"Let's get some food before Kurt polishes it off," Eric said.

The meeting resumed. "You two okay?" Kylie asked Roe and Eric. Both smiled at her and held hands. "Great. Now I thought we could tackle the problems that have been hitting us lately. We started with Eric and Roe. But Eric, please be careful. I can't have Cinderella and the Prince not getting along. That would be disastrous for the play."

Roe spoke up. "Eric and Jaimie have been friends for a long time. Maybe, Eric, you shouldn't confront her with anything until the play is over. It's only a few more weeks. Now that I know what happened, I won't mind."

"I see what you mean," Eric said, "even though I'm really mad. You can count on us, Kylie."

"And now moving on to you and Brad." Kurt said, "Or isn't that any of our business?"

"It's not like that exactly," Kylie said, "but a lot has to do with the castle, and I'd like to leave all of the castle stuff until the end, if that's all right."

"And Crofts," Brad said. "I don't like what's going on there. Because of camp this summer and other things."

Kurt nodded soberly, for once not turning the situation into a joke. "It was crappy the way Roe was treated."

Kylie told them what Aniya, Imani's sister, had said. "Imani isn't sure she wants to go to Crofts, even though she could get in easily. She says the kids are a bunch of snobs."

"Well, maybe not all of them, but being there has been hard." Roe got them up to date. "I'm going to play the part, but I haven't decided about camp yet. I'll wait and see."

Kylie, Brad, Kurt, and Eric nodded. They would all wait and see. In Kylie's case, she didn't know if she would still be considered a candidate.

"How about you, Kurt," Kylie asked. "Any problems we need to solve?"

"Now that Beth is free from that leech, I'm good," Kurt said.

"What about that, Beth?" Roe asked. "Any news?"

Beth hadn't decided how much to reveal. Her parents had cautioned against gossiping. They wanted her name kept out of the situation as much as possible. "I'm not allowed to say much," she said finally. "My parents had a meeting with the principal and Mrs. Warde. Mrs. Hunt was there, too. Mom and Dad said she talked to them about how unfair Carroll's grading of my last essay was—that it seemed to be personal. They insisted that I remain with Mrs. Hunt for social studies. This was before everything else happened, of course, and I was at home when it did."

For two days, the school had been a buzz of gossip, but no one knew the facts, other than what a few people had seen from the window—Mr.

Carroll taken away by the police. Beth did learn that it had something to do with questionable photographs taken of the girls she'd seen after school that day. She remembered how angry Carroll had been when she told him she was going to read-through instead of his meeting. He had told her she would miss photos being taken. She breathed a prayer of thanks for her friends and also for her loyalty to them. She might have avoided something awful that day.

"I guess we'll find out when everyone does," she said. "Probably in the newspaper."

"Okay. I guess it's time to talk about what's happening in the castle," Kylie said. "First of all, I was a real jerk about Brad, and I've told him I'm sorry."

Brad smiled. "I could have tried harder. It was kind of fun at first having Kylie jealous, but it got old fast. Robbie is terrific, but I think she has problems, other than being blind, although that's plenty. I don't know how much longer she's going to be staying at the castle, but I think she's part of the mystery?"

"Really?" Kylie said. Brad hadn't said anything to her about that.

"She's supposed to be Leland's niece, but I've never seen them together. And there is a whole section of the castle that's off limits—the doors are always closed. Sometimes I hear voices behind the doors—female voices."

"Robbie claimed to have helped build the fireplace," Kylie added. "I don't think that's possible, but Robbie said *she* had helped her. Robbie never said who that was."

Brad nodded. "Weird, all right. Kylie, tell them about the prompt book."

Kylie explained how the scene that hadn't been blocked appeared suddenly—in Miss Armstrong's writing.

"Okay," Beth said. "I see what you're getting at. But if you think Miss Armstrong went up those steep stairs to the kitchen—remember, she's got a broken leg."

The basement door opened, and there was Dad. "Oh, no," Kylie said. "Is it that late already?" She pulled her phone from her pocket. Ten o'clock and they hadn't even talked about the play.

Dad smiled. "You, at least, are in luck. The rest of us—not so much. For hours, while you've been plotting away, we've been treated to the storm of the season. None of you are going anywhere tonight. We're snowed in. I called your parents. Beth, you'll sleep in Kylie's extra bed tonight. Boys, between blankets, sleeping bags, and all the couch cushions down here, you should manage just fine. Mrs. Kennedy even has extra toothbrushes. He laughed when they cheered. "Don't stay up too late," he said, before closing the door again.

What a wonderful beginning to winter break, Kylie thought. Back with her closest friends! Working together, surely they could figure out all of the problems.

It turned out to be the most fun night Beth could remember, possibly thanks to her. Once Mr. Kennedy left, they never got back to castle business. Snacks and pillow fights became more important—until she remembered something. "Danny! Tomorrow is his birthday! What will happen to his party if we're snowed in?"

"Oh, no," Kurt said. "The poor kid!"

"That's all he's thought about for weeks," Kylie said. "Of course, it might not be cancelled, if the roads are clear."

Brad shook his head. "I checked the forecast on my phone. We'll be lucky if we're out of here by Sunday."

"Luckily, I brought my present for him," Beth said. "I was going to leave it here, so I wouldn't have so much to carry when I came back for the party." Kylie's parents and Beth's were good friends, and her brother Porter was one of Danny's best buddies. "Mom was certain there wouldn't be enough food and has been baking for ages. She even made the surprise birthday cake."

"The kids' party will be postponed," Kylie said, "but in the meantime he's going to have a miserable birthday."

"Unless we do something," Eric said.

And that's when the surprise birthday party planning committee convened. Shortly after midnight, after much giggling and tiptoeing around, the kitchen was decorated with streamers and balloons. Both planned and improvised gifts were on the table, and ingredients for birthday pancakes were set for the griddle.

Beth's last thought before falling asleep was that it was fortunate Roe had set an alarm for the girls, and Brad, his cell phone alarm for the boys. They had to be in the kitchen before Danny!

SCENE 13—SNOWED-IN SATURDAY

ROE AWOKE BEFORE ANYONE ELSE, ahead of the alarm. She would surprise everyone by getting started in the kitchen. Last night had been terrific! When was the last time she had been problem free, just laughing and hanging out with friends? The problems would all come back, of course, but maybe for this snowed-in birthday Saturday, she could pretend they didn't exist.

Pancake ingredients were all set, but she wouldn't start the bacon or coffee for Aunt Jane and Uncle Dan too early. The smell of both might wake everyone up. She checked the fridge. Lots of fresh fruit, so each person could pick their favorite, and she'd set out assorted toppings for the pancakes. Danny would love it, even though it wouldn't make up for missing his party.

In addition to the hockey lessons present from Dad and herself, Roe had also purchased a Spiderman video game she knew he wanted. Kylie had bought a different one, so recent Danny might not know it existed. Kurt brought a huge box of chocolates to share last night. Instead, he wrapped it up for Danny, who would be thrilled to receive candy all for himself. She didn't know what Eric and Brad had dreamed up, other than she saw them hard at work on a giant poster board card and knew they had been in serious consultation with Uncle Dan. Fortunately, Aunt Jane stored all of her party and wrapping supplies in the basement.

Quietly, the basement door opened. Roe didn't expect the boys so early and wasn't sure she was pleased. "Oh, it's you, Eric. That's okay then."

Eric grinned. "The guys are snoring too loud to hear us. Need a helping hand?"

Roe put Eric to work heating the griddle and finding interesting toppings for the pancakes. When he started to ask questions about her mom and the Crofts play, she stopped him. "Not today. In honor of the snowstorm, I'm giving myself a problem-free vacation. Honestly, Eric, last night was so much fun. I haven't had that great a time since our cast party, and that seems ages ago."

"Considering all that's happened, it was ages. It's a deal, Roe. Only cheerful talk today."

Once everything was ready, including the bacon and coffee, Eric said he'd rouse the boys. "And you wake up Kylie and Beth."

"Aye, aye, sir! And I'll have Kylie escort the birthday boy downstairs."

"What about Mr. and Mrs. Kennedy?"

Roe smiled. "We'll let them sleep, if they can. I'll bet the noise will be enough to force them downstairs. I never knew how much I could love snowstorms!"

Kylie tiptoed into Danny's room. "Sound asleep, are you, you old slug?" She shook him hard. "Rise and shine!"

"Go away," Danny said. "What are you doing?"

"Wishing you a happy birthday, dear brother. Come on, everyone is waiting, and pajamas are the correct attire."

"Everyone? The party isn't until this afternoon." But Danny got out of bed.

"Sorry," Kylie said. "Look out the window." She probably should have put it more gently.

"Oh, no!" Danny wailed. "I can't see anything out there."

"We are totally snowed in," Kylie said, "but so are your friends. It looks like you're going to have more than one birthday this year. At the moment, you have a date in the kitchen."

It went even better than Kylie expected. Hearing their footsteps on the back stairway, the boys and girls must have taken cover fast. When Danny opened the door, they all jumped out and began to sing. Kylie had never seen her brother so surprised.

After seating Danny, Roe presented him with an enormous stack of pancakes, with candles on top, along with all kinds of possible additions: chocolate chips, coconut, pineapple chunks, whipped cream. Then she lit the candles, and they all sang again. They were eating happily when Kylie's parents joined them.

"Oh, my," Mom said.

"Don't worry, Mrs. Kennedy," Brad said. "We are also the cleanup committee."

"Actually, I was thinking how kind you are." She gave her son a hug. "Happy birthday, dear."

Danny gave her a whipped cream, chocolaty smile. "My birthday is a little different this year, Mom," he said.

Mom said she'd call his friends to reschedule the party. Kylie thought, though, that Danny seemed fine with the change in plans. "Time for presents," she said.

Danny's eyes popped when Kylie's friends made their presentations. He ripped open the wrappings on the videogames and had to be restrained from going to play them immediately. He was overjoyed by the box of candy and politely thanked Beth for the board game. The rest complimented Beth on her artwork, especially Kylie's parents.

"I never knew you were so talented, Beth," Kylie's mom said.

"A regular artist," Dad said.

"Maybe later we can all play," Kylie said, worried that Beth might think Danny didn't like her gift. But Beth winked at her; she understood little boys. The homemade Castle Bluff Monopoly would mean something long after Danny had grown tired of the video games.

Kurt, it seemed, had another gift besides candy and handed Danny a card. "Consider this a challenge," he said. The challenge was for a snowball fight that afternoon. "Boys against girls," Kurt concluded. "What do you say, Danny? It's supposed to stop snowing later, but we still won't be able to go anywhere."

Danny grinned. It was a wonderful present.

Last, Brad and Eric presented their card. "We got your dad's permission," Brad said. Inside was an invitation for that night—a winter campout for boys only—in the Kennedy's backyard.

"It won't be easy to pitch a tent," Eric said, "but we'll do it! And Mr. Kennedy has plenty of camping gear for cold weather."

"It will be great!" Danny shouted. Then he looked worried. "But what about the girls? Won't they be sad?"

How sweet, Kylie thought. She shook her head. "No way. We'll be plenty happy in our own warm beds." Adamantly, the girls nodded and exchanged grins. None of them thought the boys would make it through the night.

Then Danny looked expectantly at his parents. Didn't they have a present for him? He had thought they might give him hockey lessons, but Roe's father had taken care of that, as well as the equipment he needed.

Dad smiled and put his hand into a shirt pocket. "Unfortunately, the weather means we can't give you our present today and probably not tomorrow, either. The best we can do is a photo. This will be your present from Mom and me."

Dad handed Danny the photo, and to Kylie's amazement, Danny's eyes filled with tears.

"For me, Mom and Dad, really? For my very own?"

"If you take care of him," Mom said.

"Oh, I will. I promise!"

At that, Kylie and Roe insisted on seeing the photograph, too. It was a puppy—a darling puppy. Maybe a cocker spaniel, or at least a relative of one—brown and white, with floppy, soft-looking ears, and the prettiest face Kylie had ever seen.

"He's beautiful," Roe said. "And Danny, even if he is your dog, Kylie and I will help you take care of him whenever you need us."

Kylie nodded. "What will you name him, Danny? As if I couldn't guess."

"Bingo," Danny said.

"Of course," Kylie said. Danny had wanted a dog ever since he had learned the Bingo song when he was only a toddler.

"Winter is a strange time to be adopting a puppy," Dad said, "but this little fellow needs a home right away, and we thought you were the right person to give him one."

Danny was not one for hugs but made an exception this time. "Thank you," he said. "This is the best birthday I've ever had!"

Beth smiled at the success of her board game. Everyone was having a grand time, visiting the familiar spots of Castle Bluff. Instead of jail, landing on a wrong square could send you to detention at CBMS, where you couldn't get out again unless you performed some kind of antic described on a card. Being snowed in was such a welcome relief from reality. Mr. Carroll and the unpleasantness at school seemed so far away.

Earlier, Beth had received a text from Marla Gray. As unlikely as it seemed, the two of them were becoming friends. "Mom finally bought me a phone!" she wrote. "R U snowed in? I am." Beth responded that she, too, was snowed in but at Kylie's house. "Lucky," Marla said.

Beth knew there wasn't much to be happy about at Marla's house. Mr. Gray had been found and was being returned to Castle Bluff to stand trial. Because he was considered a flight risk, he'd be held in jail and not allowed to go home, even if his family had wanted him. That story would hit the papers next week—probably something about Mr. Carroll, too. Beth had been told her name would not be mentioned, although she might have to testify.

"Castle Bluff Middle School has become a hotbed of crime," Marla had said the last time they spoke in person. Maybe it was because Marla had been supportive of her during the Mr. Carroll stuff, or maybe it was because of Marla's enthusiasm for Beth's artwork—she wasn't sure why—but Beth wanted this friendship, even though she wasn't ready to tell the others, especially not Roe. Perhaps if Marla were to apologize? Well, Beth wouldn't mention it. There was nothing less sincere than a forced apology.

"Call U Monday," she texted back.

Marla responded with a smiley face.

Beth returned to a game Danny seemed likely to win. "I kind of wish Imani were here, too," she said.

Kylie nodded. "I agree. Next time."

And Marla, Beth added silently.

After joining the boys outside for a bonfire and marshmallow roast, Kylie, Roe, and Beth went upstairs for some girl time. Kylie could tell Danny was thrilled to be one of the big boys.

Roe giggled. "Aunt Jane is so nervous I'll bet she and Uncle Dan don't get any sleep."

"Mom will be sending Dad outside all night to check on them. I think every spare blanket we own is out there, in addition to sleeping bags and hand and foot warmers—"

Beth shook her head. "I'll bet a quarter that none of them last the night. When we get up tomorrow, we'll find Danny in his bed and the boys in the basement. And I'll bet they sleep until noon." She sighed happily. "It has been such a wonderful day. I don't care if we can't get out tomorrow."

Tears filled Roe's eyes.

"What's wrong?" Kylie asked. "I thought you were having a good time, too."

"Oh, I am. It's just the thought of going back to everyday problems. It's been so horrible."

"I've been thinking something like that since last night," Kylie confessed. "Not that I've had to face anything as bad as you and Beth—just a ton of stress. I think the three of us need to make a vow."

"A vow?" Roe and Beth repeated.

"Yes," Kylie said. "We need to promise that we'll share our problems, so they won't seem as big. And we'll stop being super serious about things that shouldn't matter so much—like being in plays and boyfriends and, well—"

"I like that," Roe said. "If I had talked about what was happening with Crofts and my parents, I might not have felt so alone." Although she wasn't quite ready to tell them about her mother's dementia. Even that wasn't as hard to face as the knowledge that her mother had never loved her. My life has been a lie, she thought.

"Thank goodness I told Kylie about Creepy Carroll," Beth said, "but it would have been better if I had said something sooner." But she wasn't ready to talk to Roe about wanting to be friends with Marla. It's not like I won't be keeping my vow, she thought. I'll tell Roe eventually.

"And about Brad and me—lots of people knew about Robbie. I didn't have to suffer in silence for so long." But I'm still keeping something from them, Kylie thought. My suspicions about Miss Armstrong. Earlier, when they were all together, she'd finally figured out who fifteen-year-old Robbie looked like. She mentally added years to Robbie's appearance and added a few gray hairs. Robbie looked exactly like a much younger Miss Armstrong. But it was all too ridiculous. She needed more proof. Miss Armstrong couldn't be in the castle, could she?

Roe's phone startled them. How late was it? Nine thirty—not so late since it was vacation. "It's this girl named Norma," Roe said. "She's in the play at Crofts. I don't think I want to talk."

"You should," Beth advised. "And we're right here next to you. Whatever she wants, you won't let her get you down."

"Hello?" Roe answered. "Yes, of course I remember you. How are you, Norma?"

Roe listened while Kylie and Beth exchanged concerned glances. In spite of their fine talk, they weren't sure how much more Roe could take.

"Manuel Hernandez? Oh, that is too funny!" Roe burst out laughing. "Well, good, Norma. I'm glad you understand why I'm laughing. Yes, I will, but could I ask someone to come with me. I'm not comfortable yet—Oh. Okay. Thanks. Bye."

Roe turned to the girls and laughed until the tears came, but her tears were different this time. Yes, they were tears of mirth, but they also expressed deep cynicism.

"What in the world was that about?" Kylie demanded.

"You will never believe this. A boy named Manuel Hernandez has been chosen to take over the part of Peter. As one of my fellow Latinos or Hispanics or whatever, he shouldn't mind kissing me. Have you ever heard anything so hysterically funny in your life?"

"As long as you're not hysterical," Beth said. "You're right. It sounds like more prejudice."

Kylie nodded. "Probably, but give him a chance. You've decided to keep the part, and it's not Manny's fault he was picked. I've met him. He's a good actor and a nice guy. He wanted the part in the first place but couldn't audition because of his schedule. Maybe something changed."

Roe looked hopeful. "You think?"

Beth shrugged. "But what did Norma want? You asked if you could invite someone."

"She's having a Hanukkah party next Friday night and has invited the director and whole cast so we can block the Hanukkah scene. She said she understood why I was laughing because she's Jewish. She said the whole cast was mad at Devin. I didn't ask why no one stood up for me sooner, but I said I'd go. Would you mind if I asked Eric instead of one of you?"

They shook their heads. "Eric is a good idea," Kylie said. "He never puts up with anything." When the former vice principal, Mr. Hasting, was being so mean, Eric was Roe's staunchest defender.

Outside, they heard loud laughter. It sounded as if another snowball fight was starting up, and they could hear Mrs. Kennedy shouting out the door, "Boys, you'll get all wet again!"

Beth grinned. "I don't think we're going to get much sleep tonight, either, so let's keep on talking until we're all talked out. First, we should make the vow, Kylie."

Solemnly, Kylie said, "We promise that we will always share our problems and help each other the best we can."

They held hands. "We promise," they said.

SCENE 14—PROMISES TO KEEP

"DARN IT, BINGO! BRING ME that slipper! Good thing you're so cute!" Kylie grinned as she heard Roe race down the hall after the newest family member, who had totally disrupted their lives. Bingo was adorable, and Danny was exhausted trying to train a little fellow who clearly did not see the need of training. Fortunately, Bingo was housebroken and didn't seem to mind going outdoors, but he loved to steal, just for the joy of the chase. Bingo's story would have been a sad one if Dad hadn't found out about him in time. He had been marketing when he overheard a man and woman discussing their plight. They had to move because of their small son's health issues, and they could not take their puppy along. Taking a risk, Dad came to the rescue.

Her whole family was different since September, Kylie reflected. Mom was no longer frazzled about working and was much more laid back. Dad was happy again, realizing he would start a new job right after the new year. Roe had become a sister both to her and Danny, and all three of them had grown so much, at least inside.

When not at the castle rehearsing her cast, she was next door with Mom, Roe, Brad, and Eric, helping to get the Santos's house ready to be listed. Mom had hired the boys to clean and haul out debris, rather than contracting a cleaning service. She was paying them almost as much as she would a service, and they were thrilled. Kylie and Roe were helping to "stage" the house for a showing. This was a different kind of staging than they were used to. Basically, it meant getting rid of everything personal and making each room attractive. Strangers must be able to picture themselves living there. Mom was an expert at this, they discovered. Kylie had thought removing family items would be painful for Roe, but she seemed okay. "I'm moving on," she said. Valuable small items were stored in the Kennedys' attic. Other things were packed into Mom's station wagon and taken to Goodwill.

Kylie and Brad had found nothing amiss at the castle, although they had gone downstairs and peeked inside a few doors. Of course, Miss Armstrong wasn't there; the idea was ridiculous. But how did the missing blocking suddenly appear in the promptbook? Brad decided Kylie must have been mistaken. Well, maybe—but she didn't think so. It wasn't necessary to share her suspicions about Robbie's identity yet.

Thanks to Beth, Marla, and Pryanka, the props were almost ready, and Gee had completed the costumes. Jen Yu knew a boy at the high school who, according to her, was a techie genius. He had offered his light poles and lights and said he would work both lights and sound. Kylie sighed happily. If nothing went wrong, the show would be ready at the end of January. Their performance would be one week after Roe's show at Crofts.

"Kylie!" she could hear Roe shouting. "Get out of bed this instant! Honestly, if it wasn't for me, I think you'd sleep forever."

"Aye, aye, Sir Ma'am!" Kylie stretched herself to the floor. Time for another day.

"It's here," Marla whispered to Beth. The two girls were adding the finishing touches onto the fairy godmother's magic wand and bag.

"Oh, gosh," Beth whispered back. "Is it as bad as you expected?"

"Worse," Marla said, handing Beth the local newspaper.

"Put that away fast!" Brad rushed over and grabbed the paper.

"Why?" Marla asked. "What are you doing?"

"I have no idea," Brad admitted. "Leland told me it was absolutely essential that Robbie not see this newspaper. Where is she?"

"In the kitchen, I think," Beth said. "But Brad, she can't see. And even if she could, it's not like she lives in Castle Bluff."

"I agree that it doesn't make sense, but ditch it anyway." And Brad resumed painting the pumpkin coach he and the other boys had constructed.

Beth shook her head. "Maybe Leland doesn't want Robbie to overhear us talking about it. I want to read what happened, though. At least, I think I do. It's warmer today. Let's take a break and go outside."

The story about Marla's father was pretty much what they expected. He had been apprehended staying with relatives in Nebraska and had been denied bail. The amount of the fraud against the school district was astronomical.

"I'm so sorry, Marla," Beth said.

"Yeah, it's bad, especially for my sister, who still loves him. Mom wants to leave town but can't afford to. I guess all the talk at school will start up again, but this should distract the gossips." She pointed to the other front page article.

Beth gasped. There it was, worse than she feared. *Local Pedophile Teacher Arrested!* Under a mug shot photo of Mr. Carroll was the article.

> *Castle Bluff Middle School teacher and newspaper sponsor removed from school in handcuffs after revealing photos of students found in his possession. The minors involved are receiving counseling.*

It appeared that Mr. Carroll had a record of questionable behavior, and the writer of the article was appalled that CBMS had hired him without doing a proper background check.

The names of the minor students were concealed, but Beth knew who they were. "Thank God for you and Kylie," she said. "I could have been one of them."

Marla shook her head. "I don't think so. You were having your doubts and pulled away in time. You took your essays to Mrs. Hunt and confided in Kylie. That awful, disgusting man! He's even worse than my father."

Beth smiled gratefully. They were such unlikely friends, but it had happened. Cute, freckled, red-headed Bethie and elegant, somber, dark-haired Marla Gray were true friends. Some of the kids were starting to call them the Red and the Black. Beth needed to talk to Roe. And speaking of Roe, there she was, coming up the back path.

Beth and Marla together? Interesting, Roe thought. Well, they both were good artists. Maybe they had been working together on something for the play.

"Hi," she said. "Aren't you cold out here? I came to watch a rehearsal. Kylie inside?"

"Somewhere," Beth said. "We're going back up, too." She opened the door, holding it for Roe and Marla.

As they were starting up the steep steps, Marla seemed to have come to a decision. "Beth, you go on up. I'd like to talk to Roe for a minute—if that's okay with you, Roe."

Roe wasn't sure whether it was or not, but what could she say to the girl who had been her greatest enemy? But she nodded. "See you later, Beth," she said.

Marla patted the step next to her. "Sit," she said, but in a friendly way.

Reluctantly, Roe obeyed. "I see you've got the newspaper. Unbelievable about Mr. Carroll, but at least Beth is out of it."

Marla nodded. "That's why we were outside—to talk about both the articles. Brad said Leland told him to keep it out of the castle. Why, I have no idea."

"Odd that it was Leland. If it had been anyone else, I would have said that they were worried it would distract the cast from the rehearsal."

"Maybe." Marla cleared her throat before stuffing the newspaper into her bag. "Look, Roe, I need to say something, and I need to say it fast before I lose my nerve. I am so sorry for everything I did to you. I was horrible and you didn't deserve it. I hope someday you'll forgive me."

Roe didn't answer. She wasn't certain she could. Even though so much had happened since, the unhappiness and fear of those days was still fresh in her memory. It hadn't been that long ago.

Marla tried again. "I'm not making excuses, but I want you to know I wasn't myself. My family problems had become so ugly that I guess I turned ugly, too. I figured out that my father doesn't love me, and I stopped loving myself. Thanks to Gee, Kylie, Beth, and the rest of the cast, I'm starting to accept myself."

Roe squirmed. She understood quite well where Marla was coming from. "I read the article," she said. "I am sorry."

Marla shrugged. "I'll survive. The only decent thing about the Mr. Carroll story is that the kids at school will be more interested in that than me. And at least the stuff about my father is old news."

In spite of her pretending indifference, Roe could tell how much Marla was hurting. Then, as improbable as it seemed, Roe found herself telling Marla about the Santos family—Mateo and the drugs, her mother's dementia, and everything. Marla said nothing; she just listened. When Roe was finished, she was amazed to see Marla in tears.

"So, you see," Roe said, "I understand how you feel. My mother isn't my mother, and she never loved me. My whole life has been a lie."

"That's exactly how I feel," Marla said. "I'm sorry, Roe—about everything. You sure didn't need me making things worse."

"You had no way of knowing," Roe said. And after finally telling her story to the least likely person in the world, she knew she would be able to tell the people who cared about her.

"Do you think you'll be able to forgive me?"

"I'm starting to already. But let's take it slow, Marla."

Scene 15—Roe's Opening Night

BACKSTAGE IN CROFTS' GREEN ROOM, waiting for Mr. Warner to gather the cast, Roe shivered in anticipation. She was ready; so was everyone. She had total confidence the play would be terrific. And those who truly loved her were in the audience: Dad, Uncle Dan and Aunt Jane, Danny, Beth, Eric, and especially Kylie. In fact, the whole cast and crew of *Cinderella, Cinderella* had come out full force. She grinned. They should see this Green Room, off limits to those not connected with the show. Properly painted green, with all the amenities, including a bathroom—although they were warned not to flush until the performance ended. Instead of only a speaker, there was an actual monitor. They could watch the show when they were not on stage, although Anne was most of the time.

Hanukkah at Norma Kaplan's had turned things around. Having Eric beside her made all the difference. His family attended the same synagogue as the Kaplans, and he already knew them. In time, Roe thought, Norma might become a good friend, and she planned to attend camp, too. It was kind of funny. Norma, a Jew, was playing Miep, the woman who helped the Franks and others. And she, Catholic and Hispanic, was Anne. Roe thought Anne Frank would approve. The party was both fun and helpful to the play, as they took part in lighting the menorah with a family that celebrated Hanukkah. In that atmosphere, blocking the scene was easy. At the end of the party, each guest received a plastic dreidel to take home. Roe gave hers to Danny and taught him to play.

Other cast members had apologized, saying they didn't understand why they hadn't stood up to Devin. Laura Lee, who played Margot, was especially sheepish. "I knew it was wrong," she said. "I was mad when I didn't get Anne, but that wasn't your fault. I never should have taken it out on you." Roe thought of the Germans who had not stood up against the Nazis. Maybe some of them couldn't understand their inaction, either. She decided to keep that thought to herself.

Manny Hernandez as Peter turned out to be a good actor. His main problem was trying to get his non-theater girlfriend to understand why he had to kiss Roe. "I don't feel anything," he'd insisted. Well, Roe knew better. Some of those kisses had been unusual until she told him to stop. But that was her secret. Things might change someday, but for the present, Eric was the right boyfriend for her.

"Only one week to go," Kylie whispered to Brad. "Do you think we'll be ready?"

"Don't you remember what Miss Armstrong used to say? You always think you need two more weeks." He took her hand and smiled. "We'll be ready. We don't have a choice."

Thanks to her best CBT workers, Beth, Marla, and Priyanka, who had slaved exhaustingly all Winter Break, as well as Gee and the light and sound crews from CBHS, the technical aspects had been covered. Roe had pitched in, too. She, Beth, and Imani's dad had taken care of programs, tickets, and posters. Splendid posters had been hung on the walls of schools and in downtown windows. The programs wouldn't be ready until the last minute, but Roe assured her they were perfect. Priyanka had come on as Stage Manager, and soon the play no longer would be Kylie's. She would be sitting in the audience, a nervous wreck.

But tonight belonged to Roe. The Kennedy home would resemble a funeral parlor, Kylie thought, noticing all the bouquets. Roe's father, whom Kylie now called Uncle Carl, held red roses.

Seated on Kylie's other side was Eric, who seemed to relax when Jamie left to find a restroom. Kylie smiled sympathetically at his great sigh. "Thank you for hanging in there. It will be over soon," she said.

"Yes, over," Eric said. "Then I'll set her straight. At least Roe understands that she's my only girlfriend."

"I'm glad she stuck with this show. Do you think she'll decide it's been worth it? It's only been a couple of months."

Eric shook his head. "I think the time between our *Mouse* cast party and Hanukkah felt like years to her. No, if she had the chance to do it again, I think she'd skip this. I'm not sure she still wants to go to camp."

Beth was both amused and worried by the expression on Kurt's face. He gazed in wonder all around the fine auditorium, admiring the plush seats, the wide proscenium and gold velvet curtain. He turned around and stared at the light booth and actually counted the number of hanging fixtures.

"Ellipsoidal, Fresnel, par, strip, scoop—they've got everything. I wonder if Roe could show us around backstage after the show."

"I'm sure she will if it's allowed," Beth said.

"This is where I'll be next year," he said. "You'll see me on that stage— I guarantee it."

"It's a deal," Beth said. But would she be in the audience? For the first time, it hit her that she and Kurt would be in different schools, and other than helping out occasionally, she knew theater wasn't for her. She had already spoken to the sponsor of the art club and planned to attend the next meeting. "Are you sure you want to be an actor, Kurt? Shouldn't you have a Plan B if it doesn't happen?" Her father always talked about having a Plan B.

"There is no Plan B," Kurt said. "I will succeed."

Beth wondered how many people knew this side of Kurt. Most thought he was an amiable clown—always fun, funny, and light-hearted. But Beth knew that when it came to theater he was totally serious. Yes, he was a comedian, but he worked hard at his comedy, and his timing was amazing. And he had received a full scholarship to the camp and was certain to be accepted to Crofts. His family was behind him all the way, too.

"What about you, Beth? You could come to Crofts—after eighth grade, I mean. They've got a wonderful art program."

"Yes, Imani told me. Her father is one of the teachers. Maybe I will. We'll have to see."

But Beth had become acquainted with some of the kids from Castle Bluff High and was learning about the programs there. The CBHS students were somewhat bitter about Crofts receiving all the glory. "We do great shows. You should come and see them," they said. When Beth asked about the opportunities in art, she heard of many classes that interested her. She would never receive a Crofts scholarship. Why should her parents, who had other children, too, pay so much when she could go to CBHS for nothing? It didn't make sense. But would Kurt still want be her boyfriend?

She opened her mouth to ask, but the warning bell sounded, lights dimmed, and up went the curtain. Kurt would be in another world until long after the performance ended. Asking that question was probably a mistake anyway.

Offstage, Roe waited for the first scene to end. Miep presented Mr. Frank with the diary, and then he began to read. How odd to hear her own voice joining his, and then proceeding on its cwn. This part had been taped, of course, weeks ago. *You could do this and you could not do that. They forced Father out of his business. We had to wear yellow stars.* The scene was over, and they were back in time. Soon she would enter. All she had to do was curtsy and shake hands, before going up the stairs to investigate her attic room.

Then she heard her cue line, delivered by Mr. Kraler. Oh my gosh, she thought, what's my first line? She almost panicked until she heard the carillon playing the quarter-hour. Thank goodness for sound cues.

It's the Westertoren! she shouted. After that, she ceased to be Roe. Anne took over until the final curtain.

Soon Kylie forgot she was watching a play and that Anne was only Roe playing a part. That's how good Roe was. Her Anne was fun and silly and judgmental and wise—often at the same time. The audience laughed and cried. The play must have been a surprise for those who thought it was going to be super sad all the time. The whole cast was great, Kylie decided.

At intermission, she, Eric, and Kurt stayed in their seats, barely talking—not wanting to break the mood. The rest of the group headed for the lobby, where Crofts' parents were serving refreshments.

Brad brought her back a cookie "All set for Act Two?"

Kylie nodded. "Thanks."

While it hardly seemed possible, the second act was even better. By the time curtain call came, all of them were in tears, even the boys and Jaimie. Roe got the biggest applause of all.

Suddenly Brad grabbed her arm "Kylie, quick. Look back."

Although unwilling to take her eyes from the stage, Kylie turned around. There in the doorway next to Mr. Warner stood their missing director, Miss Armstrong! Miss Armstrong saw them, too. She gave a start—and fled.

Kylie stood. "Come on, Brad, let's go after her!"

SCENE 16—UNSATISFACTORY ANSWERS

TOO LATE! MISS ARMSTRONG HAD disappeared. "It's no use, Brad. At least we know she's in town. Let's go congratulate Roe. Then we'll go to my house."

Now Kylie was certain Miss Armstrong was staying at the castle. She and Brad would march over there in the morning and insist on confronting her. Was she worried or relieved or angry? Maybe all three.

The Kennedys and Roe's dad were surprising Roe with a party at the Kennedy's house. All her friends from CBT had been invited. After the last performance on Sunday, Roe would attend Crofts' cast party at a grand hotel in the next town. They didn't even have to strike. A professional group would take care of it. Kylie shook her head. Taking apart what they had created—laughing and crying with friends—that was one of the best parts of a CBT show. She wondered what it was like at the public high school.

Kylie and Brad joined the swarms of fans surrounding Roe. When it was finally her turn, Kylie hugged her tight. "Roe, you were absolutely perfect. I forgot you weren't Anne." That was the highest compliment Roe could have received.

Roe and her father stopped for ice cream on the way home—the Kennedy's home, that is. Her father was staying in their old house, although he had been told quite firmly by Aunt Jane that he must not make a mess. They had grinned at that. Roe's dad wasn't exactly the messy type. Both hoped the house would sell soon.

"This must seem like a letdown to you," Dad said. "Ice cream with your father."

"Not really. It's good to relax."

"You were wonderful, Roe. I'm proud of you."

Roe smiled. She was proud, too, although she would be glad when it was over. "Thanks, but it will be good to get back to just regular school. It's been hard doing both. After the cast party, it will be time for Kylie's big event."

"No more theater this year?"

Roe shook her head. "Just the musical, and a frog sings better than I do. I might sign up for a crew that doesn't take much time. Eric and Jaimie will audition; they're the only singers in our group. Kurt was cast in a community theater show."

"Well, what do you say we pick up a gallon of ice cream to take back?"

"Good idea, but better make it quarts of assorted flavors."

The Kennedy house was dark when they pulled into the Santos's driveway. No cars were parked in either one. "That's odd," Roe said. "They must have gone out." That hurt. This was her big night, and she should have been invited, even though ice cream with Dad had been a treat.

"Let's go check," Dad said. "Maybe they're back in the kitchen."

Roe shrugged. It didn't seem likely, but she followed Dad. On the top step of the porch, she guessed. Not a brilliant deduction on her part—the sounds of shushing from inside were unmistakable. It was her turn to have a surprise party.

Early the next morning, Kylie and Brad made their way to the castle. "Your theory seems pretty far-fetched," Brad said. "I'll let you do the talking."

"Okay, but I'm glad you're with me."

Leland answered but just stood there waiting.

"We've come to see Miss Armstrong," Kylie said.

The butler nodded. "She's been expecting you. Mrs. Grainger is here, too."

Kylie threw Brad a triumphant look. Gee's presence was a bit of a surprise, but on reflection she decided there was no way Gee wouldn't have been involved, as well as Leland and Mr. Markey. Too much planning had gone into the cover-up—or conspiracy. Perhaps they would finally learn the truth.

"I believe they're upstairs," Leland said.

Outside the kitchen, they heard hearty laughter coming from Gee. Brad quietly opened the door.

"Oh," Gee said, flustered. "Maybe I should leave. You'll want some privacy."

Kylie shook her head. "Please stay."

"Sit down," Miss Armstrong said quietly. "You deserve an explanation, but I hardly know where to start." The pause that followed was too long.

"I suppose for me," Kylie said finally, "the beginning was when I bumped into you rushing out of the school. Is that when you broke your leg? You seem to have recovered." Kylie hadn't meant to sound sarcastic but seeing Miss Armstrong flush, she must have.

"A slight exaggeration," Miss Armstrong admitted. "I did sprain my ankle. I suppose I thought it more poetic or theatrical when I wrote 'break a leg.'"

"And that was necessary, why?" Brad asked.

Miss Armstrong and Gee looked at each other and remained silent.

"It was because of Mr. Carroll, wasn't it?" Kylie said gently. "You left school because of him."

The director nodded. "Yes, I was afraid of confronting him. Afraid he might remember me."

"He did remember. What did he do? Did he—" Kylie began.

"Oh, no, not me—my sister! And he threatened to hurt her further if we said anything."

Kylie was almost there. It was worse than she expected, but it was starting to make sense. "Robbie was one of Mr. Carroll's victims?"

"Sister? You're kidding!" Brad said loudly.

Kylie nodded. "I guessed you were related."

"I was terrified of him discovering her. We never reported him, but he knew we could have. We'd been living with my aunt in Long Meadow. I thought about us leaving the state, but I wanted to stay nearby because of what he might do to others—and the play and—"

"Is that why Robbie is blind? Did Mr. Carroll cause it?" Brad interrupted, shaking with rage.

Miss Armstrong shook her head. "No, that happened later. She was terribly ill with a high fever, although the abuse she suffered might have triggered her illness. But she's starting to regain her confidence. I couldn't take the chance she'd see him."

"And so you went to the castle to hide," Brad continued. "How did you manage that?"

"I didn't know it at the time, but Leland and my aunt used to be great friends. More than friends, actually. It was her suggestion. She got in touch with him, and he arranged with Mr. Markey for the three of us—Aunt Janet, Robbie, and me—to come here. Later, Gee discovered us, so we let her in on it. Then I made an anonymous call to school."

Kylie and Brad stared at each other, neither daring to speak. Finally, Kylie gathered her courage. She was furious, but she needed to remain calm and respectful. "Miss Armstrong, I'm sorry about what you and Robbie went through; I'm sure it was awful. But didn't you think about Beth and the other girls?"

"Beth?" Miss Armstrong exclaimed.

Oh, right. Miss Armstrong wouldn't know about Beth. Names weren't in the newspaper article. Kylie hurried on. "Beth managed to escape, but the other girls—three of them were photographed without their clothes on. They're going to be testifying against Mr. Carroll, and they're so embarrassed by what happened, I don't think they'll ever return to school. I'm glad you made that call, even if it was anonymous, but I think you owed us more."

Miss Armstrong dropped her head. "I understand how you feel," she said.

"And you knew about this, too, Gee," Brad said. "I'm afraid that the adults in charge kind of let us down."

"Well, everything worked out," Gee said, "so we can let it go."

Kylie remembered her mother's warning about Gee when they first began rehearsals. Something about Mrs. Grainger being a nice lady but that she made up the rules as she went along. Now Kylie understood.

"Yes, let's put this behind us," Miss Armstrong said. "I truly appreciate all you've done for Robbie—especially you, Brad. And Kylie, you've done a wonderful job with the show; it's certain to be a big hit. Showtime next week! Lots to do!"

But why didn't you come back after Mr. Carroll was arrested? Kylie wanted to ask. Abruptly, though, Miss Armstrong and Gee left before Kylie could. "I don't know what to do," she whispered.

Brad shook his head. "Me neither. All our parents, especially Beth's, would flip if they knew the truth."

"I don't want to tell them, do you?" Kylie was so overcome her voice shook.

"No, even though we should. Miss Armstrong must realize she broke the law."

"Really?"

"Aren't teachers required to report anything or anyone that could be a danger to students?"

Kylie gasped. "Would she be arrested?"

Brad shrugged. "Hard to tell. Definitely fired."

Kylie made a sudden decision. "Brad, even if we're wrong not telling anyone, let's not. If it comes out eventually, it won't be from us. Mr. Carroll is gone, and Miss Armstrong and Robbie have suffered enough."

"I agree, but I'm glad there won't be any more plays this year and that we'll graduate in June."

"Me, too. Miss Armstrong isn't the person I thought she was. I always thought she was so perfect."

Brad nodded. "I guess she's like most people—terrific in some ways but not in others."

"**K**YLIE, SUCH WONDERFUL NEWS! WAIT until you find out!" Roe burst into Kylie's room, flushed with excitement.

Sitting at her desk attempting to block the curtain call, Kylie grinned. "You're so anxious to tell me, I won't have to wait long. What's up?"

"It's Miss Armstrong. I just found out she's accepted a teaching position at Crofts next fall. She might be one of our teachers. Isn't that super?"

No response. "Kylie?"

"I guess," Kylie said slowly. "I'll have to think about it. Will she be on staff at camp this summer? Not that I'll be going, of course."

"Well, no. She said she's going to travel with her aunt and sister, but at least if we go to Crofts, she'll be with us next year. Weird that she and Robbie are related. But Kylie, you don't seem pleased."

"Oh, it's fine. But I've got to concentrate on blocking the curtain call for dress rehearsal. It's harder than I expected. And I've got tons of homework."

"Well, okay . . . I'll let you get on with it then."

Kylie had been acting strange ever since last Saturday, Roe thought. Maybe she was worried about the play. Or maybe she was sad because she thought she'd lose her partial camp scholarship. Roe smiled. What a surprise her friend would have soon!

In private, Roe had spoken to both Mr. Warner and Miss Armstrong about Kylie's role in *Cinderella, Cinderella*. "It's not fair that people don't know Kylie gave up her part to direct," Roe said. "She could lose her scholarship when she's done more for CBT than anyone else this year."

The two directors agreed, and Mr. Warner met with the head of the school. They determined that Kylie deserved a full camp scholarship, once they checked that she was earning top grades at school.

What only Roe, Imani, and the printer knew, though, was that Kylie's name was listed in the program as director.

Roe had decided to attend camp, although she hadn't totally made up her mind about Crofts next year. Her dad advised her to wait and see. That's just what she would do.

Beth was glad Miss Armstrong had taken over the difficult job of aging Imani for her part as Fairy Godmother. "Watch carefully, Beth, so you can do it in the future. Stage makeup is an art, too. You should volunteer to be on the makeup crew for the musical."

"Mmmm, maybe," Beth murmured. Miss Armstrong was acting almost too friendly. The director had never paid so much attention to her before. It was as if—no, she couldn't possibly know about Mr. Carroll. But it was good to have Miss Armstrong back, even though her explanation for going away seemed weak. She said that her leg had taken longer to heal than expected and she wanted to help her sister adjust to her seeing-eye dog. But Miss Armstrong didn't even limp, and Brad was the one who'd helped Robbie. So Robbie was her sister, but was Robbie really related to Leland? Beth shrugged. It was all very strange.

"It's just as I always said, the first dress rehearsal is difficult, but the second one is fine." Had Miss Armstrong been talking all along? Beth had better tune in. But the teacher hadn't noticed her lack of attention. She was talking with Imani.

"There." Miss Armstrong finished. "You look grand. I am glad you're playing the role."

"Thank you," Imani said.

"You're perfect," Beth said, anxious to leave. "I'd better see how Marla is doing." Beth was learning to pay attention to what made her uncomfortable.

Marla, of course, was handling her own makeup. "Marla, you look absolutely wicked! Your eyes are going to bulge out and hypnotize the whole audience. They won't see anything else."

Marla gave an intentionally evil grin. "That is the plan," she said. "So did you find out if you can go Tuesday night?"

"Yep. My parents think it's a great idea, especially since Imani's mother will drive."

Beth, Imani, Marla, and other members of Art Club were going to CBHS's Arts Festival. Beth was determined to make new friends—classmates who would be with her next year in eighth grade and who planned on attending the public high school. If she didn't, she'd be lonely after her old friends graduated. Marla would attend the high school, of course, but Beth planned to keep an eye on her. Marla was interested in a boy who went there—one who was often in trouble. She would always be attracted to trouble, Beth feared.

"Ten minutes," Stage Manager Priyanka called.

"Thank you, ten," Beth said, not noticing how naturally she had used the correct theater response.

Kylie sat at the back of *their* theater, sometimes called the Markey Castle ballroom, and stared at the program. Her name was listed as director! Now everyone would know. Tears formed, and she grabbed a tissue in time to keep them from falling. No wonder Roe kept the programs hidden until the last possible minute. The cast and crew had meant it as a surprise for her. Inside, in place of the traditional Director's Note, were messages of gratitude from all of them, surrounded by smiley faces and hearts.

Perhaps—Kylie began to hope—perhaps this would satisfy Crofts, and she would be able to go to camp after all. Her family's financial situation had improved, and her grades were right where they needed to be. Did she want to go, though? Yes! Her doubts had crept in when she didn't think it was possible. Brad needed to bring up one more grade, but he was well on the way to doing it. He'd already earned so much money that his parents promised to give him the remainder as a graduation present. Roe, Eric, Kurt, Brad, and Kylie—with three wonderful weeks at camp ahead of them, and then the rest of the summer to decide about next year. Time was what she needed. Time to think about all of the things that occurred this year—positive and negative. Then she would trust herself to make the right choices.

The lights dimmed. It was time for Cinderella in the castle. Then, after two more performances, Cinderella would take off her elegant gown in favor of ripped jeans and a sweater. Finally, Cinderella would return to middle school.

ACT THREE - CAMP SHAKESPEARE

And one man in his time plays many parts.
—William Shakespeare, *Hamlet*

SCENE 1

Something's Rotten . . .
—William Shakespeare, *Hamlet*

KYLIE KENNEDY BREATHED A SIGH of relief. Not bad, she told herself—except for that one question. The directors and casting committee said she'd read okay, had good stage presence, and that her improvs were adequate. Kylie smiled. For them, "adequate" might mean lousy, but for her, it was great! Thank goodness Drama Club had decided to concentrate on mime and improvisation this spring. It had been the sensible thing to do, considering that a substitute teacher took Miss Armstrong's place. Castle Bluff Theater without Miss Armstrong—hard to imagine!

Kylie had been at Camp Shimmer Lake, Crofts' performing arts camp, for three days, and it felt like three weeks. But only two weeks ago she hadn't even graduated, still caught up in school assignments that had been pushed aside in favor of chairing the costumes committee for the spring musical and working on decorations for the eighth-grade dance. Other than modeling the new CSL T-shirt imprinted with drama masks, a shining lake, and sandy dunes on a blue background, she hadn't glanced at the other material from Crofts, figuring it contained a list of clothing and stuff she'd need to pack. Kylie wasn't concerned. After attending plenty of camps, she was certain to have everything. Roe, though, had squirreled herself in her room the moment the information arrived. For the most part, she had opted out of spring social events at middle school.

"I wish she'd told me we had to memorize a monologue for audition," Kylie muttered, knowing she wasn't being fair. Roe had tried to warn her, but Kylie didn't want to miss a second of the last days at Castle Bluff Middle School. She had more exciting things to do—than discovering she had to memorize Shakespeare!

> *Shall I speak ill of him that is my husband?*
> *Ah, poor my lord, what tongue shall smooth thy name*
> *When I, thy three-hours wife, have mangled it?*
> *But wherefore, villain, didst thou kill my cousin?*
> *That villain cousin would have killed my husband.*
> *Back, foolish tears, back to your native spring!*

And on and on forever. Juliet was only thirteen. What thirteen-year-old girl talked like that? Or what thirteen-year-old boy? Kylie giggled, remembering that boys had taken the girl parts back in Shakespeare's day. But that question! What if it really mattered?

"You did that well," the director had said, when she finally finished the monologue.

> *There is no end, no limit, measure, bound,*
> *In that word's death; no words can that woe sound.*

Kylie had put all the emotion she could muster into that ending. "Now tell us what it means."

"What it means?" Kylie didn't know. She'd memorized the whole thing on the bus coming to camp and had been proud that she'd applied herself, instead of taking part in her friends' fun and foolishness. Was it her fault they'd read *Macbeth* and *Hamlet* in middle school, instead of *Romeo and Juliet?* She guessed she could have rented the movie, but there hadn't been time to watch it. Kylie ventured a few possibilities before admitting she had no idea what the monologue meant.

The director was patient. "Understanding your role is important," she said. "Keep that in mind next time." Kylie wondered if there'd be a next time.

Everything about camp was different from what she'd expected, Kylie thought, as she sauntered down the wooded path toward her assigned cabin. The thick woods of sugar and red maple and the log cabins brought back memories of old Camp Chippewa Bay in Wisconsin, but the main building there was a rustic lodge, not a starkly modern building called Crofts House that looked as if it belonged on a sterile junior college campus. The theater inside was terrific—huge stage and equipment that would do credit to Broadway. The complex included a scene shop, a props room, a wing for building costumes as well as storing them, and many rehearsal areas and a main lounge. Campers ate in a large cafeteria, not a place that would ever be called a mess hall. They could go swimming, of course, but in an indoor pool—not in a lake with swimming tests to see who might be allowed to go out to the rafts. For some reason, Shimmer Lake was out of bounds this summer. No one Kylie had talked to seemed to know why.

The campgrounds reminded Kylie of spokes on a bicycle wheel. The main road was paved and led to the theater and a large parking lot. Then shooting off in a circle were paths leading to the cabins and other sites not yet explored. Kylie shared space with five other girls—Roe and Jaimie from Castle Bluff Middle School—and three older, Megan, Charlotte, and Jean. Megan, age nineteen, a college student and a graduate of Crofts performing Arts High, was the cabin leader. So far, they had been too busy to meet with their younger charges.

Kylie might have continued drifting along in a dream world if she hadn't become aware of voices. Could they be coming from the spirits of the woods? Unlikely. No, just other nervous actors practicing their monologues in various coves off the trail.

> *There is a willow grows aslant the brook,*
> *That shows his hoar leaves in the glassy stream.*

Jaimie's voice. Should she tell Jamie she'd better know what the words meant? Nope, each girl for herself! Jaimie, at least, had the advantage of having read *Hamlet* recently in English class. Kylie continued down the trail, suddenly aware of the sweet smell of pine. At least the odors were like her Wisconsin camp. This area of Michigan had more sand dunes than woods. She looked forward to seeing them.

> *Now the hungry lion roars*
> *And the wolf behowls the moon;*
> *Whilst the heavy ploughman snores,*
> *All with weary task foredone.*

She didn't know what play that was from, but Kurt sounded really good. Even though he was a major clown in real life, he was serious about acting.

He was determined to get into Crofts—and maybe even go to New York someday.

All of the CBT boys were nervous. Back home, they were practically guaranteed good parts because there were so few of them. Here, there were as many boys as girls.

The walk seemed especially long today—maybe because Kylie was anxious to see if she had any mail. Each person in the cabin had weekly chores. Hers this week was dusting and sweeping out the cabin. Megan had mail duty and would take letters and packages from the main office to the cabin, where each girl had her own mailbag attached to a hook on the wall.

> *Tomorrow, and tomorrow, and tomorrow*
> *Creeps in this petty pace from day to day,*
> *And all our yesterdays have lighted fools*
> *The way to dusty death. Out, out, brief candle!*

Oh, gosh, Eric was so lucky! Kylie softly recited the rest of the line along with him, even though neither could see each other.

> *Life's but a walking shadow, a poor player,*
> *That struts and frets his hour upon the stage,*
> *And then is heard no more. It is a tale*
> *Told by an idiot, full of sound and fury,*
> *Signifying nothing.*

Eric wouldn't have any trouble explaining what his monologue meant. Not after studying practically every word of *Macbeth* and taking all those quizzes. And it was a nice, short, monologue, unlike hers. But she wasn't in competition with Eric. Brad had auditioned before her. Kylie knew he didn't know anything about his speech, either. It was something famous from Julius Caesar that both had heard before.

> *Buenas dias. Como esta usted?*

Bewildered, Kylie took the path leading to a familiar voice that had progressed to counting to ten in Spanish. And there, sitting on a log next to a fire pit, with headphones covering her ears, was Kylie's best friend.

"Roe?" No answer. Kylie tapped her on the shoulder and Roe screamed. Calmly, Kylie removed the headphones.

"Kylie! You scared me!"

Kylie grinned. "I noticed. I overheard you on the trail. That was not Shakespeare."

"Not even close," Roe admitted. "I'd like to be able to say a few words in Spanish when I finally get to meet my grandparents. Too bad I took French because my Spanish sounds French, but my *mother* insisted. No Spanish for Rosita. Crazy! So why did she name me Rosita? Oh, right, she didn't."

Kylie winced at her friend's bitterness. She knew how hard it was for Roe to talk about the woman who had turned out not to be her mother, so she changed the subject quickly. "Everyone but you is going nuts preparing for auditions—unless they're done. Then they're going nuts waiting for the results."

"Mine is right before lunch. I'll just take whatever comes. I don't expect much anyway. How did yours go?"

Kylie shrugged. "Not sure. There were three directors, and they did say I did well and that my improv was okay."

"That's great, then."

"Well, maybe." Kylie paused. Should she say anything? Roe was her best friend. It wouldn't be like telling Jaimie. "Roe, they asked me to explain my monologue—to tell them what Juliet meant. I didn't have the foggiest idea, and I might have really blown it. Do you understand yours?"

Roe nodded. "Yes, I studied it before I started to memorize. It's a famous speech from *The Merchant of Venice*—Portia talking about mercy. I love it. I didn't have time to read the whole play, but I read some and checked out the Cliff Notes. I think I can explain it okay. But, Kylie, don't worry. Neither of us will get more than an extra. Haven't you figured out that we're the youngest here?"

"I guess you're right," Kylie said. "Some of the campers are college students. I feel like a little kid again."

"To them, we probably are, and major nuisances besides. Kind of how we felt last year about seventh graders—the bottom of the heap. We'll be freshmen next year, so we might as well get used to it. We're back to 'no small parts' again." Roe checked her watch. "I sure miss my phone, but it doesn't work unless I'm in the lounge."

"Even there, the Wi-Fi is awful," Kylie said. "Time for your audition?"

"Almost."

"Well, break a leg!"

"*Adios,* Kylie."

Roe and Kylie departed in opposite directions. Roe hoped they would remain best friends, but it was likely they'd continue down different paths in the years ahead. The mail had arrived, and Roe's letter from her father included a photo of a large *Sold* sign in front of their house. Even though she'd been living with Kylie's family for months and was loved and cared for, the photo made Roe feel homeless. Her father had rented a small studio apartment in Castle Bluff, but it was uncertain where he'd decide to live next. Where would she belong? Mother wouldn't want her, even if she were to recover. Home was with Dad, wherever that might turn out to be.

Auditions were running behind, so Roe looked over her monologue in a small waiting room next to the stage. She was engrossed in Portia's argument that mercy is greater than power when she became aware of voices outside the door. Voices she soon recognized as Cress Morgan, an old acquaintance, and Norma Kaplan, the girl who played Miep in *Anne Frank*.

"I don't get it," Cress said. "Everything—absolutely everything— is being run on a shoestring budget this summer. No modern plays, no big musicals."

Roe pricked up her ears. She knew there would be two plays and a musical, but what they were hadn't been announced. The auditions were unified, which meant they were for all of the shows.

"All of a sudden, it's like the camp is broke. Even the food is crappy."

Roe agreed with Norma about the meals. They were worse than Castle Bluff Middle School's lunches.

"And Shakespeare—that's crazy! As if most of the kids here, especially the younger ones, can handle Shakespeare or want to."

"*Dear Brutus* isn't Shakespeare, Cress."

"No, but it's so old and fits in. And the other two shows are *The Dream* and a musical written by a few of the college students. And get this, it's called *Lost in Arden Woods!*"

"Shakespeare again." A pause as if the girls were thinking. Roe shook her head, confused. The shows they mentioned were not written by Shakespeare.

"I've got it!" Norma said suddenly. "Now I understand! *Brutus* and *Dream* are in public domain."

"And they won't have to pay for the rights to the musical, either, since some kids wrote it."

"The set designers and construction crews are complaining that they'll be building only one set—a forest scene. All of the plays will use the same set!"

"Everyone is totally pissed that we can't go swimming in Shimmer Lake."

"Or boating. Camp Shimmer Lake without a lake. Crummy."

"Something's rotten in the state of Denmark," Cress said.

"You mean in Michigan," Norma corrected.

Laughing in a way that sounded forced and cynical, they walked away. Shrugging, Roe put down her monologue. It was her turn.

SCENE 2

Wilt thou reach stars because they shine on thee?
— William Shakespeare, *The Two Gentlemen of Verona*

"TWO LETTERS!" KYLIE GRABBED THE envelopes sticking out of her mailbag and collapsed on her bed to devour them. A skinny one addressed in an overly-large print from Danny, and a thick, probably juicy one from Beth. She skimmed through Danny's. Lots of fun with friends . . . swimming at the pool . . . learning how to skateboard. "Mom makes me wear a helmet, which is not cool!" he complained. Good for Mom, Kylie thought. With her full-time job and Dad commuting to Wisconsin, Mom had a lot on her plate. The rest of Danny's short note was about his dog Bingo's tricks and antics. "From Danny," he abruptly signed off. "Love" would have been way too daring for the eleven-year-old.

"Now for Beth."

> *Hi, Kylie!*
>
> *Hope you're having a great time at camp and end up with a lead. I will try to talk Dad into driving me up to see the performances, or maybe I can get a ride with your folks. Let me know the date.*
>
> *It's hard to believe that you and Roe have been gone for such a short time. A lot is happening here. Marla and I are working on another show. Really! The park district and the high school are doing it together. It's a comedy called "Play*

On!" about a group putting on a show in which everything goes wrong. It's kind of a play within a play. Marla has a small part, but she's happy because the competition was fierce. Most cast members are juniors, seniors, or adults. Marla and I are working on painting sets. The tech director has given me lots of compliments and says he hopes I'll help out when I'm a student there. The show will be toward the middle of July, so you'll probably get to see it. Only two performances, though. I've made new friends from the high school, and I kind of wish I was going there next year instead of pokey old middle school. But I shouldn't complain. I'm having more fun than I expected with you and Roe away and Imani visiting her grandparents in London.

I went down your street the other day. A big SOLD sign was outside Roe's house. It looks really sad and final. I wonder who your new neighbors will be. Baby sister is crying, so the tired babysitting big sister must go to the rescue.

Love,

Beth

P.S. I don't know if anyone told you but Kurt and I broke up the day before you left. That's why I haven't mentioned him. I get upset when I think about it, so I'm glad he's not around right now. Just wanted to say something, so you're not mad if you see him with some other girl.

Wow! For someone who decided not to act anymore, Beth was sure good at a dramatic exit. But she was a writer and an artist. Both required dramatic flair. Kylie returned the letter to its envelope. She'd share it with Roe as soon as they had some privacy.

Beth and Kurt. Well, Kylie shouldn't be surprised. They had always seemed an odd pair, but it wasn't that weird when they were both in middle school. Soon Kurt would be a freshman at Crofts and Beth only in eighth grade. Kylie wondered who had done the breaking up. Good thing Beth had plenty to do this summer.

The door of the cabin opened. "Jaimie, how did your audition go?"

"Scary. I knew enough about Ophelia since we read Hamlet last year, but I didn't know what hoar leaves were. Do you?" Kylie shook her head. "At least they were more interested in my singing than in my acting."

"You'll probably make the musical then, but everyone knows you can act, too. You were a perfect Cinderella."

"Thanks, Kylie. That was so much fun. I'll bet Mr. Markey misses us."

Kylie agreed. "When I write to Beth, I'll ask her to visit him."

"Yeah, Beth. Kurt told me they broke up. I thought he'd get sick of her. Such a baby!" She gave a little grin before examining her mailbag. The grin quickly turned into a frown. "Nothing. Only reason I came back to the cabin."

"It's only been a few days," Kylie said. "I didn't get much. Maybe we should go to lunch now." She almost mentioned Roe but stopped herself. Jaimie bristled every time she heard Roe's name—because of Eric. Jaimie liked Eric, but Eric liked Roe. Eric was a singer, too. He and Jaimie were likely to be cast together once more. Kylie thought about the smirk following her nasty comment about Beth. What was Jaimie up to now?

The gang sat together in the cafeteria. While the girls looked askance at the greasy grilled cheese sandwiches, lumpy tomato soup, pickles and celery sticks, the boys wolfed down everything and then looked around for dessert. "I'm going to gain a ton this summer," Kylie whispered to Roe.

Roe nodded, although she wasn't worried for herself; she could use a few more pounds. She was still thinking about Cress and Norma's conversation. It must be expensive to feed all these hungry actors, especially since so many were on scholarship. Maybe the people who ran the camp were in financial trouble. The artistic director and owner, Mrs. Crofts-Baker, hadn't made an appearance yet—not even to welcome them.

As soon as packaged cookies were served, the head counselor, Jay Wilson, made an announcement. "After lunch, only a few more auditions to go. Those who are finished, enjoy your free time until dinner. Then I'll lead you on a flashlight hike before our final lights out. The directors said to tell you they are very pleased with what they've heard so far and will announce their casts tomorrow afternoon."

Free time. To do what? Kylie considered returning to Barrymore Cabin for a nap or joining the others in the large student lounge, where it was certain they would be trying desperately to rejoin the world of Wi-Fi.

"Hey, Kyle. Got any plans?"

"Hi, Brad, I can't decide. A nap or the Internet are my only ideas."

"A nap will mean you won't sleep tonight, and the lounge is packed. Let's explore instead. Eric and Roe's idea—mainly Roe's. She's got something definite on her mind."

They met Eric and Roe on the main driveway outside of Crofts House. "Should we ask Jaimie and Kurt?" Kylie wondered, although she'd rather not.

"Interesting development," Eric said. "They're in the lounge together and being very cozy. Something's going on with those two. At least I'm being left alone, for a change. If it weren't for Beth, I'd be jumping up and down."

"Kurt and Beth broke up," Kylie said. "I don't know whose idea it was."

"Hope it was Beth's." Eric said.

"Well, are we going or not?"

Roe sounded impatient—unlike her. "Something bothering you, Roe? Explain," Kylie insisted. "Right now."

"Let's get to a path first, then I will."

"Cress and Norma really sounded like something was wrong with camp—" Roe had related what she overheard—"that maybe it was going broke and the plays were chosen because they could be done cheaply. I've never heard of them, have you?"

They shook their heads. "I wonder why they thought all the plays had to do with Shakespeare," Brad said. "The monologues were awfully advanced for an audition, at least for us."

"They said the plays are in public domain. I'm not sure what that means."

"So old no one has to pay for the rights anymore," Eric said. "No royalty or script costs. All of Shakespeare's plays qualify."

Roe nodded. "Which means cheap. We'll probably get photocopies or sides, instead of a full script. Also, they said some of the tech people are mad because the same set will be used for all three plays."

"Actually, I think one set is a cool idea," Brad said. "It will save time as well as money. But the thing that interests me most is Shimmer Lake being off-limits. The camp brochure advertises the lake as one of its main attractions."

"That's what I thought," Roe said. "And did you notice all the bottled water in the cafeteria? We've got some in our cabin, too."

"With signs saying be sure to use it for drinking," Kylie added.

Eric pulled a map from his pocket. "So we hike to the lake. I was hoping for the dunes, but we'll do that another day."

With Eric's map to guide them, they determined what spoke in the camp's wheel, using Kylie's analogy, would lead to Shimmer Lake. "Should be just under a mile," Eric said, checking his watch. "Two now—let's plan to be back no later than five."

It was good for the four of them to be together again, Kylie thought. When the path was wide enough, they walked four abreast. Other times they divided into twosomes—not necessarily boy and girl—and sometimes, single file. Curiously, auditions and casting didn't seem that important now. Kylie guessed they all knew their parts would be small.

Instead, they talked about the few letters they'd received from home and elsewhere. Brad had heard from Leland with news about Miss Armstrong and Robbie. "They're seeing a specialist in Germany, who thinks Robbie's sight might be restored with a new kind of surgery."

"That would be wonderful," Kylie said, remembering when her main feeling toward Robbie was jealousy. She told the group about Beth and Marla's theater activities.

"Sounds fun," Roe said. "Maybe more than we're having."

Kylie waited for Roe to share her news about the house selling, but she stayed quiet. Oh well, that was Roe's business. Eric was strangely quiet, too. Maybe he hadn't heard anything from home yet. Kylie told them about Danny's note. All of them had a special interest in him after the surprise snowed-in birthday party last winter.

Eric laughed. "Danny skateboarding? Broken bones ahead!"

Kylie shuddered. "I hope not."

Eric stopped. "We're here," he announced. The path ahead was roped off with a crudely written Keep Out sign attached. "Now what?"

Brad shrugged. "The sign doesn't look very official."

"And it doesn't say dangerous," Roe observed. "I think we should go under the rope. What could they do to us, anyway?"

Whoever they were, Kylie thought. It was unlike Roe to be so daring. Normally, she and Eric were the sensible ones. All agreed, though, and held up the rope for each other. "I never expected a drama camp to be so dramatic." Kylie giggled nervously.

The path grew narrower, so they proceeded single file through brush and sticker bushes until there it was—Shimmer Lake, not nearly as large as the lake they knew, Lake Michigan, but still sizable. Boats were chained along the shore, and the rafts Kylie had hoped to swim to were at various, challenging distances. But the lake, which should have been alive with pleasure seekers, was deserted and lonely. In spite of the sunshine and crispy cool weather, the lake did not sparkle as one might expect from a lake called Shimmer.

"I don't understand," Roe began, but Brad sniffed the air and held up his hand.

"Wait here," he insisted, before walking cautiously to the water's edge. They watched him cup his hand into the water, sniff, and then wrinkle his nose. Polluted," he reported. "Gross!"

"But according to Cress and Norma, they swam here last summer," Roe objected.

"And the lake is featured in the brochure." Kylie shook her head. "This is recent, and it's almost like the people in charge of the camp don't want anyone to know."

"Someone needs to know," Brad said. "I'm coming back for a sample as soon as I can find a jar. Then we'll decide who can figure out what it is."

"My dad," Roe said softly. "He's coming soon. My mother is in a place near here, and he's going to see how she's doing. He'll visit us, too, for Kylie's and my birthdays. You can give him the sample, Brad. He'll turn it over to one of the men in his lab."

"Wish we didn't have to wait so long," Brad said. But they knew that as the CEO of a large pharmaceutical company, Mr. Santos was the very person to help.

Water too dangerous to drink or to swim in—that could ruin the camp, Kylie thought. Cleaning the lake would cost a fortune. "Let's go back," she said quietly. "Brad, be sure to wash your hands."

"With bottled water and lots of soap," he agreed.

It was hard to concentrate on anything else, but Roe thought a flashlight hike at night would make a good diversion. Most of the campers were bundles of tension about the casting. She, Eric, Kylie, and Brad had the polluted lake on their minds as well. If the water was truly dangerous to drink, the warning signs should more serious—maybe something like "Danger" or "Poisonous"— and definitely an announcement made at Crofts House. Then she felt a hand in hers. "This is cool, Roe. Try to relax and enjoy it."

She squeezed his hand. "I'll try, Eric."

The college counselors led the entire group down another spoke in the wheel, briefly through woods, which suddenly gave way to land that belonged in a Star Wars movie—bleak, almost Sahara-like—the sands of the famous Michigan Dunes. The last glimpse of sun giving a fiery goodnight made the entire coastline eerie, mysterious.

"We'll wander a bit until it's completely dark," said Jay, the head counselor, "but stay off the dunes. They're fragile and take thousands of years to develop. Natural erosion is enough of a problem without our causing the sands to shift."

"Camp Shifting Sands," Roe heard someone whisper, maybe Cress. That would be a good name for the camp, if they could no longer use the lake. But if the water is poisonous, there shouldn't be a camp, she thought.

Then she and Eric walked to *the* lake—mighty Lake Michigan, almost large enough to be an ocean. Eric pointed to the southwest. "If we had a sailboat and headed that way for miles and miles and miles, where would we be, Roe?"

"Castle Bluff," she answered softly. Which may not be my home much longer but is a place I'll always love, she thought but didn't say.

"Okay, everyone," Jay shouted. 'Find a spot and lie down." An odd request, but laughingly they obeyed. "Now, close your eyes and turn off your flashlights—not necessarily in that order. On your backs, if you aren't already, and then open your eyes. Look up!"

"Oh!" Everyone gasped in wonder.

Stars, more than any Roe had ever seen, filled the whole dome of sky. Millions and millions of stars and galaxies! One of the counselors began pointing out familiar constellations.

Roe gazed contentedly. For the first time in weeks, she felt unafraid. "Eric," she whispered, "if nothing else goes right this summer, I'll have this. This moment will make everything okay."

Scene 3

All the Men and Women Merely Players
— William Shakespeare, *As You Like It*

THE NEXT AFTERNOON KYLIE SAT in the large auditorium, awaiting the cast announcements. She was not used to this method and didn't think she liked it. Normally, lists were posted, so you could grab a quick look and rejoice or go hide somewhere. Or, if you were really scared, you could talk a friend into looking and delivering the happy or tragic news. But announcing your name in front of everyone? Scary! Suddenly those butterflies that had invaded her stomach during auditions returned full force. She crossed her fingers and hoped, although she didn't know for what. How weird to audition for three plays at once, without knowing what they were. It had been tiresome spending the morning playing the childish theater games she'd learned in sixth grade, but now, finally, they would know their fates!

The audience clapped as a small group came onto the apron—a distinguished-looking elderly woman and three middle-aged men. The woman stepped to the microphone and spoke first. Although her voice was somewhat thin, it had such power Kylie was certain she had once been a fine actress. "Welcome to Camp Shimmer Lake," she said, arms flung out as if to embrace them all. "I am Loretta Crofts-Baker. One hundred years ago, my grandfather founded Crofts School of Performing Arts, and forty years later, this camp. The Crofts family is proud to carry on his legacy. I wish you a wonderful, fulfilling summer and do hope that all of your dreams come true."

Everyone applauded. What a nice person, Kylie thought. She's not in the least bit snooty. She determined to find out more about her. Then Mrs. Crofts-Baker introduced her two sons, James and Lawrence, and nephew Brian, who were, Kylie decided instantly, complete and total snobs. Lawrence was the spokesman.

"I second my mother's wishes," he said. "I'm sure it will be a successful summer, especially if a better job is done adhering to the rules. I am compelled to remind you that Shimmer Lake is off limits this summer. Regretfully, we were not able to acquire sufficiently trained lifeguards." Kylie and Brad exchanged looks, with Brad muttering *what an asshole*. So that was their story. "I'm appalled and disappointed that yesterday fresh footprints were discovered beyond the roped-off area. It is possible that people other than you theater students are responsible, but just in case—" Lawrence Crofts didn't seem *compelled* to complete the warning.

How arrogant he was, Kylie thought, but she was worried. Brad needed to get a water sample soon if they were to give one to Roe's dad. Was it too great a risk? There might be more security in place now. Then she noticed a curious expression on Nephew Brian's face. Sneaky and mean, she thought, wanting to ask the others what they thought.

As soon as the family left the stage, the three directors seen during auditions entered, each carrying a list. Jay, who was becoming a familiar face, made the introductions, then left the stage.

A woman named Miss Carlson stepped to the microphone and announced that she would direct *Dear Brutus* by James M. Barrie.

"Peter Pan," Kylie heard the whisper, loud because so many people were saying it. A show like *Peter Pan*? A children's play? That might be fun. The director began reading the names, which didn't mean anything to Kylie. Mr. Dearth (sounded like Death, she thought) would be played by Jay, and Mrs. Dearth would be Megan, the head counselor of Barrymore Cabin. The suggestive whoops and whistles at that made it clear Megan and Jay were an item. Kylie hoped so; she liked both. Cress Morgan would play Joanna Trout. Miss Carlson read off names of people Kylie didn't know, and then the last character of all. "Margaret will be played by Rosita Santos."

The crowd reacted strongly to that, both in approval and dismay. A girl behind Roe reached over and patted her shoulder. "Good going," she said.

Roe must have a lead, and it looked as if, once again, everyone else in the cast would be older.

Miss Carlson congratulated them and announced the number of the rehearsal hall and the time they were to meet the next day.

The second director was a man. "Guy Canfield," he said, adding that he hoped they'd just call him Guy. "Hey, you, would be fine, too," he quipped. His play was *A Midsummer Night's Dream*, "both challenging and fun."

So *The Dream* was a shortcut, a nickname—kind of like *Mouse*, instead of *The Mouse That Roared*. More Shakespeare. This would be her play. She'd be a fairy, which was okay, but she didn't think she liked Mr. "Call Me Guy." Mr. Canfield reminded her of Mr. Carroll at CBMS, the one arrested for child pornography. But, surprisingly, from their group, only Kurt and Brad were cast, both with good roles. Kurt went ballistic when he heard he was to play Puck, and Brad was quietly pleased to be cast as one of the Rude Mechanicals.

The only thing left was the musical, but Kylie was not a singer. She hadn't considered the possibility that she would only be going to classes and not cast in anything. That probably meant no scholarship to Crofts next year, either. She thought of Beth's letter and Roe's remark. Maybe the public high school wouldn't be so bad.

The last director, Mrs. Harrington, appealed to Kylie the most. Smiling, the director got right to the point. "Our musical also has to do with Shakespeare," she said. "We're proud of our former students, Andrea Cox and Ben Lookup, for writing *Lost in Arden Woods*. The old-timers in the audience cheered. "The girl campers will be played by—" Jaimie and Kylie were among the names read, and Eric was listed as one of the Lord Chamberlain's Men. Mrs. Harrington chuckled at the gasps in the audience. "I know some of you are saying 'but I can't sing.' You probably can but don't know it yet. Don't worry. This is more a play with music than a musical. Those who are singers will sing, but there are plenty of lines for everyone else."

Well, good, Kylie thought. Certainly she could play a camper, and she was pleased to be cast by the director she liked best.

The assembly adjourned. The day had been long and exhausting, disappointing as well as exhilarating. The theater campers, flashlights on, tiredly made their way back to the cabins.

SCENE 4

To unpathed waters, undreamed shores
—William Shakespeare, *The Winter's Tale*

ROE WAS EMBARRASSED, ALTHOUGH SHE had no reason to be. Margaret must be a lead, or at least a very good part, for people to react that way. Most seemed happy for her, but others were, well—jealous. Until she learned more about Margaret, she wouldn't decide how she felt. She would have been okay with a fairy in *Dream* or a camper with Kylie in the musical. She was pleased both Kurt and Brad had great parts. Those two alone would have made a fine showing for CBT, she thought, imagining how proud Miss Armstrong was going to be.

Jaimie had been the last to arrive back in the cabin. "Finally," Megan said, taking inventory. "Now I can go to bed, too."

"You didn't have to wait," Jaimie said peevishly. "I just wanted to congratulate Kurt. He's so excited about being Puck."

"I do have to wait," Megan said patiently. "That's my job. Try not to forget it."

Shrugging rudely, Jaimie grabbed her toilet kit and headed to the sink.

Already in her bunk, Roe rested on an elbow watching her. In seventh grade, she and Jaimie had been friends. Eric still considered her one—although Jaimie often made it difficult. Why did she have to be so silly?

Then she noticed Jaimie filling her cup with tap water. Bad idea. "Jaimie, stop."

"Stop what?"

"Don't drink that water. Open one of the bottles."

"Oh, really. Too much trouble, and what difference does it make? Bottled water comes from ordinary lakes, anyway, and a lot of it is stolen from Native Americans. The whole bottled water thing is a scam, and as for the plastic waste . . ." She completed brushing her teeth by drinking the entire glass. Jaimie screwed up her face but said nothing.

"Not too tasty, huh?" Without waiting for an answer, Roe faced the wall and fell into a sound sleep—until she was awakened a few hours later by agonized groans.

"Oooo, it hurts! Oh, my stomach! Make it stop!"

Jaimie? Roe was about to go to her bunk when she heard Megan. "What in the world? Jaimie, what's wrong?"

"My stomach. I feel awful!"

"You drank the water, didn't you?"

She sure did, Roe thought. Well, let Megan handle it—her job.

"Yes, but so what? Ouch! It hurts so bad!"

"I heard Roe warning you. Even if you didn't read the signs, why didn't you listen to her?"

Jaimie groaned. "It's her fault I drank it. It's Roe's fault I got sick."

Still, Roe pretended to sleep, but she fumed inside.

"It's Roe's fault you're sick because she warned you not to drink the water. Do you know how ridiculous that sounds?"

"Ow!" Not answering Megan, holding her stomach, Jaimie dashed to the bathroom. Soon, Roe heard violent retching.

Roe leaped from her bunk and started to follow, but Megan stopped her. "Wait. I think she'll be back soon. Then we'll decide if she should go to the infirmary." Megan returned to her bed, patting the mattress as an invitation for Roe to sit next to her. As head counselor of Barrymore Cabin, Megan's bunk was located in a corner away from the other sleeping campers.

"Thanks," Roe said gratefully. "She wouldn't appreciate either of us going in there, especially not me."

"Any reason why you're her special poison?"

Roe blushed. "A silly reason. We used to be good friends—until Eric decided he liked me. Jaimie always considered Eric her property."

Megan responded with a rude noise. "And you're what . . . fourteen?"

"Almost," Roe admitted. Her birthday was one of the reasons Dad was coming, but she didn't want a fuss made of it. Jaimie wouldn't be fourteen until the end of August. "Oh, I know what you're saying, Megan. We're too young for—" She stopped as a pale, shaken-looking Jaimie returned from the bathroom.

"Jaimie, are you okay?"

"I guess, no thanks to you."

"That's enough," Megan said firmly. "Jaimie, either I'm taking you to the infirmary, or you're going to bed. Perhaps tomorrow you can tell me why Roe warning you not to drink the water was the reason you got sick—from the water." Roe opened her mouth, but Megan held up her hand. "And it better not have anything to do with a torrid, unrequited love affair at age thirteen. I will not have that kind of nonsense in my cabin. We've got enough problems this summer without—never mind. Any more jealousy, and I'll recommend that the two of you be sent home. And don't think people won't listen to me!"

Alarmed, Jaimie and Roe looked at each other, becoming, for a split second, almost comrades. Without a word, both returned to their bunks.

Kylie, pretending to sleep, had followed the whole thing. Because of the dim light coming from above the sink, she had caught Roe and Jaimie's exchange of glances. She grinned. Wouldn't it be funny if Megan's scolding ended the almost yearlong feud? She wondered what unrequited meant. She'd never heard the word before.

In small groups, the campers from Barrymore and other cabins dragged themselves sleepily up the path to the cafeteria, open until ten to accommodate the various schedules. Roe's *Brutus* rehearsal was first, so after giving Jaimie, still sleeping soundly, a worried glance, she joined Megan, also in the cast.

Cautiously, Roe brought up the topic of last night. "Megan, I'm sor—"

"No, Roe, I'm the one who should apologize. You didn't do anything wrong. This is hard to admit, but the main reason I was angry was because I've been acting in much the same way as Jaimie about someone, and I don't have the excuse of being only thirteen."

Megan might have said more, but a few campers from other cabins, also cast in *Dear Brutus*, joined them. Roe wondered if she'd figured it out anyway, when she saw Jay holding hands with a girl named Gretel. Megan's expression, accompanied by a blush, told the whole painful story. Megan liked Jay, but so did Gretel. No, "liked" wasn't the right word. Megan was nineteen, not almost fourteen, and Jay was twenty. Megan, almost past being a teenager, was in love with Jay. And they were a married couple in the play. At least, they had the same last name. Ouch! Roe thought.

Jay smiled at her. "Hi there, Roe. We met on the hike last night. So you're going to play my daughter."

"I never heard of the play," Roe admitted. "I know *Peter Pan*, of course, but I didn't know James Barrie wrote anything else. Is it another children's play?"

Gretel laughed, but it wasn't a kind laugh, and Roe didn't think she was going to like her. But maybe that was because of Megan. "Hardly," Gretel said. "It's filled with sex, angst, and betrayal."

"In other words, true to life," Megan said bitterly. "Come on, let's get moving or we won't have time for breakfast; I'm starving." Leaving the group, she rushed on ahead.

Gretel was wearing a smug look of triumph while Jay seemed clueless or, perhaps, indifferent. "She's right," Jay said. "It's late. Don't worry, Roe. Margaret is a dream of a part, in more ways than one." He chuckled good-naturedly, and the others joined in.

"How are you feeling?" Kylie asked. Jaimie looked green and probably should spend the day in bed.

"Not good," Jaimie said, "but I'm not about to miss the first rehearsal— or any of them."

Kylie made sure the cabin door was closed since they were the last to leave. "Maybe you'd better keep breakfast simple."

Jaimie nodded. "A toast and tea affair, my grandma would say." They walked awhile in silence. "So you heard everything last night?"

"Enough," Kylie said.

"Enough so you think I'm a complete idiot?"

Kylie grinned. She and Jaimie often came close to understanding each other. "Well, maybe not a complete one, but it was monumentally stupid of you to blame Roe for making you sick when she warned you not to drink the water. By the way—how did it taste?"

Jaimie grimaced. "Disgusting! I think the water should be turned off until they fix whatever is wrong."

"Look, Jaimie . . ." Kylie paused, uncertain how much information to divulge. She stalled by pushing aside a branch that was about to give them both a fierce swat. "There's a lot going on right now that we wish we could share with you and Kurt, but you two have kind of pulled away from us, and—do you really want two boyfriends?"

"Kurt isn't my boyfriend. We're just—well, I suppose we're using each other."

Even if it cost them breakfast, Kylie wanted answers. She walked slightly ahead and plopped herself on what campers called Halfway Bench. "Explain," she said firmly.

Sighing, Jaimie sat, too. "Kurt and I aren't together," she said. "You might say we're propping up each other's egos."

"Why?"

"Well, Kurt's feelings were hurt when Beth dumped him."

"So, that's how it went down. I didn't know. Normally, Kurt does the dumping. How about you, Jaimie? The usual? Just trying to make Eric jealous again?"

Jaimie nodded, head down, ashamed. "I know it sounds dumb. You wouldn't understand, Kylie. I—"

"Moi?" Kylie hooted. "Not understand? Don't you remember what a fool I was when I thought Brad was sneaking around with Robbie?"

"Oh, yeah—that."

"That," Kylie agreed. "Maybe we'd better go, even though breakfast will be like all the meals here—lousy."

"Better than nothing, I guess." Again in silence, they walked on, while Kylie figured out what else needed to be said. Her goal was to make things better.

"Jaimie, I think you've got this crazy idea that Roe and Eric have this hot romance going. Okay, so they sometimes hold hands and go to school dances together, but I don't think they've even kissed. And have you ever heard their conversations?"

"I guess not."

"Listen to them sometime. They're the most boring couple ever. Book reports, world news, school assignments—if they're not running lines, that's it. It's like they're in love with each other's brains."

"But she always has it so easy," Jaimie whined. "She always gets everything she wants."

"Oh, does she? Like a mean, crack-head brother who died in a car accident, nearly killing her in the process? Or a mother who goes crazy and rejects her? Maybe you don't know that she's not her mother after all. So her father has a lot of money—did you know he just sold their house? She doesn't even have a home anymore? Does that sound like someone who gets everything she wants?"

Jaimie flushed. "Well, she got to play Anne at Crofts—"

"Where her castmates treated her like garbage. Most of the time she was miserable."

"I didn't know."

"And don't forget when her so-called friends, including you, decided she was a thief and responsible for causing the damage at school. That's when Eric took her side and decided to help."

Jaimie gave a slight teary smile. "Eric, always to the rescue, whether it's a stray cat or a wounded bird or a—"

"Or a hurting person," Kylie finished.

"He's always been like that," Jaimie said. They'd reached the cafeteria. "What should I do, Kylie?"

"Try thinking for once. If you decide to make things right, join us for lunch. We need the whole gang back together."

As they entered the cafeteria, Brad and Kurt came out, heading for their rehearsal. "I did it, Kylie," Brad said. "Woke up before anyone and got the water sample. The jar is hidden in my duffle. I've told Kurt everything. See you at lunch."

When the gang, including Jaimie and Kurt, gathered next, they were too excited about their plays to notice or care that the food was even less appetizing than usual. Momentarily, they also forgot that four of their members, Roe, Jaimie, Eric, and possibly Kurt, had reasons to be uncomfortable with each other.

Roe was quietly pleased with her role of Margaret, even though she was the youngest, alone again with none of her friends in the cast. It turned out that *Dear Brutus* had several connections to Shakespeare. The characters experienced magical changes while getting lost in the woods—kind of like in *The Dream*. The title was from a line in *Julius Caesar*—*The fault, dear Brutus, is not in our stars, but in ourselves, that we are underlings.* It was sort of hard to understand, but she thought it meant that people were responsible for their own actions. Margaret only appeared in the second act, but it was a terrific part with lots of lines. Roe vowed to learn them quickly, so she'd have free time to study Spanish. When she finally met her grandparents, she hoped to speak to them in their own language—or at least a few words. *Hola, Abuela. Como esta usted?* It was a start.

"Roe? Come back, come back, wherever you are . . ."

"Oh, sorry. Jaimie?"

"That's me!" Jaimie attempted to sound jolly but came off as nervous. Roe noticed her hand shaking. "But I'm the one who's sorry, Roe, about everything. Will you forgive me?"

For what? Roe almost said, but why prolong the embarrassment? *Everything* just about covered it. "Of course," she said. "I'd like us to be friends again."

Kurt sighed loudly. *Lord, what fools these mortals be!*

Brad groaned. "We shall be stuck with Puck for the rest of the summer, if not longer."

"Until Midsummer's Eve at least," Kurt said, grinning. "Stuck with Puck! I like that!"

A loud bell rang. "Time's up," Kylie said. "Swallow whatever you can stand. Back to rehearsal!"

Though she be little, she is fierce.

Brad grabbed Kurt's arm. "That's what I meant. He's going to drive us all bonkers. Come on, Puck. See the rest of you later."

SCENE 5

(Exit, pursued by a bear)
— William Shakespeare, *A Winter's Tale*

AND THE DAYS PASSED. THEY'D been at camp for almost two weeks, the days falling into a familiar pattern. Rehearse, eat lunch, take class, break, rehearse, supper, evening free—but not really free. Break and evenings were for working on lines and writing letters. Many of the actors used this precious time in the lounge, where they had a chance at Internet access.

They'd be sorry on Monday when they had to be completely off book for all three plays, Kylie reflected. Most of her afternoon break time was spent helping Brad. Memorization had always been difficult for him, even though he was a terrific actor—at least in her opinion. He loved Snug, his part in *The Dream*, especially when he got to be the Lion in the hysterical "Pyramus and Thisby" scene.

"Snug is supposed to be 'slow of study,' so it's the perfect role for me," Brad said.

Kylie was a "quick study." Lines were not causing her problems. She'd be solid, even on her long monologue, by Monday.

"I don't have a large part," she'd written her parents, "but I like it." Without giving too much away, she gave a simplified explanation of the plot. "*Lost in Arden Woods* takes place at a girl's theater camp. The camp is in trouble financially and, maybe, legally because there's been a fire that destroyed the main theater. The camp director is suspected of arson." Ironic,

Kylie thought, considering that Camp Shimmer Lake seemed to be in financial trouble, too. In the play, in order to keep costs down, the girls were required to do scenes and monologues from Shakespeare but were not happy about it. "I fracture the 'To be or not to be' monologue from *Hamlet*," she wrote. "Things are bad until magically the Lord Chamberlain's Men, including Shakespeare, come out of the woods to help the girls prepare for their show. I also play one of the witches in *Macbeth*. I'm learning a lot of Shakespeare in a fun way."

If only Jaimie liked her part. Kylie had been surprised it was smaller than hers. After always getting leads in school musicals—since sixth grade— Jaimie and her friends assumed it would continue here, too. Jaimie was a sweet, pure soprano, but the older actors blew her out of the water. Kylie could tell the difference now. A sweet voice, but it wasn't—Kylie searched for the word—it wasn't rich.

"Kylie, wait up." Roe rushed to join her. "Boy, you must have been far away. I've been calling your name for ages."

"Oh, sorry."

"Going to the cabin, too? I want to see if the mail has come. Not sure why? It's not like I'm going to get anything."

"Well, your dad is coming tomorrow. That's something. I haven't heard anything from Mom or Dad for over a week."

"They must be super busy," Roe said. "People just aren't used to writing letters today. It's like we're back in time, before texting."

"And emails and Snapchat and Instagram."

"And even regular phone calls," Roe finished, laughing.

Kylie laughed, too. "At least letters don't come by Pony Express. People back home aren't living in the dark ages. We're not going to get many letters." Kylie was trying to make Roe feel better—as well as herself. She should have heard from Mom and Dad.

"Hey!" Kurt's voice was the loudest, as usual, but the whole gang followed behind, carrying bags of assorted sizes.

"Hey yourself," Kylie said. "What's up?"

"And why aren't you working on lines?" Roe said.

"And what's with the bags?"

Eric smiled and took Roe's hand. Jaimie turned away, but at least she didn't look angry or unfriendly—maybe a little embarrassed. Kylie wished Eric would cool it when Jaimie was around.

"Your birthday surprise," Eric announced, "for you and Kylie."

"A birthday picnic in the woods," Brad explained. "The bags are full of goodies, edible and otherwise."

"Food? Where from?"

"Ah, Roe," Kurt said. "Paranoia does not become you. This is not from our beloved local cuisine but from packages sent by generous parents and a certain Grandma Gee."

They stared at him. While they were used to Kurt being in love with the sound of his own voice, he had become too fond of elegant speech, and it was becoming annoying.

"Lots of cards, too," Jaimie added.

"This is so nice," Kylie said. "Roe and I were feeling neglected."

"Lead on Macduff," Kurt ordered.

Roe laughed. "For once you're wrong, Kurt. Actually, it's 'Lay on Macduff,' and it means to attack."

"That works, too," Kurt said blithely. "I'm ready to attack Gee's brownies."

"The site we've chosen is about half a mile away," Brad said. "And since we're supposed to be practicing our lines, how about each of us take a turn at entertaining. Since I thought of it, I'll go last. With any luck we'll be there before it's my turn."

Eric nodded. "Birthday girls first. Kylie?"

Kylie cleared her throat. If it was one thing she was sure of, it was her monologue. "I play Delaney, a girl who takes everything seriously and doesn't understand Shakespeare at all."

"Well, the second part is true anyway."

"Hush, Fool," Brad scolded Kurt. "No more interruptions. Go for it, Delaney."

Kylie glared at Kurt, and then cleared her throat again. She began:

To be or not to be: that is the question.

[So what kind of question is that? Should I kill myself, or should I just forget about it? No! Don't do it, Hamlet!

Not only is it wrong, but it's stupid. You won't be around to find out if everyone is sorry. You won't find out if they say, 'Oh, poor Hamlet, I didn't know him after all. I should have been kinder to the poor boy.' Look Hamlet, I knew someone who committed suicide. He stepped in front of a train. Believe me, it wasn't pretty! And what about your girlfriend? Can't you consider Ophelia? You drive her nuts, you know. I mean, literally and clinically. (Sighing.) Come on, Delaney! Try again!]

> *To be or not to be, that is the question:*
> *Whether 'tis nobler in the mind to suffer*
> *The slings and arrows of outrageous fortune*
> *Or to take arms against a sea of trouble*
> *And by opposing end them. To die, to sleep*
> *No more – and by a sleep to say we end*
> *The heartache, and the thousand natural shocks*
> *The flesh is heir to.*

[Awful! I don't even want to think about it].

> *'tis a consummation*
> *Devoutly to be wished. To die, to sleep—*
> *To sleep—perchance to dream: ay, there's the rub,*

[It sure is. Man, did I have a nightmare last night.]

> *For in that sleep of death what dreams may come—*

[What Dreams May Come. I saw an old movie called that. It's about this man who jumps into the ocean and finds his dead wife. Delaney! You're losing focus here…]

> *When we have shuffled off this mortal coil.*

[That would make a great soft shoe dance. Shuffled off this mortal coil, shuffled off this mortal coil. (Trying not to trip, Kylie started a dance routine, then caught herself.)]

[What the hell is a bare bodkin? I'll never get this![

All of them applauded. "That was great, Kylie!"

"Thanks. That's pretty much the part, though. Only a few other lines, but I'm okay with it. You're next, Roe."

"Let me," Jaimie insisted. "I'd like to get it over with. I don't have any monologue and not many lines either, but I get to sing one of Ariel's songs with some other girls. It's weird but kind of pretty. I wish I could play Ariel, but a senior got it. At least our costumes are nice." Then without waiting for Roe to say anything, Jaimie burst out singing.

> *Where the bee sucks, there suck I*
> *In a cowslip's bell I lie;*
> *There I couch when owls do cry.*
> *On the bat's back I do fly*
> *After summer merrily.*
> *Merrily, merrily shall I live now*
> *Under the blossom that hangs on the bough.*

"That was nice, Jaimie," Roe said quickly, and the others nodded.

"I'm sure the only reason you're not Ariel is because you're new here," Kylie said. But she didn't mean it. Jaimie's voice needed a lot more training before she would ever get out of the chorus, and she might not ever have enough humility to accept that.

"Maybe I should round out the musical before Roe switches plays," Eric suggested.

"Good idea, and we're getting closer and closer to our picnic site." Brad, who had suggested the impromptu performance, no longer seemed eager to participate. "Go ahead, Eric."

"Well, I play Richard Burbage, one of the Royal Chamberlain's Men. All of the men have lost their memories, at least about their own wives in their own day. I fall for Delaney, played by the lovely Kylie. And I sing this song from *Twelfth Night.*

> *O Mistress mine, where are you roaming?*
> *O stay and hear! Your true-love's coming*
> *That can sing both high and low*
> *Trip no further, pretty sweeting,*
> *Journeys end in lovers' meeting —*
> *Every wise man's son doth know.*

What is love? 'tis not hereafter;
Present mirth hath present laughter;
What's to come is still unsure:
In delay there lies no plenty,
Then come kiss me, Sweet-and-twenty,
Youth's a stuff will not endure.

"Wow!" Kurt expressed everyone's opinion. It was obvious that Eric had a good part but was, typically, modest about it.

Kylie thought it amazing how much they had all improved—probably because of the daily rehearsals, even on Sundays. And they were all pleased with their parts—except for Jaimie, who must realize she was not as good as she thought she was. Kylie thought that was true of her, too, but it was okay. It was not necessary for her to be a great actress at age almost-fourteen. Other things were more important—like being a good friend and loving her family.

"I guess I'm next," Roe said. "I was kind of hoping to skip it because, like Jaimie, I don't have a monologue either. I play Margaret, a dream child, and I'm only in the second act. I'll put some of my lines together to give you an idea." Suddenly Roe seemed several years younger.

Hold me tight, Daddy. I'm frightened. I think they want to take you away from me. I don't know. It's too lovely, Daddy—I won't be able to hang on to it. The world—everything—and you, Daddy, most of all. Things that are too beautiful can't last. Do you think I am sometimes too full of gladness? To be very gay, dearest dear, is near to being very sad. Something in me is afraid. Daddy, what is a might-have-been? Am I one? How awful it would be, Daddy, to wake up and find one wasn't alive.

Silence until Kylie said, "Whoa, that gave me the chills!"

"Weird," Jaimie said. "I didn't really understand what that was all about. Guess I'll have to see the play."

Roe nodded. "You'll find it strange, even then. I'm just starting to get it. And of course I strung a lot of lines together because I don't have any long ones."

"You play opposite Jay, don't you?" Brad asked. "What's he like?"

"Talented and very nice. I'm his imaginary daughter—what his life might have been like if I'd been born. You see, Dearth, that's Jay, is an alcoholic. His life is a mess, and he doesn't get along with his wife—"

"Played by Megan," Jaimie interrupted. "Would that be life imitating art, or art imitating life?"

Kylie and Roe exchanged troubled glances. Jaimie was with the group again, but she didn't really fit in. Kylie wished she hadn't come. There was no reason for Jaimie's continued nastiness.

"We're almost there," Kurt announced, gleefully breaking the mood. "And I've decided on my line and insist I go last. So, Brad, you are next, whether or not you want to be."

To their surprise, Brad let out a mighty roar, totally breaking the somber mood. "Then listen to the Lion," he commanded.

> *You, ladies, you, whose gentle hearts do fear*
> *The smallest monstrous mouse that creeps on floor,*
> *May now perchance both quake and tremble here,*
> *When lion rough in wildest rage doth roar.*
> *Then know that I, one Snug the joiner, am*
> *A lion-fell, nor else no lion's dam;*
> *For, if I should as lion come in strife*
> *Into this place 'twere pity on my life.*

"Perfect," Kylie breathed. "You got every word right, Brad."

Brad winked at her. "Thanks to you.".

"Just around the corner now," Kurt said grandly. "And even though Puck has lines I like better, this one seems to fit."

> *I'll follow you, I'll lead you about a round,*
> *Through bog, through bush, through brake, through brier:*
> *Sometime a horse I'll be, sometime a hound,*
> *A hog, a headless bear, sometime a fire;*
> *And neigh, and bark, and grunt, and roar, and burn,*
> *Like horse, hound, hog, bear, fire, at every turn.*

Roe thought the spot chosen for the birthday picnic perfect— a wooded area with fallen logs for seats but still near the dunes and their own Lake Michigan. As far as she knew, Brad hadn't returned to Shimmer Lake since he'd sneaked out for a sample. At the moment, the water crisis seemed far away. Perhaps nothing but their overactive imaginations. The only thing she wanted to think about now was this crazy, impromptu birthday party.

"Presents or food?" Kurt asked.

"Both," Brad said.

"I'm awfully thirsty," Kylie said.

"Me, too," the others declared, so Brad opened the cooler of sodas and brought out sandwiches as well. "Birthday cake later," he said.

The presents were fun and, for the most part, simple. Kurt gave Roe a huge chocolate bar. Her favorite kind, she said. Jaimie gave her a note, promising a milkshake at Smithy's when they returned to Castle Bluff. "I'll look forward to it," Roe said, realizing Jaimie had to come up with a present at the last minute. That was okay—at least she did something thoughtful. Brad gave her a small book of Shakespeare quotations. Eric's gift was special—a silver charm bracelet filled with theater-related charms and a tiny heart. Roe insisted he put it on her wrist and vowed to wear it always.

Eric cleared his throat. "Now for Kylie," he said, presenting her with a bottle of water and a hand-made certificate. "Guaranteed pure," he assured her.

Kylie laughed. "I'll keep the certificate as a memento, but the water will be gone by the time we get back. I don't know when I've been so thirsty."

Jaimie gave Kylie a framed photo of the cast of *Cinderella, Cinderella*. "My favorite part of all time, and my favorite director," she said.

"It was great," Kylie said. "Sometimes scary but mainly fun."

Kurt's contribution was another candy bar, and Brad gave her a locket with his picture in it. So romantic!

Also packed in one bag were many birthday cards the sneaky friends had managed to confiscate. No wonder they hadn't received any mail. Both girls opened cards and letters from Imani, Jen, Marla, Gee, Mr. Markey, and Miss Armstrong. Nothing from Kylie's parents or brother—or Beth. Maybe tomorrow, Kylie thought, not knowing whether to be hurt or angry.

Roe looked at her watch. "This was the best birthday party ever, but we'd better get back soon for rehearsal."

Kurt pulled out the cake while Roe and Kylie put their gifts into bags. "The cake is already sliced," Kurt said. "We didn't want to bring a knife, and—"

A great noise and rustling in the woods interrupted him. Brad yelled, "Run! Don't take anything!"

Kylie and Roe grabbed their gifts, though, and they all bolted from their picnic area. Roe, hoping for a false alarm, gave a quick glance back at a large black bear, celebrating their birthday without them. It would be the only one to enjoy their pre-sliced chocolate cake.

"Exit, pursued by a bear!" Kurt yelled, out of breath, as they fled to their cabins.

Scene 6

Double, double toil and trouble
— William Shakespeare, *Macbeth*

THEY BARELY MADE IT TO rehearsal on time—much less have the chance to decide whether to report the bear. Kylie hoped they wouldn't, even though maybe they should. After all, the bear had more of a right to be in the Michigan woods than they did. What did Kurt mean by that strange exit line? Kylie shrugged. With Kurt, one never knew.

"Miss Kennedy, may I speak to you for a minute?"

"Of course, Mrs. Harrington." Was something wrong? Maybe not; the director never used first names.

"Let's go into my office, if you have the time."

"It won't matter if I'm late for supper."

Mrs. Harrington sat at her desk, shuffling papers around as if searching for the right approach; Kylie sat across from her and waited patiently, although she was becoming nervous. Obviously, there was a problem.

"I know you and Miss Jelinek come from the same town," she said. "Are you friends?"

This was about Jaimie. "Most of the time. We've known each other since we were little. Jaimie played Cinderella in the play I directed last year."

"Did you find her cooperative?"

"Yes," Kylie said. Jaimie was always cooperative when things were going her way, but she wouldn't tell Mrs. Harrington that.

"Well, perhaps you would be willing to talk with her about how she is behaving in this show." Mrs. Harrington shook her head. "I know I'm asking a lot of you, but if her attitude doesn't change—I am finding her difficult to direct, and I simply don't have the time to deal with temperamental children. I'm considering asking one of the extra fairies from *Dream* to take her role. Miss Jelinek doesn't seem to realize that a new non-scholarship student rarely has even a small solo."

"I thought—" Kylie stopped. Jaimie had told everyone she had a full scholarship—that long after the awards ceremony, her family had received a letter from Crofts, apologizing and saying there had been a mistake. Jaimie had lied, probably because of embarrassment and pride. She was the only one attending from their middle school without a full or partial scholarship. Her parents must have paid a bundle. "I'll try talking to her, Mrs. Harrington. I don't know how successful I'll be, though."

Mrs. Harrington smiled. "I can't ask for more than that. You'd better get to your supper now." Kylie stood to leave. "And Miss Kennedy, you are doing a fine job with your part. I appreciate your being off book so soon."

"Thank you, Mrs. Harrington." Troubled, Kylie rushed to the cafeteria. How in the world was she going to tell Jaimie? Maybe she'd ask Eric for advice—once she could get him alone.

The buzz at their table was about the bear. Kylie was surprised the whole table knew what had happened. So much for talking about it first! Soon everyone in camp would know, including the directors.

"You guys," Kylie hissed. "Why did you say anything? Do you want the dunes area to be off limits?"

Gary, one of the boys also cast in *Dream*, overheard. "Don't worry. This is my third year, and there's always a bear sighting. We'll just get a warning about taking food into the woods. Notice that all the garbage cans in camp have bear safety locks."

Kurt shook his head. "We'd have been done for if old Smokey hadn't wanted the chocolate cake more than us. Good thing we had food."

"A definite dilemma when dealing with bears," Gary said. "Personally, I would never go into the woods without a backpack full of marshmallows. I use them as grenades while making my escape."

Everyone at the table laughed. Kylie could see why Gary and Kurt had become friends. They were two of a kind.

"An excellent plan," Kurt said, "for the next time we must exit, pursued by a bear."

"That's the second time you've said that as if it means something," Roe said. "Why?"

Kurt told the group that "Exit, pursued by a bear," was a peculiar stage direction in Shakespeare's play, *The Winter's Tale*. "No one quite gets it today," Gary interrupted. "There is a bear who eats one of the characters, but no one does a good job staging it. An actor dressed in a bear costume turns the whole thing into a farce. Maybe with some modern lighting visuals—"

"Except the whole play is pretty crazy," Kurt added, "even without the bear and weird stage directions."

The barely adequate meal of dry thin hamburgers consumed, the friends discussed evening plans. Kylie would attend an impromptu rehearsal of the three witches scene from *Lost in Arden Woods*. "We're meeting in a clearing near our cabin. Jay is going to light a campfire. It's going to be so much fun."

"More rehearsals may be your idea of fun but not mine," Jaimie said, speaking for the first time since supper began. "I'm going to the lounge to connect with the outside world."

"But Jaimie—" Kylie began. She was about to remind her that the rehearsal would be run by Helen, the student director, and that Mrs. Harrington planned to stop by. Jaimie was one of the witches, and her absence would be a problem.

"'But Jaimie' will see y'all later. It wasn't on the schedule, so no more rehearsals for me today." With that, Jaimie left the table while Kylie exchanged worried glances with Eric.

Eric planned to meet some new friends for a game of chess, and Brad, Kurt, and Gary were getting together with other boys in *Dream* to work on their parts. Roe had no plans and decided it would be fun to watch the witches rehearse.

While scraping dishes into the garbage bin, Kylie managed to grab Eric's arm. "Could we talk a second?" she asked. "I've got a few questions about our scene." No one would wonder because they did play opposite each other.

Outside, Kylie told Eric what Mrs. Harrington said about Jaimie.

"Phew!" Eric said. "And she's going to blow off a rehearsal tonight. I know it wasn't official—she isn't required to go, but still—"

"Mrs. Harrington wants me to talk to her. What do you think?"

Eric shook his head. "I've known Jaimie practically my whole life," he said. "She's the nicest kid in the world—if she gets her own way. But if she thinks she's going to Crofts and then become an actor—As hard as it's going to be, Kylie, she has to learn. And I'm afraid it will have to be the hard way."

Roe shivered in excitement—a spooky campfire and the three witches of *Macbeth!* She wondered how many of the lines she'd remember. They'd read *Macbeth* in seventh grade English, and she'd played one of the witches for a special project. She loved her part as Margaret, maybe even more than Anne Frank, but that was because everyone in the cast was nice to her, especially Jay, who played her father. Roe had a slight crush on him—nothing serious since he was six years older. Just the same, it was kind of thrilling. But sometimes she wished she could have a small part and be in a show with kids her own age—like when she was a tourist and the page in *Mouse*.

Both Roe and Kylie were shivering by the time they reached Barrymore Cabin. This time from cold, though. "Brrr," Roe said.

"It will add to the atmosphere," Kylie said. "Let's wear hoodies."

The fire, with a large cast-iron pot placed in the center, was going strong when they arrived. Jay, the fire starter, grinned at Roe and held up a bag of marshmallows.

"Everyone here?" Helen, the assistant director asked. Roe and Kylie looked at each other, shaking their heads. Let someone else give the bad news.

"Except for Jaimie," Becky, the third witch, said.

"Anyone know about Jaimie?" Helen called out. Again, Roe and Kylie kept still. "Well, we need to get started. You—" Helen pointed at Roe. "Fill in for Second Witch until she decides to grace us with her presence. Someone hand her a side."

Kylie, who was off book, handed Roe her scene, whispering the simple blocking. "All we have to do is circle the fire, starting with my second line. I'm First Witch, Jaimie is Second, and Becky is Third. We'll keep going around until Hecate enters. That's Dolly, a Crofts senior. She'll have a line and then a song called 'Black Spirits.'"

Roe nodded. Luckily, Witch Two was the part she had played. It would be okay.

"I enter Stage Left after the thunder. Just follow me."

The witches took their places and Helen said, "Thunder. Enter Three Witches."

FIRST WITCH: *Thrice the brindled cat hath mew'd.*

Roe followed. She let her long, dark hair fall into her face while she stooped over and spoke harshly.

SECOND WITCH: *Thrice and once the hedge-pig whined.*

THIRD WITCH: *Harpier cries 'Tis time, 'tis time.*

FIRST WITCH (starting the circle): *Round about the cauldron go;*
In the poison'd entrails throw.
Toad, that under cold stone
Days and nights has thirty-one
Swelter'd venom sleeping got,
Boil though first i' the charmed pot.

Roe was having a great time. The lines had all come back. She wouldn't have to look at the rest of the side, other than peeking occasionally.

ALL: *Double, double toil and trouble;*
Fire burn, and cauldron bubble.

SECOND WITCH: *Fillet of a fenny snake,*
In the cauldron boil and bake;
Eye of newt and toe of frog,
Wool of bat and tongue of dog,
Adder's fork and blind-worm's sting,
Lizard's leg and owlet's wing,
For a charm of powerful trouble,
Like a hell-broth boil and bubble.

ALL: *Double, double toil and trouble;*
Fire burn, and cauldron bubble.

From the corner of her eye, Roe saw that Mrs. Harrington had arrived and was conferring with Helen. Jay, too, had joined the conversation. Then it was the

Third Witch's turn, another *Double, Double,* and then Roe's turn again—a short line this time. Then Hecate entered with her line and song. Dolly was a magnificent alto, and the song fit the scene perfectly. As soon as she left, Roe delivered the last line, her favorite.

> SECOND WITCH: *By the pricking of my thumbs,*
> *Something wicked this way comes.*

Helen gave a few notes and then had them run the scene twice more. This time, they were all off book.

Roe was reciting the *Fillet of a fenny snake* line when there was a loud interruption. "Wait! What's going on? How come she's doing my part?"

Roe flushed. This was hardly her fault, but Jaimie would not see it that way.

Helen, in charge of the rehearsal, calmly said, "Jaimie, how nice of you to join us—just as we're coming to an end."

"Well, I didn't know—" Jaimie started, but it was an obvious lie. "I was busy," she said lamely.

Mrs. Harrington took over. "Very well. We'll run it one more time. Please take your place, Second Witch. Miss—" She whispered a question to Helen, who whispered back—"Miss Jelinek. And thank you, Miss Santos, for understudying. Now begin, please."

A deliberate and cruel slam—Mrs. Harrington pretending not to remember Jaimie's name. Beet red, Jaimie joined the other witches Off Left. "Be good, Jaimie," Roe whispered, crossing her fingers.

But Jaimie did not know her lines. And as it was now dark, except for the flames of the fire, her reading was halting. Everyone could tell she was a poor comparison to Roe. No one spoke when it was over.

Mrs. Harrington arose from her fallen log seat. "Have a fine campfire," she said. "Don't stay up too late. And have a wonderful break this weekend, but do try to pace yourself. Remember, we'll be totally off book Monday." With that, she and Helen, heads together, walked slowly back up the trail.

Jaimie stalked over to Roe. "You just have to have everything, don't you? First you take my—" She stopped. Too many people watching. "And now you want my part? It's not enough that you have a lead?"

Roe felt her eyes welling. She had thought she and Jaimie might be friends again. "I . . . I just came to watch. I didn't know . . . I don't want—"

Becky, the third witch, came to her rescue. "You weren't here," she told Jaimie, "and we needed a second witch. Roe was helping out."

"Sure she was," Jaimie said meanly.

Jay, in his role of Head Counselor, ended the argument. "Jaimie, you're being absurd and ruining the campfire for everyone. Maybe you should get to work on your parts before your accusation becomes a reality."

Jaimie was about to respond when a frail figure came forward and a surprisingly commanding voice took over. "I wonder, Dolly dear, if you might walk me back to my rooms? This has been quite educational, but I confess I am weary."

Mrs. Crofts-Baker! How long had the camp owner and director been there? "Of course," Dolly said, offering her arm.

"Oh!" Head down, Jaimie rushed in the other direction.

"Now, how about we roast some marshmallows?" Jay said. "Everyone gather some likely sticks."

They obeyed, trying to be cheerful, but the evening soon came to a close. The campfire had been spoiled. As Roe and Kylie started to leave, Jay stopped them. "Kylie, Mrs. Harrington would like to see you right after breakfast tomorrow. She said it wouldn't take long."

"Trouble, too much trouble," Kylie said, as she and Roe headed to the cabin.

Roe nodded. "Double, in fact. First because of Eric, and now the Second Witch."

They grinned ruefully and recited together. "Double toil and trouble."

SCENE 7

Jealousy: the green-eyed monster, which doth mock the meat it feeds on.
—William Shakespeare, *Othello*

BETH THREW HER STUFFED BACKPACK into the trunk of the Kennedy's car. "I can't wait to see Kylie and Roe. They're going to be so surprised!"

"I certainly hope so." Kylie's mother laughed. "And I hope the surprise of seeing us will take away the sting of thinking we forgot their birthdays."

Marla had come to see Beth off—amazing considering how early it was. "They'll probably just think Roe's father is bringing the presents. But I told you, Beth, you should have sent cards."

Coming out of the house with the rest of the luggage, Mr. Kennedy overheard. "Hindsight is a fine thing," he said. "It will all work out, and this train is now departing. All aboard!"

"See you Monday, Marla," Beth said, and then surprised both of them by giving her unlikely friend a hug. "Stay out of trouble!"

Marla grinned. "Who me?"

"Yes, you. Be good!"

Beth sat in the backseat with Danny. She'd brought along her sketchbook and soon was taking requests for drawing action figures. She thought the long car ride would be more bearable for all of them if Danny were amused. As she placed Spiderman and his enemies in a campsite, she mused about Marla, whose main problem lately was being boy crazy. Almost like she thought boys were trophies instead of people. As far as Beth could tell, Marla wasn't really fond of any of them. But she and Marla had become good friends and would miss each other when they were in different schools. Beth was no longer sorry to be left behind, though. She needed to be with friends her own age and couldn't wait for Imani to return from London.

Danny yelled out, "That's super, Beth! Mom and Dad, look!" Mrs. Kennedy glanced back, praised the cartoon, and suggested that Dad wait until they stopped for a break.

"I'd better keep my eyes on the road," Dad said. "We're going to pass through some heavy rain."

"Plenty of time later," Beth said, "and Danny, you can have everything I sketch on this trip."

"The whole sketchbook?"

Beth laughed. "We'll see." Beth enjoyed being with Danny and his friends. Maybe she'd be a teacher when she grew up—an art teacher. That was something to think about. It made more sense than being an actor, like Kylie, Roe, and Kurt. Kurt. Would she see him? Probably not. The Kennedys planned to meet Kylie and Roe at a hotel restaurant for the surprise birthday celebration. They hadn't talked about visiting the camp. And then she, Kylie, and Roe would share a room overnight at the hotel. It would be terrific! No, she would not see Kurt, and that was just fine!

"Happy birthday, Roe," Kylie whispered.

Roe smiled. "Happy birthday to you, too, Kylie."

The rest of their cabin mates were still asleep, but Kylie and Roe had decided the night before to make each minute of their birthday weekend count. They'd also agreed the night before not to draw attention to their double birthdays. The party with the bear would be memorable enough. In truth, it was only Kylie's birthday; Roe's would be the next day. But for as long as they could remember, they had celebrated both days as one long birthday bash.

As they headed up the path to the cafeteria, Kylie expected Roe to mention Jaimie's behavior the night before, but either Roe had forgotten or didn't want to talk about it. When they had returned to the cabin, Jaimie was in bed, turned to the wall, asleep—or at least pretending to be. Quietly, Kylie and Roe had followed her example.

"What time do you think your dad will be here?" Kylie asked.

"Well, he drove up last night and planned to visit Mother this morning." Roe still referred to Mrs. Santos as Mother, even though that wasn't the case—in genetics or emotions. Even when Mrs. Santos wasn't ill, she had never been interested in the girl who was actually her stepdaughter. It had always been Kylie's mom who had orchestrated the girls' birthday activities until they were old enough to do it themselves. "I think Dad should arrive around four. Then he plans to take us to a nice hotel. I'm not sure where."

"Can you imagine having a good meal and sleeping in a comfortable bed again?"

Roe nodded. "Probably our best presents this year." But she looked down at her new bracelet in a way that said what the best present was.

"Hey, girls, wait!" Brad came running up the path toward them.

"Brad, you're up early, too," Kylie said.

"You have no idea," he whispered, looking around carefully. "I think I'm being watched. Just go along with whatever I say." Then he said loudly, "I decided to join you for your birthday breakfast. Happy Birthday!"

"Thanks," they chanted.

"Fourteen at last!" he said loudly. "I'll have to give you your birthday present before you leave today. It's something for you to share."

Brad stared a warning at them. Oh, right. They had to play along with him, even though they'd already received his presents.

Kylie linked her arm through Roe's. "No problem. We like to share."

"The card will make it clear," Brad said quietly, before dropping the subject. "I wonder what will be served this morning: stale cornflakes and skimmed milk, soggy oatmeal . . ."

They continued the breakfast guessing game until they arrived at the almost empty cafeteria, where they helped themselves to pancakes with warm syrup and bacon—almost crispy enough to please them. This was more like it!

"Oh, don't forget," Roe said, "to give me—"

Brad stopped her. "Yes. Don't worry,"

Kylie was certain Roe was about to remind Brad of the water sample, but for some reason, Brad didn't want her to mention it. Roe nodded. She got it, even though she didn't understand. Brad's odd behavior had something to do with the polluted water sample they would give to Mr. Santos when they saw him later.

More tired campers drifted in as Kylie and Roe finished their breakfast. Brad had zipped off earlier to meet with the person in charge of costuming *Dream*. Actors were excused for the weekend, but all tech crews would be hard at work.

"What should we do now, Kylie?"

"I'm supposed to see Mrs. Harrington right after breakfast," Kylie said.

"About last night?"

"I don't know," Kylie admitted. She hoped not.

The girls planned to meet back for an early lunch, and then they'd pack and wait for Roe's father. Getting up so early might not have been such a good idea after all. Hours with little to do remained.

"Sit down, Miss Kennedy," the busy director invited. "I image you're curious about why you're here."

"Yes, Mrs. Harrington. Is it about last night?"

"I do have a few questions. First, were you able to talk with Miss Jelinek after our discussion?"

Kylie shook her head. "No, we were never alone. Right after dinner I left for rehearsal, and I think Jaimie went to the lounge."

"Did she mention not attending the rehearsal?"

Kylie nodded but remained quiet. She did not appreciate being put in this position. It wasn't fair.

"I know this is difficult for you," Mrs. Harrington said. "We'll move on. Why was Miss Santos at the rehearsal?"

"She just wanted to watch. She didn't have anything else to do."

"She couldn't work on her part?"

"I guess not," Kylie said. "She has worked hard and knows all her lines, and the only scene she's in is with Jay, and he was busy with the campfire."

"Right. She plays Margaret. The reason I'm wondering is because she was so good as Second Witch, and Miss Jelinek accused her of trying to take over the role."

"Jaimie wasn't being fair. Helen asked Roe to fill in because she was the only girl there who wasn't in the cast. Roe knew the lines because she played the part once for an English assignment and is really good at remembering. Really, Mrs. Harrington, Roe did nothing wrong, and now she wishes she hadn't gone."

Mrs. Harrington sighed. "It's really unfortunate that Mrs. Crofts-Baker was there and witnessed Miss Jelinek's behavior. She feels that I must drop her and give the part to Miss Santos."

"But Roe can't sing. She's awful!"

"I'm not suggesting she take over the entire role; just the witch scene. You say she's solid on her part in *Brutus*, and Jay says she's wonderful to work with. I just don't see how the audience would accept her sudden appearance as the witch."

As troubling as the situation was, Kylie couldn't help considering a solution. Her experience helping with *Mouse* and directing *Cinderella, Cinderella* had made her used to problem solving. "Couldn't she wander in occasionally as an extra camper? Maybe a few lines, and she could join in when we all speak at once or adlib."

Mrs. Harrington smiled. "That would work. I'll send for Miss Santos and then get busy on the script right away."

Kylie hesitated, returning to reality. "The thing is Roe might not want to do it—because of Jaimie. You see, they used to be friends, but there was a problem. Here, they've been getting back together again. I don't think Roe will want to lose a friend over a part."

"Not much of a friend if that's the case," Mrs. Harrington said.

Mrs. Harrington was right, of course, and whatever happened would be between her and Roe—and Jaimie.

"Please ask Miss Santos to come see me as soon as possible."

Roe walked slowly out of the main building. This birthday was not off to a good start. Mrs. Harrington had made a flattering offer, and Roe was tempted. She'd enjoy being in a play with her friends, and she knew she could handle both roles. But if she accepted, she might as well give up thinking she and Jaimie could be friends again. Mrs. Harrington had made it clear that Mrs.

Crofts-Baker wanted Roe to play the witch, and it was also clear that as camp owner, she had the last word. Mrs. Harrington had given Roe the weekend to decide.

Roe was relieved Jaimie hadn't been in the cabin when Kylie came with the message. She supposed she should return and let Kylie know what had happened, but she wanted to be alone for a while. A walk to the dunes and the lake might help clear her head. Strolling along Lake Michigan helped her to think—it was kind of like being home.

But someone else had sought the lake for privacy. Eric! Talking things over with him might be better than being alone. "Hello, stranger," she said, and then laughed when he jumped. "Sorry. You must have been miles away."

"About two hundred sixty," Eric admitted.

"Back home," Roe said. "Everything okay?"

"I don't know. I'm afraid—That is, I hope so. But I'm glad you're here. Happy Birthday."

"Thanks, I think."

"What's wrong, Roe." Typically Eric abandoned his own troubles when he saw someone else was unhappy.

Roe explained what had taken place the evening before and about her talk with Mrs. Harrington. "I'd like the part," she said, "but Jaimie is certain to blame me."

"Phew! When it was her decision not to go." Eric sat on the sand and pulled Roe down next to him. "Kylie told me there were problems, and I said it was time for Jaimie to learn the hard way. I might have made a mistake."

"What do you think I should do?"

"Take the part. She's going to lose it anyway. In fact, I wouldn't be surprised if she lost her other parts in the show, too. Her attitude stinks, and she's doing a lousy job. She seems to think she's owed a lead in everything she does."

"Two musicals at CBT, *Cinderella, Cinderella,* and the stage manager of *Mouse.* That should be enough for anyone. And she doesn't have a scholarship, Eric. She lied about it."

"Oh, Jaimie." Eric sighed. "If she doesn't wake up and change, jealousy is going to cost her everything, especially her friends."

"Mrs. Harrington has given me the weekend to think about it."

"And you'll be with your dad. What time is he coming?"

"He said around four. It's going to be a long, strange day, and everyone seems to be acting weird."

Eric grinned. "Starting with you and me."

"And Brad."

"That's for sure," Eric said. "I tried to get him to go back to the cabin with me, but no dice. Then I suggested a hike. He said he planned to stay at Crofts House all day. And he was carrying his backpack—on a Saturday!"

Roe decided not to mention that Brad planned to give Kylie and her another birthday present. Whatever was wrong with Brad, he seemed to want it to remain private—for now. She shrugged. "And what's up with you, Eric?"

He looked troubled. "I don't know. Just a feeling that something bad is going to happen."

"Like a premonition?"

"That sounds a little dramatic, but yeah, I guess."

"Too much Shakespeare," was Roe's verdict. "Camp Shakespeare."

Both started laughing. "We've walked farther than we thought," Eric said, "and it's starting to rain. Come on, before we get drenched." Hand in hand, they ran back.

Kylie and Roe took their overnight bags to the student lounge, where they would wait for Mr. Santos. Kylie was worried. "I haven't seen Jaimie all day."

"I haven't either but can't say I wanted to." Roe told Kylie about her conversation with Mrs. Harrington.

"I'm not really surprised," Kylie said. "You wowed them last night."

"But I didn't mean to. I was just helping out and having a good time. It might have worked out if Jaimie had kept her temper and—"

"Knew her lines. Yeah, even after she blew up at you, she might have been okay if she'd given a decent performance. You can't blame Mrs. Harrington for putting the play first. What are you going to do?"

"I don't know," Roe confessed. "I'll probably take it. It's not like Jaimie and I will ever be friends again."

"I might not be her friend much longer, either."

"He's here!" Brad rushed into the lounge with his announcement. "Roe, your dad's out front. Are you ready?"

Kylie grinned. "Anyone would think you were going, Brad. You're more excited than we are."

Brad refused to take the bait. "You're signed out, right? Let's go!"

Shrugging, both girls followed him out to the Santos's car. Roe sat in front with her dad, and Kylie crawled into the backseat with the luggage. Finally, Brad leaned toward her and opened his backpack. First looking both ways, he gave Kylie a medium-sized birthday gift bag and a card.

"Heavy," Kylie said. "Thanks, Brad, but what about—"

He held up his hand. "I'm getting soaked. You'll understand when you open the bag. Open it much later." And then he said loudly enough for the whole camp to hear, "Happy birthday!" He closed the door and rushed back into Crofts House.

"Happy birthday, indeed," Mr. Santos said, merging onto the main road out of camp. "What's gotten into Brad?"

Roe shook her head. "He's been acting strange all day. The weird thing is he's already given us our birthday presents, and he was supposed to give us something different. Maybe it's in the bag. Open it, Kylie."

Kylie hesitated. "No, I think we'll do what Brad said. He usually makes sense, so he must have a good reason." She tried to change the subject. "Where are we going, Uncle Carl? Somewhere close by?"

"Depends on what you define as close. About 150 miles—Traverse City. You'll like it. We're staying at Tamarack Lodge. Nice place—I've stayed there before."

"As long as they have good food and firm mattresses." Roe giggled. "What we call a perfect birthday present."

"It's a guarantee," her dad said.

They became lost in their own thoughts. Kylie was used to Roe and her dad's long periods of silence. She found a map of Michigan on her iPhone and studied it. They were moving due north along Lake Michigan and would eventually arrive at Traverse Bay. Other than the southern shore, she didn't know Michigan. Could be a cool family trip sometime to go around the state. She surely wouldn't see much today because of the rain.

"Dad, how's Mother?" Roe ended the quiet.

"Not good. She's hardly eating anything. She's calmer and seems to have adjusted to the place, but I don't think she recognized me. Pleased to have a visitor—that's it." He chuckled. "She's still reading that damn book upside down."

"Did she ask about me?"

"No, honey. I—What the heck?" He grabbed hold of the steering wheel as an old, muddy, pickup truck appeared out of nowhere and attempted to ram their car off the road. Kylie awoke to the sudden danger. They were on a bridge crossing an inlet. The bridge had railings, but they were built as a warning, not a protection. And the road was slick from the rain.

"Dad! Oh, no! Help!" Roe began to whimper. This was not the first time she'd faced something like this.

"I'm doing my best, honey. You girls protect your heads the best you can. Kylie, get down."

Rather than obeying, Kylie tried to see the license plate, but the truck didn't have one—at least not in front. She tried to see the driver and his companion, but the windshield wipers made it difficult. A loud siren brought the crisis to an end. In spite of the slippery road, their attacker zoomed away a few short moments before a motorcycle policeman pulled up next to them.

"You folks okay?"

"Thanks to you, we are," Mr. Santos said. "You might have saved our lives."

"I got word from helicopter patrol. They're trying to track the driver now, but the truck went into the woods some miles ahead. Those woods are mighty thick. Won't be easy to see anything under the canopy of leaves. Did you happen to get the license plate number?"

Kylie shook her head. "I tried, but there wasn't any front one." Kylie thought the driver seemed familiar, but she couldn't tell. Probably not.

"Well, that's a clue, anyway," said the officer. "Could you tell how many people were in the car?"

"Two men," Kylie said with certainty.

Officer Mike Warren and Mr. Santos exchanged cards. Mr. Santos explained that they were going to Traverse City and would stay at Tamarack Lodge, "if they were needed."

Making certain their car could move safely back onto the highway, Officer Warren resumed his patrol.

"You okay, girls?"

"I guess," Roe said, still shaking and trying to hold back tears. "But there's been too much toil and trouble."

"Quadruple by now," Kylie agreed. "I think maybe we should stop somewhere, Uncle Carl. It's time we opened Brad's mysterious present."

"McDonalds okay?" Dad asked."

"A shake and fries for me," Kylie agreed.

"And a bathroom break," Roe said. "But let's not all go in at once."

"Surely you don't think we're still in danger," her dad said.

Roe shrugged. "Probably not, but why take chances?"

The girls went inside first and presented Mr. Santos with their menus—chocolate shakes and fries—when they returned. After insisting that the car stay locked, Mr. Santos took his turn and brought back the treats. "I brought hamburgers as well," he said. "Just a hunch that you didn't eat much today, and dinner won't be until late."

"I never fully appreciated McDonalds before," Roe declared, as soon as nothing was left but empty sacks and boxes. "Now I think we should open Brad's curious present."

"Wait," Kylie cautioned. A truck resembling the one that had put them in danger had pulled into a gas pump. Fortunately Mr. Santos had parked in a somewhat concealed location, and they didn't believe the driver had seen them—yet.

"There's no license plate in front," Roe said. "It could be the same one." Then the driver got out and examined the pump in disgust before storming into the restaurant. Kylie didn't think he was the same man she'd seen before, but it sure looked like the same truck—almost too muddy for her to determine the color.

"Whoever he is, he must not want to use a credit card," Mr. Santos said. "Well, he'll be in a long line inside. We'd better take off."

"First we need to get the license plate number," Roe said, "but we shouldn't get out of the car."

Her father nodded. "I can do that." Quickly, he drove around to the back of the parked truck, and Kylie copied the number. Then he returned to the highway and took off as fast as permitted. Reaching into his pocket, he handed Roe a card. Quickly, Roe used her cell phone and gave Officer Warren the license number and truck location.

"We're on it," he said. "If we don't get there in time, we might get lucky with closed circuit camera."

Then Mr. Santos did the unexpected. He took the next exit into a small town and parked at a convenience store. "We'll take back roads to Traverse City," he said. "No one, other than Officer Warren, knows our destination. It will take awhile longer, but we'll arrive in time for our dinner reservation. Must make a phone call." He called the hotel, explaining that they would check in later than planned, and then he sent a text message. Finally, he returned to the road and said, "Now, what's going on?"

"It's a long story," Kylie said, "and probably doesn't have anything to do with what just happened." Kylie decided she hadn't seen the driver before, after all. "It doesn't make sense that anyone was trying to kill us."

Roe shivered. Kylie's word "kill" changed everything. If the policeman hadn't come in time, they would have been forced over an embankment—probably killed. "It was horrible—like being with Mateo again."

"Trying to kill us might be a stretch of the imagination," her dad said. "After all, the rain was coming down hard and the bridge was slippery. Now, about Brad—shall I pull over again?"

"No, go ahead and drive, Uncle Carl. I'll read Brad's note." Kylie opened the birthday bag. "Not a present," she said. "Two jars of dirty water."

"Two?" Roe asked.

"They're labeled. One is a sample of water from Brad's cabin, and the other from Shimmer Lake, dated this morning."

"This morning? Not over two weeks ago? Read the note, Kylie."

"Please," said Mr. Santos. "I don't understand any of this."

"Okay. Brad's handwriting, so be patient."

> *Dear Kylie,*
>
> *I am staying in Crofts House today, so I'll be able to get these samples to Mr. Santos. Last night, I went to put the original jar into a paper bag, but the jar was empty. Early this morning, I returned to the lake. A lot more ropes and signs than before, so I filled the jar fast and got out of there. I felt like I was being followed, so I got off the path and hid. Two*

*men rushed by. I hid behind bushes and trees until I got back
to the cabin. I decided Mr. Santos should see what the water
in the taps was like, too. By then, the sun was coming up, so
I started up the trail to the lodge. That's when I bumped into
you.*

*I'm going home with Gary for the weekend. We'll
return Monday morning, too. I hope you and Roe have a
great birthday celebration, and that we are all making
something out of nothing.*

Take care,

Brad

"I'm beginning to understand. Something is wrong with your drinking water."

"And Shimmer Lake, Dad." Roe told him of the warnings not to drink the water and their not being allowed to even go near the lake—much less swim or go boating. "And the lake was advertised in the camp brochures. The older kids say this is the first summer it's been out of bounds."

"We're hoping you can have the water tested," Kylie said. "We're kind of wondering if someone at Crofts is covering it up."

Mr. Santos's cell phone rang. "It's Detective Warren," Roe said, answering. "Hello, Detective Warren. My dad is driving, so I'll put you on speaker."

"Well, we tracked down the truck," the detective said. "It belongs to a local farmer, but he didn't have anything to do with what happened to you. His truck was stolen for a few hours, and then returned—almost out of gas. The farmer was furious. Probably a couple of delinquents out for a joyride and not paying attention to the slippery road."

"Thanks for letting us know so quickly, Officer," Mr. Santos said loudly. "That's certainly a great relief."

Promising they'd keep their eyes open for further problems with the culprits, Detective Warren said goodbye.

"I'm glad that's over," Mr. Santos said, but Kylie and Roe just looked at each other and nodded. The close incident hadn't seemed like any accident to them.

"Back to the water problem," Kylie said. "What do you think, Uncle Carl?"

"Well, it wouldn't be the first time something similar has happened." Mr. Santos told them about a woman named Erin Brockovich and her fight against industrial pollution. Roe and Kylie listened with open mouths. "Oh, dear, I'm not helping the situation, am I? Try not to worry. I'll take some extra time here and go to one of my labs in Ann Arbor on Monday. Like Brad said, it could be nothing." He grinned. "Much ado about nothing."

Roe and Kylie nodded. It could be nothing, but neither of them believed that.

SCENE 8

There was a star danced, and under that was I born.
— William Shakespeare, *Much Ado about Nothing*

THE BIRTHDAY SURPRISE CREW HAD also given McDonalds their business. "What time do you think we'll get there?" Danny asked, as he swallowed the last bite of his burger.

Mr. Kennedy checked his watch. "About three, I imagine. Check-in time is two. We'll get there before the others even leave camp. None of us has been to Traverse City. We might walk around a bit if it stops raining; our dinner reservation is for seven."

"I've got an idea," Beth said. "Let's make sure the restaurant has a birthday cake for Kylie and Roe. If they don't, maybe we can get one at a bakery."

"And we can decorate their hotel room with streamers and balloons," Danny suggested.

Beth smiled at him. "Great idea, Danny."

As soon as they returned to the car, Danny insisted Beth sketch what the decorated hotel room might look like. "Then we can write down what supplies we need." They put their heads together and got to work.

Mrs. Kennedy turned around and watched them. "Beth, I have a thought you might want to consider. A friend of mine is in charge of our park district camp. It will meet in the morning the last two weeks of July. She wants Kylie to assist in dramatics but still needs someone to help with art. If you're interested, I'll recommend you. I've been trying to talk Danny into attending, but—"

"Hey! If Beth goes, I will, too," Danny declared.

"That would be wonderful, Aunt Jane. I'd love to." Beth's summer was taking shape. She was becoming her own person, no longer depending on her friends to make room for her.

Kylie didn't want to alarm Roe and Uncle Carl, but she had seen enough of the men in the truck to be certain they were adults—not teens out "joyriding." And the driver had seemed familiar, although she wasn't able to place him. Just as they entered Traverse City, she put her thoughts into words. "I'm still wondering if the driver connected us with the water sample."

"That doesn't seem likely," Uncle Carl said.

"No, but—"

"Kylie's right, Dad. At least we should be careful. Brad was scared enough to remain at Crofts House until he could give us the jars and the note."

"And he thought he was spotted filling them at the lake. And then followed. I didn't tell anyone about Brad ever getting the sample, did you?"

"No, just you, me, Brad, Eric—"

"We never told Jaimie, thank goodness. But Brad did tell—"

"Kurt!" Both girls shouted.

"Well, that's all right then," Mr. Santos said.

"No, Dad, it isn't!"

Kylie agreed. "Kurt means well, but he's the biggest gossip in the world. And he brags all the time. He can't resist an audience for his tall tales."

"He'll change the story until it's almost unbelievable, but a few might believe him, if they already know or suspect the truth."

"Someone was listening," Kylie said. "Oh, what were we thinking? Jaimie can keep a secret better than Kurt can."

"What's done is done." Mr. Santos pulled into the front of the best hotel in Traverse City. "Put it on hold for a while and try to enjoy your birthday celebration."

Kylie gasped. "This is our hotel? It's grander than Markey Castle! Will we have time to clean up before dinner?"

"Nope. We have three minutes to get to the restaurant. You ladies must perform your acts of beauty magic right here. The staff will take our bags and park the car."

Kylie and Roe rustled into their purses. "The jars?" Roe reminded her father.

"Locked in my briefcase, which will stay glued to me," he said. "Santos," he told the head waiter as soon they were inside. They were led to a table, set for seven.

"Must be a mistake," Kylie said, when out from another room came— "Mom, Dad, Danny, Beth!" Kylie rushed into her mother's arms.

"Surprise!" Beth and Danny yelled.

This was a birthday party they'd never forget. Roe and Kylie didn't know at the time that it was the last birthday they'd share for many years. The steaks were juicy, the cake elegant, and the gifts creative. Beth gave each a painting: Roe's was an oil of the Santos's and Kennedys' houses, side by side. For Kylie, a watercolor of Markey Castle—in winter, of course. Danny gave both booklets of word searches and crossword puzzles that he had devised himself. "Let me know if you can't solve anything," he said. "I could have made mistakes."

Kylie's mom and dad gave the girls clothes—more summer shorts and shirts and jeans and sweaters for back to school. Roe thought it a little strange that her father hadn't given them anything, but he was always generous and had paid for the restaurant and hotel expenses. She and Kylie would continue their long birthday tradition when they returned to Castle Bluff—shopping, with an agreed-upon amount to spend, each buying something special to give the other. The first time they'd done this, they had only a dollar to spend.

They were about to leave for their rooms, nagged by Danny's "wait until you see!" comments, when Roe's cell phone rang.

Annoyed, she looked at the caller ID. "Guess I'd better answer. It's the camp office—Hello? Oh, Eric . . . what's wrong? Oh, no! I'm so sorry! Well, I'm not sure. My dad wasn't going back until sometime next week. Let me talk it over with him and the Kennedys. Someone will call right back. Yes, I understand. That does complicate things. Will you still be in the office? Okay."

"Roe?"

"It's Eric's dad," she said, fighting tears. "He just had a heart attack, and he might not make it. Eric has to go home. He needs a ride there. But Dad isn't going home."

"That won't be a problem," Mr. Kennedy said. "A tight squeeze, but we can make it work. We're sorry, Beth. We know you were looking forward to your overnight."

"One more thing," Roe said. "Jaimie. Eric says she's very upset and wants to go home, too."

"I don't understand—" Mr. Santos started.

Kylie nodded. "Jaimie has known Eric's family her whole life. Mr. Stein is like an uncle."

The adults conferred. The Kennedys would not have room for four passengers—Eric, Jaimie, Beth, and Danny—plus their luggage. The Kennedys didn't understand why Roe's father couldn't drive until he said he had important business at his lab in Ann Arbor. Only Roe and Kylie knew what that business was.

"I have an idea," Mr. Santos said. "Let me make a few phone calls, including one to Eric, and then I'll let you know. I'll take care of the bill and meet you upstairs in your rooms. Jane and Dan, it makes no sense driving anywhere tonight; the roads might still be slick. You wouldn't reach the camp until past midnight. I don't think you'd be allowed in. Tomorrow morning will be soon enough." He had told the Kennedys about the incident on the bridge. All the adults, at least, had dismissed it as a mere accident.

Even though they weren't so sure about the accident part, Roe and Kylie smiled. Mr. Santos would surely fix everything, and at least they'd have their birthday overnight.

Danny was so pleased with the girls' reaction to the decorated room that he was allowed to stay with them for a while. Beth whispered that the whole thing had been his idea and that it would be cruel to exclude him. They had brought the leftover birthday cake to the room, and the first order of business was to polish it off. Time later to talk in private about Eric and Jaimie—and everything!

Just as Roe announced she couldn't keep her eyes open for even one more minute, there was a knock at the door, and her father entered. "Looks like we've got a plan," he said. "First thing in the morning, the Kennedys will drive to Shimmer Lake, pick up Eric and Jaimie, and return home to Castle Bluff."

"Oh." Beth and Danny groaned. "Too crowded," Danny said.

"That's right," Roe's father said. "Way too crowded, so it's not going to happen. Danny and Beth will go home with me when my work is completed—and they will be guests at the camp until that happens."

"What?" all four yelled at once.

"Uncle Carl, explain," Kylie insisted.

"I thought I had. It's really very simple. I talked to Mrs. Crofts-Baker, and she approved. Beth will take the place in your cabin vacated by Jaimie, and Danny will take Eric's, although I guess there are extra bunks in each cabin if Eric and Jaimie return."

"Does that mean I have to sing Shakespeare?" Danny cried in alarm.

Kylie laughed. "Of course not, silly. I don't know what's going to happen to the play. Mrs. Harrington will decide that. But Danny, you'll have fun. You can hike and swim in the pool and watch the rehearsals—"

"You'll love seeing the stage combat classes," Roe added. "And you'll be with Brad and Kurt—" She stopped and looked at Beth, who seemed troubled.

Mr. Santos cleared his throat. "Well, Danny. I think the girls need some time alone now. Suppose you and I check out our room and find a movie to watch together."

Roe and Kylie sat on either side of Beth. "It will be okay, Beth. You probably won't see Kurt that much. He's not in the plays we're in."

Beth shook her head. "Don't worry about me. It's not like I'd never see him again. I just didn't expect to so soon. Maybe Kurt and I should talk. I wouldn't mind going back to being friends again."

Silently after muttering goodnights, the girls got into bed—Kylie and Beth in the king-sized and Roe in the twin. Tired, they intended to go right to sleep but, of course, ended up talking practically all night long.

SCENE 9

---

*Our doubts are traitors, and make us lose
the good we oft might win, by fearing to attempt.*
– William Shakespeare, *Measure for Measure*

"HEY, SLEEPYHEADS!" NO REACTION. DANNY, determining which bed lump was his sister, stealthily put a hand under the cover and tickled Kylie's feet.

"What? Why you—" Kylie sat and glared at a small imp with a devilish grin. "Danny, it's the middle of the night. How dare you wake us up?"

A head emerged from the lump in the twin bed. "Wait! What time is it?"

Mr. Santos, once Danny had done the dirty work, wheeled in a cart loaded with trays and opened the curtains. "It's ten o'clock, my darling daughter, and we have brought you breakfast in bed."

"Beth, wake up." Kylie nudged her friend. "Suddenly I'm starving. But what about you and Danny? What about your breakfast?"

"We ate hours ago with Mom and Dad," Danny said.

"Mom and Dad—where are they?"

"They left right after breakfast."

"Oh," Kylie said flatly. It wasn't anyone's fault. Uncle Carl had to stay if the sample were to be analyzed. And of course Mom and Dad had to help Eric get to his father. She wasn't so sure about Jaimie, who could not be trusted and might be using this as a way to get closer to Eric. Kylie shrugged, suddenly homesick. "So what's next?" she asked.

"Danny and I have been doing things and making plans," Roe's dad said. "We'll give you one hour to eat, dress and pack up. Meet you in the lobby at eleven."

Roe made a face. "I thought we were staying here another night. Are we going back to camp?"

Mr. Santos led Danny out of the room. "Nope," he said, before closing the door.

Curiosity, even more than hunger, drove the girls into action.

A brand new cream-colored Audi was parked in the entrance as Roe, Kylie, and Beth waited for Mr. Santos and Danny to join them.

"I'm not a car person," Beth said, "but what a car!"

"Worth more than four years tuition at Crofts, I'll bet," Kylie said. "It will have to move before Uncle Carl can park there. That's probably where he and Danny are now—waiting to pull up."

"All set, gang?" Mr. Santos's voice rang out, almost on cue.

"Dad! Why aren't you in our car?"

Danny, hardly containing himself, was jumping up and down. "Wait until you find out!"

"Dad?"

"Change of plans. Our car would be a bit on the cramped side, so I rented a larger one. One of my employees will retrieve ours and drive it back to Castle Bluff. He has some work to take care of there and will drive the rental back after we get home. He's quite pleased, actually."

Roe and Kylie exchanged looks, both wondering if comfort was all he had in mind. Perhaps Mr. Santos wasn't totally convinced it was an accident, either, or at least didn't want to take a chance.

"We'll have to wait until that gorgeous car moves," Beth observed, "and I'll bet whoever owns it will leave whenever he feels like it."

Danny nearly choked with laughter. "That's our rental!" he sputtered. "I knew you'd be surprised."

"Dad, you didn't!"

"It's fine, Roe. The dealer owed me some favors. All aboard for Ann Arbor to find answers to our questions." When the girls looked anxiously at Danny, he added, "Danny's old enough to understand, so I filled him in about the water problem."

"I never thought I'd help solve a real mystery," Danny said. "Awesome!"

During their late-night chat, Kylie and Roe had managed to get Beth up to date about the near accident—if it was one—the polluted water, and their belief that Kurt couldn't keep his mouth shut.

Beth sighed. "Kurt always means well. If he was responsible for what happened, he'll feel terrible."

"He wasn't responsible," Roe said. "He's got a big mouth, but he didn't pollute the water or try to drive us off the road. I'm wondering about Jaimie. Is she really upset about Eric's dad, or is she still trying to get back with Eric?" She shrugged. "Maybe both."

Kylie wondered if Jaimie realized she could lose her parts in the play. Maybe going home was the out that allowed her to save face. Eric was solid on his part, and his dad's heart attack wasn't his fault. If Mr. Stein was okay and Eric returned soon, she doubted he would be recast. The main thing to worry about now wasn't the play, but their dangerous mystery. Did someone try to force them off the road, and did it have anything to do with the polluted water at Shimmer Lake?

Driving distance between Traverse City and Ann Arbor was close to four hours. They were talked out and bored before two hours had passed. Danny, who had been the most excited about his first big adventure, was growing tiresome with his constant *How much longers?*

Then a ding on Mr. Santos's phone provided a change. "Stratton, the man driving our car back to Castle Bluff, is trying to reach me. I need to return his call at the next tourist stop. We'll have lunch, too."

"Yes!" Danny cried.

Kylie, Roe, and Beth also indicated a desire to stretch their legs and eat. The young people headed for the rest rooms, agreeing to meet in the restaurant. When Mr. Santos joined them, they could tell something had happened.

"Dad? What's wrong? Is it Mother?"

"Quickly, order something we can take with us," her father ordered. "We can't stay here." At their looks he added, "I'll tell you in the car."

Back in the Audi, he remained quiet—and everyone, including Danny, stayed still, waiting. Finally, Kylie couldn't take it anymore. "Uncle Carl, you're making us really nervous!"

Mr. Santos sighed. "Sorry. Just trying to figure out what to do next. I'm not sure if you're safe being with me. For two cents, I'd take you back to camp."

"Then consider us broke, Dad. You don't get your two cents. Tell us what happened, so we can have an opinion."

"Something about your friend, Uncle Carl?" Danny prodded gently.

"Stratton is in a hospital back in Traverse City," Roe's father said finally. "Taken there by ambulance. Someone tried to drive him off the road, too."

Roe gasped. "Is he okay?"

"Banged up, but he assures me he'll be fine. Our car is totaled, though. I blame myself for not considering the possible threat to him."

"Did he get any information?" Beth asked.

"Car description and license plate number. It wasn't the truck this time—an old green Ford. The police are trying to trace it, but so far no luck. Again, there were two men, but Stratton was unable to describe them. I'm not sure what to do next. I think whatever is going on has something to do with my company rather than your camp. Possibly an attempt at espionage. It happens. For two cents, I'd take you all the way home to Castle Bluff."

"Not a single penny, Dad. Look, whoever it is doesn't know about this car or our destination. I say we continue on to Ann Arbor. At least we'll get some answers about the water."

"And we shouldn't go back to camp until tomorrow morning," Kylie said. "It would look weird if we suddenly changed plans. And we just can't go home, Uncle Carl. The play is less than a week away."

Mr. Santos opened his mouth, possibly to object, but Roe stopped him. "She's right, Dad. We can't let our casts down."

Kylie suddenly thought of Brad, spending the weekend at Gary's because of safety worries. She sent him a simple text. *Ok. Some danger. Tell u soon. b careful.* She muted her phone, so no one would hear it beep in reply. She didn't have to wait long for a thumbs up and a heart. Let Uncle Carl think the "accidents" had to do with his pharmaceutical company. She didn't agree, but at least he would have the water tested.

"So here's the plan," Mr. Santos said. 'I had thought we'd just pull into a motel for the night—somewhere between Ann Arbor and camp—but we need better security. Thus, we're going to treat ourselves to another 5-star hotel in Ann Arbor. We'll check in, and then I want you four to lock yourself in one room, and I'll take a taxi to the lab. I'll return immediately. Do not open the door to anyone but me. We'll order room service and stay in the hotel until very early tomorrow."

"But—" Kylie started, but Roe shook her head. Kylie understood. When Roe's father made up his mind—that was it. The alternatives were either returning to camp immediately or a long ride back to Castle Bluff. Neither was acceptable. She was disappointed, though. It would have been interesting to see the lab and find out how they were going to test the water.

"They won't start testing until tomorrow, and it will take a few days to get the results," Mr. Santos said, perhaps guessing Kylie's thoughts.

A few days, Beth mused. She wondered if she should have come at all. She could be back home working on props and scenery, or at the pool with Marla. Instead, she was stuck in Michigan—possibly in danger—and facing an unwanted reunion with Kurt.

Late that night, Kylie received a long text from her mom saying that Eric's dad would be okay. He'd received a wakeup call to take better care of himself—to exercise and eat properly. Eric would return to camp, but Jaimie had decided not to. "She was impossible on the ride home," Mom wrote. "I question her mental stability."

"That's a relief," Roe said. "I mean about Eric's dad. I'm not sure how I feel about Jaimie. I sure won't miss her." Then she giggled. "Aren't adults funny? They think texts should sound like real letters."

SCENE 10

Foul whisp'rings are abroad.
—William Shakespeare, *Macbeth*

MR. SANTOS ACCOMPANIED THE GROUP DOWN the path to Barrymore Cabin. The girls would drop off their luggage before returning to Crofts House. Danny would hang on to his bag until Brad could escort him to Sondheim Cabin.

"Now, I don't want any of you to come here alone," Roe's dad cautioned. "Preferably travel in a large group. I feel certain you're safe, but it would be wise not to take chances."

"Don't worry, Dad," Roe said, pulling a note from her mail sack. "We are going to be so busy with tech and dress rehearsals, we won't have time for anything else. This note is a request from Mrs. Harrington saying I should see her the minute I return. I guess that minute should be now. Rehearsals start in one hour."

Beth shared glances with Danny. Both seemed uncomfortable. "Are you sure Danny and I belong here? You'll be busy—we won't fit in."

"Danny will be fine once we see the boys." Kylie tried to assure them. "Beth, let's see if they need more painters on stage. I'll bet there's still plenty to do."

Beth nodded but didn't seem convinced.

"And Beth," Mr. Santos said, "you might be the right person to talk to Kurt about what he might have revealed. You know him well enough not to let him get away with anything."

Not a good idea, Dad, Roe said silently. But her father had no way of knowing the situation between Beth and her former boyfriend.

"What will you do next, Uncle Carl?" Kylie asked. "Go home to Castle Bluff?"

Mr. Santos shook his head, as if trying to organize his thoughts. "Not yet. Probably not until we all go home together. I didn't tell you, but I got an emergency call this morning from my wife's doctor. I might have to make some medical decisions. Also, I've got to return the rental car, purchase a new one—fortunately I should be fine with insurance—and see how I might help Stratton. And wait for the results—of something."

They all got it, Roe thought. It was not wise to talk about the test results—not yet and not here. As for medical decisions, that didn't sound promising, but she didn't want to talk to Dad with the others around.

Back at Crofts House, Kylie offered to wait in the lounge with Beth and Danny while Roe went for her meeting with the director. Her father offered hugs all around. "I hate leaving you here," he said, "but it seems my only option. All of you have my phone number. Text me if anything is wrong. Roe, honey, I'll let you know about Mother as soon as I know more."

Roe nodded, wondering how she'd feel if this truly was the end.

Beth squirmed. She wondered how long she'd have to wait for—well, for whatever was coming next. As exciting as it all had been, she wished now she had crammed herself into the Kennedy's car and gone home with the others. Danny looked unhappy, too. Neither of them belonged. "How long will Roe be?" she asked.

Kylie smiled. "Not long. We have rehearsal in a half hour. You can come, too."

"What about me?" Danny said. "I thought I was going to see swordfights and stuff."

"Be patient," Kylie said. "As soon as we see Kurt or Brad, you'll go with them."

"Speak of the devil," Beth breathed, as Kurt came bounding over to them.

"You're back," he said, "with some unexpected company." Enthusiastically, he thrust out his hand to Danny. "Put her there, buddy!" And then more subdued to Beth, "This is a surprise, Beth, but welcome."

"Thanks," Beth said. "Danny and I came up for Kylie and Roe's birthdays, but things happened."

"My parents took Eric and Jaime back with them," Kylie explained, "and there wasn't enough room in the car for Danny and Beth. They'll probably go back with Roe's dad as soon as he finishes his business."

"Well, that's great. I hope you'll get to see the plays."

"Oh, there's Brad," Kylie said. "Good, I can't wait for Roe any longer. I've got to get to rehearsal. Brad, I'll get you caught up later. Danny, you go along with Kurt and Brad. Coming, Beth?"

Beth shook her head. "Not just yet. I'll wait for Roe, and I'd like to talk to Kurt for a few minutes. Okay?"

"Okay. Gotta run!"

Brad picked up Danny's bag. "Are you ready to see me in a lion costume, Danny? Guaranteed funny."

"All right!" said Danny.

Beth did not want to do this, but Mr. Santos said it would be safer for her than the others. "Is there somewhere we can talk, Kurt? Somewhere private."

Kurt shrugged. "Is it necessary? I thought you said everything you wanted to back home, and I've got a rehearsal."

"It's necessary, and it's not about you and me. One of the reasons Danny and I are here is because someone might have tried to kill Kylie, Roe, and her dad. Now, where can we go?"

Kurt dropped his offended ex-boyfriend act and led her outside and a short way down a path. "So what happened?"

As quickly as possible, Beth gave a shortened version, concluding with the attempt on Mr. Santos's driver and the destruction of his car.

"Do you think it has something to do with the water?"

Beth shrugged. "We don't know, but it might, and we can't help wondering if you told someone about it?"

"Me? Of course not! I would never—"

"Kurt, are you sure? Couldn't you have changed the story to make it more exciting? That's the kind of thing you do."

Kurt flushed. "Well, maybe. There were a bunch of us in the cabin, and I spun a tale about the water being poison, a plot by aliens to take over the camp to create the first outer space amateur theater. Honest, Beth, it was so farfetched no one would have believed me."

"That is farfetched. I don't see how that could cause anything to happen. Anything else?"

Kurt started to deny it, and then turned pale. "Oh, no! I am so stupid! I said the reason Brad was leaving was because a real scientist was going to test the water."

"And first Brad was in danger, and then someone must have seen him give a large package to Roe and Kylie. Oh, Kurt!"

Kurt groaned. "I'm an idiot. What can I do?"

"Probably nothing, except not say anything more. Any idea who might have heard you?"

"Just the guys in the cabin. Oh—one of the leaders is Mrs. Crofts-Baker's grandson. I guess it's possible—"

"Don't say anything more, Kurt. Let's go back now."

"Wait, Beth. I did overhear something. The grandson, Joe, was talking to some people outside a rehearsal room where you can hear everything. He said maybe there wouldn't be a camp much longer because someone wanted to buy it for a lot of money—some steel manufacturer. He said he didn't think his grandmother would sell, though."

"That could be very important. I'll text Mr. Santos right away."

"The lounge would be the best place, and there won't be many people there now. I'll show you. And I'm really sorry, Beth."

"I know, and I'm sorry, too—that I hurt your feelings, that is. It's just that you're going to Crofts and I'll only be in eighth grade, and, oh, Kurt, can't we be just friends again?"

Kurt smiled his puckish best. "That would be terrific," he said.

"Thank you, Miss Santos—Roe. That will be a big relief to all of us." Mrs. Harrington handed Roe a binder. "You'll find all the sides you need to learn in here. Fortunately, you already know the Second Witch. The rest is just when you walk on with other campers and ad lib and react when they do."

"The song?" Roe asked fearfully.

Mrs. Harrington laughed. "Not a problem. Miss Drew will take over the singing role Miss Jelinek vacated. And Roe, Mrs. Crofts-Baker will be so pleased I'm sure you'll receive a scholarship to the school in the fall. You already live in Castle Bluff, correct? Boarding won't be a problem."

Roe nodded but didn't respond further. Whether or not she remained in Castle Bluff, she was now certain she wouldn't attend Crofts School of Performing Arts. Between *Anne* last winter and all the problems at camp, she didn't think Crofts was the right place for her. Besides, she didn't want to be an actor after all. It was fun in middle school and maybe she'd try out for plays again somewhere, but that wasn't the future she wanted. She was only fourteen, so she didn't have to decide now. She'd like to concentrate on learning Spanish, and maybe someday she could do something to help minorities that were discriminated against. "I'll see you at rehearsal, Mrs. Harrington."

The director grabbed her promptbook. "Which is right now!" She bustled out of the office.

Roe looked around . She had been with Mrs. Harrington far longer than she expected. The lobby and lounge were empty except for a few students she didn't know. She shrugged. Oh, well. She'd catch up with everyone later.

SCENE 11

We will meet; and there we may rehearse most
obscenely and courageously.
—William Shakespeare, *A Midsummer Night's Dream*

IN SPITE OF A FULL day of rehearsals, Kylie managed to get Brad up to date before everyone retreated to their own cabins to fall into an exhausted sleep.

Brad turned pale and, uncharacteristically, grabbed her into a hug. "Kylie, you could have been killed!"

Kylie nodded. "We were all in danger—including you. You were right to stay at Crofts House. That's what we intend to do now—stay with a group always. At least we're loaded with rehearsals. That will keep our minds occupied and the rest of us safe."

"We have to remain on guard," Brad said, "and never go down the paths or to our cabins alone."

"Yes, that's what Uncle Carl said." Kylie also told Brad about Beth's discussion with Kurt. "He feels awful about blabbing."

"Well, he should," Brad said, "but that's Kurt for you. He'll be careful now, and he's keeping Danny amused."

"And Beth," Kylie added. "I think both of them are really happy to be friends again.

Once again, rehearsals all morning— no chance for any of them to talk until lunchtime. Roe was so hungry she didn't mind the cafeteria's almost tasteless food. Double rehearsals were double the work, if not double the trouble, she reflected. But she was grateful to have something to concentrate on, other than worrying about Dad and Mother. Roe and her friends were fairly safe here, keeping their eyes on each other, but Dad might be in danger every second. He was a smart man, though, and had had plenty of warnings. She hoped his friend Stratton was doing okay. Poor Dad had way too much to handle.

She looked for Kylie and Beth, but the first person she saw was—Eric! "Eric, what are you doing here?"

"You forgot why, where, and most important—Who?"

Roe laughed. "Yeah, all of that."

"Grab a tray and let's sit. I assume the others will come soon?"

With sandwiches and chips in front of them, Eric explained that his father was doing well enough for him to return, although his family would not be able to come to a performance. "I hardly care about that anymore," he added.

Roe nodded. She knew what he meant. "How did you get here?"

"Your dad. No, he didn't go down and drive me back. He booked me on a plane to Traverse City. It didn't cost much; my mom paid for it. The Kennedys took me to the airport, and your dad met me in Traverse City and drove me here just a few minutes ago."

"Dad did? Why didn't he stop to see me?"

"I'm not sure. He said he may get test results tomorrow or Thursday and will be in touch. Roe, I know you and he haven't always hit it off, but I think he's terrific."

Even though Roe's relationship with her father had changed in only a few short months, she hadn't forgotten his neglect for such a long, miserable time. "Things between us are a lot better," she said quietly. "Now do you think—"

"Eric! You're back!" The whole gang—Brad, Kurt, Beth, Kylie, and Danny—descended, with everyone demanding explanations.

"Later . . . later," Eric pleaded. "Now get me caught up on the plays. I hope I haven't missed too much."

Beth had had a wonderful two days helping in the scene shop and was excited for her friends to see her contributions, especially the tree in *Dear Brutus.* "Wait until you see Margaret's magical tree!" she told Roe.

Only one cast could use the stage at a time, so many students had decided to watch all of the tech rehearsals. *Brutus* was first. All three plays used the same forest backdrop. Smaller unit sets were wheeled in as needed. *Brutus* required a simple exterior garden set and, later, the special tree. However, each play was only allowed one smaller unit, so distinguishing Margaret's tree from the others was difficult. But Beth had solved the problem.

With a few glitches, the garden scene went fine, and so did the rest of Act One. Margaret would come in at the beginning of Act Two and go immediately to her magical tree. But when the curtain opened again, the trees were no different from what they had been before—a group of evergreens and a large but ordinary oak in the center—well painted but boring. "I suppose the oak is my tree," Roe said, clearly disappointed.

"Just watch," Beth said, as lights received their cue.

The whole area was dimmed, and then new lights came up, directly on the tree.

Suddenly it began to shimmer and sparkle. Colored circles and other shapes made it look as if it were wearing a fruit salad from every tree imaginable.

"Lights alone couldn't do that," Brad said. "I don't understand."

"It's a black light," Beth said, "but I used a special kind of paint."

Roe beamed, looking even happier than Beth. "That is Margaret's tree—exactly how I dreamed it should be."

"Beth," Kurt said, "where did you learn to do that? Not at CBT."

"The high school tech kids taught me," Beth said proudly. "I've learned so much about scene painting this summer. They're even going to let me help at the high school this year, even though I'll still be in middle school. They say I'll be their apprentice."

"I am impressed," Brad said.

"I guess I'll learn about it at Crofts," Kurt said.

Roe shook her head. "Not if you're in the acting track," she said. "Crofts talks a lot about well-rounded theater students, but they don't really mean it. It's not like middle school where you get to help out with everything."

"Or the high school," Beth added

"Or the high school," Brad echoed quietly.

Danny decided to make his presence known. "Beth is the best artist I know. She gave me one of her sketchbooks to keep forever. But I like the plays that have fighting in them best, and the scene with Brad playing a lion is so funny!"

He's thinking about not going to Crofts, Kylie thought. Soon they would all make a decision. Brad was doing a good job with his part in *Dream*, but she doubted he'd receive a full scholarship to the prestigious school. If not, he wouldn't think it fair for his father to pay when he didn't plan on becoming a professional actor. Not fair when there were so many children in Brad's family.

What about me? She wondered. I still love acting and think I'll always do it. But fulltime as a job—maybe the same part over and over for a long time? Well, she wasn't sure. Three or four performances were exciting, but then she always looked forward to the next part in the next play. And was she certain to be awarded a full scholarship? There were no guarantees in spite of what Cress had told them last year. Most of Kylie's friends would be at CBHS or still in middle school. That was something to consider.

Out of their whole group, Kurt and Roe were the only ones certain to have a place at Crofts. Not only had they received full camp scholarships, both had been noticed here. Kurt was irrepressible and loved, of course, but he was also a perfect Puck, always following directions implicitly while still putting his own creative stamp on the character. Like Kurt, Roe had started out with a lead but had gone the next step by adding a second play to her already demanding schedule.

Kylie sighed. In spite of all the problems last year, she missed middle school.

"Kylie?" Megan interrupted her thoughts. Kylie hadn't seen the busy cabin leader around lately since they weren't in the same play. "Kylie, just want to be sure you're coming to dinner tonight."

"Nowhere I'd rather be. You look pretty excited, Megan. What's going on?"

"You'll find out," Megan said, dashing off.

Roe was on mail duty but hadn't had time to deliver the small stack to the cabin and, more important, no one was available to go with her. She had not forgotten her father's advice to stay cautious and safe. She wished she could be alone, though, because of a letter that had come for her. She examined the stamp and return address on the envelope that had come all the way from Spain! Someone from her birth mother's family had written to her—a family she hadn't known existed until a few months ago. No time or privacy to read it now. She put it into her bag for later. Meanwhile, she would deliver what mail she could, starting with people gathered in the lounge.

"Megan," Roe called out, holding up a letter. Not just Megan but other cabin mates gathered around her, including Kylie.

"Thanks," Megan said, glancing indifferently at the letter. "Roe, you are coming to dinner tonight?"

Others in the group laughed. "We'll be there," Kylie said. "Like how many times do you have to remind us?"

"Just checking," Megan said, leaving to approach another group.

Kylie shook her head. "What do you suppose that's about?"

Roe grinned. "I could make a good guess, but I think I'll wait and see. A letter from your mom, Kylie."

Kylie tore it open. "They're coming to Saturday's matinee," she read eagerly. "Oh, but then they're driving straight home afterwards and taking Beth and Danny with them. I hope they won't be disappointed."

Roe shrugged. "Beth wants to get back to work on her play."

"And your dad will come to the Sunday matinee, and we'll go home with him. And then it will be over, Roe."

But would it really? Both wondered. What if the mystery weren't solved?

Roe held out the other letter. "From Jaimie," Kylie said. "Didn't expect to hear from her. Florida postmark. Do you know anything?"

Roe shook her head. "Eric has kept quiet, and I didn't want to ask him."

Kylie browsed quickly. "She sends best wishes for the play and, get this, 'I'm with my grandparents outside of Orlando for the rest of the summer. They have a wonderful theater program in their town, and I'm going to help with costumes and props. It is so much better than Crofts. Some of the actors get jobs at Disneyworld. Wouldn't that be amazing? The director is sorry I didn't come sooner so I could be in the musical. And one of the actors is very cute and interested in me. Please tell everyone how I'm doing. Break a leg, Kylie! Love, Jaimie.'"

"Tell everyone," Roe repeated. "Like Eric?"

"Doesn't sound like she's learned anything," Kylie said.

SCENE 12

Small cheer and great welcome makes a merry feast.
—William Shakespeare, *The Comedy of Errors*

EXCITEDLY, THE ACTORS FILED INTO the cafeteria. They had heard that dinner would be more festive than usual and the food decent. According to rumor, it was being catered. "It smells good!" Roe said to Eric.

"I think I smell fried chicken," he said, and then whispered, "I've noticed that none of the food since we've been here has relied on water for cooking—just one of the reasons the food is so bland and basic."

"Almost worse than fast food," Roe agreed. "I heard it wasn't this way other years."

"No pasta, no soup—dishes probably are washed in polluted water, which is bad enough."

"There's Kylie and Brad," Roe said. "They saved us a place."

This would be the campers' last main meal together. Because of four performances over the next three days, only platters of sandwiches and bowls of chips and fruit would be available for lunches and dinners. Tonight was an occasion with farewell speeches and whatever Megan had up her sleeve.

As soon as all had been served, Megan—and Jay—stood and addressed the group. "I know Megan has been making sure you would all be here," Jay said, "although I think the smells of this terrific meal would have been enough enticement." All laughed and applauded. "I thought you'd like to know of a few decisions we've made. You won't be surprised that in the fall

I'll continue with my directing program at U of I, but you might be that Megan is transferring there and will continue working on her theater education degree."

The group at Roe's table looked at each other and shrugged. Interesting news, perhaps, but hardly worthy of a big announcement. Roe smiled knowingly. She knew—she just knew what was coming.

Then Jay continued. "Oh, and by the way, Megan and I are engaged. She said yes!"

Megan grinned and held up her left hand. Great whoops and wild applause accompanied Megan's friends rushing to hug her. Roe glanced at Gretel, who had been pursuing Jay since camp began. She seemed fine, but how did she feel inside? You could never tell, Roe thought, how somebody felt inside.

Finally, the happy couple sat and dinner resumed. Seated next to Roe, Kylie gasped, before grabbing Roe's arm. "Look," Kylie said, pointing.

Seated at the head table were Mrs. Crofts-Baker and her two sons and nephew. "It's him," Kylie whispered. "Lawrence Baker. I knew I had seen him before."

Roe didn't need to ask who. Kylie could only mean one thing—the driver of the truck that had tried to force them off the road. "Careful," she whispered. "He's staring right at us."

Both studied their plates as if they'd never seen food before.

What was more dangerous? Contacting Uncle Carl or not? Surely texting was safe enough. Kylie had to take a chance. First, she used her phone to take a few photos. Many kids were doing that, so it didn't look suspicious. A smiling happy Megan and Jay, her friends at their table, and when she was sure they weren't looking her way, the family at the head table. Roe looked at her questioningly, but Kylie shook her head in warning. She typed a quick text, asking Uncle Carl to bring the police at once, and attached the photo. That should do it. She was about to show Roe the text when she stopped abruptly. Instead of hitting send, she deleted it.

What was wrong with her? The driver was Lawrence Baker, and she thought nephew Brian was the passenger. They were dangerous—guilty of attempted murder and maybe deliberately polluting the water. It was also possible that Mrs. Crofts-Baker and the other son were involved, too. Uncle Carl and the police should come immediately. What had stopped her? Why had she behaved so irresponsibly? Ignoring Roe's nudging, Kylie thought it over. The truth seemed trite and shallow, but she couldn't help it. It had been deeply imbedded in her that the show must go on. Unbidden, Kylie thought of a Shakespeare quotation: *The play's the thing in which we'll catch the conscience of a king.* Could that happen in this case?

"Kylie?"

"We'll talk later, Roe." The show must go on, Kylie decided. Then they'd see what happened. She'd contact Uncle Carl before the last show Sunday— or maybe Saturday night.

A large cheer interrupted Kylie's thoughts as a huge cake was wheeled into the room. This was more like it! Cake, instead of stale chocolate chip cookies! Then Mrs. Crofts-Baker stood and demanded attention. "I'm pleased you're enjoying our last dinner of the season," she said. "I, of course, am thrilled with Megan and Jay's news. To think they first met right here in this room. We wish them every success and trust that they will be with us next summer." Kylie was certain she saw the men exchange looks at that, but did Mrs. C. know her camp might be gone? "You have made Crofts proud this summer, and I am certain your performances will be well received. I thank you with all my heart. Break a leg!"

Kylie and Roe joined the cheering. They liked Mrs. Crofts-Baker.

Before returning to the cabins that evening, Roe and Kylie managed to gather their group together and explain what was going on.

"Are you certain they looked directly at you?" Beth asked. Both Roe and Kylie nodded yes. "Then you aren't safe. None of us are, especially you two and Brad—maybe even Kurt. We've got to stick together."

"Danny will be with one of us at all times," Brad said. "And I think we'll walk with you girls to your cabin before we go to ours."

"And we'll pick you up there tomorrow morning," Kurt said, so seriously Beth hardly recognized him.

"Maybe we should plan on staying at Crofts House all day tomorrow," she suggested. "Your costumes are there. Just take everything you'll need for the whole day, and we'll follow the same routine after the show tomorrow night."

It made sense. The next few days would be very long ones, and they should be prepared for anything. All of them agreed that Kylie and Roe *should* ask Mr. Santos to contact the police, but the plays . . . How could they be responsible for ruining the plays? "We'll just be very careful and look out for each other," Brad said.

SCENE 13

I have heard
That guilty creatures sitting at a play,
Have, by the very cunning of the scene,
Been struck so to the soul that presently
They have proclaim'd their malefactions;
For murder, though it have no tongue, will speak.
With most miraculous organ.
—William Shakespeare, *Hamlet*

KYLIE SHIVERED. SO FAR, OPENING night seemed to be going well. A few overly-long pauses, a couple of lines dropped but neatly covered by an older actor. Soon she would make her entrance, relaxed, not in the least bit frightened. Why? She shouldn't be calm! Her heart should be pounding—her mind frantically trying to remember that first line. Then she understood. For the first time, no one in the audience was there just for her. Danny and Beth were, of course, but they had seen the show so often Danny had started mimicking the lines.

Tomorrow's matinee would be different. Mom and Dad would be in the audience. Thinking about that brought on the jitters—just in time for her entrance. What was her first line again? Oh, no!

She stepped out on the stage, trusting that the line would come to her in time.

Seated next to Uncle Dan and Aunt Jane, as she had called Kylie's parents her entire life, Beth felt safe again. Last night, she was certain they had been followed to the cabin after the show. All of them were scared, even the boys. She almost insisted then that Kylie text Mr. Santos, even if it meant the rest of the performances might be ruined. What did plays mean compared to people's lives? At least she'd be home soon. Tonight, after getting caught up with her parents and having a long talk with Marla, she would be sleeping in her own bed. But would she sleep, or would she lie awake imagining what was happening here? Reluctantly, Beth had agreed not to tell anyone what was going on until it was over. She wondered what over would mean, exactly.

Dream had gone well, especially when Kurt said, *Give me your hands, if we be friends . . .* That gave her goosebumps. Of course it was really the character Puck speaking, but Beth decided Kurt meant it for her. She was glad they were friends again. Maybe they'd be more than that someday, but for now, it didn't matter.

The next best thing for Beth was the magical tree in *Dear Brutus.* She had taken tons of pictures to show her art and theater friends back home. Home—where *Play On!* would be in final rehearsals, and the art counselor job at the park district camp awaited her.

Soon Roe would make her final entrance as Margaret—next to Anne Frank, her best part ever—but all she could think about was Dad. Late last night, Kylie had finally sent him the text and photo. Was he in the audience? And was he alone? *Dear Brutus* was the closing performance in the line-up for this concluding Sunday matinee. Then they would pack up and leave—with Dad if he had made it—whether or not the mystery was resolved. But what if he hadn't come? No! He must be out there!

The curtain opened, and the lights flooded Beth's wondrous tree. That was Roe's only cue for her strangely prophetic opening line. *Here is the place, Daddy. Come—look at me!*

Even though it was bad luck, Kylie peeked from the curtain. The stress was unbearable, and she could no longer concentrate on the play or Roe. Was anything happening out there? Had Uncle Carl arrived? She hoped he'd seen her performance, but that didn't matter now. The only thing that did was—what was next?

At last it was time for the entire company to take the stage for the final curtain call. The Crofts family, seated in the front row, had just led the audience in a standing ovation, when quickly, efficiently, a few policemen came down the aisle. Kylie watched Officer Warren and three others lead Lawrence Baker and Brian out of the theater. Mrs. Crofts-Baker and James followed. Only those seated near them noticed anything. The curtain call concluded as the cast gave homage to the lights booth. Whatever just happened meant it was over for them, Kylie thought, and somewhere in the audience Uncle Carl was waiting.

Kylie and Roe had packed earlier, taking their belongings to Crofts House that morning. Safety had become second nature. They said goodbye to a few important people—Megan and Jay especially—and told Brad, Kurt, and Eric they'd see them back home. Kurt's family, including his grandmothers Gee and Bee, had come to the show. Eric was going home with Brad's family. "Be sure to let us know what happened," Brad said. At that point, though, Kylie and Roe were as clueless as Brad.

As they left Crofts House, Kylie saw Mrs. Crofts-Baker, standing near the front desk. She seemed lost, alone, and very old. Kylie gave her a slight wave and a half smile. The broken woman seemed to pull herself together before giving Kylie a proud nod. Had she lost everything? The camp, certainly, but it was hard to know what would happen to the school. Looking back from the car window as they drove out of camp, Kylie whispered, "Goodbye, Camp Shimmer Lake." To think she had once wanted it more than anything.

On the way home to Castle Bluff, they stopped at a restaurant to regroup, even though Kylie and Roe didn't think they were hungry. At first they ate silently, Mr. Santos's lecture about their failure to contact him sooner still burning in their ears.

"Girls, in time you'll remember the positive parts of your camp experience," Mr. Santos said, apparently ready to forgive and move on.

"Positive?" Kylie asked dully.

"You and your friends gave fine performances. I was proud, especially because of all the worry you were carrying. And you should be proud you helped bring true villains to justice and kept greater harm from being done. It will take a long time for Shimmer Lake to be clean again, but at least it won't get worse, and people will be warned from using it."

"I feel sorry for Mrs. Crofts-Baker," Roe said.

"Yes, she was betrayed by her youngest son and nephew. They made a deal with the neighboring steel business to sell the camp and to allow the lake to become polluted with hexavalent chromium, highly toxic, nasty stuff. The managers of the steel company are under arrest, too."

"I've read about that chemical," Roe said soberly. "Everyone who attended camp should be tested, Dad."

He nodded. "I'm sure everyone will be notified."

Kylie couldn't take in the science part. She was more interested in individuals. "Will Mrs. Crofts-Baker be okay, Uncle Carl?"

"In time, perhaps, if it turns out she's innocent. Fortunately, she has her other son's support, as well as the faculty in Castle Bluff. The school will survive. Perhaps she'll be able to reestablish her camp elsewhere someday."

"I hope so," Kylie whispered, although she was now certain she didn't want to be a part of either.

"Dad," Roe said, "about Mother?"

"About the same. We'll talk later. Now, completely changing the subject"—he grinned—"it's about time I gave you two your birthday present. Note that I said one present."

Kylie protested. "Uncle Carl, you've given us too much already."

"No more than you've given me." He took a long envelope out of his briefcase and handed it to Roe. "Open it," he said.

Roe examined the papers inside. "Plane tickets? For me, and for Kylie, too? Kylie, we're going to—Mexico?"

"What?" Kylie shrieked. "Where? Why?"

Roe's father laughed. "To visit my parents, who are also Roe's grandparents. Also a large assortment of aunts, uncles, and cousins, who can't wait to meet you!"

SCENE 14

Last scene of all, that ends this strange eventful history.
—William Shakespeare, *As You Like It*

OUTSIDE THUNDER CRASHING DIDN'T FAZE the partygoers in Kylie's basement hideaway. The whole gang was there, with the addition of Marla and Imani, to celebrate Beth's thirteenth birthday. Gifts had been opened, cake and ice cream consumed.

Three weeks had passed since Kylie, Roe, Brad, Eric, and Kurt had returned from camp. As far as they knew, their roles were over—all culprits arrested. Beth and Marla's play also was over, and both of them would begin assisting at the park district camp the following week—Beth to guide children in arts and crafts activities and Marla, surprisingly, taking Kylie's position as theater assistant—because Kylie and Roe were going to Mexico!

"Time to clean up and go home," Brad said, gathering paper plates and plastic forks.

"So soon?" Beth asked, just as they heard a mighty clap before the room plunged into darkness.

"I keep telling Dad we need a generator."

The door opened, and the glow of a flashlight offered some relief. "I couldn't agree more," Kylie's dad said. "Maybe next summer. At least we'll be cool enough tonight without the AC."

"We should get going," Eric said. "I wonder how extensive the outage is."

Mr. Kennedy shined the light onto his own face so they could see his grin. "Afraid not, my friends. The storm is wild. Supplying your own racket down in this dungeon has kept you from hearing the tornado warnings. The weather has decided on a repeat performance of your winter party—with different lines, of course. You aren't going anywhere tonight."

Everyone except Imani, who didn't understand, cheered and laughed. Marla was especially pleased. "That time you were snowed in sounded like so much fun," she said. "Now I'm a part of it."

Whoever imagined Marla would become a friend? Kylie thought. Jaimie at her grandparents' house in Florida was now the outsider. Maybe they shouldn't lose hope on her, either.

"We rounded up all the flashlights we could find," her father said. "Your mother, Danny, and I will have to join you if the weather gets any worse."

"Don't take chances, Uncle Dan," Roe said.

But they hoped it wouldn't be necessary—that the weather would be bad enough to keep them together, but not so bad the adults and Danny would join them.

At first everyone was giddy, shining flashlights into each other's ghoulish faces and making shadow figures on the wall. Then Roe stopped them. "Let's shine our lights on cleaning up first," she said. "Otherwise, we're going to find frosting all over the place tomorrow."

"Right," Eric said, taking a director role. Kylie, with Brad's help, pulled the sleeping bags out of the sports supply closet.

"If we want anything to eat later," Roe said, "we still have sodas and chips on the counter. We should keep the fridge closed."

The games and fun continued until tiredness crept in and, as often happens during sleepovers, the conversation grew serious, as they sprawled out on sleeping bags.

"We never talked about Crofts next year," Brad said. "I got my letter; I suppose the rest of you did, too."

"I'm going!" Kurt exclaimed. "And I can't wait!"

"Great news, Kurt," Beth said. They all chimed in, pleased for him.

"Anyone else?" Kurt asked.

"I was accepted," Brad said, "but no scholarship. That's okay. I already decided I want to go to our high school. I was impressed by what Beth's learned this summer."

"Me, too," Kylie admitted, and then answered their surprised looks. "I was accepted with a partial, but I think I'd be happier at CBHS. Way more fun. And after all that happened this summer, I've lost a lot of respect for Crofts." That last part was hard to say. She didn't want Miss Armstrong for a teacher again, either. Her beloved theater teacher's behavior last year still hurt. "Eric, what about you?"

"The same," Eric admitted. "I got a partial but won't take it, especially because my family has to be careful with money because of Dad's medical bills. Our health insurance isn't so hot. And I've been talking with Marla about CBHS. It sounds really cool."

Roe didn't think she'd ever seen a real smile on Marla before, but she was beaming now. She had noticed Eric and Marla having an earnest conversation. It would be just fine if Marla were Eric's newest stray puppy. He was kind and good—exactly what Marla needed. As for her—

"I got a full scholarship," Roe said quietly, but held up her hand to stop the cheers. "I'm not taking it, though, because, well, I guess it's time for my announcement. I haven't even told Kylie because my dad and I had to work it out. At camp I got a letter from Spain. You know, my birth mother came from there. The letter was from her brother—my uncle. My grandparents are alive, and I've got aunts and cousins, and—"she choked up—"it's scary and wonderful at the same time. My uncle and aunt invited me to their home outside of Barcelona, and I've decided to go there for school next year."

"What?" Kylie shouted the loudest. Her best friend leaving Castle Bluff?

"We can write and skype," Roe said. "You'll always be my best friends—all of you—and I will come back. But between going to Mexico with Kylie and then living in Spain, I'll finally find out who I really am."

"We understand, Roe," Eric said softly, "but we already know who you are. You are terrific."

Magically, the lights returned. "Right on cue," Kurt said. They laughed, happy the difficult conversation was over.

Again, the door opened. "All clear, folks," Mr. Kennedy announced. "But it's three a.m. Suppose you boys stay down here, and you girls can divide yourselves up between Kylie and Roe's rooms."

Oddly enough, Kylie and Kurt, both late sleepers normally, were the first awake and in the kitchen the next morning. "Let's recreate history by making a birthday breakfast for Beth, which I'm certain she'll be glad to share."

"Bacon and coffee last," Kylie said, "so the smells won't wake everyone. Pancakes first."

They busied themselves opening and emptying the refrigerator. Kurt grew thoughtful. "I like what Roe said. I mean that we'll always be friends, no matter what school we attend."

"Or what country we're in," Kylie said. Losing Roe was going to be hard, no matter what anyone said. She would not be in the next room, as she'd been for almost a year. They wouldn't do homework together or go shopping or share confidences or—so many things. She shook off those thoughts for later.

"And just think, Kurt, you are the only one who has kept the dream of going to Crofts. I think you'll be a great actor someday."

Kurt grinned. *If we shadows have offended, think but this and all is mended, that you have but slumber'd here, while these visions did appear. And this weak and idle theme, no more yielding but a dream.*

Kylie laughed. "Okay, Puck, hold fast to your dream. I think we should have another celebration just for you. How about a milkshake at Smithy's tomorrow? "

"Vanilla or chocolate?"

Everyone had grown in the past year—everyone, seemingly, but Kurt. In a way, that was comforting. "Any flavor you want, Kurt. My treat!"

About the Author

MARILYN LUDWIG HAS TAUGHT THEATER to young people in Downers Grove, Illinois, for over forty years. *No Small Parts* is her tenth novel but the first about the theater. *Lost in Arden Woods*, which the characters perform in this book, is Marilyn's unpublished play, *Camp Shakespeare*, performed by her advanced students a few years ago. She is a member of the Society of Children's Book Writers and Illustrators (SCBWI).

9 780099 674228 3